Cuts
like a
Knife

a Kristen Conner thriller

by
Dee Dee Apple

SYDNEY
LANE
PRESS
Brentwood, Tennessee

Cuts Like a Knife
A Kristen Conner Thriller
Copyright © 2009 DeeDee Apple, LLC
www.deedee-apple.com

ISBN: 978-0-975866-20-7

Sydney Lane Press
A Division of Mark Gilroy Creative LLC
Mailing Address:
2000 Mallory Lane
Suite 130-229
Franklin, Tennessee 37067

Jacket and Interior Design: Bobby & Kimberly Sagmiller, Fudge Creative
Cover Photo: Bobby Sagmiller

The characters in this novel are purely fictional and do not reflect the life and events of specific real life individuals.

Printed in the United States of America

for
Caroline

The End of March

It was one of those March days when the
sun shines hot and the wind blows cold:
when it is summer in the light,
and winter in the shade.

Charles Dickens

Chapter 1
March 31, 9:59pm

I should have stayed in California. It was like seventy degrees in San Diego yesterday. Almost orange on the weather map. It freaking snowed here last week. And then the DePaul kids showed up at Wrigley in swimsuits today. Oh how I love children. NOT. The screaming brats distracted me from a pretty decent game. One idiot spilled beer on my scorecard. I could have killed him. If I see him again and he's still yelling at sleezy drunk girls in bikinis the whole game, I will. That's a promise, kids.

I just can't figure out what to wear in this forsaken wasteland of broken asphalt. I left my jacket home this morning and froze. I put it on this afternoon and was sweating like a dog. Edit that thought. Dogs don't sweat. Wonder what genius came up with that brilliant word picture. Chicago weather is definitely a mystery but it does set the mood of the story. My story. I bought a book on writing. Waste of time. If you're a writer you just write.

A new chapter opened. His quest for immortality continued.

Quest for immortality. Nice. I like that. Writing is a lost art, which is why I got to do this myself. Yep, it's a new day. Time to turn the page and start a new chapter. The weather is now officially irrelevant. Relief is so close at hand.

His days of living in a self-imposed limbo were coming to an end. Six months of restraint and anticipation were painful. Excruciatingly so. Denial of what was rightfully his felt like torture but such was his power of discipline that he would not jeopardize all he had established for an easy reprieve. But that's what made him different. Unique. Special. A name beyond all others.

They don't have a clue as to all I've accomplished yet. Losers. With a capital L. I know they know I'm out here but they're too stupid to do anything about it. Someone is sitting behind a computer right now looking for me and wondering where the heck I've gone. I bet I'm driving him out of his freaking mind. Or hers. Serves him or her right. I have more taste for a her. Hers are so much better out of their minds. Sooooo dumb. I love it.

Tomorrow is April Fools Day. Fools indeed. Especially cops. If I'm ever going to get the press I deserve I'm going to have to send the fools some clues. They make me do everything.

He sat at the precipice of his next great work. Ready. He was back.

The Month of April

April is the cruelest month.

T.S. Eliot

Chapter 2

Mom, I told you this isn't a good time. I've got to go."

"Honey, it's never a good time."

"I know, Mom, but it really isn't a good time this time. I have to go. Now."

My partner is looking at me with utter incredulity. He's just slammed the gear shift into park and unbuttoned his sports jacket. He flips the snap on his holster for easy access to his Glock. I shouldn't have picked up Mom's call but I thought I could get off the phone fast. She keeps carping that I never pick up. Now I'm going to hear about how I'm always the first to hang up. I can't win.

"Mom, I'll call you back. I'm getting off right now. I have—"

"You'll be at Danny and Kaylen's Sunday?"

"Yes, Mom. I have—"

"And church?"

I don't get to answer because Don reaches over, snatches my cell phone from my hand, and hits the red end call button. I wonder if it's possible to make the sound of slamming the phone down by hitting the "off" button with force. If so, Don just did it.

"Momma's going to have to wait, Kristen. He isn't going to hang around all day waiting for us to say hi. Let's get in there now."

A surge of adrenaline courses through my body as I step out of the car, touch the gun that's holstered on my side one more time just to make sure it hasn't mysteriously disappeared, snap and unsnap the top strap, and head into the Gas & Grub, game face on.

As we walk through the door the two guys working the cash register look up at us nervously, probably wondering if they're about to get busted for selling cigarettes to minors again. We pulled into the parking lot in our unmarked mud brown Mercury Crown Victoria, which is not the world's greatest disguise for detectives who want to make a collar by entering a public establishment under the radar. Maybe it's the extra antennas on the trunk lid. Might as well put a billboard on the roof that broadcasts Chicago Police Department in neon letters. We're here to serve but we do have a way of making people nervous—and disappear.

My partner, Don Squires, gives a nod as he heads down one aisle and I take the one next to it. I quickly round two corners to cut off our suspect's line of escape. Don is three feet away from him on one side and I position myself an equal distance away.

"Don't move. Leave your hands where we can see them." Don uses his menacing voice, the snarl he puts on for moments like this, which I might add is very menacing.

An EMT from one of the ambulance services recognized the punk's description from an APA bulletin while pumping fake nacho cheese sauce on a half-pound, buck-fifty Polish dog they sell at Gas & Grub. He goes to the same church as me and fancies himself a junior crime fighter, so he put the call straight to my cell phone. It's not the right time to lose focus, but I wonder to myself how Lloyd got my number. He's got to be pushing over three hundred pounds and, as I've already promised him numerous times, I am going to kick his butt for eating all those congealed fats and animal parts on a bun. He just smiles and says mustard is lo-cal. The butt kicking will have to wait for later.

The punk, late teens or early twenties, is a retro eighties piece of work. He's wearing a black t-shirt with a skull and the name of a group that I don't recognize in jagged, blood-red letters. UberDeath. Clever. He's got the chain hanging out of the front pocket of his black jeans, connected to a what I assume is a wallet that he doesn't like to use, based on his current little crime spree. All he needs is those black boots with the metal and leather straps, but unfortunately for me and my partner he has on a pair of comfort shoes that look like what we used to rent at the bowling alley; all black, of course, but you can see the stitching. Footwear isn't going to slow him down if he bolts, I think to myself. I quickly take a glance up and down the aisle. Not going to be an issue; he has nowhere to go.

Neither Don nor I have pulled guns because the convenience store is packed. Doesn't mean our hands aren't touching the brushed metal grips, however. There must be twenty gas pumps out front on a busy street. The back door services walk-ins from a blue collar, working class, urban neighborhood. So we've got people coming and going from every direction. No sense starting a panic. We have a CPD mandate that prohibits us from taking risks that are likely to result in collateral damage.

I'm not letting my eyes leave the punk's hands. If he even twitches anywhere near a pocket, mandate or not, my Beretta 96 is coming out in a hurry, whether it starts a stampede for the door or not.

The kid looks up and locks eyes with Don with a glare of anger and hatred. He soundlessly mouths something to Don that I can't make out, but I'm guessing he's not complimenting him on his choice of ties this morning. Don bristles and they face off. Don was a running back in college and still hits the weights a couple mornings a week. He's got the start of a paunch around the middle, but he has a lot of arm and chest muscle to keep his proportions right and project a serious formidability.

The punk is probably six foot one in height and less than 170 pounds soaking wet. Did I mention the tattoos and slouch? Even if he wasn't into armed robbery, which turned lethal for the seventy-seven-year-old victim who fought back and just passed away after a couple days in ICU at Rush Presbyterian Hospital for his efforts, I still wouldn't like this kid just on sight. We're obviously not supposed to profile, but my daddy didn't raise a fool. This is a kid who is screaming anger and rebellion at the world without having to move his lips.

My money is on Don if this takedown gets physical. Heck, my money is on me if Don decides to turn around, pour himself a cup of coffee, and leave the heavy lifting to me. I can take this punk. I've taken every hand to hand combat course the Chicago Police Department offers. I don't score well on the pistol range—which is why I traded the standard issue Glock 22 for a Beretta last week—but I do get superior marks on hand to hand.

The punk breaks eye contact with Don and then turns toward where I block the other end of the aisle. He looks me up and down slowly and smiles. He puckers up and blows me a kiss, and then he flips me off as he pushes a spinner rack filled with chips and other snacks in Don's direction, and vaults over the condiment counter between us. Nacho cheese sauce and pickle relish fly everywhere. He knocks two people down by the dairy cooler and crashes through the back door in a frantic sprint out the back door. I'm wishing like crazy he wore his boots with the silver rings today because we're going to be running. I'm not supposed to even think the thought but I do wonder if I can hit a moving target with the Beretta while running hard myself. Inflicting a flesh wound is all I'm thinking, of course.

I am furious and want to do him bodily harm, which as an officer of the peace I am prohibited from doing on the basis of me not liking him and him making me mad. But I'm half hoping he wants to play rough, because I'm ready. This won't be the first time I ask God to forgive me for a bad attitude today—or tomorrow—but I swear I want to be the one who cuffs him. Tightly.

Don and I are outside in a flash, bumping shoulders in the doorway but not losing a step. Don's wearing a black summer weight wool suit, Italian cut—that often means no vent in the back he has told me at least fifty times—with shiny black leather wingtip shoes, which are not good for speed. I think they're his Allen Edmonds, which cost over three hundred bucks, he reminds us in the detective's bull pen regularly. I'm sure Allen makes a great shoe, but that still doesn't make them good for a track meet. Don will be crying for a week about what the job does to his clothes and how we need a real expense allowance for clothing, just like the guys in uniform.

I have no sympathy. I've told him forty times to get some Rockports or Eccos with a soft, flexible, comfortable sole. He just looks at me in abject horror. I've got on my Eccos, the very best comfort shoe in the world the clerk at Timberline in the mall said. Dad always told me to buy American, but I'm not sure that's possible anymore, and I've got to say, those Danes or Scandinavians or whoever it is that does Eccos, make a great shoe you can actually work in. My sister Klarissa agrees with Don on matters of fashion and looks at my shoes with undisguised disdain. I think Nike makes a custom cross training high heeled model for her to wear to the health club.

That's why she's the weathergirl on WCI-TV and I'm a newbie detective who's about to rock some punk's world.

The kid is surprisingly fast. Real fast. I wish some nice high school track coach could have got hold of him before he got into all this trouble. He's clearing the alley behind the Gas & Grub and turning right on a residential street of classic Chicago row houses, and Don and I are still fifty yards behind. Don's a sprinter so if the kid makes us run more than half a mile he'll be out of the race. I, on the other hand, was a soccer player and middle distance runner in college. I may still complete a marathon some day. Depends on getting my surgically repaired right knee stronger.

I was my dad's third daughter, bless his heart. Mom couldn't have any more kids so he was never going to coach a son in football, basketball or baseball, the red-blooded, testosterone filled, All-American sports. I give him credit for making the best of a tough situation. No tea parties or Barbies. It was basketball, volleyball, year-round soccer, and track for me. For us.

For a while we thought I might be the next Mia Hamm. After a couple of torn ACLs and the slow-dawning acceptance that I never could hit a good left footer anyway, I started thinking about a day job. My dad was a cop. Why not me?

When Klarrisa the weathergirl begins a sentence, "Just because Dad was a cop," I know what is about to follow. Something to the effect of "It doesn't mean you have to rub shoulders with the city's lowlife." I never let her finish anymore. "Don't go there, weathergirl," usually stops her in her tracks.

I hear Don's labored breathing as we turn the corner. I've broken a sweat but I'm still breathing easy and can go like this all day if necessary. I've got to get serious about running the Chicago Marathon in October, I think to myself. I've done the half-marathon a couple times. The punk's still forty yards ahead, not a good thing, so its time to turn it up a notch. My partner won't like it, but this is no time to make sure his male ego gets proper care and attention. I'm breathing easy—this is just a warm-up on the elliptical machine—so I start to leave Don behind. Then he says it; gasps it is more accurate. I was hoping against hope he wouldn't, but the words rasp out: "Let's fall back and regroup. Too dangerous."

I nearly stop just so I can argue with him. He's barely wheezing the words out but I understand loud and clear what he's saying: girls aren't tough enough to be cops. No way would he have said that if his partner was male. At least I assume he wouldn't.

I don't know what gets into me, but as I ignore him and pick up the pace I suddenly want to flip him the bird. Honestly, I'm not a big time feminist. The right guy asks me out, he can open every door in the world for me if he so desires. More to the point, I'm not crude or profane. I'm not a bird flipper; it was definitely not allowed in my house growing up. Dad may have had a nitty gritty job, but we did the Ozzie and Harriet thing as a family. No R movies and not many PG or PG-13 either. Sunday school and church every week. Mom took us to Wednesday night Bible Study, though Dad let me miss if I had an athletic event. Mom didn't like that and I think Klarrisa and Kaylen, my older sister, resented that a little bit. Okay, a lot. However, it didn't mean they were going to go out for the softball team, especially Klarrisa, so they were in youth group every Wednesday night. Bottom line, no cussing and no bird flipping in the Conner home.

Like I said, I don't know what gets into me. I don't think I have an anger issue. I do have a temper, but it's never crossed the line professionally or personally. But I've been getting mad at people pretty easily lately. I wonder if it's an occupational hazard.

Don's a great partner and I won't stay mad. It helps that he is a big time family guy. He's got an almost stay-at-home wife and a girl and a *boy*—bless my poor dad's jealous heart. Talk about a committed guy, Don doesn't smoke, drink, cuss—at least not without major provocation—and great for me as a partner, he doesn't flirt and would never think about fooling around on his wife. I'm not trying to be presumptuous, but let's be honest, when you're a female in a male dominated work environment, inappropriate things get hinted at. And sometimes not hinted, just said outright.

Don and I are friends and we have work chemistry, but we're all business. I think his wife gets just a twinge of nervousness about our relationship— I've seen her size me up when she doesn't think I'm looking—but Don and I don't have this tension hanging in the air where he's trying to make something happen. What is it with some guys always testing the waters? Sometimes the married ones are the worst.

I make no obscene gestures at Don for which I'm grateful. I'll not have to apologize to him later, and now I am closing the gap on the punk. I'm not going full speed but I've lengthened my stride and am on pace to run a six-minute mile I think.

The punk turns into another alley and I'm less than half a basketball court away—top of the circle and taking it to the hoop, baby. I barely slow down as I round the corner and now he's in my sights. He's rolled two metal trashcans in my path. *Amateur.* Did I mention that I did hurdles for my high school track team, too? The effort has slowed him down, but not me. Doesn't make any difference, I am going to be catching him soon any way you look at it. He senses this and makes his decision. Fight or flight?

Fight.

The punk turns to face me and he's got a knife in his hand. He's full of surprises. Not only is he fast enough to make any high school track team in the city but he can just as easily get a part as a Shark or Jet in the school's rendition of *West Side Story*.

I shouldn't be surprised and I am mad at myself that I am. The knife has been his MO in all three of his robberies. Known robberies. Being surprised at a moment like this is not a good feeling. I put on the brakes fast or I'm going to run myself right into his range of attack. I'm reaching towards the small of my back for my dainty little Beretta, but the punk is already moving in on me. He's red in the face and breathing loud, but he lunges quickly to close the gap before I can de-holster my weapon. He's made his decision to fight alright.

On cop shows and in the movies all you have to do is employ a series of martial arts moves to deflect and negate slashing metal. I don't care if you're Jackie Chan's cousin, it doesn't work that easily. When two people fight and one has a razor honed blade, the person without the weapon, even if that person is a superior fighter and ultimately prevails, is going to lose some blood.

I have on my anti-cling black slacks and suit top, a very comfortable lycra-type material that fits and wears well—and allows me to move freely. I got both at a great sale at Marshall Fields. Half off of half off. I'm not thinking of the suit right now, but I am concerned about the skin underneath it. I've got noticeable scars around my knees from the ACL surgeries, but otherwise, God forgive me for my vain pride, I've got great skin. Even Klarrisa, all five foot nine and one hundred and ten pounds of her, is jealous of my skin. She doesn't have bad skin of course. But constant dieting and TV makeup do exact a cost.

His first slash catches the sleeve of my suit coat and pops the button off.

No problem. I can get it sewed back on. The good news is he got no skin.

I'm on my toes and jump back and dance to the left. I've had to pull my right hand from across my body where I was reaching for my gun, so now I have to start over trying to pull my weapon out and into a firing position while keeping him at bay. He's circling and giving head fakes in my direction, which indicates he's played basketball, too, and he's trying to make me lean the wrong way on his next charge, so he's making it next to impossible for me to get my firearm.

Well, if the punk can go on the offensive, so can I. I feint to my left and he leans with it. I quickly spin to the right and let loose a round-house kick that I'm guessing is beautiful to behold and would film well. Not as good as what Jackie Chan's cousin might do, but well executed.

The punk doesn't look like a fighter but he's obviously been around the block. He partially ducks under the kick intended for his head, so I catch a lot of shoulder and hit him with a glancing blow to his jaw. It staggers him, but just barely. He stays in ready position and makes another lunge at me. We're still too close for me to reach my gun with the confidence that I'll have it in hand and in firing position before he reaches me with the knife, so I just forget about trying for it and keep my hands in fighting position. I'm crouched and ready to spin in either direction. I'm looking for my opportunity to attack. Our eyes meet and lock.

His eyes dilate. He drops the knife and raises his arms. Wow. That was easier than I thought.

Don walks past me calmly, his gun in both hands, aimed at the center of the punk's chest.

"Keep your hands where we can see them, kick the knife to the side and get down on your knees." There's a nana-second of hesitation and Don shouts, "now!"

"Make it easy for us and I'll make it easy for you," I add as I push him flat on his face, maybe with a little extra nudge, and cuff his hands behind him.

Don's on his cell phone calling in the uniforms.

"Good work, we got him," he says to me as he snaps his flip phone shut. "You okay?"

Don, you better not go there, I think, but hold my tongue.

"We?" I ask him, but not loud enough or with enough conviction to start a fight. I know it was *we* who got the guy, but I wouldn't mind getting singled out for getting the call and getting to him first. I can already hear sirens heading our way. No time to fight with the partner.

God, forgive me for my bad attitude … and the next one I am about to have.

Chapter 3

It's seven a.m. Saturday morning and I'm waiting behind three people to order a grande four-shot soy latte at JavaStar. There are no cars in line at the drive-through, but I refuse to pay almost five bucks for a cup of coffee and foamed milk substitute and not get at least a little ambience to go with my caffeine. Of course I've got to be at the soccer fields in thirty minutes, so at most, I am going to get five minutes to sit in a corner chair, savor the image of coffee beans overflowing from burlap sacks on terracotta wallpaper, watch sleepy people in sweatshirts read their papers with combed or uncombed hair, and listen to a soundtrack with number one hits by the Beatles, sung by people like Bono, Jessica Simpson, Frank Sinatra, and Justin Timberlake. Justin Timberlake doing some kind of rap version of "Let It Be?" Frank Sinatra crooning "Lucy in the Sky with Diamonds?" Jessica singing "Eleanor Rigby?

Someone in Seattle has very weird taste in music. Just because you're good at coffee doesn't automatically make you good at music. I did like that Ray Charles album somebody gave me for Christmas a year or two ago. I think it was Klarissa—or maybe her boyfriend, Warren.

"What can I get for you this morning?" a guy with a tongue stud and a green apron asks me a little too earnestly.

"Quad-shot, one Splenda, grande soy latte," I answer carefully and clearly. If you don't say things in the right order, you'll be explaining that no, it's only one Splenda, not four, and yes, four shots of espresso, not one, for the next five minutes.

He writes my order on the cup and asks if he can get my name. It's just after seven on a cool, sleepy morning and there is no one behind me in line nor currently awaiting their order. I am about to ask him how hard it's really going to be to identify me and make sure I get the right drink when it's finished, but I'm working on my attitude, so I answer nicely, "Kristen."

He asks if Kristen is spelled with a "K" or a "C" and it's all I can do not to threaten him bodily harm if he doesn't have someone start grinding beans and pushing buttons on the space ship consul they use to make coffee. I answer, "K."

He asks me if I'd like a piece of coffee cake or a cheese Danish to go with my latte. I've got a five dollar bill in my hand, clearly visible and my drink is more than four bucks. The case of pastries and instant oatmeal is right in front of me, so it's obvious I know my options. What's the deal? Does he get a spiff on his paycheck if he up sells me a pastry?

"No thank you," I answer with all the earnestness I can muster. I have a very good attitude this morning and that is spelled with a capital "A."

It's been a tiring week. We arrested Jared Incaviglia, the punk, but Don ruined a three hundred dollar pair of shoes, which the department is not going to reimburse him for, and he was in a foul mood all day Friday. I looked it up online and told him that Allen Edmonds will refurbish his shoes for free if he'll pay for the shipping each direction. That only helped a little.

"Those bad boys were brand new," he told me. "I don't want refurbished."

"Can you tell a difference?" I asked him.

"Doesn't matter. *I* know the difference."

Okay.

I ended up doing all the paperwork for the arrest, which is only slightly more appealing than jumping into a tank of sharks after shaving my legs with a dull razor, but Don did brighten up in time to smile widely and vigorously shake hands with the Deputy Commissioner of the CPD, who wanted to personally congratulate us for our fine work. Commander Czaka thanked me too, but my handshake was a lot shorter and less enthusiastic. Could that have anything to do with the heated exchanges he and I have been sharing? Being the ace detective I am, I suspect yes. I think he gave me a dirty look. I think I returned the favor.

I'll give Don credit. He carefully pointed out that I was first on scene and that I was the one who got the tip in the first place. I still accused him of being a glory hog afterward. His mind was still on his shoes—and he's worried the drycleaner won't be able to get the nacho cheese sauce off a silk tie he really likes—so he hasn't taken the bait and fought with me. Sissy.

Then, twenty minutes before closing time, Captain Karl Zaworski, head of detectives for the Second Precinct, called me into his office. He let me know that Jared, the punk, felt his civil rights were violated by the "excessive force" of my grinding his face into the ground.

Excessive force? Jared better hope I don't get to spend time alone with him in an interview room.

Once the phrase "excessive force" is added to your personnel files, the CO has the option to immediately suspend you with or without pay pending further review, which Zaworski didn't do. But my work on the case just got a whole lot tougher. Some defense attorney is going to claim the arrest wasn't righteous and that all evidence is tainted. After a terse meeting with the captain, I logged back onto my computer and went back over the paperwork, making sure I dotted every "I" and crossed every "T" twice.

Internal Affairs will be called in to investigate me, Zaworski informed me, and as every cop in America will tell you, IA is not your best friend under such circumstances. Meetings with them are rarely pleasant. Of course, I'd be in a bad mood if I spent all day trying to fire cops, too. Okay, I'm not being fair. There are bad cops who need to be booted off the force.

The timing for this kind of scrutiny is never good, but based on a few conflicts I've had, namely with Czaka, this couldn't come at a worse time.

"Kirsten," my barista announces loudly enough for the crowd across the street at Dunkin' Donuts to hear. I am literally five feet away from him and he is looking right at me. Is there the start of a smug smile on his face? Since he got my name wrong, Kirsten instead of Kristen, I hope he at least said it with a "K."

I ask for a java jacket to keep my fingers from burning off, which for just under five bucks should have been slipped on the paper cup without my asking. Java jackets are now in the same category as having a clean new towel each day of an extended stay in a hotel. You can have it but not without feeling a little guilty for destroying the planet. I'm not feeling guilty today. I consider sitting a minute in the corner on a funky orange plastic chair, but look at my watch and head for the door.

I wonder again why I am not sleeping in. That would, of course, be because I'm the coach of my niece's soccer team. Her name is Kendra. All the girls' names in my family start with the letter "K." I guess we're just special that way. A guy friend from my high school days called us the Special K girls. I don't think he meant it as a compliment since he would usually add that Special K girls deserve special education.

Kendra is seven. My older sister, Kaylen, thought it'd be great for Kendra if Aunt Kristen was her coach. I played competitive soccer after all and neither she nor Danny ever played the sport. To satisfy his competitive impulses, I think Danny was on the chess team and was a regular at the science fair for his school. I'm not joking.

I wanted to ask Kaylen if seven-year-olds need someone with my playing experience as coach, or if having a parent, preferably one with infinite patience and a low stress job, wouldn't be better. Probably smart that I kept my thoughts to myself as Kaylen would explain that being a full time mom has its own stressors. Instead I made the mistake of asking how much time is required. Seven-year-olds are only allowed to practice one night a week and all games are played Saturday morning, she asserted triumphantly, confident that the deal was sealed. Her optimism was rewarded.

Our team name is the Snowflakes—Coach Kristen wasn't consulted— and our uniforms are naturally, uh, yellow. Wasn't there an old Frank Zappa song that warned us about yellow snow?

The zinger was when Kaylen asked if it would be too much for me to pick up Kendra for pre-game warm-ups with early games. That way Kaylen could sleep in a few extra minutes. She wouldn't miss any of the games of course. *Of course not.* And since their house is only a few miles—and more than a couple of traffic lights, I might add—out of the way, it really wouldn't be any extra work for me. Did someone tape a sign on my forehead that spells s-u-c-k-e-r?

I said yes, of course. Kaylen and Danny are the nicest people in the world. He's a pastor. They're really busy and need a little help with their two kids. Mom told Klarissa that Danny and Kaylen are working on number three. I wonder if I should ask her how much work is really involved.

Since I spend my days chasing thugs like Jared in back alleys, I need to be with a group of Snowflakes, I guess. Despite my expert training—and being the only coach of seven-year-olds who insists that the team show up thirty minutes early for warm-ups and drills—we've lost all our games so far, but it's a new day. The girls don't seem to mind the losses as much as the parents. Or me. I wonder if I would get turned in for doing an extra practice session the next couple of weeks.

The girls are actually having a lot of fun and I've only had one run-in with a parent. Tiffany's dad would like to see more scoring—especially from Tiffany—and was getting quite loud from the sidelines the first couple of games. He explained to me he was just motivating the girls. When I explained that screaming at seven-year-olds wasn't encouragement in my book, he tried to intimidate me with the knowledge that he had played sports. I just pulled a concept from my cop training on him: repeat if necessary, but never explain. He backed off.

I look at my watch. I'm going to get Kendra and me to the fields on time for warm-ups, thank God, without having to do more than ten miles over the speed limit. I'm five minutes away from Kaylen's and switch to a news station. A young woman has been murdered. I wonder which precinct has the case. If it's ours, I wonder who Zaworski and Czaka will give the lead assignment to. Zaworski knows Don and I get the job done. Czaka doesn't like me. Czaka is a Deputy Commissioner. His commander rank wins tie breakers. It doesn't take an ace detective to know that.

Then I think about Incaviglia and Internal Affairs again. It's conceivable I won't be working for the next month or so. Then I think there's no way I'm going to be in serious trouble for this. Incaviglia has a couple of major assaults and a recent murder under his belt. I just don't know.

Chapter 4
April 3, 8:19am

I *can't sleep. I popped that little blue pill from her cabinet and it didn't help a bit. I'm so wired. My heart rate must be at a hundred and twenty sitting still. I've missed this. My heart is happy again.*

He couldn't sleep. He'd lain awake all night with the euphoria.

I like that word. Euphoria. Wish it would never wear off. Not the word; the feeling. But it always does. That's when the cravings will start again and it'll be time to find another girlfriend. Maybe blonde this time. One I saw earlier in the night was smoking hot. I didn't like her tattoos though. That's not very classy.

He wondered what the newspapers would say about him in this new city. The television and radio stations were usually attentive after his great work was established but these were temporary forms of media. Not newspapers though. Newspapers were lasting. Paper and ink don't fade so fast. A man of destiny, he was acutely aware of building a lasting legacy. A monument to the free spirit.

I can go back and read them over and over again. I can relish every word even though they get the facts all wrong. They think they're all that with their story angles. Idiots. If I read one more thing about me and my mommy I'll puke. There's only one person on the whole festering planet who can tell my story. And It's ME.

Even without the credit to his name he would be proud of his work though the ongoing burden of anonymity gave him a feeling of wistfulness.

I had a shrink who was really fat and smelled like tuna tell me that I had a problem with self aggrandizement that I needed to work on. Work on your own problems, starting with deodorant and a diet, Dr. Stink Bomb.

But it was a new city. A new arena of conflict and conquest. No one was writing the stories yet.

But they will. The cops will eventually figure it out, slow as they are. But not fast enough to find me or to understand all the things I've accomplished in other somewheres. So many somewheres.

Drawing on a quaint American colloquialism, he noted that it felt good to be back to work; back in the saddle again.

Yee haw, baby! Giddy up!

Chapter 5

"No Kendra! The other way! That way! Kendra! Dribble the ball that way!"

I bellow and wave my arms like a crazy woman. Tiffany's dad is watching me with a smug look on his already smug face. Better take it down a notch. Or three.

The score is tied 3-3. According to my stopwatch, we only have two minutes before the ref blows his whistle to end the game. We need a win. I want a win. I could deal with a tie, but a win would be so sweet.

Kendra has scored two of our goals. Since then she's been getting mugged. The other team is tugging on her jersey. She's been tripped four times. These are sweet little seven-year-old girls, so the other coach has got to be instructing them to foul. He's got to be, no way are they thinking of this on their own. My blood is boiling.

I'm giving the coach a piece of my mind in my imagination when Kendra, who has lost the ball, steals it back and becomes a yellow streak set to score a breakaway goal. She's not old enough to keep dribbles close to her feet, and the other coach—Attila the Hun—is screaming for his goalie to leave the box and charge the ball. Apparently her name is Heidi, as anyone within a mile of the soccer complex can attest.

It's going to be close. Kendra isn't quite in control of the ball. It's about equal distance between her and the goalie when you consider the speed of the roll. I'm praying, really praying for a miracle, for a win. Does God hear the prayers of sports fans? What if two people rooting for opposing teams are praying equally hard? I'm not a theologian so I just keep praying. Even if God is laughing at me or just not listening, I doubt He's angry. And just maybe my faith can move mountains and win games.

Please God, help her to be first to the ball.

Maybe it was my prayer that did it. Kendra redirects the ball with the outside of her left foot—and any coach of seven-year-olds will confirm that this is a miracle, especially when you consider she is right footed—leaving her all by herself in front of the goal. She taps the ball in for the winning score just as an opposing player tackles her from behind.

The goal counts. I start to run out to check on Kendra but she bounces up and appears to be fine. The girls high five her as they head back for the other side of the field. The parents have erupted and are yelling, whistling, and hugging. As the Snowflakes line up for one more kick off, the ref, with everything his ample pot belly can muster, blows the whistle to end the game. We get the win, but I'm still furious with the other coach. After the girls form a line, shake hands with the other team, run through the tunnel formed by two lines of parents who have linked outstretched hands into an arbor, and then head towards the cooler with space age juice pouches that have little straws attached—the highlight of the game for many of my players—I am in the other coach's face.

"Hey, pal, you better get your girls under control before someone gets hurt," I say as I stick a finger at his chest.

"What are you talking about, little lady?" he storms back.

Little lady? I may have to cuff him. Maybe his license plate has expired and I'll arrest him in the parking lot.

"You know exactly what I'm talking about, big guy," I answer. "I'm making sure my girls don't get injured because some goon is teaching seven-year-olds to trip and push."

"You're out of your mind." His face is a dark storm. It crosses my mind that he may be right on that point.

"We'll see who is out of their mind. This is going to the commissioner. Good thing I had a parent taping you on the sideline to show him what you're doing."

I just made that up. Okay, I lied and I know that's wrong. What gets into me? Sometimes I excuse myself as the victim of occupational hazards. It's especially handy for explaining away my temper.

He looks thunder-struck. His head wheels around to the sideline where his team and parents sat, but it has cleared out now, so he can't verify whether someone was really taping him. He looks at me through narrowed eyes, appraising and suspicious. The ref, who has no sense of the drama unfolding before him—almost as oblivious as he was to the game—walks up and sticks a game card in my face.

"Need your 'John Hancock' on the bottom line," he says.

I sign. Attila signs.

"Good game coaches," he says as he trots toward the referee hut.

I look over at my Snowflakes. They are contentedly slurping juice and munching on granola bars. Danny is uncomfortable and won't make eye contact with me. Kaylen will. She is scowling.

I know it happens in professional sports all the time, but I wonder how often volunteer soccer coaches get fired mid-season.

Chapter 6

"Kristen, you've got to get your temper under control," Kaylen says to me. We have our own table at Pizza Palace for our celebration lunch. It is only ten thirty, so I guess we're having pizza brunch.

Eleven girls are munching pizza contentedly at a long table we've created by pushing some together. The parents, including Danny, have morphed into groups of four or five at surrounding tables.

I guess I'm at the time-out table because it's just Kaylen and me. I have an untouched piece of pizza in front of me and have taken just a couple of sips of my Diet Coke as I get chewed out by my older sister.

"Kendra could have been hurt," I protest. "That guy is ruining things for the girls."

"Maybe so, but he wasn't spitting and yelling and the girls are doing just fine," Kaylen says, pointing to the girls who are laughing and shoving food into their mouths. Kendra is now standing on her chair and is rotating her hips like she is twirling a hula hoop. I hope that's what she's doing at least. She is explaining to the other Snowflakes how she scored the winning goal. I guess that is her celebration dance.

"Kendra!" her dad barks and she is immediately back in her seat, a sheepish expression on her face. I can tell she's trying not to smile. I'm doing the same thing because I know how she feels. I'm in trouble, too. No smiling allowed.

"Where did she learn to do that?" I ask Kaylen, hoping to change the subject. Doesn't work.

"Kristen, I'm serious. You're thirty and this in-your-face anger has got to stop. You were almost as bad as Tiffany's dad today."

She looks up to make sure he didn't hear her. "Check that, worse," she continues in a lower tone. "He was very well behaved and only cheered today, per coach's order."

Ouch. I'd argue that her comparison was a low blow and that I didn't spit. Problem is, she is right. Not about the spitting. But I've always had a temper. I've always been in-your-face. But it's never been so relentless and as personal as lately. I don't even know how long lately is. And I've never lost it in front of the kids. I'm a good girl. I don't smoke and I don't chew, and I don't go with guys that do. What's happening to me?

I start to apologize when my phone begins playing Tchaikovsky's "1812 Overture." I am going to ignore the call but I recognize Captain Zaworski's number. The boss rarely calls on the weekend. I'm hoping this doesn't have anything to do with Internal Affairs and the punk.

"Conner," I answer, turning away from Kaylen and putting a finger in my free ear to buffer the noise. She is watching me with suspicion. She obviously thinks I'm trying to escape this conversation. I listen for half a minute, tell him it will take me twenty, my eyebrows furrowed enough to cause permanent wrinkles, and hit the red "off" button.

"Kristen, you can't get away this easily; we need to finish this conversation," Kaylen begins. I knew that was what she was thinking.

I cut her off. "But not now. There's been a murder and I'm on the case."

I'm already standing up and pulling car keys from my purse. I'm about to leave without a word, but I stop myself.

"I'm sorry," I say as I turn and hug Kaylen close. "I am. Honestly. Just say a prayer and don't be mad at me. I've got to go right now."

"Bye Coach!" eleven voices chirp in near-unison. I turn and tell them they played a fabulous game and circle around the table to give a little love to each one. Kendra hugs my neck hard as I bend down to kiss her. Kids can be very forgiving.

There is almost a tear in the corner of one of my eyes as I walk out the door and into the sunlight. Man, it's bright today. I blink it away. I thank God for my Snowflakes.

As I near my car it crosses my mind that Kaylen's reference to me being thirty was definitely a cheap shot. Almost thirty is not the same as thirty.

Chapter 7

I flip stations the whole way over to the precinct. I know more about who to call for all my insurance needs and save money, but don't catch a peep about our murder case or the score of the Cubs game last night, the only two items of vital interest to me. The media usually gets it screwed up anyway—and so do the Cubs—so better to start with a clean slate and no false information or hope embedded in my mind.

I consider stopping by my place to grab a sixty-second shower and a change of clothes. No time.

I'm still the last person to the conference room after parking, entering the back door with my electronic key, and pounding up four flights of stairs to Homicide in the Second Precinct. I was too impatient to wait for an elevator. I look around and realize this could be about a hundred different rooms in our precinct. Gray table and chairs. Gray walls. The white ceiling must have been the interior designer's idea of a contrast. A couple of the ceiling tiles are cracked or chipped at the corners. Several tiles are rust-stained from a leak on the floor above and look like they are ready to cave in. I used to drink water from our antiquated porcelain fountains when I first joined the force. I shudder and thank God for bottled water.

"Grab a seat," Zaworski says barely nodding at me and without further greeting. I sit next to Don. He looks dapper in designer jeans and a white mock turtleneck. Summer weight. Loafers with no socks. You've got to be kidding me. Does he not have to clean the garage or mow the lawn on a Saturday morning?

Four other men are at the table besides Zaworski and Don. One is in uniform with sergeant stripes; I think his name is Kincaid. Then there are two detectives from another precinct that I recognize, both wearing jeans with one in a cotton pullover and the other in a couple layers of t-shirts to protect against the howling winds of April. I don't know either by name. Finally there is a very nice looking man, maybe early thirties, in a suit way too fine for local law enforcement. Except for Don, of course. Navy blue with a light blue stripe, white oxford shirt with button down collar and monogram on the chest pocket, and a pale yellow tie with a diagonal blue strip. This guy has got to be a federal agent or a salesman for IBM. I am suddenly self-conscious of my worn out soccer shorts and ratty NIU sweatshirt. I wore my cleats to the game but have switched into a pair of Crocs with Mickey Mouse smiling on one and Minnie Mouse on the other. Christmas present from Kendra.

I don't catch myself in time to not take a quick glance at the Fed's ring finger, which is naked. I think he catches me looking, which is very embarrassing. I kick myself for looking because I have a sort-of boyfriend who is madly in love with me—at least that's what he tells me quite often. The problem is I'm not crazy in love with him. So I don't reciprocate with the words he longs to hear. Every time I try to break up, he assures me that he's very comfortable just being very good friends and that he is willing to wait for me to feel the same way for him that he feels for me. Did I mention that he keeps a one caret diamond in the consul of his car just in case I have a change of heart and suddenly want to marry him?

Captain Zaworski makes the introductions.

Nice suit guy is FBI, like I guessed, and his name is Austin Reynolds. Austin. Did his mom go through an English phase? The sergeant's name is Konkade, not Kincaid, so I was close. If he has a first name other than Sergeant he's not giving it out. The detectives are Bob Blackshear and Antonio Martinez. We all shake hands, say our "heys," and nod.

The mood is somber and I resist any temptation to crack a joke. Don't know why I would think to do so in the first place. We're talking about murder—and no one laughs at my jokes anyways. Except for Kendra. She thinks I'm hilarious.

Captain Zaworski passes photos around the room. A very pretty girl in the alive photos; a very disfigured girl in the crime scene shots. No details were given on the radio. Good thing. She died at the hands of someone very nasty and very good with a knife. Nope, no jokes today.

"How long have we been on the scene?" Konkade asks.

"A little more than two hours," Zaworski answers. Don and I look at each other in surprise. Konkade purses his lips and runs a hand over his bald scalp.

"Why aren't we there?" Don asks for both of us. "Time's wasting and the bugs are eating our clues."

Don's quick in meetings. My mind works fine; it just doesn't send messages to my mouth soon enough for me to speak up so that I look alert and contribute clever insights in a group setting.

"Soon enough," Zaworski answers. "Everything will still be there unmoved, including the body, when you get there. We're going slow on this one. Blackshear and Martinez got the first call and they got to walk around a couple minutes before we pulled them out for this briefing. They'll share some impressions in a moment. The deed was done right on jurisdictional lines." Zaworski pauses and continues, "we're not sure if the Second or Third Precinct owns it, so you'll be working together."

Uh oh, I think. Sharing and police work rarely go hand in hand.

"We're not sweating the politics," he adds, looking pointedly at me. "This one gets even more complicated." He looks around to make sure he has our undivided attention. "The second our initial report hit the data ports, a red flag went up in D.C., at FBI Headquarters. They've tagged a guy with a very sophisticated crime pattern. He's been killing lots of people and moving to new cities for a couple of years now. They think he's been a member of our community for the past six months, getting ready for his first victim in Chicago and a good number to follow."

Oh, man.

The captain goes on, "Major Reynolds was flown in by the U.S. Army this morning in order to assist us in our investigation. He's going to fill you in on what the FBI knows about our perp and help us apprehend him. Not only are we going to work well between precincts but also across agency lines. That order has been jointly issued from the director of the FBI and the CPD Commissioner. The mayor's office strongly endorses it."

Reynolds is a major. I guess that's impressive.

"Actually, I wish we knew more about who the perp is and how we're going to apprehend him, but we don't," Reynolds begins, clearing his throat. "About six years ago we got some extra software programming money from the Department of Homeland Security. We hired some geniuses from Silicon Valley to create a specialized search engine to cross-collateralize and correlate a number of local, state, and federal databases. The purpose was tracking terrorist activity, but some other good things came out of Project Vigilance."

Reynolds pauses dramatically for a sip of water and I whisper to Don, "wow, it's got a name. Project Vigilance; just like a spy novel." Don leans away, frowns, and arches his eyebrows to let me know I need to keep my mouth shut, which is appropriate and fair.

We all wait as Reynolds sets his water bottle down slowly and picks up his papers again. I can't pull off the pregnant pause like he's doing because I live in a constant state of fear that I'm putting people to sleep when I talk. There's precedence to support me on this one.

"PV is one of the biggest breakthroughs in profiling unsolved crimes," he continues. "Obviously, it connects the dots between federal, state, and local investigations. It gets people talking. One of the key ideas was to make information available whereby other law enforcement agents and analysts could study and make suggestions on a case, even if there was no solid line of connection with something they were working on. PV stole a page from a business textbook and has become a kind of a 'best practices' online symposium."

"I bet that goes over real good with the guys working the case," Martinez chimes in. "Sounds like one more way everybody in the world wants to second guess you and look over your shoulder if you're a cop."

"You'd be surprised at how well it works and how well it's been received, Detective Martinez," Reynolds answers. "I guess advice doesn't offend as much when someone's nose is in your case from a thousand miles away. But the unexpected positive outcome from Project Vigilance is that it has revealed to us almost one thousand connected cases. PV has correlated crime events that were once treated as singular and jurisdictional-specific crimes into non-isolated crime streams."

What did he just say? Jurisdiction-specific? Non-isolated crime streams? I'm writing this stuff down. I think I'm back at NIU in an advanced level Criminal Justice seminar.

"So boss, how come we aren't on Project Vigilance, if it's so good?" Martinez asks, turning to face Zaworski.

"It's still under review," the captain answers curtly with a steely look that suggests further comments and interruptions are not welcome.

I look straight down at my notebook. No way am I going to snicker. Don must have been worried about me because he kicks me under the table. Ouch.

"So did you start this Project Vigilance? Do you run it?" Blackshear asks Reynolds.

"I wish," he snorts. "No, I'm a single investigator who has benefited from someone else's vision and work."

I'm impressed. He is dutifully humble.

"I do have the distinction, however," he continues, "of identifying thirty-seven streams; more than any other investigator. I've spear-headed seventeen busts nationwide."

So much for being humble.

"But I've had my eye on one stream from the first day PV went live," he says after a dramatic pause. "This particular stream is pulled together from six unsolved crime factors. And by factor, in this case, I mean each of the cities that have experienced multiple murders—and all at the hands of the same perp, who I'm about to tell you about."

"How many murders in all?" Konkade asks.

"There are now six factors, which means six cities," he answers. After a pause he continues, "there are now forty-seven known murders. It's possible PV has missed some of his handiwork so there could be more."

Everyone is still. Blackshear gives a low whistle. Don whispers, "Sweet Jesus," under his breath. Martinez crosses himself and mumbles something in Spanish, which I can't quite hear but I assume is a prayer.

"Today's murder is just the first he has planned for your city," Reynolds continues. "We believe Leslie Reed is victim number forty-eight."

I can't help myself; I gulp. An hour ago I was poking my finger in a coach's chest for encouraging rough play. Now I am saying a prayer for help with something that really matters. Okay, that matters, too, but this really matters. Someone has committed forty-eight murders and is running free. How can that be?

"We haven't seen our friend for almost seven months, so we were afraid he had changed his *modus operandi* and disappeared from PV's ability to detect patterns. Honestly, I was starting to go a little crazy with the thought that I wouldn't get another shot at him. But last night tells us—or at least strongly suggests—he's back."

Reynolds continues to speak. The phrase "he's back" repeats itself in my mind as he lays out details of forty-seven murders in six cities and why last night's murder in my city looks like a fresh start and a new factor.

"If this guy's so smart," Blackshear interrupts, "how are we going to catch him and then convict him when we do? Chicago's a big city with plenty of judges who are quite fond of criminal rights."

"The catching part is tough. No one in this room is going to argue with you on that point," Reynolds responds. "But once we do, this guy is so delusional that he'll probably have his confession written out, printed, and bound in leather. Sociopaths love narratives. As long as they're the star of the story, of course. But I can assure you, we are going to do everything by the book." He goes on to tell us about the perpetrator's childhood and adolescence; about what makes him tick.

Forty-seven murders in six previous cities. Murder number forty-eight has happened in my precinct—or at least right next to it. Holy cow.

I hate when bad people go free. Klarissa says I get too uptight and worry about things I can't control. Dad said that makes me a good cop.

Chapter 8

I turn the ignition on my '97 Miata; it starts right up. That's a good thing because it's been acting real funny for the past couple of months. I keep meaning to get it in the shop tomorrow, but tomorrow becomes today and I keep looking for parking spaces located on inclines, so if it won't start, I can roll it backwards and pop the clutch in reverse. I'm glad I couldn't afford an automatic transmission when I bought this thing slightly used.

Don looked up my car online for me and says a salvaged starter will cost about two hundred bucks. I could actually afford the starter if that was the total bill. But that doesn't cover labor, which will be at least the same amount. I almost had enough put aside when I decided to switch from a standard issue Glock service revolver to a Beretta. It's my third handgun in the past three years, so the CPD Armory only paid half the bill. Half of seven hundred bucks is serious change on my salary.

I've also procrastinated on getting my car fixed because there's the question of spending the better half of a day in the waiting room of an auto shop drinking burnt coffee out of a Styrofoam cup. Isn't that what work is for? Based on the selection of magazines last time I went to Phil's Phast Auto, I have no burning desire to catch up on the monster truck circuit or how to build pecs that will drive her wild. Who reads that stuff anyway? Maybe I'm just jealous because the one guy with the huge pecs in the weight room at the Y doesn't notice me. But the competition is stiff and he only has eyes for his own reflection in the mirror.

I look at the cracked leather passenger seat and think about how hot this thing used to look. No major body damage but a dent in the back left corner. There's a little rust there now. Something else I don't have money to spend on right now. I frown.

Where has my newfound good attitude gone? It didn't even last half a day. Shoot, it didn't survive a soccer game with seven-year-olds.

I look down at my cell, which I left in the front passenger seat. Six missed calls. This is not good. I've been at the crime scene for four hours, still decked out in my paint-stained sweat shirt with a couple holes in it. I realize now that I forgot to call Dell, the guy with the diamond in the consul of his Lexus, to let him know something had come up. He's been after me to drive out of town about two hundred miles to see a historical Amish village. I've been putting him off forever. I think my new case qualifies as a good excuse, a great excuse, in fact. But after having used several lame excuses in previous weekends, he'll just feel put off again. I could be honest and just tell him I'm not interested in nineteenth century customs and furniture, even if everything is made without metal nails or the aid of electricity. I'm such a Philistine.

Dell feels put off pretty easily even if he fights hard not to show it. He's not that hard to read. Of course, I am a detective. Wonder if he feels put off because I always put him off? I met him at church six months ago, which I've been told is a great place for single adults to meet members of the opposite sex with shared values and beliefs. I agree with all that, but it certainly doesn't mean I'm morally obligated to fall for a guy just because he's good looking, has a great job, drives an expensive car, and is very spiritual, all of which Dell is or seems to be.

Maybe it's the pressure I feel from everyone, including my sisters. Maybe it's his name: Dell. I am thankful I haven't been asked to meet his parents yet, because there's a good chance I'd bring the name thing up. Maybe it is Dell's earnest patience with me that sabotages my feelings for him. He basically says he's there for me and is willing to wait until I feel the same about him.

Kaylen says that's incredibly romantic. I hate to admit it, but it's actually a bit of a turn off for me. And what's with the Amish village thing? My mom says I always knew whether something was going to be fun or interesting before I gave it a chance—and that I was often wrong. I don't remember the being wrong part as much as she does.

I've missed one call from Kaylen and five from Dell. Three voice messages. I just hit the call back option for Dell. I'm not crazy about him but I do think I should explain what's going on. The ring tone bleats four times then clicks into voicemail: "You've reached the phone of Dell Woods…"

I jab the "off" button with my pointer finger. Better to listen to my voicemails from him first anyway. I do believe this is the first time Dell hasn't picked up my call within the first two rings. I guess I made him mad. Good for him. I should make him mad. I don't treat him as well as he deserves. If I don't feel guilty, it's because I'm honest with him, except for the Amish village thing. Besides, six months isn't very long to really know who someone is.

I'm on the entrance ramp to the cross-town expressway that will deliver me to my apartment and hot shower in twenty minutes. I work through the gears quickly and have it in fifth before I've merged onto the actual highway. The Saturday night party crowd is still at home getting ready, so I have pretty light traffic to weave through.

Austin Reynolds of the FBI was pretty thorough on what we should expect when we got to the victim's trendy townhouse. But I don't think you can be thorough enough to prepare someone for the shock of what we saw.

I've been in homicide two years now. Got that and my gold detective shield a year earlier than my dad did. So I've seen my share of death and destruction. But whoever this guy is, he's a sicko. He's evil. I'm not positive the case is going to stay with Don and me, but I have some intense feelings coursing through my body and soul. I can physically feel something from the top of my head to the soles of my feet. I'm angry, but it doesn't feel like the lousy kind of anger I've been mired in the last couple months. Maybe I'm feeling a little of the holy anger Mom likes to brag about when talking about Democrats and the liberal bias in the media. All I know for sure is that I want to be the one to bring this guy in before he does any more damage.

I wrap one towel around my body and one around my hair after a thirty-minute shower. Got every last ounce of hot water there was. I'm fading fast now. I want to do my nails, but may not have the energy. I plop on my couch and pick up the remote. I'm debating between watching a TV show or just hitting the sack.

I grabbed an oven roasted turkey sandwich at Subway on my way home and then did a workout in my living room to blow off steam. I started with eagle jumps but they make too much noise and I didn't know if the old guy who lives below me was home or not, so I only did one set of thirty. I shadow boxed for ten minutes, keeping my fists at chin level the whole time—my arms were on fire the last two minutes—and then did crunches. I worked up quite a sweat before hitting the shower.

I look at my cell phone. No new messages. Dell still hasn't called back. I left him a pretty detailed explanation, leaving out crime scene details, of course, but I suspect he has had his fill of my explanations and is being a little passive aggressive. Good for him.

Sometimes, no matter how long of a shower you take, you just can't feel clean. I toss the remote on my couch and head to the bedroom. I pick up a John Grisham novel I got at the library. I only make it through ten pages before my eyes get too heavy to continue. I don't do well on books when I keep getting interrupted. I turn off the light.

Chapter 9
April 2, 6:03am

```
DEATH IN THE CITY: NEW IN A THEATRE NEAR U!
By ChiTownBlogger
```

>   ChiTownBlogger—ChiTown's numero UNO source 4news that matters—is a 24/7 legend 2u and 4u cuz he never sleeps!!! Good thing he's all seein cuz this town is going n2 a death spiral in2 Lake Meatchicken—don't flush!—if some1 doesn't start payin attention. With Heir Daniels as Mayor this is an ISSUE. (Poly Sci 101 told me 2identify "KEY ISSUES" so I'm identifying baby.) QUIZ: if a tree falls in one of our incredibly unsafe forest reserves and the CTB isn't listenin does it make a sound?????! We'll never know, cuz CTB doesn't sleep. But I bet some1 got mugged ;op

Started hearin some chatter on the police bands last nite. Very interesting chatter. So CTB started reachin out 2the people who know. That eliminates u and any1 on ur payroll, MAyor Daniels, so consider this a clue as 2one of the birdies who whispers tweet TWEET in my ear....!!

Somebody woke Das Mayor up from his beauty sleep. No easy task!! Sleeping Beautys been out for the count while crime and violent crime is up in Chicagoland 4a 3rd straight year!! What got the Mayor's attention? Yes, ur guess was same as mine. He had 2have finally caught the old lady who keeps lettin her dog do a nasty deed on the sidewalk w/o scooping it up in the leftover produce bag from Frankie's Fine Foods. but NOPE. That wasn't it.

I know. But do u? Not if u follow the city from 1of the serious news sources that sold their soul 2Mayor DAnny and his electioneering investors from AmeriCo. So I turned 2WCI Radio cuz I'm such a big fan of comedy. Sure nuf ChiTownBlogger fanz, its Professor Daniel's yard boy, the police chief, himself speakin. A fair maiden of our city was MURDERED and he's assuring us that he and our boys in blue r on it. If that doesn't sober u up and scare the dirty deed out of u, I don't know what will. I might start bringing 1 of those pooper scoopers with me on walks if CPD Chief Ferguson (Daniel's twin bumbler separated at birth???) is gonna talk 2me that way.

But WAIT. there's more here folksies. ur gonna get it 1st from moi. NOT WCI. NOT WGN. NOTa Nimrod's new conference. HERE. Just here. Now. Cuz some little birdie went tweet tweet in CTB's ear!!!! And CTB has got soul. Aretha and Marvin kind o' soul. If u want ur chicken and news battered, ur gonna have 2get it from Ike—or Mayor McDaniels.

U c, this isn't just DEATH IN THE CITY on the small tube. This is a theatrical release!!!! Our fair maiden wasn't just killed, though that seems 2make 4a sufficiently busy evening on date night. Seems this killer has peccadillo for BLOOD. A propensity for GORE. A penchant for SHARP objects that go slice slice SLICE in the night.

Need I say more???? Naaaah. I'll let the hacks from WCI play catch up and pretend they broke a story, a real story, 4the 1st time since urz truly hung his shingle out on ur internet pathway of life and u fell in love with his voice of Truth. Don't b coy. Admit it. U can't help urself. u love me! u really love me!!! Chief Ferguson got his feelings hurt a couple weeks ago and called me a muckraker with a capital M. Hey Fergie, how come no1 loves u? Cuz I think they really really really love me.

It ain't noon on a saturday and I'm already showing the mainstream media how 2do it. My eyes and ears r open throughout the city ... I hear and c all... so rest easy dear fans ... Ciao! and XOXOXO ... from ur fav blogger! ChiTownBlogger is out but never down!

Can't wait 2read ur responses. Who goes first? Who is it? cuz FIRST POSTER gets 2 free gallons of fuel from my homeboys at the GAS & GRUB on Halstead. (The only thing Mayor Daniels makes go up faster than crime is gas prices!)
>

Chapter 10

I look at the clock on my nightstand. How did it get to be 9:40 already? Did I just sleep ten hours? Well, since I tossed and turned all night and never really drifted off, I guess the question is whether I've been in bed ten hours. I've overslept big time. My feet hit the floor with a start. I told Kaylen I would get to church early to help her with Kendra's Sunday School class. Soccer coach; class helper; what next? Weekend babysitter? Oh, I've already done that, too. Many times.

I slide into the pew next to Kaylen. She's singing and barely acknowledges me. That means she is not happy with me. She finally looks over a stanza or two later and gives a half-hearted nod. I don't think her smile is totally sincere, but she's gorgeous and is developing the cutest baby bump and she's my older sister. I immediately feel better even if she's being pouty; not real nice for a pastor's wife I think with a smile. I missed all of Sunday School and I'm fifteen minutes late for the worship service. That means another ten minutes of singing. All standing up. The words are projected on a screen. I understand contemporary church services are designed to appeal to contemporary people like me, but it wouldn't kill us to sing a couple verses from the hymnal—sitting down preferably. Ten minutes of announcements and the offering will follow. Danny will preach about thirty-five minutes.

We're usually out the door at noon sharp. The Baptists have all the good restaurants tied up by then—the Charismatics will follow in waves at one thirty or so. We're in the no-man's land of Sunday dinner timing, so we always eat at Danny and Kaylen's house. We used to do it at Mom and Dad's house, but there is more room at Danny and Kaylen's. Mom will be there. Tradition can be a good thing. Like I said, it wouldn't kill us to pick up a hymnal and sit down for a song or two. I think the hip and contemporary train left the station without me. Klarissa, my baby weathergirl sister, got in the first class car.

I'm leaning hard with two hands on the chair in front of me. Kaylen's giving me sideways glances and decides to forgive me for slinking in late. I get a sideways hug.

My mind sometimes wanders in church, but not today. It stays focused. Just not on church. I'm thinking about yesterday's meeting at headquarters. After Reynolds' presentation, Captain Zaworski recapped the FBI profile of our alleged perp. Male. White. Very methodical; maybe an accountant or engineer. He's intelligent. Watches TV, because he leaves next to no trace of his existence at the scene. All those shows on forensic evidence have seen to that, even though technically, every human encounter does leave some physical record of having occurred. He blends in well. Probably helps old ladies cross the street. Will say hi to new neighbors, but won't engage. His relationships won't be in his neighborhood. He's a good actor.

How the FBI has identified his bonding issues, desire for narrativity, and a childhood filled with an alienating, abusive, and neglectful father and an absent mother—left the family? Died?—is beyond me. And as I like to tell Don and anyone else who will listen, I'm not just muscle and good looks. I am a college graduate. Not *summa* or *magna cum laude*, but *cum laude* by the skin of my teeth, and that's still honors in my book. I'm on the slowest boat possible towards a master's degree in criminal justice. That means I sign up for three classes a year and usually drop one of them on the exact date that doesn't count against me grade-wise, but where I don't get much of my tuition money refunded. My mom gets after me but I'm on my own dime now.

I'm not sure how all this psycho data is going to help us actually find him. But Reynolds does have one clue we can actually work on. In five of the six known cities our murderer has worked, multiple victims attended Alcoholics Anonymous meetings. This apparently confused the FBI a lot at first because the profiling doesn't suggest someone who abuses alcohol or drugs. Someone finnaly suggested the obvious; he is pretending to have a drinking problem. All the pieces fell together.

Of course, we're putting a lot of confidence in a computer program called Project Vigilance. We're assuming Virgil—I've given the program a name of my own—hasn't missed other cities that would reflect a broader or emerging pattern of behavior. To be fair to good old Virgil, he's only going to be as good as the input he has to work with.

Reynolds is convinced that the connection of the forty-seven previous crime scenes is valid and that we are factor number seven. Not sure why he just can't say the seventh city. Our perp has been hibernating for six months and is ready for serious business again and might be pretending to be a recovering alcoholic.

Leslie Reed and many of the other victims didn't attend AA, but enough did—thirty-one to be exact—that it's a major priority in our investigation.

Kendra has switched spots with her mom and is at my side. She tugs on my sleeve. How long have I been the only one in the congregation standing? Kaylen looks over and stifles a laugh. I guess long enough to be noticeable. Is Danny giving me a dirty look from the pulpit? I'll remind him that pastors aren't supposed to do that. I'm sure his message is scintillating as he starts off with a good joke that people find very funny but my mind wanders away again. It's yesterday.

We agreed that the four detectives in the room would start attending a couple AA meetings a week. I don't drink—okay, I've had a sip of Klarissa's white wine on occasion—but I've heard enough sob stories from winos when I walked a downtown beat in uniform that I can fake it good enough. For that matter, there are enough cops with drinking problems—self-medicating with alcohol is one of those occupational hazards that come with keeping the peace—that everyone on the force most likely has first hand experience themselves or with someone who has been in or should be in AA. We considered putting out the word that any department employees who already attend AA meetings need to keep their eyes open. We couldn't quite figure out what they were to look for—or how to keep that kind of information from getting leaked to the press, so we scrapped the idea.

There was nothing else but the crime scene. We dispersed quickly and all seven of us headed out in separate cars to caravan over to a small apartment house in Washington Park. I didn't even mess with the starter on my Miata, I rolled it back and popped the clutch.

I'm back in church. Danny is winding things down up front. He asks a couple of questions about the current state of our soul in the matter of anger. That wakes me up. If I had paid attention I wouldn't have been so surprised that he wasn't talking about having too much bad anger, which is a problem for me right now—at least that's what Kaylen says and I'm starting to agree—but rather not having enough Godly anger. Holy anger. Righteous anger. My mom's kind of anger. Things that make God mad are supposed to make us mad.

Okay. I can embrace that. First of all, I already feel lousy about myself right now, and it's nice to not feel judged for once lately, especially at church. But even more so, I was at a crime scene unlike anything I've ever witnessed. Worse than any of the films they showed us at the academy. Slasher film bad. If that doesn't stir some Godly anger, I don't know what will.

We pray the benediction as I stretch and arch my back; I think I sigh out loud because Kaylen gives me an elbow to the rib. Not very nice of her.

Danny says "amen" and I turn into the aisle. I see Dell about six rows back. Our eyes lock. I pop mine wide open and tilt my head to the side plaintively to give the "I'm sorry" expression. He takes a step backward and half turns as a twenty-something puts her hand in the crook of his arm. He looks back at me, trying to stifle a look of triumph.

Okay. Unexpected. But you go, Dell. I had that coming.

Chapter 11

The crime scene.

We should have carpooled but no one wanted to lose anymore of a Saturday afternoon in the salt mine.

We pulled into a narrow street in Washington Park. Three and four story houses, each two units wide; the classic Chicago row house neighborhood. A few double-wides were spotted throughout the neighborhood; small apartment houses. It was one of those streets that is timeless; it could pass for elegant '50s or as Neo-Bohemian, early twenty-first century. The side yards weren't much more than the width of a sidewalk and maybe a row of tomato plants. A back alley serviced small parking lots behind each house that could accommodate maybe six cars. That meant half the street's residents parked out front. It was one of those enclaves undergoing gentrification. Everything was well cared for and a lot of expensive cars were on the street.

There were already six or seven black and whites with blue lights rotating but unseen in the bright sunlight, a couple of dark brown Crown Vics, indicating the brass had arrived, an ambulance, and two crime scene vans. Both of the vans were wedged on the strip of grass and sidewalk in the front.

As we approached the front steps, we could hear a neighbor explaining to a uniform that the vehicles would damage the lawn and somebody was going to have to pay for it. The kid, stoic in a starched blue, was looking right in the lady's eyes, but obviously not listening.

Two of the uniforms had set up sawhorse road blocks a couple houses away in each direction. One of the guys had pulled the barrier aside to let our train of cars trail in. Our entourage officially finished filling in the center of the street. I thought I was last to pull up, which I figured was good because it would be easier to get out when we were done.

I had forgotten about Major Reynolds' car. He drove a rented Cadillac in behind me. I didn't think the government approved luxury cars on expense reports. I figured he's either more important in the Bureau than we already suspected or he's going to explain that Hertz double upgraded him because they didn't have the full-size car he reserved.

The seven of us huddled at the front steps and he explained the latter; the Caddy was an upgrade. I was relieved to know he's a humble everyday officer of the peace, just like the rest of us. Not. He looked like he should be picking up a date for dinner rather than visiting a bloody crime scene.

Blackshear offered each of us a cotton ball dipped in a little ammonia mixture, if we needed something to help us with the smell we were about to encounter. No one wanted to be the first to touch a drop above the lip and beneath the nose because it would look weak. An EMT staggered through the front door, leaned over the rail, and sent his breakfast and lunch spewing. Maybe even his snack from the night before. We applied the ammonia in unison.

Martinez led us up the steps into the foyer. The security door was propped open. We walked past twelve white buttons underneath twelve, dull brass-colored mail slots; each about four inches wide and eight inches tall. That meant four two-bedroom apartments per floor. I did a little calculation in my head and figured at least two thousand square feet each. Probably storage cages and a laundry room in the basement. Twelve foot ceilings on the first floor. A wide circular staircase and a small three to four person elevator dominated the lobby. Everything was in great shape, including the elevator with a black button, the size of a checker, for each floor. I poked my head in and rejoined the circle of investigators in the foyer.

"According to the neighbors, our victim lived alone," Blackshear started.

"Nice apartment and furniture. She appears to be a very neat person. No sign of anyone breaking in. We've checked all ground floor windows and front and back doors. For right now we're assuming the victim knew the perp and let him in voluntarily."

"Or her," I said. I thought it was a good point and worth noting. You know, not starting with any assumptions on anything, including gender. No one commented.

"Our victim," Blackshear started again, but Don interrupted—

"What's Leslie's age?"

"Late twenties, early thirties," Blackshear said. He flipped back in his black notebook. "Thirty-two. I'm not good with ages anyway but her attacker didn't make it easy to tell." He paused and got his train of thought again. "She's single; an accountant in a big firm downtown. She's got the title, 'vice president,' on her card. Must be smart to be a VP this young."

"Divorced? Married?" Don interrupted again.

"Our uniforms have been covering the neighborhood and making calls. We got the human resources director from her firm into the station and he's being very helpful. She's divorced. No kids. And before you interrupt again, Don, we've already got a call in with the ex but no answer yet. He doesn't live here anymore. He's in the L.A. area. Maybe he slept late."

Don just nodded calmly at the rebuke. No big deal. I need to learn poise from him. It was just the type of comment that I would have perceived as a major slight. I would have stewed the rest of the day.

My mind went to the ex-husband. Family is always going to be first suspects. Especially an ex. If he was sleeping in, he was about to get a wake up call from the LAPD.

"He took her cell phone just like every other time so we have to wait on the phone log," said Blackshear. "If Major Reynolds is right, the log isn't going to help us anyway. No sign of forced entry in her third floor door either. And incidentally, no one we've talked to remembers hitting the entry buzzer to let a stranger in yesterday."

That's the oldest trick in the book for burglars. Hit buzzers until someone answers. Tell them you're UPS delivering a package or you're dropping a cake off for your aunt on a different floor. People hit the entry button because they don't want to be hassled. Of course, after a murder, who is going to admit they were the one who opened the door for a serial killer to get in the building?

"Time of death?" I asked.

"Not official, of course," Martinez chimed in, "but probably a six hour window between seven p.m. yesterday and one a.m. this morning. The techies got her body temperature about ten this morning and it was down about fifteen degrees. Jerome was looking at dilation of her pupils and thinks time of death is closer to one a.m. Once the ME has her on the table, he'll be able to see how long the bugs have been nibbling on her."

"Didn't take long for someone to note that a person living alone is dead," Konkade said. "Is there a clue there? Who found her?"

"A neighbor on the second floor," Blackshear answered. "They run together most Saturday mornings. She confirmed with Ms. Reed that they'd meet at eight in the morning. That was at six thirty last night. We think she is the last person in this building to see or speak to her."

"Except for the perp," Don added. Everyone nodded.

"Yeah, except for him," Martinez shrugged. "*Este tipo es un loco bastardo.*"

I don't speak Spanish but I have a pretty good idea that Martinez wasn't being complimentary.

"Are we assuming that she died from the cutting wounds?" Don asked Blackshear.

Reynolds had just caught up with us and answered for Blackshear: "If the perp is who we think it is, then yes, he's bled her to death. It'll take a little time for your ME to confirm, however, because there will be a list of pharmaceuticals to factor and rule out, and his binding method does suggest asphyxia."

"Yeah, what he just said," Blackshear said with a nod of his head at Reynolds and a little shrug of his shoulders. "We've got more to give you," he continued, "but let's get everybody upstairs for their own look before the body really starts going bad. It's been a nice cool March, but the perp turned up the thermostat all the way. That's why Jerome's being shy on his time of death guess."

"It's April," I said.

No one commented. Oh well. I turned and was first in the elevator.

"Let's do the stairs," Blackshear said with a nod away from the elevator, "unless you've got all day. That thing is slow and we can't all fit in there."

We trudged up after him, me with my face burning red and feeling quite sheepish. Don wouldn't have given it a second thought.

The place was neat and stylish. Except for the corpse on the bed. Reynolds had reported in the profile session that the killer did not have sex with his victims. Possibly some foreplay. But apparently he—or she— got jollies in inflicting pain and cutting up women. He would drug them, secure them with duct tape, and spend a lot of slow, seemingly deliberate time with his knife; for most of that time they would be alive.

Toxicology reports from the various cases could not declare definitively the extent to which the victims were conscious and aware of what was happening to them. On the majority of victims that followed the pattern we were looking at, there were signs of struggle on the wrists and above the ankles, the main areas where they were taped down. But this could simply be in keeping with someone who is drugged but not quite knocked out putting up a last minute fight. The abrasions were not so severe to suggest the kind of frantic thrashing that someone in intense pain would exert. Back in the pre-crime scene meeting, Konkade had said that maybe our guy has a streak of mercy in him. Looking at Leslie Reed in the middle of her bed I doubt he's buying or selling that now. Maybe our killer has some kind of a code but mercy isn't in it.

We all took our time searching for clues, moving room to room and lingering in the main bedroom, while the two techies, Jerome, who guessed the time of death, included, waited patiently to bag the body and get it down to the morgue. I did a solo version of a line search, starting in one corner of each room, moving to the far corner, and then taking one step to the right each time so that I was sure to cover every square inch visually. Furniture makes this an inexact survey method, but with four detectives and a horde of other cops in the apartment, finding the proverbial needle in the haystack isn't what I was getting paid to do. No one was thinking the murderer had dropped his business card and it fell behind a seat cushion on the sofa.

I did my total pass through the apartment—town home is probably a better descriptor because the place is big and roomy—and then went back to the primary crime scene and just looked and breathed, doing my best to imagine what might have happened. I went back through every room, just trying to get a sense of the world of the victim and what might have drawn a killer to her—or her to him. I didn't have to struggle too much to come up with an answer as to what drew him to her. She was good looking, successful, neat, and had a great taste in art and furniture.

My mind can jump around and do crazy things and at one point I actually wondered if she had an interior designer help her decorate. The place was almost too well put together. But the indelible image burned into my mind during and after our crime scene review was the victim herself. Leslie. A real person with a real life, filled with joy and sorrow, dreams and disappointments. And she was gone.

We are a product of our upbringing and mine was very religious. There were signs of that scattered through the modest little Chicago row house I grew up in, from the picture of Jesus knocking on a door that hung by the thermostat in the hall leading to our three bedrooms, to the big beat up black leather Bible that sat on the nightstand on Dad's side of the bed. Leslie had no such imagery anywhere. My mind started wandering toward thoughts of the afterlife but I forced myself back on task.

Konkade left first and when we exited the building he could be seen talking with the uniforms that were first on the scene, probably reviewing protocol on how potential witnesses were separated and the evidence protected.

We reported to Zaworski on the front lawn and then Blackshear barked out orders to a group of ten uniformed officers. The two youngest were put on garbage pull. Seniority does have a few rewards. The rest were given a few instructions and assigned to help us start canvassing the immediate and adjoining blocks. When we met together three hours later, all of us had the same story. Nobody remembered seeing anything unusual last night. We didn't talk to anyone who actually knew Leslie Reed. Chicago is supposedly a city of neighborhoods, but this section of Washington Park wasn't being very neighborly right now.

I went home, did my makeshift workout, and took a long shower. I read through my notes. I cried. I prayed. I tried to read Grisham and turned off the light. I fell asleep with light jazz playing in the background to soothe my frazzled psyche. I had put on an old Larry Carlton CD, *Solid Rock*, which I like a lot for the tunes, but also because it is guitar rather than sax driven. I like sax fine but a little guitar is a nice change of pace in today's jazz landscape. I'm really not into jazz that much but it does serve as my kick back genre. But sleep didn't come even when Larry played "Deacon Blues." Just thoughts of Leslie. I don't know what time I drifted off but it wasn't that far away from time to wake up. No wonder I was late to church.

Kaylen didn't know that. I'm not mad at her. I love my sister, both of my sisters, fiercely. I wish they understood me a little better.

I wish I understood me a little better.

God help me understand everyone a little better.

Chapter 12

"So what gives with Dell?" Klarissa asks.

I am chewing a large piece of grilled chicken, my second helping, so I don't answer right away. I've already devoured the twice baked potatoes, fruit salad, broccoli and cheese, three Sister Shubert's dinner rolls with plenty of butter, and a couple bites of Kendra's macaroni and cheese.

I think that macaroni and cheese is all the kid eats. And not just any brand. It has to be Kraft or the noodles don't taste right, she claims. Her parents need to make Kendra eat green stuff—and not just lime jello. If I had to eat vegetables growing up, then Kendra needs to, too. If they'd make her eat more healthy foods, I'd eat healthier, too, especially when I sit next to her at Sunday dinner.

My weathergirl sister is carefully cutting another microscopic sliver of chicken, probably not big enough to choke a lab rat. She puts it silently in her mouth and starts to chew slowly. She has to be going through the motions because there's not enough meat to require more than two to three bites before swallowing. Most of her food is still on her plate and there wasn't much to start with.

Good thing I was busy chewing and couldn't answer or I would have smarted off something about what's up with the Warren. Warren is her on-again, off-again boyfriend. He's the sports guy at a rival television station.

They met at a local media awards banquet. He's about ten years older than Klarissa, but fit and handsome. Great teeth. All good gifts come from God, but not those teeth. Is it possible to have teeth that are too good? Too straight? Too white?

Apparently he was a good enough college quarterback at Western Illinois that he got drafted by the Redskins. He has told me that he stayed in "the league"—which means the NFL, he explains, in case as a mere woman I get confused about sports lingo—for three years; numerous times. He doesn't mention the fact that he never took a single snap in a regulation game, but now I'm being snippy again. If you were good enough to get drafted in the NFL then you were one heck of an athlete. He's been a sportscaster since his playing days ended at the ripe old retirement age of twenty-six. Not that he ever played in a regulation game, I think again.

"Well?" she asks again. Klarissa isn't going to let this drop.

I chew extra slow and finally answer her question after a fake cough and long drink of Diet Coke with a clever question of my own: "What do you mean?"

"You know what I mean."

"About what?"

"About Dell." She's trying not to get exasperated.

"What about him?"

"He was at church with someone else. I didn't know you two had broken up."

"I didn't know we two were together."

"Well, excuse me, but he's been coming to Sunday dinner for the last six months and last I heard, which was exactly one week ago, you two were dating. So what happened?"

"Kaylen didn't tell you?"

Klarissa's head swivels accusingly toward Kaylen who is no help to me as a diversion. She rolls here eyes and shrugs her shoulders.

"Don't ask me," she says with a bite of food still in her mouth, jabbing an accusing finger at me. "I know nothing. She's just trying to get off the hook."

Klarissa turns back toward me.

"Did something happen when you went to the Amish village?"

I laugh out loud and spit Diet Coke on my now empty plate. Kendra and Daniel think that's hilarious and screech in delight. Klarissa is not amused.

"Give it up," she demands. Now everyone at the table is looking at me soberly, including Kendra's little brother, Daniel. Dad is Danny, so son is Daniel. I think they got something turned around on the name thing.

"Where's Mr. Dell?" Daniel asks me earnestly. "I like him."

"That's because he gives you a dollar for your piggy bank whenever he comes over," I answer him.

"He does?" Kaylen asks, surprised. Daniel's head bobs up and down but he doesn't make eye contact with his mom due to an instinctual understanding that too much discussion could lead to the end of a good situation. I think it might be a good time to change the subject, but now Danny is curious.

"Dell seems like a good guy. He's obviously crazy about you. What happened?"

Do I sense an undercurrent of recrimination in his tone? It's no secret that Dell has done all the work in our relationship. Honestly, I'm just not crazy about him. I like him. But that's it. I've never been dishonest with him or led him on. So why are people trying to make me feel guilty? Everyone is looking at me, including Mom, so I guess I'm trapped and have to say something. But it's not like this has been a big deal to me. The younger than me twenty-something was more than a bit of a surprise, but hey, maybe she likes learning about farm implements from another century.

"I wish I could give you guys the scoop," I say. "But there's no story. Everyone move along. Nothing to see here."

"Did something happen yesterday when you went for the drive over to the Amish colonies?" Kaylen asks. Is there a retro obsession with horse and buggy culture? Is the energy crisis that bad?

"Well, we didn't really take a drive."

"Oh?" Klarissa's eyebrows are arched upwards. Should I tell her that will cause wrinkles? That would give her something more important to think about. Everyone is staring at me, including Daniel.

"What?" I ask. "I just said we didn't go."

"Did Dell have to go in to work?" Mom asks. "Because I know he's really been looking forward to seeing the Amish colonies."

"Actually, I got called into work, Mom. Right after Kendra's soccer game. I have a job, too. And I might as well let everyone know, I caught the case that's on the front page of today's paper."

"You're doing security when the President comes to town?" Mom asks.

"No. The murder in Washington Park."

"I didn't catch that story," Danny says. "That sounds awful."

"Yeah, I heard two of the producers talking back in the production room," Klarissa says. "A boyfriend shot her or something?"

"No guns were involved."

"Well that's good," Mom says. "Now tell me again why you didn't take the drive with Dell? I think he's a sweetheart."

Daniel saves me. He kind of liked the Diet Coke trick, so he spews milk in a fine mist all over the table. Kaylen is up in a flash and his smile turns to a plaintiff wail to let her know it was all a big misunderstanding. She marches him from the room with a swat on his butt. Kendra knows she's not supposed to smile but does so anyway. Danny gives her a look and she frowns appropriately. Mom looks at me from the corner of her eyes without turning her head my way. I know she thinks I'm being a bad influence on the kids. Hey, my beverage malfunction was an accident; Daniel did his on purpose I want to say. After a moment of awkwardness, Danny gets the conversation rolling again. He's good at that.

Thankfully the table has lost interest in Dell and Amish folkways. The Washington Park murder is forgotten, too. We talk about the Cubs and about the great spring weather, even though it has been all over the charts temperature-wise. We discuss why some people believe in predestination and eternal security for a few minutes, which somehow segues to a new discussion on whether Klarissa should consider interviewing for the weather job with the number three television station in New York City, which would be one step closer to a national position.

I want to hear more about predestination because I'm wondering how it is people do the things they do. Especially evil people who cut up innocent women; innocent being a relative term, of course. I also want to ask Danny if he thinks it is ever okay to tell a lie, like when it is for a good cause or just by omission or part of the job description as a detective. But once the conversation transitions to Klarissa's career and then back around for another go at the weather—Mom says that the wind yesterday really cut like a knife—I stop paying too much attention. I do listen carefully to a joke Kendra tells me in a loud whisper when she loses interest in big people talk.

"Knock knock."

"Who's there?"

"Canoe?"

"Canoe who?"

"Canoe come out and play?"

I laugh enthusiastically and interrupt something Danny was saying for just a second, but he soldiers on. I do fear Kendra has inherited the same gene I got on joke telling. Hopefully she'll have a better left foot in soccer than I ever did.

Kaylen and Daniel return—he no worse for the wear—as Danny tells everyone about Kendra's three goals. She beams. I beam. Daniel is ready for some attention and insists that he plays soccer, too, and that he scored ten thousand goals yesterday. I love my family.

But all I can think about is Leslie Reed and the family she left behind—a mom and dad in Columbus, Ohio, a brother in San Diego, and a sister out in Lake County.

God, help us tell them we caught her killer.

Chapter 13

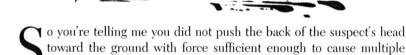

S o you're telling me you did not push the back of the suspect's head toward the ground with force sufficient enough to cause multiple abrasions and bruising to his facial area?"

"No sir, that's not what I said."

It's Monday morning and I wasn't in the greatest mood to start with. I'm not a Monday morning groaner as a rule. I don't go out partying over the weekend as a few of my colleagues are want to do—and it sure shows on their faces on Monday mornings. I wasn't in a sour mood because I don't like my job. In fact, I love my job.

This particular Monday morning just started wrong. First of all, after not enough sleep on Saturday night and church and Sunday dinner with my family, I spent most of Sunday afternoon and early evening in the situation room back at the precinct. Ever since the advent of CNN and around-the-clock cable news, plus a new generation of cop shows, you have to name things with a little more flair. It's not good enough to go to a conference room. It's got be something dramatic, like a *situation room.*

I got home at eight, ready to do a light workout with my home exercise equipment, which consists of a floor, gravity, and the weight of my body. Then I was going to relax with my favorite TV show and get to bed early. But I procrastinated and by the time I was poised to do a set of one-legged squats Dell stopped by to talk things out. It was quarter to nine. He knows that at quarter to nine there's only fifteen minutes until the only show I watch every week comes on and that I struggle to program TiVo. He also knows I wind down by nine on Sunday nights and need some alone time after a typical Sunday with my family.

I knew the second he walked through the door I opened in response to his loud knocking, uninvited I would add, he was mad and was going to vent. And vent he did. Hey, I never pledged undying love and devotion. Heck, I never even gave a hint of reciprocity. I never let the guy steal a full hug or kiss—though that hasn't seemed to be on his agenda, which I've thought is a little weird based on previous relationships that involved a lot of hand to hand combat to keep the wolves at bay. And even if I did miss a Saturday drive in the country, for obvious good reasons—and admittedly, I didn't make that much of an effort to get hold of him and explain—it wasn't me who brought a revenge date to church. Why am I the bad one?

After I had heard enough of his pain and suffering at my hands and a little bit of analysis on my inability to bond, I came back with both guns blazing. Not literally, of course, because I am already in trouble with the department over my temper—and based on my latest shooting range score, he wasn't in grave danger anyway. I explained clearly that any pain and suffering he was feeling was self-induced. I let him know I liked him, but reiterated that I did not return the level of feelings he professes toward me. I let him know we had covered this territory before. And I let him know that I thought his church date was cute and that perhaps he needed to devote his considerable attentions in that direction.

His response was interesting: "You know it's only you, babe. I was hurt and just wanted to get your attention. It was stupid to bring Carrie to church. Will you ever be able to forgive me?"

I don't think he was listening. I may not like a guy showing me up and putting me under the spotlight with my family, but there is nothing to forgive. I pushed him out the door at eleven. I was so tired I didn't brush my teeth or hang up my clothes. I just fell in bed and squirmed under the covers. When I woke seven hours later, it felt like my teeth had a film to rival barnacles on the underside of a cruise ship. When I stumbled to the bathroom and took a look at myself in the mirror it was downright frightening. That's how I greeted Monday morning after my alarm went off like a tornado warning at six.

It didn't help that when I arrived at my cube, with just fifteen minutes to spare before my interview—or is that interrogation?—with Internal Affairs was to begin, there was a large Post-it Note on the center of my computer screen with a carefully scripted message written in all caps:

DEAR DETECTIVE CONNER—HAVEN'T MEANT TO LEAVE YOU OUT! JUST WANTED TO LET YOU KNOW THAT YOU ARE ALWAYS WELCOME TO BE A PART OF AARP! (ANGRY AND RAGING POLICE PERSONS.) WE FEEL YOU'VE GOT LOTS OF PROMISE. YOU'RE EVEN BEING CONSIDERED FOR A MENTORING ROLE. DETAILS TO COME!

That was bizarre. Who would write that? I looked around a couple times and then crumbled it up and threw it away. I wasn't going to give someone the satisfaction of seeing me get angry. For once.

I am in an interview room usually reserved for suspects. I guess that makes me a suspect. Tom Gray of Internal Affairs and I have been sparring in a twelve by ten room, complete with a six-foot folding table centered in front of a large mirror, which I and the two billion humans beings who have ever seen a cop show know is a one-way glass, for ninety minutes now.

If anyone from my detective squad—and the curiosity, and yes, embarrassment is killing me—has been watching, they've got to be close to nodding off. I'm not a cooperative suspect. Just as I was leaving my cubicle, Zaworski and Konkade stopped me and in hushed tones advised me to say as little as possible. That had me wondering if I should be worried. I'm still asking myself the same question at a time when the interview should have been long over.

After introducing himself just as Tom Gray, no rank given, which is not typical of an officer of the peace, he proceeded to open a thick manila file and leaf through it for almost ten minutes in complete silence. I knew he was trying to create an awkward silence where I would blurt out a confession of premeditated and unmitigated brutality.

Is it fair for me to suspect Mr. Gray of such subterfuge? That's a joke, of course. That's exactly what he was trying to do. It's what I would do if I were in his shoes.

I wanted to say, hey, Tom, thanks for coming prepared and respecting my time. Instead I sat quietly, very atypical of me. The whole time he leafed through files I so wanted to tell him that as a big city cop I knew what he was doing. Say nothing and rely on an intimidating silence to get the suspect talking. I guess that's why Zaworski stopped by and told me to keep it zipped. Finally the Internal Affairs sphinx spoke and we struggled through ninety minutes of tortured back and forth.

I think we're coming to the end—maybe wishful thinking—and make myself refocus.

"I don't understand," he says. "You said that in cuffing the alleged robbery perp, you pushed him to the ground while your partner covered you with a drawn weapon. If the threat was nullified, why push?"

"Tom, the punk may be an *alleged* smash and stash perp to you from the comfort of your office, but the knife he waved in my face and with which he ruined my favorite suit top in an attempt to pierce my also non-alleged skin was very real. You've been studying the report like its tomorrow's final exam, so I think you know a lethal weapon, brandished at a police officer by a suspected murderer was recovered and the punk's prints were positively identified. How many times do I have to repeat that?"

"I understand exactly what you're saying about the knife, Detective Conner," he says as if speaking to a child who is a slow learner. "But I don't understand the contradiction in your testimony."

"Tom, there is no contradiction in my testimony, just in your questions."

He looks up, closes the folder, places one hand atop the other on the table, and raises his left eyebrow with a polite quizzical expression. I'm not going to answer an eyebrow, so he is going to have to ask it. We face off for thirty seconds, and I know that for a fact, because I counted from one-Mississippi all the way up to thirty-Mississippi.

He breaks the silence, asking, "how so?"

Ever difficult and actually not understanding what he's asking, I respond, "How so what?"

He stifles a sigh and asks politely, "how are my questions contradictory, Detective Conner?"

"I'm glad you asked, Tom. When you asked if I used excessive force, the answer was 'no.' When you asked if I pushed my attacker into the ground, the answer was 'yes.' So maybe the questions aren't technically contradictory, but neither are my answers. Yet you seem to find something contradictory there. I think your questions are ignoring an important qualifier. The qualifier is that the punk, someone who is suspected of murder, wielded a weapon with deadly intent and needed to be restrained."

"And yet your training specifically prohibits using retaliatory force once an alleged perp is remanded."

"But he wasn't remanded. I pushed him to the ground in the process of remanding him."

"But why with sufficient force to create contusions and abrasions? You said yourself that your partner had a gun trained on him."

"Well, Tom, when you're in the field, you learn that a lot can happen between the time a dangerous criminal is initially subdued and when he is actually in handcuffs and contained in a safe space. With all the action of the previous few minutes, we didn't know if he had another weapon or would make a desperate play for freedom that might involve harm to my body. If he had chosen to make things rough again, there may very well have been a moment when my partner's gun was trained on me, not the punk."

Tom interrupts, "but he was flat on the ground. You had cuffed him. The hard push came afterward."

"Tom, let me repeat, the push was because (a) he was squirming and struggling, and (b) he was not yet cuffed."

"Are you sure? Because that's not what I'm reading."

"I'm positive that the cuffs were not secured and that I needed to keep him down to protect myself from a head butt or donkey kick. The punk was resourceful."

"Why do you keep calling the alleged perpetrator a 'punk'?"

I say nothing. We stare at each other to see who will break eye contact first. He looks down. Hah! My first win of the day.

He reopens the file and riffles through a number of papers until he finds what he is looking for. He reads it studiously.

"Well maybe this explains my confusion," he says looking up, his eyes piercing into me. "The report, signed by you and detective Don Squires, doesn't mention the alleged perp squirming or struggling. In fact, it says he went down easy once Detective Squires entered the scene with drawn gun."

"It's a police report, Major Tom. Not a chapter from *War and Peace*."

I almost smile at my "Major Tom" reference but come back to reality quickly. Now my mind is a blur. Am I going to get punished in semantics? Or did I go too far with that push on the punk's head? I don't think so, but why in the heck am I getting grilled by my own department? Am I in trouble for getting physical with a dangerous criminal? You've got to be kidding me. I was first to the scene. If I hadn't been so fast, he would have gotten away. I was attacked. Despite words like "abrasions" and "contusions," I didn't really hurt him. I should have emphasized that the punk was squirming but that probably wasn't quite true. But he was sly and dangerous and I did want physical distance, even if it meant only inches of additional separation. And yes, I was mad. I'm wondering if this will kick me off the biggest case and news story in the city.

"Detective Conner?" Gray asks. "Is there something more you want to say?"

"I didn't know you asked another question," I answer defiantly. Probably time to read *How to Win Friends and Influence People* again, an assignment my dad gave me several times in my teen years, requiring a three page report filled with life lessons I had learned each time.

Gray is apparently done. He carefully organizes the file and places it in his brief case. He snaps the clasps and then places his case on the table. He takes off his glasses and wipes the lenses on his red tie with paisley amoebas. I'm not sure it's in style.

He picks up the case and walks towards the door. I stand and stretch my back. I don't know whether to be relieved or worried. He opens the door halfway, pauses, pulls it shut and turns back to me. I am suddenly wary.

He looks at me with his deep brown eyes and says, "Detective, I knew your father. Great cop. An even better man."

I freeze. Where's this going?

"I worked in the same office with him the last year or two he was on the force. I wasn't always in IA, so I know what you deal with on the streets."

I start to mumble something but he holds up his hand to stop me.

"Your father was one of the good guys and very good at putting away bad guys." Gray is speaking softly. It's hard to hear him and I lean forward despite a burning desire to lean as far away from him as possible. He lowers his eyes. "I never once heard him refer to any of his collars as a punk. And it's not because he arrested a bunch of saints. It's just not how he went about his business. This thing with Incaviglia is done. I don't see any real problem with your conduct. But for your old man's sake, I'm going to tell you straight up, I don't like the vibe you're projecting. This is not a path you want to be on. This isn't the first time you've expressed some real anger inside the department, either. I don't have to tell you that you're not real popular with top brass right now. Now isn't the time to make enemies—or make people suspicious of whether you have your act together. This conversation should have taken less than thirty minutes. We're off the record so you're welcome to ignore me, but you might want to think about talking to someone."

I want to say something. Maybe I want to say I'm sorry; sorry for pushing the perp's head into the pavement even if the APB described him as armed and dangerous; sorry for having such a crummy attitude; sorry for not respecting that he has a job to do, too; sorry that I don't care what the top brass thinks of me after what they did to my family. Or maybe I want to challenge him for laying a guilt trip on me. My eyes are moist. I'm not sure if it's because I'm mad or I'm sad. I look up. He's gone. I didn't see or hear him go.

I stand in a fog for a full minute. I look at my watch. It's almost nine thirty. Time to work on catching a killer.

Time to get serious about my anger problem.

Hi, I'm Kristen and I'm angry.

Chapter 14
April 3, 11:00am

*T*he crime scene was certainly interesting. A simple murder and half the city's finest showed up. Sweet potatoe pie, I'm good. Such attention. Such praise. And all for ME.

The guy that got out of the Cadillac wasn't local. His suit was way too nice. From the cut, I'm guessing a Hugo Boss. Nice shoes too. Bet they're not sewn by ten year olds in China. Probably has some guy with a British accent measure his feet and then the old lady from China sews them in the back room. Navy suit. Might have had a light blue strip in it. Couldn't tell for sure. I have to get better binoculars. He's got to be Fed. FBI. No big deal. About time they showed up. The Caddy was a rental so he's not from the Midwest office. Washington knows something a lot sooner than I thought they would. I figured they had to be aware of me by now, but maybe they know more than I give them credit for. I'll have to give that some more thought. Serious thought. But if I am on the Feds' radar screen all I can say is, it's about time. I invited them out to play like seven years ago. Now, where was I?

A girl detective appeared on the scene. Exquisite. Chestnut hair that he could imagine cascading like pure silk between his fingers. She turned in his direction, not seeing him, yet sensing something forbidden that she longed for.

My intentions are always purely platonic of course. I'm such the gentleman. But man, whoever her stylist is needs to be jailed for gross misconduct.

She's tough and in charge.

Weak and insecure.

Savvy.

Naïve. With the ugliest ride I've seen in a long time. And she was messy. Wearing a sweatshirt and beat up pair of shorts. I mean come on. Where is her sense of pride?

He wanted to get closer.

Much closer. Even though I'm more than a little repulsed by her lack of neatness. Sometimes my curiosity gets the better of me.

So much for me to think about. Me. Me. Me. And I need to think about the next turn in my story. Cubs are in town tonight. Put me in Sweet Lou. Who's on deck, coach? Batter up!

Chapter 15

I'm furiously scribbling notes from phone messages on my cell and office lines while trying to scan and delete email messages that don't require an immediate response. I fear my inbox is going to explode. I stop writing and just listen to the last message on my cell:

"Kristen, this is Dell. I know you're swamped. Don't worry about calling back. Just wanted to say … just wanted to say I'm sorry. I'm reading the *Trib* right now and can't imagine what you're having to deal with. I was just feeling sorry… just thinking of myself last night. You didn't … you don't need that burden right now. I also want you to know Carrie doesn't mean anything to me. Even if you don't feel the same way about me, you're the only one in my life. I'm here if you need someone to talk to. Whenever. Doesn't matter what time, day or night. I was miserable all day yesterday. Bringing Carrie to church was a bad idea. Well I guess it's not a bad idea to bring someone to church, but you know what I mean. She's in my office and we're just friends. I have to tell you, even if you don't want to see me again, I'm still going to invite myself to Sunday dinner with your family. I didn't grow up with that. You all are amazing. I really missed you and Klarissa's weekly fight. Plus Daniel is a buck short on his college fund now. Tell him I'll pay him double next week. Please? Seriously, I've … I've never felt like this for anyone in my life and I just want to say …"

Dell never got to finish his sentence. He ran out of message time. I shook my head and laughed out loud. His life story with me; no time for him. He deserves better. I told him that last night.

Carrie's an awfully cute girl. I hope she's treating him better than I do. Not really a tall order. I promise I'm not jealous, but is there a reason he keeps bringing her up by name to me? Have I ever complained to him about Carrie in the twenty-two hours I've been aware of her existence as a person and a revenge date? Even once? I might send Dell a text suggesting he find out if Carrie wants to tour an Amish village. Maybe she already did on Saturday.

I don't have time to think about Dell. That's been my life story when it comes to guys. I get too busy to engage. Mom says I *keep* too busy. I wonder how someone can just lay their emotions out on the table like Dell does. I mean, I think his phone message is a little embarrassing; for both of us. I know he does great in business—or based on the Lakeshore condo he's in and the Porsche Boxter he drives on weekends and the Lexus he drives during the week, it appears he does. He's explained to me that he is a freelance contract worker who specializes in supply chain management. I don't have a business background, but I get the basic idea. Actually I didn't until he explained it to me. Several times. Companies need materials to make products but don't want to pay for them or store them in a warehouse until they actually need them. The key is to make someone else be the banker, is how he put it, which usually means the manufacturer or even the supplier of raw materials. Okay.

Since I work for government, I'm confident I don't understand all the nuances of his business specialty. I'm pretty certain, for example, we have a lifetime supply of paperclips at the CPD. Dell could do wonders for us—but I'm not sure he'd be safe if an armed workforce found out the name of the person who wanted to mess with their supply of Styrofoam cups and sticky notes. Come to think of it, someone keeps forgetting to order coffee filters. I might have Dell put in a call to the purchasing department.

Dell's told me he moves a lot. He has shown me pictures of a rustic home on about twenty acres he has out near Durango, Colorado. Nineteen acres of pine and one acre cleared for the gravel driveway and home site. Only about thirty minutes from Wolf Creek Ski Resort. He has been pestering me about a family trip during ski season. He wants Danny and

Kaylen and the kids to come along with Klarissa and Warren or whoever she is dating seriously at the time. I think he's trying to use my family to get close to me. There I am, using my skills of detection again.

I asked him why Durango? He said, why not. He says it's too much hassle to buy and sell houses with as much moving as he does, so he bought the land and built the cabin—that's what he calls it, but it looks more like a home to me—to build real estate equity. He seems concerned that I am worried about how the subprime mortgage crisis is going to impact the value of his investment, so he's explained—and even drew a graph on a napkin at Ed Dbevik's one night—that if he experiences some value slippage, he'll bounce back before you know it. Okay. He spends time out there a couple weeks a year and has a leasing agent try to keep it occupied otherwise.

He tells me he has never pursued anyone like this before. He has always liked the single life and women usually chase him. I guess I'm supposed to be flattered. But here's the deal. I've only known Dell six months. I'm certainly not going to do a background check to verify his story, but maybe this is exactly what he does in every port of call. Moves into a condo, visits a couple churches, and sticks with one where he meets the most attractive police detective immediately available. Major Reynolds and his friend Virgil would call that a non-isolated activity stream. My dad would have said there is a pattern.

I'm not sure how Dell and I became such an item based on my explicit lack of affection for him, but I know there's a lot of assumption and presumption involved. We met. Reasonably attractive female detective doesn't have a boyfriend. Handsome stranger introduces himself. Sweet sister of reasonably attractive detective invites handsome stranger to family dinner. Handsome stranger is liked by everyone in the family, including the detective, though that same detective has considerably less ardor toward him than any other family members, including the three-year-old who is trying to get college paid for or buy a new G.I. Joe one buck at a time. Detective has certainly not been shot in the heart by Cupid's arrow and the more he pushes the less likely that is to happen.

Handsome stranger and reasonably attractive detective go out for a meal and a movie. They show up at some church functions and sit together, and voilá, they are declared a couple.

I can understand that. But I can't understand his pacing. One month into a comfortable little pattern of getting to know each other he tells me he loves me. I spit Diet Coke out my nose at Chili's—apparently another non-isolated activity stream in my life that makes me popular with kids but not other adults. I do remember being disappointed that the Awesome Blossom was ruined.

I think I will make a wonderful wife one day. Okay, a decent wife is more like it. I think I will be affectionate and loving and mushy and affirming and appropriately attentive and jealous and all that stuff—and probably more than a little difficult to live with. But I'm not a natural when it comes to opening up my heart to just anyone. I don't have some huge heartbreak in my past that I can't let go of. It's just the way I've been; the way I am. I've had a couple regular boyfriends in the past; one in high school and one in college. Both lasted a little less than a year. I've also dated casually from time to time, but I've never been moonstruck. Ever. Does that mean something's wrong with me and I have bonding issues? Doesn't feel like it to me. The lack of being smitten hasn't changed with Dell. He says this is all new for him. But something doesn't quite add up and I don't think, in this case, I am the one with all the problem. Of course, I rarely believe I'm the one with any of the problem.

I'm not ready to buy the bonding issue, either.

You going to stare at the pad of paper all day or do you think we might get some work done?" Don interrupts my momentary reflection. Dark suit, soft blue shirt with white collar, red power tie; French cuffs with black onyx cuff links. And I do believe he has on a new pair of shoes. He's styling. Maybe he felt threatened by Reynold's power suit and he is reasserting himself as the alpha GQ male. No wonder he looks like he's bounced back emotionally. He'll give my outfit disparaging looks all day. Nothing wrong with a khaki skirt and a navy polo with a wrinkled collar in my book. Last time I had this outfit on Don said I looked like a sales girl at the Gap. So? I punched him hard enough to leave a bruise on his arm.

If it was anyone but Don dressing this way, I'd suspect he was on the take, because there's just no way to afford the clothes he wears on a detective's paycheck. I have neither spouse nor kids and I bet I still don't spend half what he does filling up my closet.

I do know he has a little secret though. I've been sworn not to tell anyone in the department, which makes it all the tougher to keep. Don's stay-at-home wife doesn't just stay at home. She also sells a little real estate on the side—actually a lot of real estate on the side—and she's quite good at it. I've asked him how it feels to be a kept man. He just smiles and tells me it feels mighty fine. That doesn't mean he wants the guys to know that his wife is pulling down six figures and at least twice what he does, though. I'm happy for him. Don and Vanessa wanted their kids in private school and Vanessa's gig pays the tuition and a whole lot more.

He looks at his shoes and beams his happy smile and then immediately gets somber.

"So how'd it go this morning?"

"How'd what go?"

He rolls his eyes, "Your group therapy at the donut shop, what do you think I'm asking about?"

"I wouldn't know."

"How'd it go with IA? And by the way, if you're going to act like a horse's behind all day, we're driving separately."

I start to smart off to him but Zaworski strides around the corner.

"I got an email from Gray," he says without preamble.

I hold my breath.

"Sounds like your interview with Internal Affairs was a roaring success."

"Thank you sir," I say, trying to hide the relief in my voice.

"I didn't announce you won a medal for bravery so there's nothing to thank me for. This whole thing from Friday is a pain in the butt to tell you the truth. Conner, I've already had to go to bat with you on Czaka—"

I start to interrupt but he immediately holds up a hand to silence me.

"And whether or not you support his decisions, I don't want to hear any more about that, either. I also don't want any repeats of you grinding a kid's face in the gravel. I'm serious. You're on a short leash. You're on the edge of administrative leave and if that happens, you won't be back in homicide in this precinct. I don't care how good of a detective you are. Understand?"

"Yeah."

"You sure? Cause I can't tell when some says, 'Yeah.'"

"Yes, sir. I understand, sir."

"Good. I'm just glad we've got this distraction out of the way. Now what say two of my finest get busy and find me the sick killer who wants to terrorize my city?"

Don and I head for the stairs in a hurry. He gives me a dirty look and keeps a safe distance in case I have political leprosy or something else that is contagious and bad for his career. I like that Zaworski acknowledged I'm a good detective but I'm seriously frosted that I just got a major reprimand in public. I would have told Don all about it anyway, but Zaworski doesn't know that. CPD protocol is that reprimands happen behind closed doors. Except when they don't. Don can shrug something like this of in an instant. I'll be stewing all day.

At the first landing he says, "we're meeting Reynolds over at FBI in the State Building. He seems to think it is a better location for our task force."

"He's probably right."

"You been over there?"

"Nope," I answer. "It's out of my league."

"I have and you're right," he answers.

"I am? About what—that it's a better spot or that it's out of my league?"

"I'll just leave it at 'you're right.'"

Huh? If I figure out that he just put me down, Don is going to have a tough day ahead of him.

We're out the back door and into the parking lot. I let him open the back door of the precinct for me so I can seize the inside position to grab the driver's side of a Tauras we've been assigned to this week. That makes me driver. Don is still looking at his new shoes and barely notices. That's disappointing.

As we pull onto Clark Street I tell him we need to stop by the CPD Armory on the way back so I can get in some practice shooting with my new Beretta. I switched from the standard issue Glock 22 to see if I could improve my hand gun scores for my personnel files—and to shoot bad guys. So far neither has happened.

"Kristen, I'm going to have to decline. I think my job is dangerous enough already."

I drive in silence the whole way over to the State Building on Wacker, more than a little peeved. It's one thing to gig somebody for something they do well; it's not allowed when you really can't shoot worth a darn. Dad always said big nose jokes were funny as long as no one in earshot has a big nose. If Don notices my pouting, he doesn't comment. He does move his feet around a lot to look at his shoes from different angles.

Dear God, help my attitude. And my shooting.

Chapter 16

"Hello. My name is Walter, and I am an alcoholic."

"Hi Walter." The circle of seventeen of us intones back.

"By the grace of God and with all of your help, I've been sober for three months, two weeks, four days, thirteen hours, and twenty-six minutes."

He is looking at his watch as he ticks off the time. We cheer enthusiastically but all the time I wonder how the heck someone could be that exact. Maybe he has a stopwatch feature that he clicks the second he takes a drink just in case it is his last for awhile? He beams and then turns serious.

"I've lost everything this year; my wife and my boy. He's six years old now and I haven't seen him for eight months by court order, which doesn't look like it's going to be lifted anytime soon."

He chokes up and pauses. I take him for early thirties. He looks beat up enough to be at least a decade older. Probably a middle class kid who lost his way, because he definitely doesn't look tough enough for the streets. I hope Walter finds his way home. He isn't going to survive out here. I wonder if his wife will have him back. Sometimes the long suffering ones hit a wall and when they finally boot him or her out, there's nothing left of a relationship to salvage. The toughest cases to process are when a hittee decides to stop getting hit and hits back. I had one of those when I was in uniform. The hittee was charged with murder. Everyone, including the district attorney and jury believed her husband had a well earned bullet coming to him, but convicted her nonetheless.

Walter talks about some job interviews he has coming up but I'm not listening very closely. Apparently this group proceeds from person to person around the circle and everyone shares something, even if only a sentence or two. In briefing for the assignment, my understanding was that all sharing in AA groups is voluntary. I start paying attention again as a twelfth person tells about a recent setback and a recent victory. Only five more chairs and it's my turn to speak. I've worked with Don, Konkade, and Zaworski to establish a role. But I thought I'd just watch and learn my first time out. I need to think of a quick story.

Eleven women from the precinct are going to attend two to three meetings a week. Seems like a long shot since our research department has established there are at least 750 AA meetings in more than three hundred locations across the city. That doesn't include other church and civic sponsored meetings other than Alcoholics Anonymous.

I googled the Chicago metropolitan for alcohol support groups and came up with more than a thousand hits. I know some of them are duplicates, but man that's a lot of meetings taking place every week. We're focusing on a five mile circle around the crime scene. That cuts the numbers down to forty-eight known weekly or semi-weekly meetings in twenty-one locations. Again, we're assuming we don't have all of them accounted for. My assignment is to cover the Tuesday night sessions at St. Bartholomew's United Methodist Church.

A married woman goes next. I'm assuming she's married because she's got a big rock and matching wedding band on her left ring finger. She's got on a tight white scoop front shirt with a pushup bra that's generating a lot of interest from the men who are present. The facilitator is carefully keeping his eyes on the ground because he knows what we're all going to think if he gives her the same kind of earnest and attentive eye contact he's given everyone else. I want to laugh but stifle it.

"Hi, I'm Bethany, and I'm not sure, but it's conceivable that I'm an alcoholic or that I more than likely just have a drinking problem."

"Hi Bethany," I say along with the group. This is going to get interesting.

She describes the various places she squirrels vodka, her poison of choice, around the house and out of her unsuspecting husband's sight. She gives a pretty detailed description of the new vodkas on the market, including a revolutionary grape-based vodka, and which ones are best for the money. One of the reasons she's not sure she's an alcoholic is that she doesn't drink cheap vodka, which she heard is one of the tell-tale signs of being an alkie—her word, not mine. I begin to wonder if she is liquor distributor and this is a marketing scheme but she finally gets down to business.

She tells us that she's explained her slurred speech and erratic behavior to her husband as a hormonal imbalance and that it will take awhile for her doctor to find the right level of meds to get her emotions back on track. She explains that no man wants to talk about a woman's hormone problems, so he's bought it hook, line, and sinker. I can actually see that being the case and nod my head meaningfully with a first pang of empathy.

Husband thinks she's with her friends playing bunko tonight. The fact that she has lied to attend an AA meeting sparks a discussion about whether it is ever right to lie to protect the innocent, which heats up and runs wild for about fifteen minutes. I look at my watch and realize this will save me from having to share—gratefully. I do wish I could have talked to Danny about this very topic last Sunday at dinner.

I've never been to an AA meeting so I don't know what most of them are like, but I'm pretty sure it's not common for an entire group to instinctively dislike someone. This group dislikes Bethany. The consensus is that honesty is a necessary requisite to getting better. Then some of the comments on the value of honesty start getting directed at Bethany and how her lying is just one more desperate way for her to mask her deep-seated problems. I'm not making this up. Someone specifically said, "Bethany you are trying to mask some deep-seated problems."

The facilitator is all for honesty too, but finally comes to Bethany's rescue. Her cheeks are flushed in anger. I don't think she was expecting to get ripped at an AA meeting. I'm no expert on drinking troubles, but I suspect she's not ready to make a go of this sobriety thing just yet anyway. Hope I'm wrong. I begin to wonder if Housewife's name is really Bethany. There I am being a cynical detective again.

My mind drifts to our murderer. Wonder what happened in his childhood to start him down this path. Doesn't matter, does it? I know it does, but I also know that at some point he embraced evil and he's got to be stopped. Heck, even if you believe in predestination or are a hardcore psychological or biological determinist, you still can't deny that you have to hold a guy like this accountable. It's been five days and so far we have only one clue—and that clue is based on the assumption that Virgil is on to something. Not all, but some victims attended AA. I mull that over. Life isn't fair. About the time you make a decision to get your life together, you get hit by a freight train with no conscious.

"My name is Jonathan, and I am an alcoholic."

"Hi, Jonathan."

I look up and over a couple seats. Jonathan doesn't quite fit in this setting. It's not that the rest of us here have dark-rimmed and blood-shot eyes, smelly clothes, slurred speech, and a variety of involuntary tics and spasms—although my partner and my sister would agree that my clothes leave something to be desired. Housewife, for instance, is neat and trim. She's got a full caret rock on her left hand. The day she pawns that is the day she'll know for sure she has a problem. But Jonathan is immaculately dressed in a pair of gray wool slacks with pressed creases, nice polished loafers with tassels, a preppy navy jacket, and what looks to be an expensive dress shirt with sleeves showing exactly half an inch below the jacket. Jonathan actually reminds me a little of Dell in mannerisms. Even Don might approve of his taste in clothes.

"I've been drinking every day since my junior year in college. Never thought I had a problem, even though my grades slipped enough to keep me out of Kellogg School of Business for my MBA. I still got a bachelor's degree from Northwestern so I rationalized my slippage away.

"Now I'm thirty-eight. I've lived all over the country but always end up back here where I grew up and went to school. I have been through seventeen jobs—I always get a new one because no one will give you a bad reference for fear of a lawsuit. I don't think I can count how many relationships I've burned through. Thank God I've never been married nor had children. I wouldn't wish me on anyone. Once girls I date discover my angry side, I'm shown the door pretty quickly. Some of you are sweet drunks. I'm an angry drunk. I've rationalized away my inability to have a relationship that lasts more than a month, too, because a lot of my friends are married and tell me how lucky I am to be single. I do want to add that I've come close but I've never, ever, ever hit a woman."

Am I supposed to stand up and applaud?

"Well, I don't have job number eighteen yet and actually, I'm the one who is jealous of the guys who have wives and kids. I'd like that for me someday. So about a month ago I finally decided to own up to the fact that I have a problem. I want to change. It's been two days since I've had a drink and I'm dying for one right about now. I especially want to thank Walter. Just knowing you've succeeded for more than a couple months is a real inspiration to me."

Walter blushes and nods in acknowledgment. After a momentary lull, the group breaks into applause.

He continues, "I'd tell you what else I'm dying for right now, but who knows, maybe there's a policeman present and not all of my substance issues are legal."

He laughs and everyone laughs with him, which is a good thing because I think I just turned red. That seals the deal for me. I'm not ready to share a story in my first AA meeting. So I sit back and listen to Jonathan finish up and the four people to my left tell what's going on in their lives right now. When it's my turn I say nothing. The facilitator politely deflects attention from me and asks if anyone else would like to say something. He looks my direction a couple times so I keep my head down. I'm mad at myself for wimping out, but more so I'm thinking about Jonathan. He fits the profile. Maybe I should have a word or two with him just to see if my internal radar sounds an alarm.

The facilitator looks at his watch and asks halfheartedly one more time if anyone else wants to give a testimony. Sixteen sets of eyes look my way and quickly glance away one more time. I guess that was my last chance tonight. The facilitator explains the importance of regular attendance, celebrating victories big and small, and having a sponsor you can call when the urge to drink is strong and your willpower is weak. We hold hands and recite the serenity prayer together and are dismissed.

A few attendees make a beeline for the door. Others saunter over to a side table to get another cup of wretched coffee and a store bought cookie or two from plastic molded trays. Jonathan awkwardly shuffles my way trying to make eye contact. In my peripheral vision I see that the housewife, Bethany, is eying Jonathan and me and is on a path to intercept him before he gets to me. Now I'm positive she's not really here about staying sober. She succeeds in getting to Jonathan first, but only because the group facilitator has cut me off. He introduces himself as Jack and asks a non-threatening question about how I like the weather we're having this spring and then if I would like the name of a female sponsor I might want to talk with if I have anything on my mind.

I tell him I need to think about it. Jonathan keeps looking over our way for an opening, but Jack is now telling me about how long he has been sober and about how scary it is to share for the first time, but how much it really helps. Jonathan gives up on introducing himself to me and heads out the door. Housewife has been rebuffed and gives me a dirty look. She should have gone to bunko night with the girls.

Jonathan graduated from Northwestern, which is just up the road from Chicago in Evanston, but didn't he say something about just moving back to town about six months ago? I think so. I think of the profile Virgil spit out. Neat. Articulate. Organized.

God, I don't care who gets the credit. But let me be the one who catches him. Oh, and help Walter find his way home.

Chapter 17
April 4, 2:00am

S *he is delightful.*

He wished she had spoken. He wished she had shared her own story.

Talk about a fish out of water. She's a babe. A total babe. Long legs and thin but still has some curves. Now that's my kind of woman. Not a Silicon Valley type. Soft and supple flesh. I like it real.

The irony was exquisite. His timing—perfect. Naturally.

I'll talk to her next time for sure. I like it here—even with the wind and the crazy temperature changes. I think I'm happy.

The group had listened in awe as he shared his story.

Not the real one of course, but I like building my other personas.

And he loved to tell it and tell it well.

Just got to keep it straight. Don't want to get it mixed up and raise red flags. I do like hearing from others sometimes, but I've got to say that dude whose chick left him was a loser with a capital L. What real man would let a girl get the better of him?

Yes I'm happy. But I want more of it. I want to be even happier. It's a catch-22 I guess. Happiness doesn't satisfy—it leaves you wanting more. And I definitely want it. And more.

He was overflowing with happiness. And he knew he couldn't keep it all to himself. He was compelled to share it with someone. Joy is for sharing.

Cubs are on the road. Sox are in town through Sunday. All night games. May have to miss one for a more pressing engagement though!

Chapter 18

Am I last on the phone chain or what? And if I am, is it by design? I don't think Captain Zaworski dislikes me, but you can never tell with him. I hate being late. Why am I always the last one to show up for meetings? My sister, Klarissa, the perfectly coiffed weathergirl, can vouch that I am not wasting time playing with my makeup. I barely put it on in the first place. A little base and usually a quick splash of red on my lips, my one cosmetic indulgence.

It wasn't the starter on my Miata either. I got a good spot on the hill in front of my apartment so starting it was easy. I just shifted into first, turned the key to the "on" position, took my foot off the brake, rolled it forward with the clutch pedal pressed to the floor, hit fifteen miles per hour with the help of gravity, popped the clutch and accelerated, and after only one or two jerks and heaves, was off to the races. Just slower than everyone else out of the gate. Nothing wrong with my Mazda's engine as I hit eighty on the cross-town highway on the way over, so I've got to be getting called last. I still need to spring for the three or four hundred bucks to get the starter replaced. It crosses my mind to call Dell to see if he knows anyone in the supply chain world who can get me a great deal on a starter, but it doesn't seem quite right to ask for help after the week we've had. Or not had.

They've started without me. Don, Zaworski, Blackshear, Martinez,

Konkade, and Reynolds are in their regular places, plus there's a couple new faces, most notably another woman.

I open the door carefully but it still creaks like the entrance to a haunted house. Everyone looks up—except for Don who keeps his head down out of fear of being deemed guilty by association with his partner. Zaworski stops speaking. I feel like a ninth grade truant and the captain looks like a displeased teacher as I bring his presentation to an abrupt halt. Everyone mumbles a polite "hey" and he introduces me to Dr. Leslie Van Guten—I am not making that name up—a colleague of Major Reynolds with the FBI.

The other new face is Tony Scalia, who I've known ever since I tagged along to the precinct with my dad on Saturday mornings as a kid. Big Tony hasn't changed a bit in twenty-some years. Of course, he looked like he was sixty years old back then, too. He still has a full head of the darkest, shiniest black hair that a bottle of Just for Men can buy. His face is pockmarked with scars from what had to be one incredible case of adolescent acne. He's at least six foot three and has the barrel chest of a weight lifter. I'll bet he goes 260 or 270 pounds. He's actually soft spoken, but then you don't have to be loud when you exude the raw strength of Big Tony. If he wasn't a cop, he would have made a great gangster or better yet, he could have played gangsters in the movies.

Big Tony, ever the gentleman, is the only one to stand up. He doesn't say anything but gives me a sideways hug and a wink.

"You know Major Scalia," Zaworski says, stating the obvious, "and this is Dr. Van Guten with the Federal Bureau of Investigation."

"A pleasure," she says, giving me a firm handshake. She is wearing a matching black skirt and jacket with white blouse, which sounds rather austere, but she has a good tailor who has fitted the outfit to accentuate her nice figure without being offensive or over the top in the conservative "man's world" of law enforcement. Her second button is undone to show off a large diamond pendant on a simple gold necklace. No wedding ring, so I'm guessing she salvaged her engagement ring after a divorce. I'm just guessing. If I'm right, that might suggest I have the finely honed instincts of a great detective. If I'm wrong, it probably means I'm just a jealous, catty, small-spirited female who has never been married.

I don't smile because I'm embarrassed beyond belief, and more importantly, the business at hand is gruesome. Pictures have been tacked to a cork strip that goes around the conference room. I'm jolted up to speed without hearing a single word. The pictures tell a familiar story. Another woman. Based on furnishings and decor, seemingly successful. Single. Living alone. Murdered. Murdered is a harsh word, but it doesn't come close to conveying or describing what someone is up to in my city. Butchered?

It's been fourteen days since I visited the first crime scene. In contrast to standard operating procedures, we are once again meeting off-site first. There's a downside. The clock starts ticking once a murder takes place and every minute, every second counts. Other than family members and close acquaintances—who account for half the homicides in America—if you aren't chasing a specific person with a name within twenty-four hours, there's a good chance the killer is going to get away. The FBI thinks we have a specific person we're after, but there's that small detail of a name. So time is of essence in this type of case.

The upside to huddling together before hitting the victim's home en masse is that we can each receive assignments that allow us to go into greater detail at the scene. At least that's what Zaworski thinks. And since it's automatic that all gathering, handling, and analyzing of evidence is going to be vigorously challenged in the U.S. legal system, this gives Zaworski and Reynolds a chance to remind us to mind our P's and Q's. No good deed goes unpunished, so if you have a question, you ask before acting—and touching. No seeking forgiveness later. Usually I chafe in this kind of environment, but I have to be honest, I am nervous as a cat on a hot tin roof. I don't have a cat so I'm not familiar with their habits, and I've never seen a tin roof, not even down by the tracks where the homeless create warrens of refrigerator box huts, but suffice it to say, the description seems apt.

"According to our experts, this second homicide proves beyond a shadow of a doubt that we have a serial killer in our city, and one who has evaded arrest and detection for close to a decade."

The call came in at four a.m. On Saturday, of course. Be at the precinct ASAP. I was whipping into the parking lot by five, the sun rising over the lake and turning the Chicago skyline from smudge blue to increasingly lighter shades of gray. My Snowflakes have two more games. I was going to get to sleep in since today's match doesn't start until noon. I need to call my assistant coach, a mother who knows nothing about soccer but is very good at organizing after-game snacks. Today she's got to coach, too.

Zaworski finishes detailing evidence protocols. Routine stuff but a good reminder that our break in this case is probably going to come through a small detail. He looks to Reynolds and nods. Reynolds clears his throat and begins.

"If you haven't finished reading the previous incident notebooks, you need to do so within the next twenty-four hours. Nothing we say leaves our situation room. That stays the same. But before we head over to the CS, we're going to give each of you an executive summary of all seven previous event notebooks. We're then going to have you put your signature on a sworn affidavit that the materials will not leave your possession, will not be shared with anyone not on the task force—even if that someone is your superior—and will be returned within twenty-four hours. We've made extra copies. I understand that one of you has stopped by twice and not been able to secure notebooks. I apologize. We've got to get everyone up to speed on this thing. No excuses."

That would be me and he gives the slightest of nods my way. There's two ways to interpret it. Positively, it may be a sincere apology. Negatively, it may be Reynolds' way of telling me to check out materials earlier. I've read five of the seven notebooks front to back. I've got an electronic key to the FBI's regional headquarters and there is a 24/7 attendant to get us the materials. I've been working twelve hour days since the first murder. Apparently that isn't enough. I don't care how long we are on the crime scene. I will not go to sleep without reading every page of the last two notebooks and the executive summaries today.

"You're going to notice a significant change in pattern with the current murder. Anyone have an idea already?"

"Time between murders," says Blackshear.

He answered way too quickly. That can't be right. I purse my lips to say something.

"Nicely done," Reynolds says to Blackshear. "He's been a once a month predator, but this time it's less than two weeks."

"Any chance we got a new perp at work?" Martinez asks in his heavy accent. "A copycat?"

"Great question," Reynolds answers. "But there's just too many signature acts for this not to be the same predator that Project Vigilance has identified and that Dr. Van Guten has profiled."

He nods deferentially in her direction when he says that. She must be a big shot. Good old Virgil is always on the job but his outfits aren't as nice as Van Guten's.

"We're going to hit the scene together," Reynolds continues. "We've got transportation lined up that will accommodate all of us."

There was a Gray Line bus with the engine running in the parking lot when I arrived. That's got to be the transportation and it seems weird and surreal. Last time I was in a Gray Line vehicle, I was in eighth grade, and me, my parents, and my two sisters were in New York City for Kaylen's high school graduation present.

"We're dropping the team off in pairs on each corner of the block. We're all walking up slow. We're going to look around. We're going to look people in the eyes. We're going to see who's watching, who's avoiding eye contact, who doesn't fit there. If someone wants to talk to any of us, we're going to stop and talk. Ask them what they saw and if anything has been out of place in their neighborhood. I know this is a different *modus operandi*, but honestly, what you're going to see at the crime scene is something you've already seen before.

"We did meet here at CPD because the media is stalking our Midwest regional office for the FBI. I don't want the circus we had at the first scene. If anyone from the media is already there, I'll assume a neighbor called or someone was paying very close attention to a very subtle message on the police band, but I'm still going to check everyone's home and cell phone logs."

I think he just looked at me. You've got to be kidding? Just because my sister works for a TV station, he thinks I'm going to give her a scoop. She's the weathergirl for crying out loud.

Reynolds introduces Van Guten and explains that she is a psychiatrist under contract with the FBI. She is a profiler and will now be an official and permanent member of the team until we apprehend our butcher in Chicago or he moves to another city.

"Five minutes and in the bus," Zaworski barks. "You got anything to take care of before we leave, take care of it fast."

"*Más le vale a ese tip que no sea yo el que lo encuentre,*" Martinez says to Don and me as we exit the situation room. *"Va a desear nunca haber nacido."*

He strides off, his jaw jutting out, and nearly knocks the door to the men's restroom off the hinges as he disappears from sight. I look to Don for help. I took French, which was probably a mistake, but my mom pushed so hard for me to take Spanish that I suddenly developed a love for *lingua François* in eighth grade. Don isn't fluent in Spanish but he is our interpreter when necessary.

"I think he wants to meet our killer in a back alley," he says with a shrug. "You never know with Antonio."

I stop to pee and take care of it fast, wash my hands—probably a mistake based on Reynold's five minute order—and hustle down the steps and out the back door into the employee parking lot. Unbelievable. It's seven a.m. and there are more than ten local TV and radio station vans with satellite equipment atop outside the chain link fence, plus what looks like a fancy Winnebago from Mars with CNN printed on the side. I take back the Winnebago part. How about a country music star's home away from home? I have a fleeting thought that it would be kind of cool to look inside there.

There is a horde of reporters with microphones, digital recorders, and even a few old fashioned flip notebooks with yellow pencils. Three squad cars block the entrance to our lot and six blue clothes are keeping the jackals at bay. I keep my eyes on the ground and hop up the three steps and into the bus.

I'm last one in. Everyone is looking at me. Reynolds and Van Guten have commandeered the whole front row. They are leaning into the aisle and speaking to each other in hushed tones. They have to stop and lift their heads so I can pass. The rows aren't close to being filled up but the aisle seats sure are. I'm reminded of the scene in the school bus from *Forrest Gump*. But there's no one to play the role of Jenny and share a seat with me. I plop into a seat by myself and look at my cell phone with horror. I realize I called Klarissa on the way over to leave a message about meeting for dinner tonight. I look forward. Reynolds is on his phone. I can only guess what order he is giving. He's going to have our phone logs checked and think I called the story into Klarissa.

I feel sick to my stomach. But not as bad as I'll be feeling in about thirty minutes.

Chapter 19

C an I see your gun, Aunt Kristen?"

"Daniel, you know your mommy doesn't think it's polite for me to brandish weaponry at the table."

Kaylen gives me a dirty look, which brings a smile to my face. I think it's my first smile of the week. But I guess Sunday is the first day of the week, so that doesn't quite account for the way the last seven days have gone.

"Please. Pleeeease, Aunt Kristen."

Daniel's persistent today, so I suggest to him, "How about after we have dessert, okay kiddo?"

He shakes his head vigorously and spoons a large dollop of mashed potatoes into his mouth. He's my kind of guy.

"Can I see it, too?" Kendra asks.

"You bet," I answer. "And if we're real careful we can take all the ammo out and I'll even let you hold it."

"Me too!" Daniel calls through a mouth filled with mashed potatoes.

"Daniel, don't talk with your mouth full," Danny instructs.

"Is it good to introduce four-year-olds to hand guns?" Klarissa asks with disdain. "Isn't that how violence gets started?"

"Guns and milk," I answer. "Seems to be a pattern or as I like to put it, a non-isolated event stream. Oh, and the media helps with the violence thing, too. You've got to talk to your station manager again. Have you seen some of the stuff they're showing during prime time family hour?"

"Funny," she answers sarcastically. "But what kids watch is up to parents—and playing with handguns should be, too. We have enough violence in this world."

"Hey, us cops don't start violence, we just end it," I answer smartly. "And if Danny and Kaylen want to tell the kids they can't look at a Beretta 9 millimeter, I will keep it holstered."

Nice move, I say to myself. Get the attention elsewhere. She rolls her eyes and carefully brings her fork within an inch of her lips with the smallest bite of salmon filet I have ever seen in my life, or at least since the last time I watched her eat. I watch as she opens her mouth and then thinks better of choking herself on a gram of fish. She closes her mouth and lowers her fork back to her plate. Now I roll my eyes. I've cut a decent sized bite from what's left of the piece of salmon I was able to nab, the largest on the serving platter, I would add, but bypass it, and spear the bigger portion on my plate and stuff it in my mouth. I'm starved. Fighting crime builds up an appetite.

"Mmmm," I moan noisily, my eyes locked on Klarissa, who looks like she might get sick. I smile and laugh.

"So Dell, you still enjoying our fair city? Work going okay?" Danny asks. I'm a little disappointed that my little melodrama with Klarissa is being ignored by everyone at the table.

"Actually, I'm loving it here," Dell answers. "Work couldn't go any better, which means the company I'm consulting for has tons of problems, and that means job security for the foreseeable future."

"What are some of the places you've lived Dell?" my mom asks.

"Better question may be where haven't I lived," he answers with a smile. "Not having family, I've just really enjoyed taking in different areas of the country. I've spent more time in Colorado than anywhere else, and that's where I keep a permanent address, but honestly, I've found something I like in every place I've lived."

"Ever get tempted to lay down roots and stay in one place?" Danny asks.

Where the heck is he going with that question? My ears are burning.

Maybe he's about to pop the question to find out what kind of dowry the family might expect to pay out if he wants me for a bride.

"All the time," he answers. "I may just be a victim of circumstances. After college I worked two years in Denver with a company that ended up going Chapter Eleven. The economy there was miserable at the time, so I took a contract job in Albuquerque. I made more money doing contract work, so when that gig was up after a year, I took a couple months off to roam the country a little, and then signed up to do the same thing in Phoenix. I think Portland was next. Then it was Atlanta. I stayed there a year after my contract was finished and got my MBA at Emory. There was work waiting for me in Colorado Springs, so I printed a business card with a phone number and email address and kept moving around. I was in Boston before landing here in Chicago. The only thing I've done to lay down roots is buy some land outside of Durango and build a little home. The problem with that is I've only been in it myself for about three months total."

I'm impressed and a little embarrassed. Am I that self-absorbed that in six months of knowing him I've never bothered to ask Dell about the different cities where he's spent time? He's glanced my way a couple times. I think this is when a real girlfriend, a good girlfriend, would quickly correct him to make him look good and say that the house he built isn't really so small. I'm neither so I say nothing.

"So the house just sits there?" my mom, ever the pragmatist, asks.

"I've got a real estate firm that leases it out, so it doesn't sit that much," Dell answers. "The two problems are that I always forget to reserve time for myself during ski season."

He takes a drink of iced tea.

"What's the other problem?" Klarissa asks.

"Well, with renting the place out and having strangers living there all the time, I've never figured out how I'd like to decorate it to suit my own tastes. As a result, I'm not even sure what they are. My tastes, that is. So my little cabin looks like a million other vacation homes. When I do spend time there it feels an awful lot like a hotel. It could use a woman's touch."

He smiles and looks at me. I'm taken by surprise and redden. I frown, shake my head, and roll my eyes. Klarissa looks at me triumphantly and smiles. Thank God for Mom. She's relentless. She could work with Tom Gray in Internal Affairs.

"Well I hope that you feel at home here. Chicago's not such a bad place to live if you don't mind cold winters."

"You all are way too kind to me," he answers. "I've never been treated better. I always find a church as soon as I hit a new town, but I've never had so many fabulous home cooked meals. I actually have to hit the gym an extra day every week just to keep the weight off."

Mom beams. Kaylen beams. Danny looks very pleased, too. Daniel and Kendra are busy shoveling apple cobbler and ice cream in their mouths. Klarissa smirks at me. I'm suddenly ready to show young Daniel my gun.

Before I can get up and make my escape Kendra says, "you never asked how I did in the soccer game, Aunt Kristen."

"I'm sorry," I say with enthusiasm, relieved to have a change in the conversation. "How did my star Snowflake Kendra do?"

"Two goals."

"I had a hundred," Daniel yells.

"Daniel, stop interrupting," Danny says sternly. Daniel gives his empty dessert bowl a pouty look.

"Very cool," I say. "And how did the rest of the Snowflakes do?"

"We won!"

"Way cool. Mrs. Kimberly must have been a good coach," I say, not believing my own words.

"She didn't coach," Kendra chirps. "Tiffany's dad did."

"Really?"

I look up at Kaylen but she is suddenly studying one of her fingernails.

"We had fun. And we won!"

I'm glad someone had fun and won.

I show Daniel and Kendra my gun. I remove the magazine and double check that no bullets are in the chamber, of course. I give a perfunctory lecture on handgun safety and let both of them hold and aim it. I put the magazine back in, holster it, and wander from the game room where Daniel is pretending to shoot bad guys with a candle stick. I push the door to the kitchen open and look over the counter into the living room. Danny and Dell are watching the Cubs contentedly and talking. Dell is filling out a scorecard just like Dad used to do. I have no problem with that at a game but it seems weird when you're watching it on TV.

Klarissa is closing her purse and getting ready to leave. She gives Kaylen and Mom long warm hugs. I get a quick, mostly one-arm embrace and a quick peck on the cheek. I really do have to get checked for leprosy or body odor. Kaylen walks her to the door and it's just Mom and me in the kitchen.

"So when are you and Klarissa going to stop fighting and start getting along?" she asks.

"Mom, we're not fighting any more than we ever have. It's just how we communicate with each other."

"Then it's time to you two start communicating better. You're like teenagers fighting over a boy."

"Well, if that's what this is all about, she wins. She can have the boy."

"What's wrong with Dell?" Mom asks with a sincerely hurt expression. "I like him."

"I know you do and I do, too," I retort. "Doesn't mean I have to marry him does it?" There's challenge in my voice.

"You are thirty, so it's not like you shouldn't start thinking about things like that. You make it sound like settling down, getting married, and having kids is a disease. You can't keep people at arm's length forever, you know."

Ouch. Not sure what hurt worse. Mom thinking I don't want to be close to somebody some day or the reference to thirty. I'm not thirty yet.

I say my goodbyes and head out to my car. I've got incident notebooks at home so I'm not going to stop by the office. I push in the clutch and turn the ignition. It grinds but doesn't start. Danny and Kaylen live on a flat street. Great. What now?

I end up slinking back up the sidewalk to ask for help. I get back in the driver's seat. How embarrassing. Danny and Dell get behind the car and push me into the street and get me rolling. I can hear them laughing. I make sure the car has enough momentum, pop the clutch, and wonder for a second if the engine is going to turn over as it pitches and sputters. It roars to life and I'm out of there. Tomorrow for sure. I've got to get the starter replaced.

I think about the crime scene all the way home.

*A*fter three solid hours of reading non-isolated event stream notebooks, I jog over to the high school football stadium a mile from my house. Forget the track. I'm going to run up and down the stairs on every aisle. My twice repaired knee will protest but I've got to do something to clear my mind. It's a jumble of Dell getting a family invite despite having done a revenge date two weeks earlier; Tiffany's dad coaching *my* Snowflakes and winning; Tom Gray from IA grilling me and invoking my dad's name in the process; and a bad man killing independent, successful, attractive women in my city and my not being able to do anything about it.

It is a cool, pleasant, early spring evening that's already dropped into the upper sixties but I sweat like it's an August boot camp in southern Georgia. My mind starts to clear and my spirit lightens just a little but I can't help thinking about the latest victim, Candace Rucker.

Help me find her killer, dear God. And thanks that the Snowflakes won.

The second part of my prayer wasn't as heartfelt as the first.

Chapter 20

The crime scene was as gruesome as we knew it would be. No one demurred when offered cotton swabs with a drop of ammonia at the door. The smell was still overpowering. Same *modus operandi*. He—I'm not arguing that we need to be thinking it's a woman anymore—did his work and then left with the heat turned up full blast.

There was a body that had been violated, so there was tons of forensic evidence. The problem is that it doesn't point us to a particular person but simply confirms a profile and provides us with everything we need to convict him if we ever find him. I kept my focus and took copious notes like a good soldier. But the only thing we really learned was that it was the same person doing almost exactly the same thing that Virgil has already alerted us was going to happen in our city. He is careful. Precise. And sick.

Candace Rucker, thirty-two years of age, a junior member of a major Chicago law firm, divorced, no kids, and no live-in, is dead.

Good weekend?" Don asks.

We spent most of Saturday at the Rucker crime scene, so it would be more accurate to ask if Sunday was good.

"So-so."

"Your girls win?"

"Yep."

"Nice. Isn't that like the first win of the season?"

"Second."

"Cool."

"We've only got one more regular season game. Who knows, maybe we'll get win number three."

"There's the Vince Lombardi we all know and love. So how'd Sunday dinner go? Dell back in the picture?"

I cock my head and look at Don across a Formica table top, a cup of steaming diner coffee in my hand and almost to my lips. I want to see if he is giving me a hard time or just being a nice, normal human being who is interested in other human beings.

"Sunday dinner was nice. Yes, Dell was there. And yes, it was a little awkward. He acted like nothing had happened. I guess that puts all the awkwardness on me."

"No surprise there." he laughs. "So, if you feel awkward being with him, why did you invite him over in the first place?"

"I don't. I didn't. My mom did."

He spits coffee out and nearly jumps out of his seat out of fear that a coffee spill will stain his starched white shirt with his monogram sewn on the pocket.

"Don't even ask why," I continue. "My mom has always had a soft spot for stray cats and lost puppies. Actually, my whole family adores him. Just for the record, Dell and I didn't drive over together. Kendra and Daniel sat between us at the dining room table. He was just there and it seemed like the most normal thing in the world to everyone. In fact, he was still there watching the Cubbies with Danny when I left."

"No way," Don says.

"Well, actually the last I saw of him, he and Danny were pushing my car down the street so I could start it with the clutch."

Don laughs again and shakes his head. "Don't you think it's a little strange," he asks, "that you, the most in control and controlling person in the world have no say in your love life?"

"Did you just say 'love life?'" I ask him, ready to stare him down as long as it takes.

He breaks the gaze, laughs, and says, "okay, let me rephrase that.

This guy looks and acts like your boyfriend and he's in the middle of your business, and you don't even know anything about him, much less what you think about him."

"Can we change the subject?" I ask.

"Hey, I'm just trying to be a good partner and I am tempted to point out that getting close to a member of the opposite sex can be a fulfilling experience. He seems like a nice guy to me."

I look up to argue, but he holds up his hands in surrender and then pokes a fork at the last crumb of pie on his plate. For revenge I want to say something about how eating dessert before ten a.m. will add inches to his waistline. But I'm worn out and don't have energy for a battle of insults.

"So how'd your weekend go?" I ask instead. He is trying to suppress a smile, which makes me think he's been waiting for me to ask.

"Need a warm up?" the waitress interrupts. We both answer yes. I peel back the top of another creamer and stir it into my now full cup.

"Vanessa sold another house on Saturday, so it was a great weekend," Don says.

"She take you shopping?"

"Maybe she did." He holds up his silk tie. I guess I was supposed to notice that it was new. It's nice, but a tie is a tie. Don doesn't look at it that way. He then turns sidewise in the booth and kicks a leg out in the aisle, high enough for me to see his foot. I'm assuming the shoes are new, too. I'm looking at a shiny black loafer with a tassel.

"Nice. New Eddie Arnolds?" I ask.

He rolls his eyes and says, "Allen Edmonds. I've been wanting to buy some Graysons. They're not made quite as narrow as the other AE models, but they still feel great."

"That's two new pairs of shoes in two weeks."

He doesn't answer but just smiles.

"What do they cost? More than a hundred bucks?"

"More than three hundred," he answers sharply, pulling his foot back under the table and crossing his arms. I've hurt his feelings. I feel a little bad for purposely gigging him.

We've canvassed the first crime neighborhood in Washington Park, where Leslie Reed was murdered, since six this morning. It'll be back to Rogers Park for Candace Rucker's murder later, but we wanted to catch the early-to-work crowd from the first murder as they were leaving for the office or airport or wherever they go on a Monday morning. It's been two weeks and we still haven't been able to interview everybody on the block yet, and if we catch someone for a second or third time, maybe they'll remember something they forgot to tell us first or second time we talked to them, we figure. Good idea before turning the corner and throwing everything into the new scene, but not very fruitful. We talked to a sum total of six people, all more interested in their wristwatches than talking to us. I wonder if anyone even remembers that a real life human being who is now dead was their neighbor just a few weeks earlier.

We have a task force meeting in thirty more minutes, so we thought it'd be a good idea to grab a bite before the possibility of lunch or dinner disappears. I had tuna salad on whole wheat. Lettuce and tomatoes, with a pickle on the side. A big glass of water and an endless cup of coffee. Don did a full bacon and egg breakfast, half a bottle of ketchup on the hash browns, with blackberry pie to chase it down. I notice that he's put on a few pounds since this serial killer thing started. He doesn't show it, but he must be feeling some stress, too.

"Have you finished reading all the notebooks from the other cities?" I ask.

"Yeah. But to tell you the truth, I didn't find anything. How about you?"

"Me neither. This guy is a ghost."

"I love that the FBI is involved and is bringing all these resources to the table," he says, "but it seems to me that we're going to catch him with old fashioned police work. And the problem is he's good and until he makes a big mistake, we're going to be spinning our wheels. I keep thinking that the AA meetings might lead to a breakthrough."

"I don't disagree. Would be nice of him to leave a business card or something, preferably with his confession written out, wouldn't it?"

"We can hope and pray, but I'm not counting on that."

"Well, tell Vanessa to pray then. You say that God answers all her prayers."

"She got me, didn't she?"

I roll my eyes. We look at our watches and get up without a word. I pull seven crumpled dollar bills from my wallet and leave them on the green check the waitress has left. Don makes a face at my offering and leaves a crisp ten dollar bill and two more ones. I'm no math wiz but that's about a forty percent tip.

"You need change?" she asks our backs.

Don turns and says, "Keep it." To me he says, "I bet she'll love that seventy-eight cent tip Scrooge."

"I'm not married to a real estate mogul," I shoot back.

I hustle out the door and down the sidewalk to the driver's side. We've got a real simple rule as partners. Whoever gets there first, drives. Neither of us like being second. I hold out an open palm and he drops the keys in my hand with a frown.

"You limping?" Don asks as we pull out of the parking lot. I don't answer but my knee is barking after last night's stair run.

Dell called last night to see if I wanted to go out for a quick dinner. I politely declined and spent my evening going through notebooks, created by a computer I've named Virgil, yet again.

It's been a tough month. Everyone I love has told me in some form or another that I've got an anger problem. Now everyone wants to know why I have bonding issues. I'm pretty sure everyone likes Dell better than they like me. Klarissa gives Mom and Kaylen big hugs. I get a polite sideways embrace and she misses the kiss on my cheek by a mile.

I wasn't totally honest with Don. My weekend wasn't so-so. It was lousy.

Chapter 21
April 26, 3:30am

CUTTER SHARK ALERT: FALL ELECTIONS NOW HAVE A SHARP EDGE TO THEM..
By ChiTownBlogger

>   Wonder how well Mayor Daniels has been sleeping lately? SWeet dreams? or nightmares? There's a killer lose in our fair city. Never a good thing 4a reelection campaign, even when ur an incumbent 8 times over ... and the geriatric set still thinks ur your daddy LOL

Ye Olde historians surely remember Harold Washington gettin voted out cuz he couldn't shovel snow from our sidewalks fast enough, spawning the Empire of Jane. Chitown is loyal and fickle all wrapped in 1 package ... albeit a bloody and bloodied package based on our newest resident.

So who is this denizen of the night? A Vampire? Werewolf? George Bush and Hillary Clinton's love child? YIKES!!! Now that's a scary thought. We do know he loves blood and has a proclivity toward sharp edges ... he's a predator ... with 2hits under his belt he seems 2b always on the move ... blown by the winds. SO I hereby dub this twisted tortured soul Chicago's very own CUTTER SHARK. (Note: that moronic morning news meddler on WCI-radio who is calling our new friend the Windy City Whacker isn't the sharpest blade in the drawer.)

It's also quite clear he has a way with our lady folk. Big shout out 2 nancy regan. She was right girls. Let him buy u a drink but then just say no ;O)

Mayor Daniels assures us our crack police force is on the case and will turn over every stone 2bring this PERPETRATOR OF PAIN, this SULTAN OF SLICE, this FAUSTIAN FIEND OF THE FLESH (I cud go all day here folks) 2quick and certain justice. I'm def buying a hand gun ... and maybe an assault vehicle 4trips 2the grocery store. Now, if our venomous villain was perpetrating a string of illegal parking citations, I have no doubt that all of us would b safer and he would b off the streets and in custody.

Well while Mayor Daniels sleeps like a baby ... his only concern a reelection six months down the road, certainly not the safety of the fair maidens of Chicago ... ur faithful ChiTownBlogger—CTB Numero Uno 2my myriad of fans—is wide awake and on the case. There's a $10 000 reward 4info leading 2this man who loves nothing better than a close shave. hey Mayor, why so generous? and maybe I'll b the big winner. Gee golly ... WHat will I buy first? I've had my eyes on a used Cavalier and might b able2 pay cash after taxes. Some people have no sense of gravity and definitely no sense of style. Make it a million if u really care. Sheesh.

My eyes and ears r open throughout the city ... I hear and c all... I would love 2hear from the man himself, Mr. C. Diddy Shark. As long as ur not my sushi chef, I am here 4u and feel ur pain ... now ur victims pain is another story altogether ... I faint every time I get a flu shot :op
Okay fans ... Toodles ... XOXOXO. Big lovin from ur fav blogger. ChiTownBlogger over and out.

Can't wait 2read ur responses. The CTB board is open 4business! 1st POSTER gets a coupon for a jumbo meal @ Devil Dog. The Sisters @ St. Mikey's claimed St. Paul said works w/o faith is dead. I'd still go for the works! Peppers, cucumber, tomatoes, and celery salt all around!!! :oD SHAZAM!
>

Chapter 22

Today's meeting is not pleasant. Captain Zaworski is not happy. The press is all over the case. The people of our city, specifically single women between the ages of twenty-five and forty who are at least reasonably attractive and gainfully employed, are afraid. They're staying home at night, which means the single men of Chicago are not happy either. Then there's the bar and restaurant owners. Everyone's clamoring for us to get off our tushies and make a quick arrest. Okay. I'll just hit that red easy button and get to it.

There was an article in today's newspaper interviewing guys who have been accused of being the Cutter Shark, the name given to our homicidal maniac by some nut job with a popular online blog. The moniker is now being repeated by every radio host and bandied about at every water cooler in the city. The guy being interviewed in the paper who wished to remain nameless was claiming that every time he offers to buy a girl a drink in the bar he is in fear of being pepper sprayed.

Mayor Daniels is not happy either, which means the Police Commissioner is not happy, so no surprise Zaworski is feeling the heat and so are we.

"We're sitting at almost four weeks and the only lead we are working came to us from the FBI. Folks, I need something. We need something. It's time to earn your retirement program."

Is that a threat?

We are back in the spacious and almost luxurious office suite of the Midwest Regional office of the FBI, located on the forty-eighth floor of the State Building. I've never considered anything but local law enforcement, but I could get used to the federal digs.

The meeting is scheduled to go ninety minutes, which is a relief. I might even get in a workout early this evening. Nothing too rigorous because my knee is aching. I did the high school stadium stair torture workout again. I'm not even thirty and I'm already complaining of aches and pains.

After Zaworski's chewing out, Dr. Van Guten spends fifteen minutes proving that Leslie Reed and Candace Rucker's murderer is the same killer who has struck in six other cities. This seems very important to her and Reynolds, but I'm not sure what that gets us. This guy is a needle in a haystack. Once we find him, the information is going to be invaluable in making sure that ten years and twenty appeals from now, someone from the state of Texas—he spent time in San Antonio and since they allow the death penalty, we're guessing that's where he gets tried—is going to stick a needle in one of his veins, but it's the finding him part that we need help on. She doesn't know what to make of him changing the timing between kills, but she wants us to know that it is still the same man based on 137 direct connections or parallels she and Operation Vigilance have discovered. She enlightens us that mathematically this is a 98.7 percent certainty. I never did well in stats class—the chi tail formula just about killed me. She already looks tired at eleven in the morning. I think she's spending too much time with Virgil. Maybe I should invite her out for dinner.

"Has everyone finished the notebooks?"

We all nod yes.

"Then it's time to start over because honestly, I'm not seeing any action from local enforcement."

She just lost her dinner invitation.

The detective teams report their current activities. Don speaks for us. I have no problem with that as long as I get to drive the car. And no question, he can deliver an elevator speech a lot better than I can.

I'm not quite sure what Tony Scalia's role on the team is, but apparently he's unofficially the liaison with City Hall and more specifically, the mayor's office. Did I mention that he and my dad once brought down a hit man hired to kill the mayor? That was about ten years ago, but Daniels is still alive and still the mayor, so he wanted someone on the case reporting directly to him that he trusts. Big Tony. Mom still has my dad's medal in one of those shadow box frames in the living room.

No question, my dad's status at CPD gave me a leg up on my first job and subsequent promotions. With the run-ins I've had with Czaka, I'm hoping his posthumous status serves as major career protection. I met Mayor Daniels when Dad got his medal. He made a big deal about me following my dad's footsteps at the time. But he's a politician and politicians are good at saying what people want to hear. I wonder if he remembers me now. Czaka is sitting down the row from me and has studiously ignored me.

They say cream rises to the top and in our group of detectives that seems to be Blackshear. I'm as competitive as anyone, but I've had my gold shield for less than two years. For all my lip, I'm actually very impressed with the team we have going and Blackshear has been sharp as a tack. He and Reynolds spend twenty minutes of our meeting going over new strategies and new assignments. Despite feeling lost and helpless, this is my favorite part of the meeting. We may not know what to do, but at least we're doing something.

Konkade goes last and reports on the number of volunteers from the force who are working the AA angle. No real leads so far—and no leaks to the press, thank God. He reminds us that this particular haystack is a lot smaller than the city of Chicago, so we aren't to skip our appointments and we should do more if we have the time. Don't forget to follow up on others who are attending.

I put my notes into a small briefcase I carry, stand up to stretch the small of my back, and look down at my phone, which is vibrating. Klarissa. I had forgotten Reynold's promise to check everyone's phone log in the hour leading up to our assault on the second crime scene. My heart does a quick somersault. Then I relax. I figure nothing must have come from checking the phone logs—if they were even checked—or I would have heard something by now.

I follow Don toward the door. Only Zaworski and Reynolds are still in the room, talking quietly and heatedly at the far end of the table.

"Conner."

I freeze in stride, halfway outside the conference room. That's Zaworski's you're-in-trouble-now voice. I turn toward the two men and step back in. Don stops just outside the door.

"Yes sir?"

"Need you to stay a minute. Squires, this is going to take a little while so you may want to head back to the precinct."

I don't think Zaworski was making a suggestion to Don. Zaworski, outside of an occasional expletive, is a very polite man. He usually asks. This is an order. The blinds on the large windows that dominate one of the interior walls of our task force's home are pulled, so they can't see Don. He looks at me with arched eyebrows, as if to ask what I've done this time. He heads toward the door leading to the reception area and out to the bank of elevators.

I know you called three times, Klarissa, but I couldn't pick up. You of all people know that there are moments when answering isn't an option."

"So you weren't just blowing me off again?"

"No! Believe me, I would have much preferred talking to you. I was busy getting my tail chewed."

"Something to do with the Cutter Shark?"

"I don't know where you guys in the media come up with names like that, but yeah, it had to do with the Cutter Shark—and you!"

"Me?"

"Yeah. Remember the morning following the second murder?"

"Sort of."

"Well, we were trying to get over to the crime scene without any media interference. Someone placed a call to Mr. or Ms. So and So and the whole world showed up in our parking lot. So Reynolds, the FBI guy, ran a check on everybody's phone log. Guess who talked to someone at WCI-TV an hour before we rolled out the door?"

"Who?"

"Me, Klarissa!"

"Who were you talking to?"

"You, you big dummy. Don't you remember?"

"Oh, the morning you decided to wake me up at four."

"It was closer to five but I didn't know when I'd have a chance to call again. I was actually planning to leave you a voice message."

"Yeah, I remember the call, but it still doesn't make sense. How could they know you called me? That was on my cell, not the office."

"You think the FBI doesn't know who pays your cell phone bill?"

"Well, that's more than a little disturbing."

"Don't go naïve on me, Little Sis. I hope you're kidding me."

"I'm not kidding. I feel like my privacy has been violated."

"Got something to hide?"

"No." she retorts immediately.

I pull the phone back from my ear and look at my watch. "Hey Sis, I don't want to be rude, but I'm getting hammered here with no results in our investigation. What'd you call about?"

"We were supposed to get together last Thursday night for dinner, which you cancelled. That's in addition to cancelling coffee yesterday. Despite my hurt feelings, I wanted to see if it might work out to grab a bite tonight."

"What time you thinking?"

"I'm not back on air until the ten p.m. Anytime between now and nine."

I look at my watch. It's six. I've got another two hours of work. I was wanting to hit my health club on the way home. I wonder if I can get everything done in an hour and meet her at seven thirty.

"Hey, if it's too much trouble," she starts with hurt in her voice.

"No. No," I interrupt quickly. "I'm just looking at what the boss wants done. Tell you what, I'll grab a cab and meet you somewhere in the middle. I'll come back and finish up. But brace yourself, because I may have to miss you give your weather report tonight and I don't want to cost you ratings."

"We're only half a point from being number one, so I can manage without you for one night. Just don't make it a habit," she adds primly.

"I won't—and it's a date," I answer with a laugh. "Where do you want to meet?"

"I like that place over in Wicker Park. Not the Italian restaurant. The one with the American-fusion cuisine."

"American-fusion?"

"Yeah. Just tell the cab to get you to Feast at the five corner intersection."

"See you in thirty minutes."

Leaving early?"

It's Van Guten. She is wearing a mauve business suit with an ivory blouse. One extra button unbuttoned. She usually wears her hair up, but it's after six, so she's let it down. Light brown with blonde lowlights. What do I know? I've never colored my hair. It may be blonde with brown highlights. I knew she was attractive, but wow. I wonder what it would be like to be as together and confident as she seems to be. There's a slight challenge to her question.

"Nah. Just going to grab dinner with my sister but I'll be back," I say over my shoulder.

"Oh, the one who works in the news department at a TV station?"

Nothing indirect in her tone this time, it is a straightforward challenge. I want to punch her in the nose. Then I wonder if she's been trained in hand-to-hand combat. It doesn't matter. I'm not even looking at anyone cross-eyed because I am one outburst away from Zaworski ordering me into an anger management program. I've heard that they cure you through sheer boredom. I also know it's the kind of thing you never get off your employment record. I'm sure Leslie will be here when I get back. Looking wonderful in mauve, of course.

"That's the one," I say.

"You didn't happen to get a chance to talk with Reynolds and Zaworski this morning, did you?" she asks with arched eyebrows. "After our meeting?"

"Indeed I did. But I bet you already knew that."

"Anything good come out of that?" she asks with raised eyebrows, ignoring my back-at-you challenge.

"I'm not sure you'd call it good, Doctor, but we did seem to clear up a potential misunderstanding."

"Good," she says dismissively. "I trust it will stay cleared up."

I have recently gone through a course in Brazilian Jiu-Jitsu outside the department. Mike Dragon's dojo. Don't ask me why I put so much energy into hand-to-hand training. Maybe because I score so well at it—Barry Soto, one of the chief CPD trainers says that pound for pound, I'm the toughest fighter on the force. I know that when I told Dad I wanted to be a cop he hammered in my brain that a life or death moment is going to come when it's going to be just me and the other guy. Right now, I am embarrassed to say, it has crossed my mind that I hope Van Guten takes a swing at me. That's a scary thought. Really. Maybe I should call Zaworski and go into anger management voluntarily.

We lock eyes in a little power stare down. She flinches first. "Later," I say to Van Guten's back, because she is already striding toward the captain's office.

Dear God, help me to stop making people in charge so mad at me.

Chapter 23

"Hi, my name is Kristen."
"Hi Kristen," twenty-some voices answer back.
"And I'm an alcoholic."
Is that lying? I don't even drink unless you count a sip of champagne at a wedding once a year. Or when Klarissa insists I take a sip of her wine. That's basically it. Mom made Dad quit drinking; against church rules. He kept a six pack hidden in the garage fridge from time to time. One sip of his Pabst Blue Ribbon when I was eleven or twelve and I was cured of craving beer for life.

It's definitely lying I guess, but my understanding is that there are theologians who have worked out the morality of lying if it's done for a greater good. Kind of like the Just War theory that Catholics have. Danny pastors a community church, so I'm not sure who he answers to other than his local board of elders. Or deacons. Or whatever they call themselves. I guess he gets to mix and match his theologians and rules. It's really no big deal to me. Mom doesn't like it because she grew up Baptist and made Dad, who was a Catholic when he met her, become a Baptist if he wanted to marry her. She also sent her first daughter, Kaylen, to a nice Baptist college in North Park. When Kaylen fell in love with a ministerial student everyone was thrilled—until Mom learned that he was non-denominational and had no intention of declaring membership.

"Oh, so you don't mind using good Baptist education and all the money that it took to build that college, but then you just get to go off and do whatever you want."

Danny's as straight-laced as they come. I somehow don't think he's going crazy with all that freedom.

"My problem began small," I intone.

Lots of nodding heads. They sense I'm going to need encouragement to keep this little speech from becoming a disaster.

"So it really didn't impact my work life or my social life. At first. At least I didn't think it was affecting me negatively."

More nods from some very earnest people. I'm looking for Jonathan but he's not been here the past two weeks. I'm still coming on Tuesday nights. I thought he might have a regular day of the week. The way he was heading my direction, I thought he might want to get to know me and might assume I had a regular day of the week, too. Maybe it doesn't work that way if you really do have a drinking problem. Maybe you hustle your butt over when you need it. Maybe you're not thinking about the new group member across the circle from you that much either. Unless you're a con artist with murderous intentions, of course.

I just wish I could remember if he said he had recently moved to town for sure. Housewife isn't here either. She came last week. Maybe they did hook up after all. Of course, if he's the murderer, that's not a good thing, though Virgil has told us our perpetrator, the Cutter Shark, almost exclusively pursues single women. In the few cases where a married woman was the victim, there was some likelihood that she wasn't broadcasting her marital status. That actually could make Housewife, who looks ready for action, vulnerable. But I'm pretty sure she did mention being married in Jonathan's presence two weeks ago. What's wrong with my memory these days?

Then again, if you're a murderer, is adultery that a big of a deal? Who knows when a human psyche gets as damaged as our killer's. His choice of single women probably is based on pure logistics and has nothing to do with morality. A single woman is more likely to live alone, which means no one else to deal with when it comes time to give into whatever demons are haunting your life.

"Maybe I've had a problem longer than I think I have. I know some people at work have called me out. But it didn't turn into an official reprimand, even though it looked like it might. And my mom's not happy with me right now because of my, ah, problem. And my sister and I aren't getting along so hot either."

Wow. I'm on a roll.

"And my boyfriend—well, not really my boyfriend, I guess—but he and I, well, I guess we are in some kind of state of limbo. I'm not really sure if we're going out anymore or not. So I guess I'm here to figure out whether I have a problem or not."

I think Walter is trying to stifle a laugh. Hey, I don't laugh at him when he gives us the updated weeks, days, hours, and seconds to his sobriety every week, do I? I see amusement in some eyes and concern—or is that pity—in others. A few people have zoned out. I'm quite the public speaker—make them laugh, make them sleep. I redden a little as I realize that what I've just said makes me sound like the world's biggest loser.

"But things probably aren't as bad as they seem," I continue quickly, in an attempt to recover. "My other sister has me work with her kids and I do pretty well at that. For the most part."

Okay, none of this is coming out right. No one is smiling now. Everyone is wide awake. I think I see some outright fear on the faces of a few women who look like they are mothers.

"I'm not saying this quite right, but what I mean is that I think things are going to go a whole lot better and you all are really helping me."

I end abruptly and plop into my seat. My ears are burning. The room is quiet. I really hadn't planned to speak but with this being my fourth visit, I figured it was time to play the part a little. I really should have written my talking points down and not tried to wing it. My sister is probably going to get reported to Children's Services for letting a drunk take care of her kids if anyone finds out my last name. Jack, the moderator, gets up and clears his throat.

"I want to thank each of you for sharing. Stick around and have a cup of coffee and a couple cookies if you can. I want to remind you that a big part of Alcoholics Anonymous is having a trusted sponsor to help you through the rough times and just to help you keep your feet on the ground. Every one of us in the room is going to experience temptation and we're not supposed to go it alone. That's why God has given us each other."

I'm pretty sure he's talking to me. One clue is that he keeps looking at me pointedly. There I am being a detective again.

We stand, hold hands, and mumble the Serenity Prayer together. "God grant me the serenity to accept the things I cannot change, courage to change the things I can, and the wisdom to know the difference."

An elderly woman comes over and gives me a hug. The moderator shakes hands with me, thanks me for sharing, and asks me if I have a sponsor yet. I assure him I'll get that taken care of next week, but excuse myself and nearly run for the door.

I'm exhausted on my drive home. It was another twelve hour day at the office. The long hours aren't a big deal. It's just spinning my wheels that wears me out. Two missed calls. Dell. Haven't talked to him since Sunday lunch. Klarissa. What's that all about? We've been sniping at each other for years and suddenly she wants to be my dinner partner. Come to think of it, Warren hasn't been around. He's never really done the Sunday thing with the family—he's the sports guy at WBC-TV, so Sunday is a big workday for him. But usually we hear something about what he and Klarissa are doing. No mention in how long? I really need to be a better big sister.

I zone out and find myself in a parking spot in front of my apartment. I park far enough away from the car in front of me that I can use the decline to start my car if it's as difficult in the morning as it has been the past month.

God, help us to get a break in this case, please. Please. And help my car start in the morning.

Chapter 24
April 29, 1:19am

*T*wo can play at this game. She doesn't want to see me … fine! Her loss! If she can't stand my presence, my being … then I can't stand hers either. I'm not calling. I swear I'm not calling. Here's my new rule: she has to call me two times before I call her back. And from now on, she has to call me two times for every one time I call her. Stupid witch.

She was lovely. She wasn't like the other girls. She was special. He wanted more time with her.

I bet I end up forgiving her. She'll like that. But I'm still not going to call her until she calls me two times. That's my final offer chick.

He had strayed from the schedule. From the plan. And he knew it was wrong.

I am a little mad at myself. I didn't think it would hurt to go again sooner. I've always been so careful to keep to a strict timetable and that's why the stupid police never catch me. One of the reasons.

I think the big one is my superior IQ. Or is it that they're really just that clueless? They need to raise the standards on their hiring practices. It's almost too easy. I'm playing chess and they're still trying to learn checkers.

He had to punish himself for this divergence. Starvation maybe.

Or no TV and Internet.

And he planned to wait two extra weeks before his next intimate encounter.

Maybe.

He knew it was important to prove his discipline and self-command once again.

Call. I said call! And I mean right now.

Chapter 25

The car in front of me left before I did this morning and someone else took the spot and put the parking brake on about three inches from my front bumper. But my trusty Miata fired right up and after maneuvering backward and forward about ten times to edge out of a tight spot, I slammed it into first, gunned the engine, went airborne over the speed bump in front of the entrance to my apartment complex and hit the road in a hurry.

I stopped at JavaStar and got a grande Americano with a Splenda, an extra shot, and no drama. I bought a copy of the *Sun Times*. They ran a banner on the front page directing readers to the Cutter Shark section, a running feature in both major Chicago papers, but at least there was no lead story about CPD incompetence. Our lack of progress does make their job harder with nothing new to report, so they've resorted to a tabloid approach. Yesterday, the *Trib* ran a three thousand word piece on new theories about what's driving the Cutter Shark murders, which included a reference to a cult of Vampires. Vampires? You've got to be kidding me. Maybe if they'd postulated werewolves I could have taken the story more seriously.

The *Sun's* big scoop this week was a story on a psychic from St. Petersburg, Russia, who apparently told her neighbors about this Cutter Shark fellow months ago—in detail and documented with date stamped camcorder that they had handy—and who is waiting for the CPD to contact her and fly her over to help solve the case. I suspect she's running a mail order bride scam. On the latter story, there is already a citizen's action committee demanding that Mayor Daniels act now if he wants to be reelected.

I haven't followed the White Sox or Cubbies so far this baseball season. Both lost last night. But the Sox are in third while the Cubbies are in last. Oh well. If I wanted good news I'd watch insurance commercials on youtube.

It was another day of spinning wheels. Our task force keeps getting bigger. We're covering the same territory in waves. But no one has any fresh ideas. We're all frustrated and growing more concerned and wary by the day. The killer went early with his last victim. Does that mean the four week clock started ticking with his first murder or his second murder? Or is the clock broken?

Blackshear, Martinez, Don and I grabbed lunch near the second crime scene in Rogers Park. That was convenient because our assignment was to ask every restaurant owner or manager if a new customer had started hanging out a couple weeks earlier. We ate at a strange little vegetarian place called Victory's Banner that serves great breakfasts all day—and even better coffee. If I was casing that neighborhood I'd sip their coffee a couple hours a day. We talked with a pleasant little Indian or Pakistani woman wearing a serape. She was not aware of anyone fitting the description—and honestly, what description could we give her. She assured us she would talk to everyone who works there and if anyone has any ideas she'll have them call one of us. Same response from everyone we chatted to in a two square mile section of Chicago.

I was in the office at eight and left exactly twelve hours later. Klarissa, who has been incredibly sweet lately, came to my office with some sandwiches from Panera. Sliced turkey and avocado on whole wheat. Yum. She was only with me a half hour when she got buzzed. Big thunderstorm rolling in and they wanted her ready to be on air for special reports pronto. She gave me a hug and scooted.

*M*y engine catches but turns over. I give 'a sigh of relief. I start driving home, mostly in autopilot mode. After a few minutes I come out of a near stupor. I remember there was something I promised myself I would do.

I look at my phone and continue an internal debate. Call back or not call back. To call or not to call. I shake my head and hit his cell phone number. He answers on the second ring.

"Well, hey stranger. I didn't think you'd ever call back. I was just thinking about you."

"Dell, I'm sorry. You know what's going on at work right now."

"I really don't ... I just can't imagine ... but I know this murder thing is all-consuming right now. That's why I've only left you one message since Sunday. Just trying to let you know that you have someone to call if you need a friendly voice. I know this thing you're working on is ... well, like I said, all-consuming. I'm trying to keep up with it in the papers, but it doesn't sound like a whole lot is happening."

"You've got that right. Hey, Dell, we really need to talk."

"I thought that was what we were doing. Let's talk. Better yet, let me meet you over by your place and we'll grab something to drink. I've had a tough day and wouldn't mind a beer and you can have your grapefruit juice."

"I can't tonight."

"How come I knew you were going to say that?"

"I'm just off work now and it's almost nine. I've got to be in the office in less than twelve hours. I know you don't want to hear this, but I'm going to work out at Planet Fitness instead of meeting with you on the way home, because if I don't get some exercise, I'm going to explode."

Explode? Oh well, whatever that means.

"I worked out this morning, but I'd love to hit the treadmill. Why don't I come over there?"

"Dell, you're not listening. That's why we need to talk."

"Am I pushing again?"

"No, you're not pushing. You're just being a nice guy. A great guy."

"Well thank you. Is that kind of like telling an ugly girl she has a great personality?"

"No. I'm serious, Dell. You're wonderful. It just emphasizes how lousy I am to you. That girl you brought to church a couple weeks ago was smoking. I can't remember her name."

"Carrie."

That was fast. Good. Maybe he has some thoughts for her and I can help them along by restating the obvious—I am not interested in spending time with him romantically or otherwise. He's got an imaginary relationship going on with me and my family is aiding and abetting it. This has got to stop. It's gotten too weird. I don't like it.

"Yeah, Carrie. Why don't you go out with her or someone who is as nice to you as you are to them? Seriously Dell, what's with me?"

I knew it was the wrong question before the words were all the way out of my mouth. In the midst of disengaging I had just reengaged.

"You mean besides your awesome good looks and your intense and smoldering personality? Because beyond those two things—oh, yeah, and your good morals and your incredibly nice family—I don't know. I'm just crazy about you. I've told you that."

"I think maybe you're crazy about my family."

"Hey, I'm not even going to argue that point. I love your family. The only downside of watching you all interact at the dinner table is that it makes me realize what I grew up without."

"Well the good news is that my family loves you. In fact, I think—no, I know—they like you a whole lot more than they do me. They seem to spend all their time grilling me about you. Especially Mom and Klarissa."

"How are things with her?"

"With Klarissa? Fine actually. We've been hanging out recently."

"I know its tough fighting with a sibling," he says.

"You have no idea until you've lived it."

"Well why shouldn't I hang around your family?" he asks, getting back on topic. "You're from that family and whose to say you aren't going to wake up one morning and be mad, crazy in love with me, too?"

"Okay, you're pushing. But Dell, I'm being serious. I'm not the girl you want to be seeing right now."

"But I do want to see you and if it's not now, I can wait until later."

The moment of truth is here. I just got to do it. Dad said that if you're going to cut the tail off a monkey, do it all at once, not one inch at a time since every cut hurts the same.

"Okay then, try this Dell, because I don't know how else to say it than to be very direct. I don't want to see you."

There's a pause.

"I understand. But you're going through a lot right now. Things settle down and maybe you do, too. You're floating along right now and I'm willing to wait."

"You may be right about me floating in my relationships right now but what you're not hearing—or simply not accepting—is that I'm pretty positive that when I do land, I'm not going to land with you."

"When you say 'pretty positive'—"

"Dell, don't do the 'I've got a chance' line from *Dumb and Dumber*," I cut him off. "We've kind of joked about this and it's not helping either of us."

There is another palpable silence on the line. I feel like a creep for being so blunt but you know what, this is Dell's doing. He's demanding an answer I won't give and he's relentless. I count to ten and then speak.

"Dell, I'm sorry."

He says, "thank you."

"For what?"

"For finally being honest."

"I don't think I've been dishonest with you prior to tonight."

"No, you haven't, but you've probably left enough wiggle room for me to keep hope alive."

"There's plenty of hope for you, Dell. Just not with me. Go call Carrie or someone else. Ask someone on a date tomorrow night. I'm being serious. Do it. Get moving."

"Okay, I hear and obey," he says with a painfully stilted laugh. "I just might make that call. But I'm not going to set up a date for tomorrow night. I see you tomorrow night."

"What are you talking about, Dell? What did I just get done saying?"

"Kendra's birthday party is tomorrow night. I got invited by the princess herself. You didn't forget did you?"

"Of course not; I just haven't looked at tomorrow on my calendar, yet," I answer with a laugh, which is almost as stilted as his was.

I get off the phone fast now. I'm still not sure Dell is really listening but I don't have time do anymore explaining tonight. Crud. Forget Planet Fitness. I've got to go get Kendra a birthday present.

What you doing?"

It's Klarissa. Apparently, my closest friend in the whole world based on our recent food and telephone activity together.

I'm going out of my mind at a Wal-Mart super center, looking for a great present for a soon-to-be eight-year-old Snowflake, is what I'm doing.

"Just picking a few things up at the store on the way home," is what I tell her.

"So you just remembered to get Kendra her present tonight?"

Busted. I pause too long while trying to think of a witty comeback, so she continues.

"Just a bit of advice, but you might want to get her something that's non-sports-related. Just once."

I look at the soccer ball and new shin guards in the cart. I roll my eyes and sigh. I've let my hair down and it falls across my face. I blow it off and run my fingers through it. I'm half a mile from the checkout line and the return trip to sporting goods is pretty close to the Wisconsin state line. I put the items on a display with electric toothbrushes. I spot a two-pack of replacement heads for my brand and put the armored plastic package in my cart.

"You there?"

"Oh, sorry Klarissa. I'm just having trouble narrowing down what I want to get for Kendra."

"I'll bet. Hey, I'm not going to keep you because I know that shopping takes every ounce of patience and concentration that you possess, but I just wanted to say thanks for going to dinner with me earlier this week and then eating with me again tonight. It was nice."

"It was, Baby Sis. If I didn't tell you already, thanks for the sandwich. Just what the doctor ordered. Oh, and you promised to tell Mom that we didn't fight. She won't believe it coming from me."

"Already done," she says. "It made her happy."

There's a long pause.

"You okay, Klarissa?"

"Yeah, I think I am. Just a tough time for me right now. Things are already looking up though. I love you, Kristen."

"I love you, too, Klarissa."

When was the last time we said that? There's an awkward silence. She breaks it.

"Go look for a present and I'll see you tomorrow night."

We hang up. I have the feeling there's more going on than she told me our last few outings and she told me a lot more than she ever has before. Warren broke up with her. That's usually not a big deal. They've broken up a hundred times. But I guess this time it was more than one of their battles of the network stars. There's someone else in Warren's life and he admitted that she had been there for a while and that things were serious. I just hope her name isn't Carrie. I need her for Dell.

Klarissa's a volatile mix of vulnerable and unconquerable. At dinner she showed her vulnerable side. I asked if there was anything else that led up to the breakup—like her seeing someone else, which has happened before—and she hesitated as if to answer for just a second, but closed back up. I circled back to that point a couple times between bites of turkey and avocado, but she wasn't going to give anything up.

I remember that Don has an eight-year-old daughter. Veronika. He and Vanessa treat her like a princess. I'm betting Vanessa can help me find a better present for Kendra than I can on my own. Don will find that amusing and give me a hard time. He'll point out that he is a better shopper than I am. I'll remind him that it's really not saying much.

Three sets each of twenty push-ups—the boy kind—and a hundred crunches, followed by twenty-five double leg jumps and eagle jumps in quick succession—I may have wakened my neighbor in the apartment below. Three three-minute planks and thirty bridges. Not a bad workout. I am breathing hard and sweating. I shower, brush my teeth with a new electric toothbrush head that I have to wrench from plastic packaging that requires an electric chainsaw to open, and plop into bed with a copy of *People* magazine. I'm not sure I care who is together or apart or having a baby or having a mental breakdown or finding inner peace in Hollywood, but it's right there in front of me.

Klarissa had it in her carry-all and was reading it when she came over to my precinct for dinner. The cover story is about a nineteen-year-old actress who is in rehab for alcohol abuse. I want to read it so maybe I can tell a better story in my next AA appearances. I'm adding a second meeting tomorrow night after Kendra's birthday party. Actually, it's more like a dinner with presents. Kendra's party, not the AA meeting.

The article's actually kind of lame and not a whole lot of help. I'm not sure I can work the horrors of growing up as child actress into my storyline.

I hit the lights at midnight, thinking I'll be asleep in a minute or two. Don't know what time I actually drift off. I can't get the faces of Leslie Reed and Candace Rucker out of my mind.

Chapter 26

Blackshear, Martinez, Sergeant Konkade, Scalia, Don, and I are reviewing notes. There are now twelve detectives and another ten techies from forensics, data, and psyche on the case. That's twenty-seven full timers from the CPD dedicated to this case alone, plus countless others taking time away from the other work involved in keeping the peace in a city of almost three million people to help with our Cutter Shark nightmare. We're trying to make sure we have covered all the bases.

We have. We've talked to every neighbor, every relative, every work associate, every club associate, and every other kind of associate of the past ten years for both victims. We've canvassed every store owner in a three mile radius of each crime scene. We've checked every phone log. We've read every report that Virgil has spit out on previous crime cities. We've read all forty-seven case reports at least a couple times each. We've talked to lead investigators from the other cities and from similar cases. We've listened to Reynolds and Van Guten hypothesize on the motivations and habits of our killer. We're all attending AA meetings.

Konkade heads up that part of the investigation. We've read the reams of reports this has generated. I think he has them memorized. We have done background checks on close to 300 AA attendees. None of them look good for this kind of crime but we did face to face follow-ups on about forty of them anyway. That means Konkade has mobilized about twenty surveillance teams to pierce the anonymity of a good and innocent organization. None of us are comfortable with it but none of us are willing to let the only viable lead go unattended. I don't know the religious orientation of the individual team members but I'm guessing anyone who prays is praying that the press doesn't get hold of our infiltration of a nonprofit service organization. That's not even factoring the response of the attendees themselves and the potential legal repercussions.

Stern and taciturn, Konkade is showing signs of stress. He keeps running a hand over the top of his head to smooth his hair back. Problem is he doesn't have any hair.

With all the effort we've put forth in this area, only one red flag remains. My Jonathan. I saw him in one meeting at one location. He hasn't been back. He fits the age profile that Van Guten has proposed. Even his story of multiple jobs and high intelligence fits. The only thing she doesn't like is that she's not sure that our perpetrator would be that forthcoming. But then again, who says the story is true? He may have just created a storyline to fit in. Who says the Cutter Shark has ever had a drink in his life? Did I just call him the Cutter Shark?

Could I have warned him off?

Scalia is old school. Just like Dad. He listens and rarely speaks. Just like Dad, again. He'll occasionally interject a question about a conversation we've had with someone who might have information that can help us understand what's going on. Otherwise, he's not volunteering what's on his mind. He's a legend on the force. Could it be that he has no ideas in mind either? That's scary.

Reynolds pops his head in the room. Zaworski and Czaka are behind him.

"Sorry to interrupt. Can we steal Detective Conner from you for a few minutes?"

"We're wrapping up anyway," Blackshear answers. "She's all yours."

Blackshear is now our official spokesperson. I am predicting a promotion for him in the not too distant future. Maybe Martinez, too. His English isn't the best but his Spanish is a very desirable trait in a multicultural city. Because of guilt by association, I may not be helping Don's cause for advancement.

I look at my watch and frown. It's eleven thirty. I was planning to get Kendra's present over lunch break. I wandered another thirty minutes last night and couldn't come up with anything. I'm going to break down and text Vanessa and see if she'll bail me out. I'll never hear the end of it from Don but desperate times call for desperate measures.

"Is there a problem, Conner?" Czaka asks, noting my frown and hesitation.

"No, sir."

We give each other an icy stare, both willing the other to speak. Zaworski isn't going to let me hang myself and smoothly turns me by taking my arm at the elbow and leading me down the hall. I feel like a fifth grader being taken to the principal's office.

I look back at Czaka and Reynolds following us. Reynolds has a puzzled expression and knowing him, he will have the full story of Czaka and my bone of contention within the hour. We enter Zaworski's office. Van Guten is already sitting comfortably in one of the wingback chairs, legs crossed, kicking a high heeled shoe up and down slowly, reading a report. She nods at Czaka, Zaworski, and Reynolds but doesn't look up at me. I guess what she's reading is too important to acknowledge a lowly detective.

I told Don after the first meeting that I didn't think she liked me. He scoffed and credited it to my female insecurity. He may be right but so am I. We all just stand around and get busy doing nothing. Zaworski scrapes at an invisible stain on his tie with the fingernail of his right forefinger. Reynolds races through emails on his Blackberry or iPhone or some concept phone that only the FBI gets to test. Czaka has opened a green file folder and is looking at a two-page report of some kind. He shuts the folder, hands it to Zaworski, and exits without a word.

Van Guten is in no hurry to finish her reading. She looks back a couple pages, purses her lips, snaps her folder shut, and looks directly at me.

"Detective Conner, after almost four weeks of scouring for clues, it appears that you are the only law enforcement officer from local, state, or national agencies who has suggested even one possible lead for our quarry."

My mind races around trying to remember what it was that I came up with. I'm hoping she will tell me what it is before I have to ask for clarification. She does.

"As I mentioned before, there are things I like about this Jonathan that you met at your first AA meeting and things I don't like. What intrigues me about your description of him is that on three separate reports you have expressed a question as to what he said about the timing of his return to Chicago."

"I think that says more about my memory over a quick remark than it does about him."

"Precisely. I agree with you on that," Van Guten says smugly. "It suggests to me that something about this person triggered a response in you that may be LCR."

I look at her blankly.

"LCR; Latent Case Relevant," she clarifies.

Okay. Everyone in the room is looking at me intently now. What the heck is going on?

"What I'd like to do, with your full consent of course, is put you under hypnosis, which just happens to be one of my areas of expertise."

I'm not sure I'm comfortable with her knowing what's on my conscious mind, never mind my unconscious; the thought of opening that part of the self to someone else is outright scary. I'm not sure even I want to know all that goes on in my head.

O God, save me from myself.

Chapter 27

So are you going to do it?"

"I don't know Don."

"I'm sure it's safe or they wouldn't ask you to do it."

"I don't know. I read a novel once where an FBI psychologist used hypnosis to murder victims."

"Did he strangle them or what?"

"It was actually a she and she didn't do it directly. She had them commit suicide."

"Huh?"

"She'd call them and speak a key word prompt she planted in their minds when they were in a hypnotic state. So there were no clues."

"Sounds like a tough conviction."

"Wasn't necessary. The good guy killed her."

"What kind of trash are you reading these days?"

"Who says I'm reading trash? It was a great book. A little farfetched but believable."

"Using hypnosis to murder people is plausible?"

"Well, the way it was written, sure. But getting back on topic, the thing that worries me most about Van Guten hypnotizing me is that … well, she doesn't like me."

"You say that about everybody."

"Well if you had even a twinge of suspicion that someone didn't like you, wasn't for you, would you want them being in control of you in an incredibly vulnerable state?"

"No, guess I wouldn't. But I do let you drive and I even go to the shooting range with you. Both are acts of courage."

Normally I'd punch Don in the shoulder. Hard. But my mind is racing. Don clears his throat and knocks some imaginary lint off his jacket sleeve while he ponders murder by hypnosis and my concerns about Van Guten.

"Then don't do it," he says.

"Right."

"I thought you said it was your choice."

"What do you think? Do I really have a choice?"

"Sure you do. You can say no—and go back to checking parking meters."

"I think I've worked every rotten job that CPD has to offer, but I actually missed the meter maid routine."

"I didn't."

I can't help but laugh. Don? Working the parking detail? How'd I miss that in my year and change as his partner?

"Don ... I'll bet we've never had a better dressed maid on the force."

"Keep laughing," he says. "Wonder what you'll be doing next."

It's Friday morning. I have to give Reynolds, Van Guten, and Zaworski an answer by ten. We've been on this case close to a month and desperation has seemingly and finally set in. Van Guten wants to hypnotize me based on my report of Jonathan at my first AA meeting. Are they grasping at straws?

Duh. Insightful question, Detective Conner.

I wonder if I was the one who got myself into this mess by embellishing my written reports on my encounter and non-encounters with Jonathan. If so, I'm going to end up in a state of mind that I abhor—absolute vulnerability.

Hey, I'm all for science and any technique that might help us catch a sick killer. But you have to be realistic, too. Hypnosis feels about one step above the work of all the so-called psychics who come out of the woodwork in the highly publicized circus atmosphere surrounding a predator like the Cutter Shark. My dad was actually intrigued by the psychics—or the psychos as he called them. He said that if you believe in the spiritual world, including angels and demons, you never know when one of the whack jobs, his phrase not mine, was going to have an insight due to a special connection with the spirit world.

Van Guten was all business in detailing the efficacy of hypnosis with me, but there's an arrogance there that still doesn't feel totally right to me. Zaworksi handed me the green folder from Czaka, which contained a liability waiver. He gave me instructions to meet with my union rep for sure and a lawyer if I wanted. CPD would pay for one hour of legal consultation. He stressed one hour about three times. I guess our budget is already shot for the year and we're not halfway into it. I talked to my union guy who said it was my call. I skipped the three hundred dollar an hour legal fee for the department.

So how'd Kimberly like her gift?"

"You mean Kendra?"

"I can't keep track of all the K's in your family. I don't want to start anything with you today, but it does make me wonder if someone in your family tree wore sheets and rode a horse by torchlight late a night."

I turn and give Don my hardest glare.

"Just kidding."

"It wasn't funny."

"I'm not the only member of this team that has missed the mark on humor on more than a few occasions."

Touché.

"She loved it," I answer Don truthfully.

Problem was the gift didn't go over very well with mommy. No one sent me the memo that Danny and Kaylen weren't getting Barbie stuff for Kendra. Don said his daughter, Veronika, loves her Barbie dolls. I guess they have a black model, but according to Don the wardrobe is still way too lily white. But no problem. Vanessa sews clothes when she isn't selling houses and buying him expensive shoes.

Vanessa got my text and was thrilled to help. She brought a Sporty Barbie to the office wrapped up in matching gift paper. She spent about ten bucks more than I would have so I felt even better showing up for the party.

Danny and Kaylen think that Barbie sends the wrong message to girls about body image, Kaylen explained to me. Seems a little severe to me, but who knows, they're probably right. I just know that Kendra squealed with delight and hugged on me the rest of the evening after opening her present. I don't think she was worried about her chest size or lack thereof—or not having six-inch heels with her soccer outfit. Maybe it will mess her up later. I somehow doubt it.

I thought I was doing well by forgoing sports equipment for something girly but missed the boat again. No good deed goes unpunished.

There now that wasn't so bad was it?" Van Guten asks me. "Kind of like waking up after a power nap, no?"

No. First of all, I never take power naps. If I put my head down when the sun is still shining, I just pass out and slobber on the pillow. Second, what I really feel is groggy and disoriented; I don't sense even a trace of empowerment.

I am tempted to tell her that I won't be able to fully answer her question until I go for a full year without howling at the moon or running down the street naked when I hear the sound of a cell phone ringing. I think there was an old black and white movie I watched with my dad where some French doctor trained an ape to kill people when he rang a certain bell. And I'm thinking about that book with the FBI psychiatrist who hypnotizes people and then calls them like a month or year later and has them kill themselves without any link to her. There is an anti-hero vigilante character named Reacher that catches her at her game and kills her. He never let her hypnotize him. Good for him. He's a better man than I am even if he is a made up character.

My head clears enough to realize that Van Guten has left the room. I appreciate her deep concern for my well being. I'm probably just jealous that once again, she looks beautiful and completely together in yet another outfit that probably costs enough to buy three new starters for my Miata. I get up and stretch my back, then gather my purse to head to the elevator bank on the forty-eighth floor of the State Building and home of the regional office of the FBI.

I hear a phone ring from down the hall and get very still. A minute later my clothes are still on and I'm not howling at the moon—or the sun since it's not lunchtime yet. Maybe it's the sound of an oven timer that is the secret trigger Dr. Van Guten has imbedded in my psyche.

Good thing I don't cook much.

Chapter 28

A unt Kristen, I like my new Barbie doll a lot."

"You do?"

"A lot! I really do. Her name is Kristen."

That throws me for a loop. I thought the doll's name was Barbie. Can you do that? Can you give a doll that already has a name another name? Could GI Joe become GI Jerry or Barry? Could the Incredible Hulk become the Incredible Larry? And do I want my name attached to a plastic doll that is *persona non grata* in my sister's house?

"So where'd you come up with the name Kristen?"

"It's your name, silly."

"My name isn't silly, it's Kristen."

She thinks that is very funny and squeals with delight.

"So you really do like the Kristen Doll I got you?" I ask.

"The mostest of all the presents I got for my birthday."

I'm about to ask her if she is hiding in her closet so she can play with her forbidden Kristen Doll without getting in trouble with her mom, but she quickly tells me bye and says that mommy wants to talk to me. Uh oh.

"I'm sorry Little Sis," Kaylen says to me.

"What are you talking about this time?" I ask with an exaggerated sigh.

Why can't I just be gracious? Kaylen has no time for my sparring today and stays on topic.

"Honestly, Kristen, I was pretty rotten to you. And I want you to forgive me."

"No big biggie—you are forgiven."

"It's just that we had wanted to keep Kendra away from certain things and Barbie was one of them."

She yammers on for fifteen minutes, explaining in detail what it does to a woman's psyche when she is objectified by men. There's a few times when I think she is actually retracting her apology. There are a few times when I think she is a card-carrying member of NOW and is about to march on Washington to reintroduce the ERA Amendment. There are a few times I think she's full of something and a few times when she makes a lot of sense. Part of the time I'm not paying attention.

I finally interrupt, "so did you call to apologize or to enlighten me on the dangers of the fashion doll industry on the psychological development of the modern pre-adolescent?"

She hesitates long enough that I know my question hit the mark. Hah. It sounded pretty smart, too. I have to get back to my master's degree.

"To apologize. And also because I'm worried about Klarissa."

She has changed the subject and I am fully attentive now.

"You too?" I ask.

"Yeah. I didn't know you were worried. Why didn't you say something?"

"I don't know if I've been out and out worried," I say, "but something is definitely going on with her. You know she and Warren broke up?"

"Yeah. But do you think that is really what's eating at her?"

Rats. I thought I might have the inside skinny for once.

"Hard to say," I respond. "I never figured they would actually make it to the altar. But they have been together for most of the last five years. That's got to hurt."

"Has it been that long?" Kaylen asks in disbelief. "I am getting older. Well, you too I guess!"

We talk another five minutes about Klarissa and Warren and Kendra and how I'm handling the pressure of working on a high profile murder case. That slows the conversation down considerably. I finally start to beg off because I've got to get something done today. While in a non-hypnotic state of consciousness and fully clothed.

"Hey, before you run," Kaylen interjects, "Did you say that Warren broke up with her?"

"Yeah. For a hot young squeeze."

"Says who?"

"Says Klarissa."

"That's weird. Warren called Danny and said that he was worried about Klarissa, too, and that it wasn't just because she broke up with him."

"Well maybe he was trying to save face for Klarissa," I say.

"Yeah, maybe," she says, "But he's always been a little more interested in his own face."

"That's true," I say with a laugh. "But then again, he was the one that called Danny to express concern."

"Good point," she says.

"I love you Sis, but got to go," I say.

"I love you, too, and I really am sorry for beating on you about the Barbie. It's just that—"

Was it wrong to click the red button before getting a recap of potential self-image crises that may be in Kendra's future the moment she unwrapped the smiling doll who likes to stand on her tip toes no matter what she's doing? I put my cell phone back in a leather sleeve I wear next to my Beretta. I look at my landline with its message light bright red. Better start calling people back.

Hey, did Kaylen make a reference to my age again? Are she and Mom working on me in unison?

Before I hit the replay button on my phone, I stand up, stretch, roll my neck, and throw a couple imaginary punches. I step outside of my cube to see what's happening in our detective warren. Someone has put a yellow Post-it Note on the carpeted wall of my office space.

DEAR DETECTIVE CONNER—YOU'VE REALLY GOT TO STOP SLEEPING ON THE JOB. NOT THAT BEING AWAKE HAS DONE YOU MUCH GOOD EITHER. YOU THINK YOU'RE SO HOT RUNNING AROUND WITH THE "BOYS" AND RUNNING THAT BIG MOUTH OF YOURS. I THINK YOU MUST LIKE MAKING A FOOL OF YOURSELF.

What the heck? Okay, Don and Martinez gave me a hard time about being hypnotized, but this is just too weird. Whenever a detective show on TV includes a note as part of the storyline, the note is always from the bad guy to the good guys and leaves clues. I'm getting trash talked by a colleague.

God, I'm sorry I make so many people mad. Please help.

Chapter 29
April 31, 3:30pm

*M**aybe she'll be there tonight. I'd like to talk to her. I think I'll go. I just want to talk is all. She's special. It's not her turn. Yet. Hah!*

He was filled with anticipation. He knew he should wait a couple more weeks and return to his perfect progress, but, on the other hand, he had already tampered with the schedule and knew that he would find the right solution to set it right. He was good at making adjustments. After all, it was her fault that things were out of alignment.

If she keeps screwing with me, it really is going to be her turn. Nah. I just can't stay mad at her.

One of his many strengths was his ability to rise above the petty irritations that plague so many people and make the world such an unpleasant place to live. He truly was a man in control and yet filled with charm and kindness.

Okay, maybe not too kind. But definitely charming. That's what the girls tell me anyway. An elliptical machine can only help me relieve so much pressure. I'm glad I forked over the extra cash to get one with a built-in video player. Good thing for this city I like old classic movies. Between Gone With the Wind, Dr. Zhivaggo, *and* Sound of Music, *I bet I burned ten thousand calories this week.*

His exertions served two purposes. His physique, toned and cut to the ultimate image of manhood, was maintained, while his energy, the source of his inspiration, was controlled through the application of fatigue. He was more powerful than ever.

I'm still wired, though. And there's only so much pressure a man can withstand. I feel trapped. I think I'll watch The Great Escape *this afternoon. I liked it when I was kid. I don't like the symbolism though. Reminds me that a day will come when I'll have to move on. That's okay. I like new cities and meeting new people. I do want more time with her first though. Game on baby.*

Chapter 30

I'm trying to look as casual as I possibly can but I'm running across the church parking lot to my AA meeting in a downpour and I'm almost ten minutes late. That started when my sporty little Miata wouldn't.

The precinct garage was full this morning so I parked in the back lot, which is completely flat, so there was no way to roll my car backwards and pop the clutch to get it started. I ended up having two uniformed officers push my car while running as fast as they could. Because of the haphazard way the CPD parks—somebody needs to be handing out some tickets back here—I didn't want to maneuver half a city block in reverse, which doesn't require as much speed, so they had to push me almost one hundred feet for me to get enough momentum to jerk my car to a start from first gear. How embarrassing. One of them was actually pretty cute. Where were Danny and Dell when I needed them most?

The problem was exacerbated because there are six plainclothes officers in three unmarked squad cars assigned to follow and watch me tonight, so this little episode will make the rounds in the office tomorrow. Great. Another yellow note is sure to follow.

I guess that under hypnosis I told Van Guten that Jonathan had indeed said that he had just returned to town. I'm guessing there are a hundred thousand people who are new to our happy little metropolitan over the past six months. Not all of them, however, attend AA meetings. Van Guten also likes his age, the main points of his story, and his physical description as related by me. She let the task force know that there are eleven additional points of convergence she has identified between Jonathan and our killer. Couldn't that be a little like six degrees of separation from Kevin Bacon?

Everyone around the table was unanimous that I wouldn't be attending this particular AA meeting solo again. I didn't argue. So tonight I am wearing a wire and have a cadre of bodyguards close at hand. I hope the wire is waterproof.

I walk down the half flight of steps into the now familiar basement of St. Bartholomew United Methodist Church. I've also started attending another AA meeting at Holy Family, a large Catholic church. It might even be a cathedral or basilica. There they put the chairs in rows and we all face forward and look at whoever is speaking. You have to walk up front to share. There's usually more than a hundred people there. The meeting room at St. Bart's is a lot smaller so we always sit in a circle and can get a good look at everyone else attending, unless they are to our immediate left or right. I don't think we've ever had more than twenty at one meeting.

There are four empty chairs, so I slide into the one closest to the door. Housewife is back. I can't remember her name. Brittany? Nope. Bethany? I think so. She is sharing and makes a dramatic pause while I get situated, not looking too happy about the interruption.

"I don't know what I'm going to do. I don't love Jeff anymore. I know he's a great guy and is a good father and husband. He definitely doesn't deserve what I'm putting him through. He thinks I'm having an affair. And to be honest, the thought has crossed my mind. If the right opportunity had come along, I probably would have already.

"But my real problem is vodka. I didn't even drink until I was thirty. We went to an office party and I had my first Cosmopolitan. All the girls I drink with now love them because they're sweet and go down so easy. Funny, but I don't need the Kool-Aid or whatever they mix in there. I just like the alcohol. It's ironic, but Jeff always wanted me to loosen up and have a drink with him. Well, I've loosened up alright. Now I don't know how to screw the lid back on.

"I guess I lied when I started speaking tonight. I haven't been sober for two weeks. I slammed two martinis on the way over here. I don't know what I'm going to do. If I don't figure something out I'm going to lose my husband and kids. The problem is I'm not sure I really care."

She stops talking, folds her arms, and stares at the black and white, checkered tile floor. A single tear rolls down her cheek. And then another. A waterfall follows. But she doesn't change expressions. Instead of looking sad, she looks angry while tears stream down her face. The kindly old woman, who always gives me a hug, stands up and walks over to sit beside her. She embraces her, but Housewife is not responsive. She continues to stare at the floor with snot and tears running onto her lightweight, v-neck blouse.

I feel bad for the judgmentalism and cynicism I've felt toward her. Our sponsor, Jack, spends a few minutes telling the group that acknowledgment is the first step toward recovery. He affirms Housewife. Her name isn't really Bethany. It's Kathy.

She doesn't respond. What is Kathy feeling? Anger? Sorry for herself? Remorse? Guilt? Numbness? Has she told us the real story? It kind of rang true tonight, but who knows.

A few more people share, but the energy just isn't there. We end our session thirty minutes early. No Jonathan tonight. I wonder what the six detectives listening in on my meeting think of Housewife. I'm ready to head home, but from out of the blue, I step forward and cut Housewife off at the door.

"Kathy?"

She looks up. Her eyes are red and puffy. She looks at me first with defiance and then softens.

"Yeah?"

"You okay?"

"What do you think?"

Okay, I admit that was a dumb question.

"Sorry," I mumble. "I guess I'm just making sure you can make it home okay."

She starts crying again and puts her head on my shoulder. I hesitantly put an arm around her and she really starts blubbering. I feel a little bad because the thought crossed my mind that I'm glad I've got an old spring weight shirt on—sleeveless with a collar that I think went out of style so long ago I can't remember when. I was thinking of getting rid of it anyway—and anytime time I get rid of an article of clothing, I have this weird need to wear it one more time. Now she's just plain snotting on me. Her mouth is right next to the tiny microphone tucked into my top and I'm guessing she's blowing out the eardrums of whoever is listening in. I don't think I'm going home early after all.

Chapter 31
April 31, 11:58pm

*S*omething didn't feel right. I don't like that feeling because I liked going there. The people were nice and had some pretty good stories.

His intuition had forewarned him. He had made a discovery. Just like him, always one step ahead.

They know where I sometimes meet my girls. Someone from the FBI has been working overtime. I know local enforcement isn't smart enough to figure anything like that out. I hope they don't feel too proud of themselves. Let's face it; it took them forever to figure this much out. Besides, it's really not doing them any good. I don't think they're any closer to me than they were seven years ago.

He harkened back to his youth. To a time when his fledgling potential had gotten him caught and put in "the system." But he always knew the right answers to their questions. He was always too clever. Alone in his genius.

But I bet they don't know all the places I like to meet new girlfriends.

Wonder if they'll figure my other hot spots out in less than a decade again. I'll have to be more careful if I'm in this for the long run. And I soooo am.

I hated The Great Escape. *It wasn't as good as I remembered it before. Plus I'm worn out from a three hour workout.*

He chided himself and resolved to exercise his cunning as much as his muscles.

No movies and no elliptical tomorrow. Time to get back to work.

Chapter 32

D o you realize how much overtime you cost us last night?"
Zaworski is angry. Real angry. He's not making eye contact. It's
only ten a.m. and he's already taken off his suit jacket. He's either
madder than I think he is or he's forgotten to put on his deodorant. Dark
semi-circles of sweat have formed on his white dress shirt, which isn't quite
tucked in right. It crosses my mind to compliment his tie, but I doubt that
will distract him. And it is an ugly tie.

"Sir, I didn't anticipate that the team would stay with me once the AA
meeting was over."

"And why wouldn't you anticipate that? Didn't we say that we would
stay with you all evening, no matter what? Are you saying that you think
we don't keep our promises? That I'm not a good and honest leader?"

"Sir, that's not what I was implying. It's just that Jonathan, or the man
who calls himself Jonathan, didn't show up."

"Doesn't mean he wasn't in the area. Doesn't mean he isn't using your
new best friend to help him recruit a victim. Doesn't mean I'm going to
leave an officer in the field uncovered."

"Sir, I'm very sorry for keeping the watch team out until midnight
and away from their homes and families. I'm sorry for the expense to the
department."

"Midnight? Try two a.m."

"But what was I going to do? She had been drinking and was in a total meltdown. I didn't feel I had a choice. She was either going to kill people in a crash because of her hysterical crying or she was going to kill people in a crash because she was going to go out and do some more drinking, followed by driving."

"Or she was going to drive home and take care of her own family business."

Or that.

"Are you always like this? Do you save kittens from trees and push beached whales back into the ocean?"

I'm thinking about pointing out that there are no whales on the beaches of Lake Michigan but he's out of steam and actually smiles. Then he laughs. I've never seen Captain Zaworski laugh.

"I can't believe you went home with her to help her tell her husband what is going on in her life."

"I can't either," I say, laughing a little myself now, not because I think it's funny but out of sheer relief for not being in trouble. "But she was on a roll and I figured I better help keep things moving the right direction."

"I've got to tell you, we were nervous as heck. Felt like a trap."

"So I kept you up, too?"

"Unfortunately, yes. Reynolds and I monitored the transmitter together all night. That's why I haven't decided whether to give you a good citizen award or fire you yet."

"I kept the FBI up until two, too?"

"I have no clue when Reynolds and Van Guten left. They were still here when I left at three."

"Wow. I feel special."

He's not smiling anymore.

"Maybe we're all getting a little too desperate," he says. "Nothing else substantial has turned up and something just felt right about this lead. The others felt it, too. Martinez was listening from home all night."

I frown. I'm now backtracking and trying to remember everything Kathy and Jeff, her husband, and I talked about half the night.

"Anyone else listening, sir?"

He frowns and then starts to smile for the second time in the eighteen months that he's been my boss. He says nothing.

"Anyone not listening?" I ask.

He shakes his head no. Now I'm really embarrassed. I get up from the chair in front of his desk, pivot on the heels of my shoes, and head back for my cubicle. I see a lot of sleepy and unhappy faces on my way there. Don's chair is still empty. He's going to be a grouch. He's the only cop I know who gets eight hours of sleep every night.

I plop onto my seat. There's a sticky note in the middle of my computer screen. Someone—and I am going to figure out whose handwriting this is—has scribbled another note:

DEAR DETECTIVE CONNER: MY WIFE SWEARS SHE'S IN A BOOK CLUB AND THAT'S WHERE SHE GOES EVERY MONDAY NIGHT. BUT I'M SUSPICIOUS…I THINK SHE'S HITTING THE BOTTLE AND SPILLING HER GUTS AT AA MEETINGS. I HEAR YOU MAKE HOUSE CALLS. HOW MUCH DO YOU CHARGE FOR: (A) GETTING HER OFF THE BOOZE; (B) MAKING HER FALL IN LOVE WITH ME AGAIN; AND (C) INVITING US TO YOUR CHURCH. PLEASE ITEMIZE AS I'M ON A COP'S SALARY!

Whoever's doing this is such a jerk. Better not show how angry I feel right now or there's going to be a lot more of this coming my way. This is yellow note number three, which already makes it feel like a non-isolated event stream.

My cell phone buzzes. A name flashes up. My new best friend. Housewife. I probably should input "Kathy."

Chapter 33

My hands are on my knees and I'm breathing hard after a tough workout. That's when it happened.

He came in fast, quiet, and furious. Within a nana-second of sensing someone behind me, he had his arms around me in a ferocious bear hug. I was going to stomp on the inside of his foot, but in a flash he had lifted me just high enough to get my feet off the ground but not high enough for me to kick back and up toward his crotch. I was too slow anyway. In a single move he stutter stepped and looped a leg forward and tripped me. Thank goodness my head didn't hit hard when we landed on the ground. The fall still hurt like crazy and I could barely breathe with his arms wrapped around me in a vise-like grip.

I was still thinking clearly on the way down and I tried to snap my head back and catch him on the bridge of his nose. He seemed to be waiting for that move and had already dropped his chin down in the center of my back, right between my scapulae, and started digging in. Oh man, he was hitting nerve endings I didn't know I had. I bucked, trying to create space so I could squirm forward and out of his suffocating hug. His chin in my back kept me pinned close to the ground. His hug kept me from using my hands. I knew I had to think of something quick or I would be utterly helpless in a matter of seconds—if I wasn't already.

I tried the head-snap again. Not even close to the mark. I inched my knees forward with every fiber of strength I could muster to see if I could sit out. He just put more weight on me. I was seeing stars. His 200 pounds plus change were now doing most of the work of keeping me pinned down as he slid his right forearm up to the side of my neck. Was he working his way to my carotid artery to apply a sleeper hold? I was about to panic. That meant he was planning to take me prisoner. I flailed and tried to muster a scream.

A whistle blew and my attacker immediately let go. I rolled over gasping for air.

"Conner, you are not on top of your game."

My breath is too ragged to say anything. Just as well. He's right. I haven't worked on hand-to-hand combat in months. Barry Soto works for CPD as a fight trainer. He's the best. Every chance he gets, he reminds us that what we see in the movies isn't the way fights really happen. They end up on the ground. Always. Either someone gets shot or knifed and goes down to stay—or two assailants engage and end up off their feet and the best grappler wins. Better know what you're doing if you want to survive. There's a reason high school and college wrestlers dominate in those pay-per-view fight games. Sick stuff—but reflective of how mean real life fights can be. I've investigated the aftermath of more than a few of them.

"Where you been?" Soto asks.

"Busy. Too busy."

"Too busy to stay in shape?"

"Hey," I flash back. "I'm in shape."

"I don't care what you look like in your swimsuit," he answers back with a sneer. "I want you to be in the kind of shape that keeps you alive."

"I'm not sure I believe you," I spar back. "Felt more like you were trying to have your goon kill me."

"May feel that way to you, but if it was the truth," Soto responds, "you'd be dead right now. Timmy's pretty good at that."

"Wow. Where's the love Mr. Barry?"

I can't help it. If I met someone on the force when I was a kid tagging along behind my dad, they've got a title in front of one of their names. Sergeant. Lieutenant. Captain. Mr. Something.

"Hey princess, you said you wanted a tough, no holds barred, crash course, and that's what I gave you."

He gives me a friendly squeeze on the shoulder and laughs. Soto is probably sixty years of age but he makes most of us look like softies. He's old school. Very few weights, but tons of pushups, dips, and pull-ups and about a hundred isometric exercises designed to torture and humble. I go to a Pilates class at my health club every now and then. Whoever thinks they've discovered some new training technique never read the old Charles Atlas books and definitely hasn't been under the tutelage of Barry Soto.

He believes that all you need for a good workout is a floor and gravity. A wall can be a nice addition. A bar or punching bag is pure luxury. Bring your own towel.

He's probably not five foot six, but I've seen him put guys that are thirty years younger and 50 pounds heavier flat on their back on a mat before they know what hit them. He's probably pushing 180 pounds. I doubt he has a thirty inch waist. Lots of muscle and lots of hair—except on his completely bald dome.

"By the way, have you met Timmy?" he asks enthusiastically, nodding to my attacker.

"I think I just did."

Timmy laughs and Soto smiles. Then his face drops into a frown.

"Hey Kristen, seriously man, you need to spend more time over here. People talk to me. I know you're into something serious and I want to be able to take at least partial credit for keeping you alive."

How about a little dinner tonight? I promise to be more gentle."

I've showered, changed back into work clothes, and am getting ready to walk out the door of the gym and grab a Subway on the first floor that I'll eat at my cubicle. Soto and Timmy have put me through a grueling combat workout with a focus on handwork. Soto's given me a pair of old fashioned spring-loaded handgrips to use at my desk three or four times a day. I can feel muscles in my abs and legs that I forgot I had.

"You know researchers have found that gripping exercises lower blood pressure," Soto said as I tucked them in my purse. Do I look like I have high blood pressure?

Now Timmy, don't know his last name, is asking me on a date. Wow, this guy is aggressive. He'd have been a real hit in the Stone Age. Club a woman on the head and drag her back to his cave for dinner by candlelight. He's enough of a savage that she might be the entrée.

"Timmy, it's not going to work out tonight," I answer.

"Then how about tomorrow night?"

Were I to say yes, I'm guessing he'd pick me up by vine and we'd swing to his home in the trees and among the apes.

"I really can't, Timmy."

"Are you already seeing somebody?"

Timmy doesn't mess around with chit chat and subtle probing.

"Well, yes, I kind of am."

"'Kind of' doesn't sound real serious to me. Why don't you think about it and give me a call if you change your mind."

He hands me his business card. I'm flabbergasted. I say nothing, turn, and head out the door. I feel his eyes on me the whole way down a short hall and around the corner to the atrium area that has a couple of food court style restaurants. Yuk. If I could think fast on my feet I would have asked him if he was best friends with another hard-of-hearing man I know named Dell.

I get the roasted turkey breast on whole wheat with tomatoes, lettuce, lots of onion—doesn't matter, I don't have a date tonight—pickles, banana peppers, cucumber, spinach, and spicy mustard. I skip the chips for a cellophane bag filled with exactly seven dried out carrots. I pull a twenty-four ounce bottled water out of a cooler. I've got a lot of extra change in my wallet and I don't think the cashier or the thirty people behind me like that I've decided to get rid of it in this transaction.

I still feel weary from the work out, but eschew the elevator and jog up the five flights of stairs. On the way up I feel a pang of guilt about Dell. Not so much that I just don't feel the same way about him that he does about me, but that I just used him to get rid of someone I don't want to go out with. I've been honest with Dell from day one, and this is the first time that I feel like I've used him.

A folder is sitting on my chair with a sticky note on it.

Need to see you asap! – Austin

153

There's asap and then there's *asap*. Which one is this? More to the point, do I or don't I eat my sandwich first?

I eat my sandwich quickly, clean off my hands with a Purell wet wipe that I keep in my desk drawer and then head toward the small conference room he and Van Guten use as a temporary office when they're slumming it and working out of our precinct. Two cubicles away I stop. I can taste the onion big time. I go back and pop a tiny breath mint in my mouth. My sinuses are instantly cleared. I crunch it and it is gone in a heartbeat. I shake two more from the container, vow not to chew, and walk toward Reynolds' work area. I stop again. Forgot the folder. How hard can I make this?

While I'm there, I pull a mirror out of my purse and check my hair. Still not quite dry, but I've pulled it back in a ponytail, so it doesn't much matter. I reapply my red lipstick.

I turn to exit my cubicle again and there is Don and one of the receptionists, Shandra Barker, eyeing me with amusement. I walk by with my head up.

"Where you heading in such a hurry there, partner?" Don calls to my back.

I'm not answering or looking back. I can hear them laughing. I make a mental note to myself to get a sample of Shandra's handwriting and investigate whether she's been ordering an inordinate amount of yellow Post-it Notes within the CPD supply chain.

Chapter 34

"You wanted to see me, Major?"

"Call me Austin."

"Yes, sir," I say with a salute.

"Hey, sorry to just leave you a file and note on your desk but you weren't around and I wanted to make sure I got your attention."

"No big biggie. What can I do for you, sir?"

"Austin?"

"No, my name is Kristen."

"Cute. You going to call me Austin?"

"I'll have to think that one over. So what have you got for me?"

"An invite for dinner on Friday night."

"Is this an official pow wow?"

"Nope. An old-fashioned date."

"You know what Major Reynolds? I'm going to have to get back to you on that one, too."

"If it'd make it easier for you to come up with an answer," he replied, "we could call this an official pow wow."

"I'm still going to have to get back to you."

"Okay," he said with his head tilted and eyes squinted, the kind of expression on his face usually reserved for studying exotic animals at the

155

zoo.

"What about the file you left?"

"I think it's just my expense accounts from the last month. I needed a prop. My visit to your cubicle generated a lot of interest."

"Oh, great."

I get asked out some. But not that much. Today it was Timmy and Austin within an hour of each other. Plus two missed calls from Dell making sure my evening hadn't freed up tonight or any other night. Then there was another missed call from Klarissa setting up coffee on Saturday morning before Kendra's last soccer game. Then I called Kathy back. She and Jeff wanted to take me to dinner. I agreed, popular girl that I am.

I love Greek food. Lamb, big and fluffy saffron rice, lots of garlic yogurt, salad with some tabouli on top, feta cheese, kalamata olives, and lots of pita bread. Yum.

I'm sitting across the table from Jeff and Kathy and am struggling to make eye contact. For one thing, I'm keeping an eye on my food. But there's also the deal that they want me to be Kathy's AA sponsor. I never thought to tell them that I'm not actually a real AA member. I'm undercover in pursuit of a serial killer that is stalking our city. The press is on top of this and people are scared, but for once I don't think the hype matches the reality.

It's Tuesday night. They wanted to take me to dinner before my weekly AA meeting at St. Bart's, which I was going to skip this week and go to bed early. I thought she was planning to go by herself but she's let me know how much it would help and how much it would mean to her for me to be there. I've been going to St. Bart's on Tuesday nights and then Holy Family on Thursday or Fridays. This is getting complicated.

"So what do you say?" Jeff asks.

Shouldn't Kathy be asking me if I'll be her sponsor? I'm not sure if it's proper for him to speak on her behalf. See, I don't know anything about this. I think there are classes and some training for sponsors. But the deal is, I don't even know that much.

"Jeff ... Kathy, I've got to be honest with you."

"Don't say no, Kristen," Kathy pleads. She has a tear in her eye.

"The thing is I just don't know if I'm qualified."

How's that for honesty?

"I feel like you saved my life the other night," Kathy says.

"The thing is I've never been a sponsor. Heck, I've only attended AA myself for a month or so. I don't think I'd know what to do."

"But haven't you had a sponsor?" Jeff asks. "Can't you just do the same kinds of things? Whatever your sponsor does with you sure seems to work. It looks like you're doing great. You are doing okay aren't you Kristen?"

"I'm not sure everybody would agree with that," I respond. "But yeah, you know I think I am doing better with my, ah … problem."

So much for being honest. I look at my watch. Our meeting starts in fifteen minutes.

"Let me try to figure this out," I say, "but we've got to get moving or we'll be late. I'll meet you over there."

"Nope. We're driving together," Kathy says with a triumphant smile. "Give Jeff your car keys and you're driving with me."

"Unless Jeff can push and steer a car while popping the clutch at the same time, he may want to stay with his Mercedes. Though I would consider a straight up swap."

"Just give me the keys," he says. "I've got it all under control."

I hesitate.

"Kristen, just give him the keys," Kathy says. "He's got a friend over here who is going to put a new starter in your Nissan."

"It's a Mazda," I say. "I don't know if I'm comfortable with that. And I am definitely short on cash these days."

"Whatever," she says with glee. "Just let us do this. We don't want you to pay. Jeff's getting a great deal and we want to do something small to say thank you for being there when we needed help. You know, you were a Godsend. Honestly, I feel like a new person since Tuesday night. I feel like I've come out of a fog and started to get my life back."

I protest some more but resistance is futile. I have no clue what I might have said a couple nights back, but it apparently it was the right thing. This is a girl who I couldn't stand seven days earlier and now I do think of her as a friend. I'm going to have to figure out how to tell them that I'm not who they think I am. Well, maybe I am, but I'm not just what they think I am.

We drive over in near silence, light jazz playing softly. She asks if I like Rick Braun. I've never heard of him. But I like the song that's on now. Jeff's going to take my car over to a friend's house who works on cars out of his garage. If he can't replace the starter in ninety minutes, he's got a car I can borrow for a day. Either way, Jeff will drive over to Saint Bart's to pick up Kathy and leave a car with me to get home.

We pull into a parking space with three minutes to spare. The door is on the side of the church and is at the bottom of five steps leading into a half basement meeting room. We enter the hall and I make a quick left into the bathroom. I smooth my hair and pop another breath mint in my mouth. Greek food is murder on the breath but probably not strong enough to cover up the raw onion from lunch. I wash my hands and splash a little water on my face. I wear next to no makeup except a little base and sometimes an eyebrow pencil and dash of red on my lips if I'm feeling frilly and feminine, but at this point in my day there's nothing left to wash off anyway.

I push open the double doors into the meeting room and spot an open seat next to Kathy. I look over and smile. Jonathan is on the other side of the empty seat and thinks I am smiling at him. He gives a friendly wave and pats his hand on the chair.

Two hours ago all I was planning to do was have dinner with Jeff and Kathy King. I wasn't planning to attend an AA meeting. I haven't told anyone from the office I would be here, including Reynolds who I spent an hour with before heading for this impromptu dinner. As bad as last Tuesday night was with Jonathan's no-show and my marathon counseling session with Jeff and Kathy, this is going to be worse.

I'm in direct violation of Captain Zaworski's orders.

I stand up with an embarrassed grimace and curtsey. I point a finger toward the bathroom door and walk across the room. I hope Kathy doesn't comment on the fact that this is my second trip in the last thirty minutes. I figure I've got five minutes to get hold of the team before Jonathan, if he's the Cutter Shark, gets suspicious and bolts. I walk into the stall and scroll down through my phone directory and hit Zaworski's number. Four rings and his voice announcement instructs me to leave a message. I do.

I call Don's number next. Same procedure. I decide to stay with task force members. Martinez. No answer but a message prompt half in Spanish and half in English:

"*La próxima vez que estés sola, ya sabes a quién llamar.* And baby, you know who you are."

I'm not even going to ask Don to translate that. I hang up and again leave a message. I hit Konkade's home and cell numbers in quick succession. No answer. Blackshear. Ditto. I'm on a roll. Reynolds. Nada. He must be busy with Virgil. Scalia. I think he goes to bed early so his no answer is no surprise. Van Guten's next. She picks up immediately.

"Dr. Van Guten, how may I help you?"

"It's Kristen." She doesn't respond. "Detective Conner," I say.

"Yes?"

"This is going to be quick. I don't have much time. I ended up going to the St. Bart's AA meeting tonight."

"Did you clear that with Reynolds?"

"No time to explain. Jonathan's here."

"Detective Conner this is highly irregular."

"Got to go."

I hang up. I flush the toilet and run the water in the sink in case anyone is listening—probably not possible but an ongoing phobia of mine anyway. I dry my hands, smooth my hair again, which is already perfectly smoothed, and head back into the group setting.

Kathy is sharing. She is beaming. Suddenly, she and everyone in the room are looking at me.

"I've never met anyone so open and direct and honest," she says.

I realize she's talking about me and blush.

"I can honestly say that for the first time in months, really more than a year, I feel hope in life. We talked and laughed and cried and prayed. She helped me and Jeff get some issues on the table and I feel like I'm in love again."

She and I sit down at the same time. The old lady who likes to hug me starts to clap. Then everyone is clapping. My face is beet red. I roll my eyes and shake my head. Jonathan reaches over and gives my hand a squeeze. I stiffen and take a quick breath of air. He feels my response and lets go.

I look over at him. He smiles and winks.

Okay, this is too hard for my little brain to figure out. Is Jonathan sincerely being affirming in the moment? Is he hitting on me in the moment? Is he the Cutter Shark and trying to lure me into his sick world of murder—in the moment, of course?

Mom, I can't talk right now. It's not a good time."

"It's never a good time."

"I know Mom, but this time it really isn't."

"Are you working?"

Kathy, Jonathan, and Jack, our AA facilitator who really wants me to have a sponsor, are looking at me with bemusement.

"I'm at a meeting."

All three stifle laughs. I've been stalling. No one I trust took my call forty-five minutes ago. Van Guten's a high powered shrink, not a cop. No courtesy text messages have shown up to acknowledge that anyone else on our task force knows where I am. I may be flying solo with a serial killer tonight.

"What meeting, honey?"

"Mom, I promise I'll call back tomorrow. I promise."

She sighs. That's the break I need.

"I love you," I blurt out quickly. "Call you tomorrow. Promise."

I click the red button. I take my empty Styrofoam cup back over to the electric coffee urn that looks just as good tonight as it did thirty years ago. I've been chatting with Jack, Kathy, and Jonathan about Kathy's breakthrough last Tuesday night. I can tell that both Jack and Jonathan are dying to talk to me alone. For different reasons, I'm sure. I know what's on Jack's mind. He wants to know how I've come to be Kathy's sponsor when I've never had a sponsor or any training myself. He's got a point.

I don't know what's on Jonathan's mind, but he's the one that breaks free and follows me to the coffee station. I don't actually want another cup of coffee. It is a wretched brew with lots of grounds floating around. At least I hope those are grounds floating around.

"Kristen," he says to my back, "I missed hearing you speak last week. I can't believe I wasn't there for your story."

Who told him I spoke last week? Did he ask or did someone volunteer that information? He's standing too close to me and I don't like it. I need my space. I know from my first sociology class in college that different cultures have different proximity standards. Heck, you can be inches from someone's face in certain Asian countries and no one thinks a thing about it. That's not where I was born. I need my space.

"And what you've done for Kathy is simply amazing," he continues. "When did you do your training?"

Crud. I don't know anything about becoming a sponsor. Is there a curriculum? Do you get a certificate? Why haven't I taken the time to find this out? I've always thought of myself as a good cop. No, a great cop. I grew up in a cop's home. And Dad was the best. He never cut corners. He got along with his colleagues. He closed more than his share of cases. I'm not sure he'd approve of the situation I'm in right now.

Time to focus. I am in the situation I am. That's all I have to work with. Jonathan is still in my space and he's taken my right hand in both of his. It's all I can do to let him speak, because what I really want to do is put a knee in the groin, push his left hand into his body and then to the outside, duck under and wrench that thing three quarters of the way up his back so I can start asking questions. Hard questions. Is that a sign of anger?

I don't even know if he's a suspect. I'm creeped out, but let him hold my hand another second.

"I don't want to be inappropriate," he is saying, less than a foot from my face. "But I'm wondering if we could go out and grab a cup of coffee. Maybe some dessert. That's all. I'd love to talk with you some more tonight. Spend a little time getting to know you."

Do I head butt him now? No. Be cool, Kristen, I remind myself. Be cool. Be cool. I pull my hand away and turn to where the powdered creamer is. I like real half and half and never use powdered cream. He probably doesn't know that. I shake some of it into the center of the black sludge. I try to look natural. I watch my hands closely to make sure they're not shaking. I'm good at action. I'm lousy at inaction. I stir the clotted mess until there's only a few clumps left.

I've gone months without being asked out on a date. I now have a testosterone-filled junior combat instructor, a major in the FBI, a devoted sort-of boyfriend who is fascinated with Amish culture, and a possible serial killer suspect asking me out in less than twelve hours. Some girls have all the luck. What's my problem?

"Jonathan …"

"Yeah?" he responds hopefully.

"I just don't go out with guys when I don't even know their last name. And …"

"Yeah?"

He looks and sounds a bit deflated but interestingly, he doesn't offer even a Smith or Jones for a last name.

"Well, there's someone else."

Am I using Dell again? Or is it Major Reynolds? I know it's not Timmy.

"I didn't think a coffee invitation was asking you out on a date," he says.

He looks miffed. Kathy and Jack walk over. They're looking at us cautiously. They sense something isn't right.

After some awkward chit chat, Kathy and I head for the exit. Jack stays back and talks to the last few stragglers. Jonathan is right behind us to make sure we get to our cars safely, he says gallantly. I figure there's no way Jeff's mechanic friend could replace a starter in less than two hours. If he can, I'll be parking on hills again in just a matter of time. I wonder what kind of car Jeff has waiting for me.

We walk out of St. Bart's into a glorious Chicago spring evening. Jeff is leaning against his Mercedes with a proud expression on his face. I can't believe it but a sparkling blue onyx Mercedes 500SE sits in front of his car. He nods to it with a smile. Now that's what I call a loaner. I think maybe I could like this being a sponsor gig.

Then all heck breaks loose.

Chapter 35

I am literally picked up off my feet. I look to my left and Kathy is being pulled to the side in an orchestrated takedown starring athletic men in black body suits and hoods. Jeff loses his smile, which is replaced by a look of utter shock on his face. An agent appears out of thin air and firmly moves him around to the other side of his car. It is an arm lock maneuver and I want to call out to Jeff that resistance is futile if he has any impulses to fight back. The hold is designed to break your elbow.

Two more men put Jonathan facedown on the ground. He is kicking and squirming and trying to yell. I know what these men know how to do. It ain't going to happen, Jonathan, just relax, I think.

I hear Kathy scream my name.

"Kri-i-i-i-i-sten!"

I am in the back of a black Chevrolet Suburban heading downtown toward the 2nd Precinct in less than thirty seconds of my exit from St. Bart's.

Chapter 36

It's two in the morning. We are in a conference room on the first floor of CPD's Second Precinct. I am there to foster cooperation. The only problem is Kathy won't look at me at all and Jeff won't stop staring at me with anger and loathing. I am wondering if this means I don't get to drive the loaner Mercedes. I've been told someone drove it over for me. The question of whether I'm a suitable AA sponsor has now been answered. Emphatically.

A bureaucrat is explaining why it is in their best interest to sign non-disclosure and non-liability forms. I didn't know Jeff was a lawyer. Kathy never mentioned it. Of course a week ago Kathy was still Bethany. Jeff's not inclined to sign nor let her sign any forms without his attorney present. I wonder why he can't just read the words and be his own attorney. Apparently, that's not how it works. His specialty is M&A, an acronym which everyone present seems to recognize, except me. Murder and Arguments? Malfeasance and Animosity? Misogyny and Apprehension?

I discreetly google M&A on my Blackberry, hoping nothing naughty comes up. Mergers and Acquisitions. Big business and high finance stuff. Okay, out of my league. But I guess if I can figure some of Dell's supply chain management business and Reynolds' non-isolated event stream mumbo jumbo, I can at least comprehend some of the basics of this.

"I'm not signing. What I am going to do is file a lawsuit against the Chicago Police Department—and a certain officer who set my wife and me up to be part of a dangerous operation."

The bureaucrat continues to speak in low tones. My guess is his response and volume are part of his training in a situation like this. Do nothing to stir emotions. Seek to be conciliatory. Appeal to the complainant's sense of duty and honor. He is laying praise for their poise and valor on a little too thick, I think.

Problem is I think Jeff has had the same training and he's not buying it. After mentioning the lawsuit, he shuts down.

I feel trapped in the conference room. I want to talk to Kathy and explain that I really do like her and that I had no idea a takedown was going to go down. I would never have endangered her and Jeff. Plus, I want to get down to the basement where the action is with Jonathan. Who's questioning him? Is he the Cutter Shark? How many awards will the mayor be giving me?

I'm hoofing it down a hall that is about as long as a city block. I was raised right, so I don't run inside. But I'm moving fast enough to get an Olympic tryout in speed walking. There are small signs over each door that are perpendicular to the wall with numbers on them. Jonathan is being interviewed in thirty-two, which happens to be the last door on the right. I am almost out of breath when I get there. I reach for the handle but the door opens first.

Don and Martinez step into the hallway. They look tired. I raise my eyebrows in question. Each shakes his head "no" and starts down the hallway from the direction I just came from. I reach for the handle again but Don calls over his shoulder.

"I'd just let things be tonight. Come on. We'll get something to eat."

I don't know who was madder, Zaworski or Reynolds," Martinez is saying, crumbs from a piece of apple pie in his goatee. Should I tell him?

"At least he was guilty of something," Don says.

"Just the wrong things," Martinez continues. "Not what we were hoping for."

Jonathan. Last name is Abernathy. First name is Andrew. Good old

AA attending AA under an alias. He's married with three children. He has worked as a broker for the same company at the Chicago Board of Trade for the past eleven years. No degree from Northwestern. He does have a math education degree from the University of Illinois Chicago Campus, which he parlayed into a job as junior trader.

There were nine grams of cocaine in his car. No previous convictions, but two arrests for solicitation. He basically admitted to liking the combination of drugs and adultery and lying about his marital status—but not murdering women in Chicago and other parts of the country.

Zaworski has already decided to cut him loose and not charge him with drug possession in exchange for his signature on the non-disclosure and non-liability forms. Abernathy is more than elated to accept the tradeoff. He keeps a studio apartment downtown and is only home in a rural community south of Lincolnwood on weekends. He wants to keep his weeknight habits a secret from the missus, so all in all, he has a scrape on his right cheek but feels none the worse for the added excitement.

"This lawyer guy isn't going to sign?" Martinez asks me for the tenth time.

"Didn't look like it when they left," I answer. Again.

"Oh man, the captain is going to be mad, mad, mad."

"At me, me, me, me, me, me," I respond. Again.

After four chirps the voicemail comes up.

"This is Kathy. Leave me a message and as long as this isn't someone selling something, I'll get back to you as soon as I can. Ciao!"

Heck yes I feel bad. But I'm starting to get mad. What did I do wrong? Yes, I attended AA meetings under false pretense but I don't think any ethicist is going to judge me for doing my job, which just happens to be in service to my community.

Okay, I shouldn't have gotten involved. But I did. So sue me. Okay, I guess they are.

Kathy's situation and circumstances were outside my assignment and expertise. But she was an absolute mess the night I went out with her after the meeting and then over to her house to talk with her and Jeff. Do you have to be a Ph.D. in psychology to help someone? Isn't peer to peer conversation sometimes the best medicine in life? I feel embarrassed now, but I actually prayed with her and Jeff at the end of the meeting. I don't usually wear my religion on my sleeve, but God knows I've been around church and Danny and Kaylen enough to have a little idea on a few things to say to someone who's in trouble. Heck, I've helped teach Kendra's Sunday School class and coached her soccer team for the better part of two years.

I wonder what Reynolds, Van Guten, Zaworski, Blackshear, Don—and seemingly everyone else in the universe—thought about that. Who cares.

Scalia—Big Tony—always had a phrase he would say when he was partners with my dad that seems appropriate right now.

"No good deed goes unpunished."

I hit the green button twice to redial. I'll leave her another message.

Dear God, help me not to get punished for this mess I've made.

Chapter 37
April 30, 2:26am

DOS AND DONT'S FOR DARING DATERS!!!
By ChiTownBlogger

> SPRING is in the air!!! and its time 2fall in love again. I know. I know. ChiTown's Numero Uno source 4the real news has already stolen the hearts of our city's fair maidens. Guys. Fellows. Muchachos. Even if i never sleep—and I don't cuz who else is gonna keep an eye on things around here??? certainly not Daniels and his gang of incompetents on that rotting corpse he calls CPD—I only have 24hrs a day here peeps. Don't blame me for my sexy self ;o) I was born with it. just wait ur turn. And hope it's me she meets and not our bloody friend, the CUTTER SHARK (cue dramatic music ::dun dun dun....::)

As the Windy City's only 24/7 source of sanguine sanity and her 1 true purveyor of protection in a city held hostage by a man with a gleam in his eye—and even more of a gleam on his highly honed knife—I offer these foolproof safety tips 4our young ladies. Free of charge. FOC baby. A lady's knight kinda thing. That's the kind of public servant I am. (Note:

Mayor Daniels, u can only dream of ever achieving my approval ratings! i don't care who ur daddy was. But I do know who your dad is. Daddy CTB, baby!) IMHO, no lady should leave home without protection.

1.   DO b ready 4an instant manicure. Why? Fingernail files are a great weapon. If it looks like a dagger and pokes someones eye out like a dagger ... suffice it 2say, its a dagger. Add this one 2your file system! LOL!

2.   DO NOT invite poorly laundered men back 2ur place 4the night. If he has unsightly blood stains on his clothing, I don't care how sharp the crease in his slacks is. (Sharp. Get it???) This guy is both a slacker and a whacker rolled into one steaming package of manhood. WAtch out.

3.   DO carry pepper spray. Do I think it will save u? Alas, prob not. But who says ur final meal has to b boring. Spice things up with a fine mist of flavor. Recommended with beef, pork, poultry, and esp fish. BAM!!! Hold the shark. (No groans please.)

4.   DO NOT carry 1of those aerosol noise makers. Think about it. U live in a big city with an inferiority complex. (Any group of people that brag 4a hundred years about bein America's 2nd city and then go in2 a decade-long funk just cuz Los Spangeles' immigrunts pushed it down 2numero tres has got self image issues. How does that make u feel Mayor Daniels? Blue? Well how does that make u feel?) Depressed people honk their horns a lot. No 1 is gonna look up when u blast that horn in the Cutter Shark's face. U r gonna really piss him off tho. Who knows what he'll do if he gets real mad... :oD

5.   DO keep ur sense of humor. So u went 4the wrong guy. AGAIN. So he's gonna leave u in the morning, just like all the others. Dry ur tears honey. Doesn't mean u can't have some side-splitting laughs with the Shark that will last u 4the rest of ur life!

6.   DO NOT count on the police. Unless u double park or jaywalk. B assured of this. Yes, the Cutter Shark will easily escape. But u will b shot, which will put u out of ur misery. Praise be.

Now that's FUnny stuff. I kill myself sometimes. Gotta keep that edge hehehe. Okay fans ... I've got 2cut this thing short—i think this cutter fella and i wud get along just grand! LOL ... XOXOXO ... from ur fav blogger! ChiTownBlogger is out – but not without his protection!

Can't wait 2read ur responses. The CTB board is open4 business! 1st POSTER gets my BUY1 GET1 FREE coupon from Pizza Palace. Every slice is a delight! LOL ...

>

The Month of May

What potent blood hath modest May.

Ralph Waldo Emerson

Chapter 38

It is pouring down rain and I'm standing in a puddle up to my ankles. I can feel mud squishing inside my soccer shoes. I think the ooze has worked inside my socks and between my toes. It actually feels kind of good. April showers are supposed to give way to May's flowers. May decided to outdo April in the showers department for my Snowflakes' last game of the season.

We're trying for win number three and are playing the team with the best record for the season—coached by Attila the Hun, of course. Rematch time. Bring it on.

The rain has not dampened the spirits of the girls; in fact they're more energetic than I've seen them all season.

They are soaked and muddy to the point that it is hard to tell the two teams apart. Before the game even started Kendra discovered that you could run at one particularly big puddle near midfield, dive forward, and slide on your belly for about twenty feet—nature's own slip and slide. Attila didn't like that too much and wanted his girls a little more serious before our grudge match. I actually agreed with him. I want a win just as bad as he does. The girls were not to be denied their fun, however. Pretty soon players from both teams were sliding past each other screeching and giggling. I winced a couple times for fear of a head on collision—it crossed my mind that Attila was telling his girls to aim for mine. Sometimes you just have to admit you are out of your mind—and in this one instance, I do because I am.

The parents were glum and in poor spirits twenty minutes before the game, but the midfield entertainment soon had everyone laughing and the video cameras came out in force.

The referees, a father and son team, I think, came three minutes before game time and asked if we wanted to cancel and call it a tie. Not even Attila and I, our lips pursed in emphatic "no" were as quick as the girls. They jumped up and down yelled, "Plaaaaaay!"

The older ref, looking stoic with mud splatters from head to toe, said to get moving then. We'd have the same twenty minute halves as a normal game, but halftime itself would be only three minutes. That way we could all go home and dry off. His kid, probably thirteen or so, and I'm guessing thrilled that he is still going to get his ten dollar game fee as a line judge— I've been there and done that at his age—looks at Attila and me and says, "it's cool when old people are still crazy."

I know he meant it as a compliment but I'm not sure I like being lumped in with Attila—and especially not old people. The kid thinks we're funny. Okay Kristen, time to chill. I shudder from the cool rain on cue.

The first half ended up in a 3-3 tie. If we were scoring this on the basis of mud wrestling, we might actually have a slight lead. When the ball hits the biggest puddle, sometimes it plops and just sits there. Other times it skips like hard rubber crazy ball. They got their second goal off a cheap bounce.

I look at my stopwatch. I can almost guarantee the old dude is going to end the game exactly on time, so we've got less than three minutes and the score is now 6-6. Tiffany and Kendra have scored three goals each. At least I think that's who those little mud balls are.

One of their girls kicks the ball out of bounds a few feet from me, so that's where we'll get to throw it in. I look behind me and see Mom, Danny, Kaylen, and Klarissa huddled together under Danny's golf umbrella. They have a couple of soaked blankets wrapped around them as well. When I took my survival training course I was taught that wet material actually drains warmth. I'm going to have to trust they'll survive these last two minutes without falling to hypothermia or wrinkled finger tips.

Kendra runs over and picks up the ball to throw it in. In a moment of inspiration I tell her, "score a goal and win and Coach Kristen will do a belly flop in the puddle with you after the game."

Coach Attila smiles and is gracious as he shakes hands after the game.
"You all really improved this year. Nice job and good win. See you in the fall if you're coaching—and no hard feelings from the first game. I apologize for letting things get out of hand."
I mumble a "nice game" back to him and try to get my own apology out but am not able to as I'm mobbed by my team. I feel bad. I was still ready to give the guy a piece of my mind and he ended up being a nice, normal parent. What does that make me—besides not a parent?
It's show time and I break away from my clump of jumping and yammering seven year-olds and run for the middle of the field. I dive and sure enough slide at least twenty-five feet. My face and hair are covered with mud. Come to think of it, I wish I had zipped my sweat suit top tighter because I think the inside of my bra is now enhanced with a couple gallons of ooze.
I hear a cheer go up from kids and parents. We didn't win the World Cup or anything but overall I think we just had a successful season.

More hot chocolate?"
"No thanks, Mom."
We were supposed to go to the Pizza Palace as a team but there was no way we could take the girls inside anywhere as dirty as they were. Dunkin' Donuts has four outside tables with umbrellas, so we all stopped for a quick sugar celebration. The rain was still coming down hard but as wet as everyone already was, players and family members alike, it didn't matter. I kept thank-you's and special awards to less than five minutes. Everyone drove home happy.
It's just Klarissa, Mom, and me finishing off a second cup of hot chocolate each. We're all getting along and at peace. I wonder if the Cutter Shark has moved on or gone into an early hibernation. Or, with his lifestyle issues, if something violent has happened to him.
Van Guten said that the FBI estimates there are fifty active serial killers in America at any one time. When Project Vigilance detected our guy they

found one person who they had previously thought was six different killers so the number might even be less. But serial killers make mistakes and tend to get caught or get killed.

I wonder if the turn of the calendar to May might not represent a turn in our fortunes with the Cutter Shark.

Chapter 39

L loyd."

"Oh, hey, Kristen."

"Just the man I've been wanting to see."

"Yeah?"

Lloyd is suddenly wary. We're on the front steps of the church. Service is over. I'm going to Danny and Kaylen's for lunch. I guess on Sundays, lunch is dinner. He squints in the bright light and looks left and right. I think he's checking for escape routes but he isn't going to get by me.

"Yeah," I say. "I've got a question for you."

"Okay. Shoot."

"How'd you get my cell number?"

"What are you talking about?"

I'm watching him closely for signs of guilt and evasion. He looks genuinely stumped so far.

"You know what I'm talking about."

"No Kristen, I don't know what you're talking about."

"You don't remember calling me about a month back? You saw a kid in the Gas & Grub that fit a wanted description on the bulletin board?"

"Yeah, I do remember that. So?"

"I'm just curious how you got my number."

He looks relieved and then his expression changes and he looks left, right, and behind him in mock furtiveness. He turns up the collar on his lightweight spring jacket. He cups a hand on the side of his mouth and whispers loud to me.

"I called your office and the receptionist gave it to me."

I'm not amused.

"Shandra gave it to you?"

"Not sure it was Shandra but someone who answers the phone for your department did. Have I committed a crime?"

He is still whispering out of the side of his mouth and playing the part of an informant.

"No. It's just against office policy."

"Well if I'd known you were going to get all bent out of shape," he says in normal voice, but just a twinge of anger, "I'd just have reported seeing that greasy punk on the general line. Thought you might like a tip. Help a friend move up the ranks, you know."

Okay, I'm not the only one who thought the punk was a punk. Lloyd does too. I feel immediately better about my questioning by Internal Affairs, but then realize that this is an awkward moment between Lloyd and me. I should feel embarrassed right now, but I don't. I have every right to be mad at Shandra—and I am.

"Lloyd, forget I said anything. It just took me by surprise is all. I haven't given it a thought since the day of the take down, but it just struck me as a little weird at the time, and when I saw you walk out the doors I was reminded to ask you."

"So you think I'm stalking you?"

I look close for a smile, but none is there. I think he's mad. Or miffed. I think miffed is a lesser version of mad.

"No, Lloyd, I do not suspect you of stalking me. Should I?"

They say the best defense is a good offense. Just not this time. I have definitely hurt his feelings.

"Or are you so far above me that there's no way in the universe I should be so worthy as to have your number?"

"Lloyd."

"Don't 'Lloyd' me. I think you were wondering how I had your number because you look down on me."

"Not true, Lloyd."

"You sure, Kristen? Because hey, I'm very aware that I'm a hundred pounds overweight—and not all of us can be perfect like you or Klarissa. Plus I don't carry a gun like you do. I just have a stethoscope and defib paddles."

"What's wrong with Kaylen? Why isn't she perfect?" I try a diversion to get this going a direction other than steep nosedive. He doesn't take the bait.

"Nothing's wrong with Kaylen. She and Danny are nice to everybody."

I'm not good at arguing the fine points of life. I'm not good at subtle. This conversation is a train wreck and it's time to hit it head on. That's what I do.

"Okay Lloyd, let's get real here. First of all, I don't look down on you. Doesn't mean I don't worry about you and want you to lose some weight. So if that gives you a vibe I don't like you or look down on you, I'm sorry. But I've been straight up with you on that point the whole time I've known you and in your own words, I've never offended you. If I have, again, I'm sorry."

"You haven't. I agree. I need to lose a hundred pounds."

Better. But I'm still on task.

"Second, we've been buds a long time and you owe me the benefit of the doubt."

"Just like you gave me?"

Touché.

"You know Kristen," Lloyd continues, "I'd almost go with you on that benefit of the doubt point, but you tell me the last time we've talked. You can't. It's been forever. You don't show up for discussion groups anymore and you are in and out of this place like a rocket. The fact that you are standing around on the front steps of a church instead of running straight for you car is a shock to me. So when someone pulls away like you have, I guess it's hard to read their motives."

I feel bad because he's right. I think my face shows it.

"I'm not trying to bust your chops, Kristen," he continues. "You worry about me and my weight. I worry about you and your Type-A, hard-nose, me-against-the-world attitude sometimes."

"I've always been that way."

"I know. And most of us actually love you for it. You've just never been this over the top for this long."

"Well, get in line, because I'm apparently rubbing everyone the wrong way."

"Kristen," Lloyd says, now serious. "You've got a lot you're working through. It's been a tough year for the Conner girls, period. Now you're in the middle of this Cutter Shark whack job case. You've always felt free to give me advice, so let me return the favor and give you some. Get yourself in a place where you can slow down and talk and even open up about hard stuff with some people who care about you. I like the Tuesday night Bible study here, but hey, you just got to go somewhere. I don't care how much you run on that treadmill of yours, you're still going to burn out fast and furious if you don't get off the angry wheel in the gerbil cage."

I'm a gerbil? I think his heartfelt advice lost some steam with that ending. I don't tell him that I've already been attending a group meeting on Tuesdays. Not sure how much it's helping.

*H*ey stranger. No hello?"

I've opened my car door to hop in to head over to Kaylen's for lunch. Kendra has just plopped into the passenger seat. He bends over and waves to her.

"Hey pretty girl."

"Hi Mr. Dell," she answers.

"Wow," he says with a whistle, "someone has fixed up their ride."

Kathy hasn't talked to me since last Tuesday night. Jeff called the office on Thursday to set up a time to drop my car off and get the keys to the Mercedes I drove for almost a whole day, feeling both incredibly guilty and amazed over the ride the whole time. I went down with my checkbook to pay for the repairs, but Jeff wouldn't even look at me, much less answer even a single question. He handed me my keys and took the keys to the SL 500SE, got in, and drove off.

I found the work order in the glove compartment. Not only did he have the starter replaced, but he had his mechanic friend do a whole laundry list of maintenance items. And then he had the car detailed inside and out. I don't know what kind of wax the guy used but the paint looks shiny and gorgeous again. Same with the black leather seats and convertible top. It drives like a charm. And it starts up immediately. I'm still in the habit of parking on hills just in case I wake up and this was all a dream. There is no price for the work and the itemization is handwritten on a generic form, so the mechanic's name and contact information is not on it.

I'll show Danny the bill and have him look over my car this afternoon and ask him how much he thinks it all cost. I know I can't pay Jeff and Kathy back in one or two paychecks but I'll start sending them something every month to settle this. I don't know what all he did to my car but I'm guessing it's stuff I should have done a long time ago.

When you're a cop, you do get some freebies. Some restaurants refuse to take your money for a meal, for example. Some cops abuse the generosity of others and start expecting everything to be for free. Others won't take anything. Ever. I've read and signed the CPD ethics policy statement. This is a gray area. Jeff didn't do anything for me based on my performance in the line of duty. On the other hand, I would never have met Kathy if I hadn't been working the St. Bart's AA meeting.

I'm going to pay them back. This doesn't have anything to do with institutional policy. I just feel lousy about how things went south so fast.

"It was time to get a few things looked at," I say to Dell. "It even starts without a long hill," I add.

"Nice."

"Are you coming for lunch, Mr. Dell?" Kendra asks.

"Not this week, sweetie," he answers.

He looks up at me with a searching glance after he says it. Is he trying to make me feel guilty for our last conversation? I don't know. Is he sniffing around for a lunch invite? Probably. And if he would lay off clinging to me, he'd probably get it. But so far he hasn't let up so I'm not going to cave.

"You take care," he says as he gives me a half hug.

He walks briskly to his car without looking back. I watch just long enough to see if he has Carrie with him. He doesn't. He probably should. I was pretty clear. With the growing polarity of our feelings toward each other I'm just not going to see him anymore. At all. Period. I cut the tail off the monkey.

Kendra and I talk and giggle the whole way over to her house. I've never seen her carry a purse to church. She shows me the reason. She used it to smuggle her Kristen doll to show all her friends. If Kendra's mommy finds out, we're both—make that all three of us if you include the Kristen doll—in big trouble.

I turn off my car and park it in a turnout in front of their house. My mind flashes back to Lloyd. When I got direct with him, I told him "first of all," but I can't remember what the second thing was. He made a comment that most people love me because of my intense personality. I wonder how many people don't.

Dear God, help Dell find the right girl for him. Help Lloyd lose a hundred pounds before he dies of a heart attack in his thirties.

Chapter 40
May 4, 11:43pm

*W*hat's taking them so long? I'm back on schedule. If they weren't so stupid they'd be all over this already. Now one of them is probably going to get all pissy and say I'm early. That's only if you count Candace. Don't any of them play golf? She's my mulligan!

They really should be paying better attention, but I don't think they are. What can I do to help them? Well, I guess I've already taken care of that. I hate it when I have to do everything but someone's got to help them with the attention deficit issues.

It had been three days. He knew a nasty surprise awaited his enemies.

It's going to be bad.

He knew they would criticize his timing, but who were they to question his infinite perfection?

And you know what? When you point an accusing finger at

*someone else, there's four fingers pointing back at you! I like that.
Too bad they won't. But government is all about blame and lack of
accountability. Family too. But who needs those meanies. Not me.
I take responsibility for my life and my action on my terms. This
message paid for by Citizens in Support of the Cutter Shark. Hi, I'm
the Cutter Shark and I approve this message!*

*I bet I would have been good in politics. Unlike the Republicans
and Democrats, I would know how to slash the budget. Hah. I've
got a plank to run on. Yes.*

He would have been a brilliant politician.

Chapter 41

Y ou went on a date with someone from work?" my mom nearly shouts down the table. "But you're going out with Dell."

Thanks, Klarissa. I appreciate you stirring up a hornet's nest. She called me again Friday afternoon to meet up for dinner Saturday night. Saturday breakfast wasn't going to work out before Kendra's soccer game. When I demurred, I could tell she felt bad, so I confessed that I was going out on a date. We've only been sitting down for five minutes at Sunday dinner, so it didn't take her long to weave that into conversation with Mom.

"Where's Dell?" Daniel asks.

"Mr. Dell," Kendra corrects him. "He and Kristen don't like each other any more."

"Aunt Kristen," Kaylen corrects Kendra.

"Why don't you like Mr. Dell?" Daniel asks me.

"What's going on with you and Dell?" Mom asks again.

I give Klarissa a dirty look. She can barely conceal a smile. She pokes at the food on her plate and manages to get a single pea on a tine of her fork. She lifts it to her mouth and begins to chew beyond any actual requirements.

"Mr. Daniel and Ms. Kendra listen closely," I say firmly. "I do not dislike Mr. Dell and I do not think he dislikes me."

"But can you be sure?" Klarissa asks.

She snorts out a little laugh and goes into a coughing fit. That girl has got to start eating. It's pollen season and she's always had allergies, but with her weight, I'm not sure she is healthy enough to fight off a cold at any point in the year. She does look marvelous on TV, however. Not just marvelous. Drop dead gorgeous. With Warren out of the picture, she'll make Chicago's top ten list for hot bachelorette babes.

"Aunt Klarissa makes a valid point, and it is possible that I'm wrong and Mr. Dell does not like me anymore. Nonetheless, I told him last week that we needed to not see each other anymore."

Everyone at the table, including little Daniel, is staring at me, willing me with their eyes to go on. Maybe I will. This is a new experience for me. I did not always get pluses for speech skills on my elementary school report cards.

"So what happened?" Mom asks. "He's such a nice kid. And I think he likes being with us."

She is relentless today. Honestly, she's never been particularly invasive in my or my sisters' personal lives—as long as we go to church and come for Sunday dinner each and every week. What's the deal with Dell?

"I think he's swell, too, Mom. But I'm just not romantically inclined toward him."

"Is romance kissing?" Daniel asks wide eyed.

"It is," I answer him.

"Gross!" he nearly screams.

"Daniel!" Danny yells sharply. "No yelling!" Daniel lowers his head and quiets down immediately but I see the trace of a smug smile on his face. He's no worse for the experience.

"So what if you don't feel romantic toward him?" Mom grills me. "It's always better to start as friends and then get romantically involved later."

"Just like you and Dad?" Kaylen asks her with a laugh.

Bless Big Sis's heart. She came to my rescue.

"That was different," Mom says defensively.

Now everyone has turned their attention her way. I believe I'm off the hook. She gets a dreamy look in her eyes and Klarissa, Kaylen, and I make eye contact at once and burst out laughing.

"What? What?" Mom asks, perturbed now.

"Mom, just go on," Klarissa urges. "What made things different for you and Dad? Kaylen's got her man, but Kristen and I obviously need some serious help."

"Seriously serious," I agree.

"You guys are just laughing at me," Mom says.

"Just tell us!" Danny exclaims to her. Then as an aside to Klarissa he says, "and you got that right about Kaylen getting her man."

Kaylen punches him but his command to Mom is probably going to carry the day. He may be an independent church minister, not as good as being a Baptist obviously, but he is a minister and that carries weight with Mom.

"We just knew the first time we met that we were made for each other. I couldn't take my eyes off him and he couldn't take his eyes off of me. My daddy was strict and I wasn't to hold hands with boys on a first date under any circumstances. And I definitely wasn't allowed to see a Catholic boy. I guess I wasn't so good that night. We met at the skating rink and held hands the whole night."

I want to laugh but the moment's just too sweet and Mom will shut down if she thinks we're teasing her. Kaylen has scooted her seat right next to Danny and he is running his fingers lightly across her pregnant belly.

Klarissa and I look at each other and sigh. Then she puts her finger and thumb in the shape of an L on her forehead. I return the compliment.

L for losers. We really are getting along good these days.

Chapter 42

You don't look down when Daniel has a certified weapon in his hands.

I'm pitching a whiffle ball to the kid. The kind with air holes to enhance velocity. He may be four years old, but man, he can already smack that ball. I'm about done throwing to him underhand. I may have to give him some chin music to move him off the plate and then throw him the curve ball away and down if he keeps parting my hair every time whacks the ball

I can't exactly claim to be a baseball fan. It's slow and tedious. Between player strikes and free agency, I barely know half the Cubbies roster anymore and not even the starting lineup for the White Sox. But I do have fabulous memories of going to Wrigley or Comiskey with my dad. I thought it was cute that he still bought a box score card and filled it out in pencil the whole game. A couple times I caught him comparing his card with the *Tribune's* the next day. He was pretty sure he was more accurate than the official scorekeeper.

First couple of minutes out here I had Kendra and even Klarissa to help shag Daniel's prodigious swats of the bat. Both lost interest pretty quick. So I'm pitcher and solo fielder, which means I'm running around and sweating in a jean skirt and short sleeve cotton shirt with some little mark

on the chest that is supposed to give the impression that it is from a bona
fide designer.

Danny's sitting on a lawn chair next to Mom on the patio, talking. She's
crying about something. I'm not about to complain about having to jump
the fence to shag Daniel's fungos; Danny's got the real work today.

I glance around. This is Chicago weather at its most beautiful. It
deluged yesterday, but today is breezy and in the lower seventies. The grass
is a velvety green. Kaylen's flowers and her tiny vegetable plot are already
bursting with color. She is showing something that is growing to Klarissa
and Kendra by the side of the single car detached garage.

My phone buzzes on my hip. I pitch the ball to Daniel and look down
to see who's calling me on a Sunday afternoon. Big mistake. Daniel clocks
me on the crown of my forehead with a scorching liner. I put my hand to
the spot where the ball hit. It feels hot and is instantaneously swelling. I'm
going to have an angry red circle for the entire world to see; an alien crop
circle on the top of my forehead. I will look like a unicorn that has had his
spear surgically removed.

Zaworski is calling and I ignore the pain on my forehead. My stomach
does a somersault as I push the receive button and answer:

"Conner."

I feel sets of eyes on me from every point in the yard. Danny is tugging
on my skirt and asking if I'm okay. I put a finger on his lips so I can hear the
details of my call.

"Got it. On my way, sir."

Chapter 43

For detectives, rule number one in investigating a murder is that you get to the scene of the crime as quickly as possible to see things as they really are with your own eyes. Even though the first officer on the scene, particularly this kind of scene, will be competent and diligent in protecting evidence—everything from segregating witnesses to establishing a traffic pattern to the victim that is least invasive to evidence—you know there is going to be corruption. If every criminal leaves a trace of his activity—so does every investigator looking for him. In our case that includes a horde of techies from the Medical Examiners office, about ten of us who are considered central to the task force, and then all the uniformed officers who secure the scene, which could probably be limited to two or three at the most. But let's face it, even if you're a cop who deals with crime every day, you're still a human being, and human beings are curious creatures. We want to know what's up.

There's a second kind of corruption; the spiritual state of the scene. I don't know how to explain it, but it is basically the mood, the psychology, the ambience—whatever you want to call it—that gives you clues on the emotions of a particular crime. Was it passionate and spur of the moment? Was it slow, methodical ... premeditated? Was it violent, noisy, and angry?

Once you and twenty-five of your friends start tromping around a crime scene, it's hard to get the feeling of the virgin situation back. It takes a weird combination of focus and imagination. You do your job and carefully go over every potential item of evidence using your powers of observation and reason, but you also try to feel the situation. Dad said that Scalia would show up to a murder scene and just stand there for as long as an hour, never saying anything, just trying to see and feel possibilities of what might have happened.

Starting with the murder of Leslie Reed, we broke the rule of being on scene post haste. The FBI flew in with some insight and information that the powers that be thought would be helpful to our murder investigation. They were probably right. The Cutter Shark, a sociopath with no conscience—who might appear to be socially adept and who might actually understand what people are feeling, though he obviously doesn't care—is no ordinary criminal. But when you break from well-established and time-proven protocols, there is always a potential downside. The majority of murders involving non-family members that are solved are solved in the first twenty-four hours following their occurrence. Why? The murderer makes a mistake that offers up a big clue. If the Cutter Shark had left a clue at either of the first two scenes, we would have allowed valuable seconds to tick off the clock.

I am first one on scene from the task force. As I stride down a long bricked sidewalk toward the front door I see Konkade and Zaworski drive by looking for a parking space. I wonder if they live close and Konkade picked the captain up. I look ahead and recognize the officer working the front door. Chuck Gibson is a tough twenty-year veteran of CPD. I nod at him.

Gibson nods back and says, "I took a look upstairs. We're past initial decay and into full blown putrefaction—maybe even a little black putrefaction. You're going to need a mask."

I grimace. The victim has probably been dead two or more days. That means the body has already swollen to as big as it's going to get and the gasses are starting to leak out. I sigh. The death odors are going to be at their very worst. It also means that even with hustling over here as quickly as we can, our team still will not be on a Cutter Shark crime scene within a twenty-four hour post mortem interval.

My bright beautiful Sunday afternoon has gotten dark in a hurry. I touch the angry welt on my forehead lightly with one finger. I think I'm stalling. I left Danny and Kaylen's and grabbed the Kennedy Expressway and connected with the Dan Ryan and then onto Lake Shore Drive South in the neighborhood of ninety miles an hour. Like I said, my little Mazda is really humming along these days. Jeff even had his mechanic put new tires on it, Danny noted to me. I need to be a little more observant of my car. I'm not going to be able to afford anything new for quite a while. I've got to put a first check to Jeff and Kathy in the mail tomorrow morning.

I walk partway back down the sidewalk, turn, and catch the grandeur of this stately three story town house just north of University of Chicago one more time. The other two places had been very nice, even high end by my civil servant standards, but this one must have cost a fortune.

Gibson hands me the mask as he signs me in at a checkpoint. I walk up the wide stairs of an impressive front stoop to the front door. I take four steps on the porch and before reaching the egress the odor is already overwhelming. I quickly pull the mask over my face. A neighbor was out walking his dog. His 120 pound chocolate lab basically dragged him to the front steps. The man took time to throw up and then called 911.

The 911 operator called the closest squad car to investigate but had a pretty strong inkling that the Cutter Shark was back in action. He called Zaworski one minute later and he started a chain of calls to rally the troops. I guess I've moved up the call chain.

I put sterile cotton slippers over my shoes. I pull the mask away from my face and hit three drops of ammonia under my nose and flinch as the chemicals make a mad charge up my sinuses and into my brain. Reynolds has ordered an extra level of care at the scenes, so I also put on a cotton version of a shower cap, similar to what the food vendors wear at Sam's Club.

I step in the front door to view a wide front door to back door hallway with four rooms on each corner of the first floor, and an ornate staircase dominating the middle of the house. All the floors are open around the staircase, with a widow's perch constructed mostly of open windows on top of the third floor, so there is plenty of light in this weird mixture of classic and contemporary architecture. A second uniformed officer, I don't recognize this one, stands in front of the staircase.

"Third floor, bedroom in the southwest corner," he says with a nod upwards.

"Anyone else up there?"

"Couple of tech guys from the ME. No detectives yet. But the tech guys will keep the scene just the way it is for you folks. The Chief Medical Examiner is on his way in, too, so they'll be running a tight ship."

What does Big Tony do when he stands motionless in the middle of a room where someone's life has been stolen from him or her? Does he see images? Does he pray? Does he hear voices?

"Dear God, help me see things I can't see myself," I pray over and over as I lightly tread up the steps. I don't think I've ever prayed at a crime scene.

Halfway up the last flight of stairs I can hear muffled voices from the room in the southwest corner. I look up and down the identical front to back hallway on the landing of the second floor. An eclectic mix of furniture and art styles. Everything is so still and muffled that the place feels like a museum—or a mausoleum today.

Even with the ammonia, the stench assaults all my senses anew as I enter the room where Gigi Baker's mutilated body is simultaneously decomposing and bloating grotesquely. Two techies look up at me. Impossible to read their expressions behind their surgical masks.

I walk to her nightstand. There's a large ten by thirteen picture of a happy couple. I pick it up carefully and turn it over in my hands. On the back someone, I assume Gigi, has drawn a heart and wrote "Alex loves Gigi" in the center of it. I hold the face of the picture out toward the lab guys.

"Is this what the victim looked like?" I ask.

"I'm guessing she's about four or five years older now," answers one who has "Bruce" stitched on his scrub top. "Pretty girl. What a shame."

"You've got that right," I respond. "Wonder where Alex is?"

"Who's Alex?" Bruce asks. "The guy in the picture?"

"Yep. And if he's still alive, he is a certain suspect, though I doubt he's the killer."

"Do you folks have any leads?" the other tech guy asks. No name on his chest. He sees me looking and says, "my name is Jerome. We met on the first scene."

We both start to put out hands to shake, but awkwardly pull them back realizing this isn't the place to touch anything that doesn't absolutely have to be touched.

I carefully set the picture back in place. I force myself to look at Gigi. Scalia, Big Tony, doesn't move for an hour or more. I've never stood still more than five minutes in my life. I am reminded of a Bible verse: "Watch and pray." Don't know where it's at and what the context is, but I make a note to myself to look it up tonight. Maybe even try to practice it.

I hear loud thumps coming up the steps. Sounds like the cavalry is about to arrive.

Martinez is first through the door. He looks paler than I do today. He is wearing one of those silk or linen button-down shirts that are popular in tropical climates—he might be fashionably early by a month or two. He has on light khakis and a pair of sandals, which are covered by the gauze hospital booties we are all to wear on the crime scene. He has somehow worked a fedora, complete with felt band and a little feather, into his outfit. He takes off his hat, which I guess took the place of the gauze headwear, out of respect for the dead, and walks slowly to the decomposing body of Gigi, his eyes downcast. The others are close behind.

"Santa madre de Dios, apiádate de nosotros," I hear Martinez say as he makes the sign of the cross. I'm not exactly sure what he just said but I'm pretty sure I agree with him. I'll ask Don later. For now, I'm sticking to "Watch and pray."

Chapter 44

"Gigi Baker. Thirty-six years old. Five foot ten, 145 pounds. Widowed a year ago."

Ouch. Blackshear is reading a summary of the victim. We are back at the precinct. We switch holding task force meetings between our place and the FBI's office over in the State Building. We can't avoid the throngs of press anymore, but the change of location cuts the mob we have to wade through in half since they can't be certain which location we're going to use.

"Deceased husband of the ..." Blackshear hesitates over the wording and gives it another go. "The deceased husband of the deceased wife is Alex. He died of lymphoma and complications from treatments on May 5 of last year. No children."

"Some cinquo de mayo," Martinez says with a whistle. "Life's not fair."

My first thought is, thank God he wasn't alive to face this. But then I realize that this probably wouldn't have happened if she was a happily married woman. And then I thank God there were no kids, but realize there might be wonderful brothers and sisters and parents left behind who would raise their kids with love. Maybe they didn't want kids. Maybe they couldn't have kids. Maybe they thought they had all the time in the world to have kids. That's probably what I think.

"She was a certified public accountant and had her own business that she ran from the first floor of her home. But she didn't have a lot of active clients. Those she did have are big accounts. Real big. Not sure how much she has to work anyway. At first glance, her husband left her well cared for financially. No relatives from her or her deceased husband's family in the area."

Leslie Reed. Candace Rucker. Gigi Baker. A simple pattern in Chicago and a pattern consistent with the stream of related national occurrences that Virgil spit out. Single. Living alone. Successful. Attractive enough. Or too attractive?

That would imply that our killer, dubbed the Cutter Shark by the sensationalistic press, is probably the same: single; living alone; successful; reasonably attractive. He doesn't force his way into these homes. There are some signs of romance and all three women have been murdered in their bedrooms. The evidence says that they haven't been moved there but have actually died there. He doesn't consummate sex with the victims, which has Van Guten in psychological profiling heaven. The possibilities for our killer's stunted development are endless.

"Has he had sex with women from other cities?" I ask.

"No," Van Guten answers. "Any ideas on what that might mean?"

"Impotent," I say timidly.

"Possible but not probable," she answers. "He's a healthy male. What else?"

Undeterred, I try again and this time pick up a little steam: "He's both fascinated by and terrified of women. He's attracted to and then repulsed by them. He goes through the motions of romance and maybe even foreplay but his heart isn't in it. Deep down he hates women. His conquests are to show who has the real power. He is unable to love."

"How'd he get that way?" she asks, looking directly at me.

I look around before answering. Konkade is smoothing his non-existent hair. Don is brushing equally imaginary lint from his shirt. This seems to be a habit. Reynolds is staring at the ceiling, broken tiles and all, with his pointer fingers forming a tent and his lips pursed.

Our date—I guess it was a date—was okay. Reynolds wanted to go to the Magnificent Mile, so we did. We ate at the Signature Room on the ninety-fifth floor of the Hancock Building. I've always liked the Hancock's observatory best, even if it isn't the tallest building in the city. The viewing windows are floor to ceiling. The outside decks leave me tingling and weak-kneed. He dressed down for the evening. Instead of his dark suit, white shirt, and red power tie, he wore gray slacks, a navy two-button sport jacket, a white shirt, and a red power tie.

"Family trauma," I answer Van Guten. "Maybe the death of a father, leaving behind a mother with damaged emotions, unable to cope. Something happened and he was taken away from her. Really, just the kind of path that Virgil has already told us."

"Virgil?" Reynolds asks, his head snapping in my direction. "Who is Virgil?"

Don rolls his eyes. Blackshear stifles a laugh. Martinez comes to my rescue.

"Just a nickname we have for Operation Vigilance," he says.

I like Martinez better all the time. What a standup guy. He said "we" instead of "Kristen."

"So where does that leave us?" Van Guten asks.

"We'll know him when we find him," I answer. "And we'll know all the right questions to ask him. But the problem is finding him. We're looking for a needle in a haystack."

A needle in haystack? That's a clever new figure of speech. Did you come up with that one yourself?" Don asks. "Or did you get that from Virgil?"

We're in the back parking lot of the precinct about to take different aisles for our vehicles.

If I wasn't so tired I'd ask him if it mightn't be a good idea for him to start using a good dandruff shampoo with the way he was picking at flakes or some other mysterious particulation on the shoulders of his suit the whole meeting.

Wow. That would put him in his place. Not.

God, help me stand still long enough to watch and pray.

Chapter 45

W hat do you want me to order for you?"
I'm at JavaStar before Klarissa on a bright Saturday morning. I catch her on the phone.

"Grande latte, skinny."

The skinny's a surprise. Not. Maybe I'll order her a slice of the extra fat cinnamon swirl coffee cake.

"Go ahead and have them make mine," she says. "I'm almost there."

"You got it."

I repeat "grande latte, skinny," to the barista. I've already ordered my extra shot grande Americano with one Splenda. I need every one of those four shots.

"Just one Splenda in that?" he asks.

"In which?" I ask.

"The skinny latte."

"No, I just asked for a Splenda with my extra shot grande Americano."

"Got it. Name?"

"Kristen."

"And on the latte?"

"Kristen, too."

"That's funny," he beams, "you're meeting someone with the same name!"

There are so many things I'm tempted to say. I wonder if he can see wheels with gears spinning in my head.

"No, I'm just waiting for my sister to come. If she's not here yet, I'll be picking up her latte for her."

"Do you want me to add her name, too, in case she gets here before the drinks are done?"

I look around. Most of the seats are taken. But there's no one else in line at the moment.

"I think I can keep it straight for both of us," I answer.

"It's no problem either way."

I promise, I was in a good mood, all things considered, when I got here. I love going out for a cup of coffee in the morning. A lot of times it is very uneventful and that's what I love most about the whole experience. Because once I get the urge to jump the counter and cuff the barista, the coffee just doesn't taste as good. Oh well.

"Hey Big Sis."

Klarissa saves me from charges of false imprisonment of a man with an ear stud the size of a silver dollar who's currently wearing a green apron.

"Name?" he asks her with more enthusiasm and delight than he ever showed to me.

"Klarissa," she beams.

"Two s's?" he asks.

"You bet, and thanks for asking Darrin with two r's," she says with a wink.

Darrin carefully pens her name with a Sharpie, a look of rapture on his face. I think there's a little lesson in this interaction I'm supposed to learn. I don't want to acknowledge it so I give Klarissa a dirty look. She sticks her tongue out at me and laughs. She grabs the crook of my arm and pulls me toward the door.

"Let's talk outside," she says.

"I'd love to," I say, still a little sullen. "You grab a table and I'll grab the drinks."

The barista looks up as she exits the side door to stake a claim on a patio table. He looks after her wistfully. I'm guessing he wishes I had gone for the seating and Klarissa had stayed to pick up the drinks. I drop a dollar in the tip box; slowly while clearing my throat. He still doesn't notice. He and the entire world would have broken into a song and dance from the musical *Mama Mia* if it had been Klarissa.

I've got to start using people's first names so I can win friends and influence people.

Mom wants to talk to you, too."

Klarissa hands me the phone. A delivery truck pulls by the patio spewing diesel fumes so I don't hear what my mom says.

"Come again?" I ask her.

"I said I am so proud of the way you two girls are getting along."

"I didn't know we weren't getting along before," I say.

"Well, you weren't," Mom answers. "And stop being difficult with your mother for a day."

Klarissa is nodding her head in agreement with Mom because she apparently knows exactly what she's saying. I guess I would, too.

"I'm not going to ask you about Dell today," she says. "But that doesn't mean the subject isn't going to come up at lunch tomorrow. I'm worried about him. He hasn't been to church for three weeks. He's lonely and he's a bit of a lost soul. Our family helped him."

"What am I supposed to do about that Mom?" I ask. "Pretend I'm mad crazy in love with him?"

"Well you don't have to make a decision on him right away do you?"

"No I don't, Mom, if he was willing to go slow—and my family would cooperate with my wishes and stop including him in all our plans. But he was pushing and, honestly, so were you guys. I take that back, you still are. That's too much pressure."

"Kristen, I told you I wasn't going to ask about him today and I'm not going to."

I sigh. Klarissa has a smug look on her face. I stick out my tongue at her.

"Did Klarissa tell you about her new boyfriend?" Mom asks.

I look up sharply at my sister. The smugness is gone in a flash. She knows what's up. She grabs the phone from my hand.

"You promised not to say anything, Mom."

My mom says something to her that I can't hear.

"Okay, I love you, too. And Kristen says she loves you, too."

She hangs up.

"Thanks," I say. "Now tell me what gives. I thought we were buds. Why you keeping secrets from me?"

"I'm not keeping secrets," she says. "I'm just not ready to talk about him yet. I've been going out with Warren off and on for five years. My family knows all about every up and down I've ever had romantically and I just want to get to know somebody without there being a big deal about things. Besides, I think he's a little shy and I'm not sure he's ready to meet the family."

"I can buy the no-family-involvement concept and might go for that myself next time around."

"You mean you're not bringing your intrepid and handsome FBI Agent boyfriend to dinner tomorrow?"

"Boy, Mom does talk, doesn't she? You don't even have to put her on the water table and she blabs everything you ask her to hold onto."

"Oh, yeah. But she really wasn't gossiping about your Austin because she wanted to talk about Dell. She's just worried about him."

"Tell me about it."

I look at my watch. I can't believe we've shot the breeze for an hour and a half. My Americano is long gone. Klarissa takes another sip from her still half-filled cup. This is like gulping for her. Her latte has got to be ice cold by now. I like my coffee like I like my clues: hot.

"You really okay with breaking up with Warren and everything?" I ask her. "I feel like I've been a lousy sister. I know you've been trying to tell me some things and I just haven't been a very good listener."

"I'm definitely okay on the Warren breakup. I should have done something years ago. We weren't going anywhere. We're too much alike, I guess."

"Hey, who broke up with who?"

"What does it matter?"

"Well, I thought you told me he broke up with you for a hot little number who does research for the news desk. Kaylen says Warren called Danny and he says you broke up with him."

"Warren called Danny? You've got to be kidding me."

"Unless he or Kaylen have suddenly become pathological liars, then indeed he did. However, I probably wasn't supposed to say anything so forget that I told you."

"Oh, so it's okay for my sisters to talk behind my back?"

"Well, I think Mom was involved in the conversation, too, so yeah, that probably makes it okay."

"Hah hah." She pauses and furrows her brow and then says, "I can't believe that jerk called my family."

"Well, you and he did date for five years. And for the record, I don't think you two are anything alike."

"I'm going to take that as a compliment," she says with a sniffle. "So thank you."

I can see the wheels turning in her mind. She's still perturbed at the thought of Warren calling Danny and that there was subsequent family discussion.

"Man, love stinks," she says, breaking the pause.

"I kind of like that song," I say. "But you're way too young to be cynical about love."

"Okay," she responds, "then how about it 'hurts so good.'"

"C'mon baby, make it hurt so good," I croon back to her.

"Nah, not quite right," she says.

"I never claimed to be able to carry a tune," I say.

She laughs and says, "it wasn't your singing that was the problem. Okay, part of the problem."

I punch her. Gently. Good thing she's a girl.

She clears her throat and picks up an imaginary microphone and belts out:

"'Cuts like a knife, but it feels so right.'"

"You're the one with the nice voice," I interrupt, "but that song hurts too good right now with what I'm dealing with."

"Oh, yeah," she says. "That Cutter Shark guy."

"Yeah, the Cutter Shark guy."

"You really think so?"

"Think so, what, Klarissa?"

"You really think I have a nice voice?"

"Yeah, you always have," I say. "If this weather girl gig doesn't work, I guarantee you could dominate 'American Idol' with your voice and looks—

unless you make Paula jealous and she kicks you off. However, that doesn't mean the coffee shop crowd doesn't think you're a little crazy. People are watching."

"'The first cut is the deepest,'" she sings, now playing an air guitar instead of holding an imaginary microphone.

"You're as good as Sheryl, but again, not the best song for me right now," I interrupt. "You are definitely on a roll."

"Hey, there's one more thing I've been wanting to talk to you about," she says and then pauses. "But you're looking at your watch so you've got to go. We can catch up tomorrow."

"Hey, I've got time now."

I fight the urge to look at my watch again. I really don't have time. I have to hit the office for a couple hours, even though it is a gorgeous late spring Saturday. I'd like to get outside and run a couple miles in daylight. I don't have any plans tonight and that suits me to a tee. I look her straight in the eyes, doing my darnedest not to look even one scintilla impatient to move on. I'm not sure I can pull that off.

"You get to the office," she says. "Let's go to dinner one night next week and we'll talk some more."

"C'mon, Klarissa, I can talk now."

"No. We've been sitting here almost two hours and let's not push it. Besides, I want to make sure you're sitting down when we talk."

"Now you've got me curious."

She stands up and says, "get going. I know you're dying to get back to work."

I stand and we give each other a tight hug. Wow. I don't think we've ever been this close. As I walk out the wrought iron fence area she points a finger at me and serenades me all the way to my car:

"'Every time you go away, you take a piece of me with you!'"

As I start my ten-year-old Miata up, I see her stride toward her brand new Porsche Carerra with all the grace and confidence of a runway model. I still can't help but think she looks so vulnerable.

Chapter 46

I t's been two weeks since Gigi Barker, victim number three of the Cutter Shark in Chicago, was murdered. We've been on the case for almost two months. It feels like a decade. We still have only one active lead and it's not one we ferreted out through our own investigative work in Chicago. It was brought to us by the national office of the FBI in Washington, D.C., on the first day we met. All we think we might know about finding him is that our serial killer has picked up many of his victims in recovery meetings, which may or may not be relevant any longer. He might have found a new hunting ground.

We keep going over the same scraps of evidence. I wonder where he is and what he's up to right now.

I push the button on my radio. What do you know, it's Bryan Adams crooning in that raspy bluesy voice the line, "Yeah, it cuts like a knife, but it feels so right."

Not in my world. Feels so wrong. I think back to coffee with Klarissa. She sang that to me last time we talked. We were supposed to get together for a couple dinners but haven't connected since. She hasn't been at church and dinner the last two weeks either. I think she's visiting another church. Mom won't like it but honestly, I think Danny and Kaylen want her to be wherever she gets the most good. I wonder if that's what she wanted to talk to me about.

Our most recent task force debate was whether to keep so much manpower focused on attending AA meetings. Ever since my Jonathan debacle, enthusiasm and volunteer attendance is definitely down.

I pull up to the security gate at the CPD Armory. The guard steps out and comes to my window to look at my ID and have me write my employment number and sign my name on a form that rests on a clipboard. I do so and pull in to find a parking spot. I'm going to spend a couple hours practice shooting.

So how'd you get onto the force in the first place?" Sergeant Mike Peterman asks me rhetorically.

He's an old friend of my dad. He used to be lead hand gun trainer but he's semi-retired now. He still comes a couple days a week and gives individual instruction. In my case, he spent three hours with me. I think I've worn him out.

"On the last simulator drill, I think you killed about ten civilians before getting yourself shot because you didn't count bullets."

"I wasn't that bad was I?"

"Almost. However, your accuracy marks improved throughout the day on the static range. You're almost up to mediocre."

"Man, I thought switching to the Beretta was going to help."

"Nothing wrong with that Glock you were using. Or the Smith and Wesson before."

"Is there any hope?"

"Definitely," Peterman says. "But mostly for the bad guys."

I give him an affectionate punch but I don't return his smile. I'm mad. I've never been good with handguns but this is ridiculous.

"Hey, don't get your feelings hurt," he says. "I'm just busting on you. Just come see me more often and I'll work with you. We'll get you up to the fifty percentile at least."

"Is that supposed to make me feel good?"

"Kristen, making you feel good isn't my job and it's not what you want. And right now, it's not what you need. You've got some work to do. You're on a dangerous assignment."

"That's what everybody keeps telling me."

Chapter 47

I've been sober for eighteen years, seven months, five days, and about seventeen hours."

I'm in a crowd pushing a hundred people at Holy Family Basilica. Not nearly as much pressure to share here. If everyone said something we'd be here all night. At St. Bart's there might be only fifteen people present, so you kind of got to know everybody and there is kind of an expectation that you ought to say something.

I'm looking for a killer and have two significant problems. First, I have no clue what my killer looks like. I'm not beating myself up over that. You don't kill forty or fifty people like our Cutter Shark has unless you blend in. Second, the guy speaking has me mesmerized. It's Big Tony. I didn't know he was working the AA meetings. He tells a much better story than I do. With the way he checked off his years, months, and hours, he might have been Walter's sponsor. I'm supposed to keep one eye on my surroundings to look for anything out of the ordinary. But all I can hear right now is Scalia.

"I know those times to be a fact because I looked it up this morning," he continues. "I look it up every day. That way I never take for granted the gift of sobriety. It also reminds me to say a prayer for the soul of the man who helped me get my life back, get my wife back, get my kids back, get my job back.

"I hated the son of a bitch. Excuse my French. But this guy was constantly in my face. You'd have hated him, too. But man did I need him. I don't know why he stuck with me, but he did. Even after I took a wild swing at him one night and broke his jaw."

I freeze in my seat. That might be a true story. Dad had his jaw broken at work. I was probably only eleven or twelve when it happened. The docs wired his mouth closed for almost three months. All he could do was drink liquids and pureed food through a straw. He was never that talkative anyway, unless the Bears were on TV naturally, but we didn't hear a word out of him the whole time. First thing he said to us when they pulled the wires out was, "I needed to lose twenty pounds anyway." That was it and then life went back to normal, the event forgotten.

Did Big Tony throw a punch at Dad?

"I hated him for making me own up to my problems. And I loved him. Like a brother. I grew up in a big family with eight kids. But no brothers; seven sisters if you can believe that. He was my brother and I thank him for what he did for me. I light a candle for him every Sunday morning. I miss him. I pray you have a friend like him. So, my name is Tony, and I'm an alcoholic. God bless you."

He makes the sign of the cross and takes a seat. A tear is running down my cheek. Don't know where it came from because my tears dried up a long time ago. The meeting goes another hour. I forget to look for my killer. I don't hear anything else anybody says.

Chapter 48

Dinner tonight? My treat."
I look up. It's Major Reynolds. We went out the one time two—or was it three?—weeks ago. We had an okay time. He did a lot of the talking, which was fine with me. He graduated with a B.A. in Political Science and English Literature, and then he got his law degree at Princeton. Quite the Ivy Leaguer. He never said it directly, but it sounded like there's a boatload of money in the family, so I get the feeling a public servant's salary really isn't going to hamper his lifestyle. Don is married to a real estate mogul and Reynolds has a trust fund. Both dress nice. Reynolds was polite and interesting. To be honest, I was tired after a long work week and the dramatic end to me and Dell so I'm not sure I reciprocated on being interesting.

"If it's your treat, does that make it a date?"

"Based on the lead up to last time we went out, it would help me if you could give a hint if there happens to be a right answer," he says with arched eyebrows. "If you'd like it to be a date, it's a date. If you don't want it to be a date, then it's just two work colleagues winding down after a long work week."

"I'll tell you what," I say. "Give me a couple hours to finish paperwork and we'll figure out what it is later."

"I'm very comfortable with that," Reynolds says. "Now, just tell me what a couple hours means. It's five now. If I picked you up at seven is that a couple hours?"

"I'm heading downstairs to do some punching. Eight o'clock is probably a couple hours."

"I'll be at your place at eight sharp."

Van Guten walks into the makeshift office as he says that. She looks at me appraisingly with just the hint of a smirk.

"You two come up with anything like a hot new lead?" she asks.

"Well if we did," Reynolds answers quickly, "it would be a first on this darn case."

I nod to Van Guten and exit in my typical graceful fashion, bumping into the corner of the table hard enough knock Reynolds' full cup of coffee over and spill hot liquid on papers all over the shared conference table. Crud.

Von Guten takes charge and orders a junior FBI officer to go get something to clean the mess up with. I hoof it back to my cubicle.

*H*it it! Hit it! Hit it! I don't feel nothing. Nothing. Give me something. Hit it!"

I'm trying to remember why I thought Barry Soto was a nice guy. Just because he was friends with Dad? He is killing me. He wanted me to break a sweat, so he put me on a steep grade climb at seven miles an hour on the treadmill. I think he forgot about me so I kept running. I did three and a half miles straight up Pike's Peak for thirty minutes. Then it was twenty minutes of core training, fifteen minutes of grappling, and then on to punches and kicks, which is where I'm at right now.

We've done the kicks. Now we're working on cross body punches. He's holding up two pads and screaming at me to hit. Let me say, this part of the workout is a great workout all by itself. When you're already at the point of fatigue, its torture.

"Don't stop. Hit! Don't you quit on me, Kristen. This guy is after you. He ain't quitting. Who's got the last punch. Hit, I said! Don't you quit on me. Hit!"

I finish my left crosses when he says "finished" and leans over. I want to vomit. I think I taste acid in the back of my throat.

"Great job, honey. Great job. Great workout. Hey, straighten up. Arms over your head. Get your lungs open. Breathe. Great job, Kristen. You still got some fight in you."

I'm gasping for air. My heart is racing. My legs and arms feel like pudding. I contemplate fainting. I would but then I'd have to get up. Soto brings a towel and wipes sweat off my face. My hands are on my knees again.

"Stand up straight," he says again. "Get your arms over your head. Breathe."

It's working. I think I'm going to live. I look up at the wall clock. Big hand on the six and the little hand halfway to seven. I'm going to have to get moving if I'm going to be ready by eight. I was going to shower here, but I'm thinking I may throw a towel on my seat so I can hustle home and get cleaned up there.

"You really are doing great, Kristen."

"Mr. Barry, I think you are trying to kill me," I say.

"No, I'm the guy who's going keep you alive," he says with a laugh. "Hope you don't have big plans because you are going to be really tired tonight."

I consider asking him to write a note that I can hand to Reynolds to establish that there's a reason I am the absolutely worst date in the universe on a Friday night. I probably should have suggested tomorrow night anyway. I'm tired most Friday nights, whether or not I've worked out with Richard Simmons' evil cousin; the one with a bald head and plenty of hair poking out his ears and nostrils.

"Just my luck," I answer him. "I've got a date."

"Then you better get out of here," he chortles. "You ain't going to make it to eleven."

We laugh and I head for the door.

"Kristen!" he calls right before I let the door shut behind me.

I turn back to him as he hustles up to me.

"No, I'm not doing another set of dips," I say to him.

He squeezes my upper arm and says, "You could probably use it. But I had a quick question because you said something earlier. Did Timmy ever hassle you?"

"No, not really," I answer a little uncertainly.

"What's 'not really'?" he asks.

"Well, this is kind of embarrassing to say, but he did ask me out the first time I met him. I thought he was a little forward, but no big biggie. Why?"

"I don't know how to break this to you kiddo, but you aren't the only one he was a little forward with. I think he asked every female in the building with two legs to her credit to go out with him."

"So I really didn't mean as much to him as I thought I did?" I say with a laugh.

"Like I said, kid, I didn't know how to break it to you easy. But here's the thing, I had to let him go and it wasn't because he wouldn't leave the ladies alone."

"What'd he do?"

"None of his references or background information checked out. We were in my office and he said he could explain everything. I said, 'Fine, explain.' He said he had to get something out of his locker and that he'd be back in a sec. That's the last I saw him. Poof. He disappeared."

I turn the ignition on my Mazda and enjoy the sound of an engine that starts right up, strong and true. Soto's Timmy story is weird.

Chapter 49

S o you've never been married, never lived with a guy, and you have no steady boyfriend in your life. How does that happen with a drop dead gorgeous professional young woman? Are the men in Chicago prone to blindness or is it more a matter of low IQ?"

We're back on the Magnificent Mile. This time it's Lawry's, an old-fashioned restaurant—I really don't imagine that the waitresses' mustard yellow uniforms looked good in the forties either—that features prime rib. They wheel a huge silver contraption, looks a little like a fancy outdoor grill to me, right to your table and carve your slab of cow right there in front of you. Reynolds looked a little surprised that I ordered the captain's cut. He shouldn't have told me he graduated from Princeton, one of those places where blue noses go to law school. Knowing he's from high society makes me suspect that (a) he can afford whatever I want to order and (b) that I'm just a curiosity to him and that he's more comfortable with sophisticated women from his social strata, ones who order the petite cut, all of which makes me a little self conscious.

I'm absolutely starving. I had a cup of coffee and half a bagel for breakfast, which wasn't a bad start to the day. But Don and I met with Blackshear and Martinez from nine to one to review notes and assignments. Someone put an apple on my desk—a peace offering from Shandra, I suspect, who knows

I am closing in on her for writing those notes for everyone to read—and that was all I had for lunch. I had a granola bar late afternoon, but that was six hours ago and all 220 calories got burned off in one tough workout.

"Or maybe in Washington, D.C. politicians will say anything to flatter," I respond.

"Touché! Not bad Detective Conner."

"Even if I'm not an Ivy League girl?"

"Actually, that would be young lady or woman; never a 'girl'. That would not be a politically correct form of expression at an Ivy institution of higher learning."

"It's taken you this long to figure out that I'm not PC?" I ask with an exaggerated roll of my eyes. "What was your GPA anyway? Did your dad buy you a spot into Princeton Law School?"

"Not hardly," he says with a laugh. "I did it the old-fashioned way. Hard work and good grades and lots of grants based on need as much as anything."

"So you're not from a fabulously wealthy family?"

"Again, not hardly. But I didn't take you for a gold digger. Maybe I was wrong. Does this mean you won't go out with me on another date?"

"I didn't know that we had defined this as a date."

"Oh, you're right," he says. "Since it's your call, you still need to give me the verdict. And just so you know there's no pressure, I'm a big boy and can take any answer you give me as long as it means 'yes.'"

I cut around the fat for another bite of melt-in-your-mouth prime rib. I don't cut all the fat off, however, and after carving just the right size, I put it in my mouth and chew slowly and thoughtfully. This would be a month long project for Klarissa. I look up at him several times. He's a good sport and has an amused and patient expression on his face. I finally finish chewing and pat the corners of my mouth with a napkin. I take a sip of water. Slowly, of course. He rolls his eyes.

"I can wait you out, you know," he says. "I'm very good at watching and waiting."

"Okay then, it's a date," I say.

I can't believe I just said that. I don't usually give an inch. I must like this guy. Or maybe I'm the one looking at him as a curiosity. His watching and waiting statement did get my attention. It reminds me that I still haven't looked up where "watch and pray" is in the Bible.

"Sure I can't pour you a glass of wine to celebrate?" he asks with bottle poised.

"Not even a drop," I answer with a smile.

"And you don't mind that I'm having wine by myself?"

"Why would I?"

"Well, some people do."

"Not me. My mom; well she would. My older sis, the preacher's wife, probably not, but she's not going to drink herself especially since she's pregnant right now. My younger sis, the most beautiful weathergirl on the planet, sips wine the same way she eats meat. She burns more calories with the effort of letting it touch her lips than what she ends up ingesting. Or imbibing as the case may be."

He laughs and asks, "What about your dad?"

Before I can answer, a shadow crosses our table.

"Well isn't this a delightful surprise?" Dr. Van Guten asks. "Austin, how nice to see you. And you, too, Detective Conner."

Reynolds stands and gives Van Guten a peck on the cheek and holds out his hand to her companion, a tall silver-haired gentleman who obviously has a good tailor. I stand up for introductions, suddenly self-conscious that my little black dress, which isn't that little, is probably ten years old—and wasn't that expensive when I bought it. Maybe it's aged well, I think to myself with a laugh. I have on some cheap imitation pearls that mom gave me for my birthday. I want to hide them and suddenly don't know what to do with my hands, but find my bearing in the nick of time, and hold out my hand boldly for introductions.

"How are you sir?" Reynolds says to the suit.

"I'll be much better when you introduce me to your friend and call me Bob in a social setting," he answers quickly.

Van Guten steps in before Reynolds can speak.

"Robert, this is Detective Conner. You might recognize her from the reports we've been sending you."

He takes my hand and holds it in both of his.

"I'm Kristen and it's nice to meet you … Bob."

I see Reynolds tense up, his eyes wide. He might be holding his breath. Van Guten purses her lips. After just a hair's breath of a pause, Bob roars in approval and gives my hand a kiss. That's a first.

"Kristen, this Robert Willingham, the Deputy Director of the FBI," Reynolds says.

"Pleasure to meet you, sir, and nice to see you Leslie."

She has made no move to shake hands or give me a polite buss on the cheek. I see a shadow cross her eyes. I don't think she is happy with the attention Bob has shown me.

"I'm sorry to interrupt your dinner," Willingham says magnanimously. "I will look forward to seeing you tomorrow morning, Austin. And Kristen, if I may be so bold, would you mind joining us?"

"Sure," I say.

"Sure you mind or sure you'll come?" Willingham asks me with a twinkle in his eyes.

"Bob, I'd be delighted to join you all wherever and whenever."

"Fabulous," he says. "Austin will tell you that the wherever and the whenever is tomorrow morning at seven."

I smile but groan inside. Soccer season is over. I was really looking forward to sleeping in. They follow the maitre 'de, the paragon of patience, to their table. Leslie has on a little black dress, too, but hers really is little, showing what I figure has to be one expensive boob job. At least I hope so—no one should be born with all that up there and so little around the waist. I think the diamonds around her throat and wrist are real, however. I really can be catty.

I had a nice evening," Reynolds says.

This is always awkward. I decide to be bold and get it over with. I stand on tiptoes, put my hands on his shoulders, and give him a kiss on the cheek. I might have touched the corner of his lips. That's it. I do notice he shaved before picking me up and he has good muscle tone that he hides under a suit jacket.

"I had a nice evening, too," I say quickly. "Thanks again for a great dinner. See you in the morning."

If he's disappointed, he doesn't show it. If he's disappointed, he'll also have to get over it. I enter my apartment, give him one more smile, close the door slowly, and then turn the deadbolt and put the chain lock in its groove.

I look at the tiny red light flashing on my phone. Three missed calls. Klarissa, Dell, and a number I don't recognize. There are three messages. I sigh. I don't want to deal with messages tonight. I'm beat. I head back to the bathroom to wash my face and hit the speaker button as I call my voicemail inbox. I'm a pretty good multi-tasker.

"Hi stranger," Dell says. "I would like to talk sometime. Would love to see you. I miss you. I think I'll be at church Sunday morning. See you then."

I hit three for delete. Mom will be happy. Kaylen, the most sensitive soul in the universe, will probably invite him to dinner. That will be weird.

"Just got in … where are you?" Klarissa asks me on the next message. "Oh, I forgot, you're out with Agent Dreamboat. Coffee in the morning? You can tell me everything. Call me late if you want or just send me a text. Let me know. I want to talk. Love you, Big Sis."

I hit delete.

"Thanks a lot for getting me fired," the third voice says with anger. "I was hitting on you in your dreams." I don't recognize who this is. Whoever it was, hung up quick. Timmy? I can't remember his voice. The yellow Post-it Note writer? I hit delete and as soon as I do I realize I should have kept the message. Oh well. I then send a quick text to Klarissa:

Yes, had nice date 2night. Got called into office 4 early meeting @7. Will call u after. Maybe coffee then. Luvs and hugs. K

Face lotion on, I gargle and floss. I let my electric toothbrush do all the work while I check the corners of my eyes for lines. I do have good skin.

I really ought to do something about my wardrobe though. I put my toothbrush on the charger, turn off the light, and go straight for my closet. I pull out the little black dress and throw it in the trashcan to force myself to buy something new.

Two to one odds that I'll pull it out and hang it back up in the morning.

Chapter 50
May 16, 2:00am

A HOT FLASH—AND IT'S NOT A MIDDLE AGE CRISIS
OR THE WEATHER!!!
A Little Birdy Told CTB the Cutter Shark Has
Been a Busy Busy Bad Boy …
By ChiTownBlogger

> Wonder why our esteemed city government and crack police force isn't tellin us everything they know about our fair city's new best friend the Cutter Shark??? (I do like Busy Busy Bad Boy and the BBBB thing—but Cutter Shark he shall remain.)

Note 2only the smart and sassy readers: Don't accept imitations. Ur faithful ChiTownBlogger—CTB Numero Uno 2my myriad of fans—was the first media mogul 2dub our master of the ginzu knife, the CUTTER SHARK. Like it? Thought so!!! Anyone else who tries 2glom credit or suggest any other genesis 4that morbid moniker is nothin more than a jealous hack—no pun intended. (Okay, maybe a little bit intended LOL)

What's the secret? This isn't C. Shark's 1st time and we're NOT his 1st city!!!! Don't b hurt. Serial killers can b such pigs when it comes 2how they run roughshod over our emotions. This chap has led us on with promises that we really were different than all the others only 2find we're in a long line of love sick and jilted lovers at his various ports of call. I just find it curious, in fact, curiously strong, that no public official ... NOT the mayor, NOT the chief of police, NOT the head of sanitation or sewage, NOT even our combo dog catcher and road kill eliminator has seen fit 2tell us that we're city #7! Oh yes, dear devoted readers, u heard that here 1st. And here we felt so ... so ... Special ... Yes, special that we were his 1st. Like I said, what a pig. Cuts like a knife doesn't it? At least that's what Bryan Adams said. (Note: Can't wait to see him in concert at the Odium. Only thing better'd b Duran Duran.)

Who's the birdy whispering 'tweet tweet tweet' in CTB Numero Uno's ear? Wouldn't u like 2know, Mayor Daniels? Seriously, in this day when our BBG, Big Brother Government 4u learning impaired schleps out there, feels enabled—or is it ennobled—when trampling on our freedoms and privacy rights, why not just ask ur cronies in the police department or at the FBI 2find a name 4 u?? I'll bet they'll put together task forces 2plug that leak while blood continues 2seep throughout our fair city.
2bad they're not doin very well finding the killer. Hope it doesn't hurt ur reelection campaign. Bet they can't find my birdy either. Tweet tweet!

Toodles ... XOXOXO ... from ur favorite blogger! ChiTownBlogger is out.

First 1 2POST on this thread gets a special prize: a Bloody Mary on the rocks, extra olives and those charming little onions LOL, at Mack the Knife's over in Old Town. Finally ... justice in our city!
>

Chapter 51

Honestly, I'm not interested in all the reasons we can't find this guy," Willingham says. "I don't care what you've done so far. It's not working. I want to know what you're going to do today. Tomorrow. This guy is about to hit again and we've got a near crisis on our hands. The local media is out of control as it relates to this discrete theater of conflict, but they still don't know we are dealing with a multi-theater phenomenon. We can thank God for small blessings. You think the rabble downstairs right now is a hassle? Wait until the journalists from Sweden and Tokyo and Johannesburg and Moscow and Tel Aviv and everywhere else start showing up."

The Deputy Director takes off his rimless glasses, pauses dramatically, and looks at each person in the room right in the eyes. I feel like he's trying to peer into my soul. I don't dare think of a sarcastic response to his "discrete theater of conflict" comment. I'm afraid he can read my mind. Van Guten breaks the silence.

"This is a fascinating case," she says. "Honestly, with the break in pattern, I thought our friend might be going into an acceleration cycle. I hate to sound crass, but that's not always a bad thing. That's when serial killers get careless, make mistakes, and start leaving clues."

I don't think she was successful in one of her aims. Leslie did sound crass.

"I know the thought drives law enforcement officials crazy," she continues with a glance at Reynolds, "but there is evidence that some serial killers burn themselves out at this stage and return to a normal life."

"Really?"

Did I say that out loud? I did. I had never heard that before and here I am a college graduate with a degree in criminal justice and I'm about halfway done with a master's degree. Actually, I'm not sure if I'm halfway done. I've started and stopped so many times, I'm just amazed I'm still in the program. Of course, I haven't seen my academic advisor, a retired judge who teaches part-time, in about five months. Maybe I've been booted out of the program. Note to self: check to see if you're still a graduate student at University of Illinois Chicago Campus.

"Let's put it this way," she says directly to me—I must have spoke out loud. "Many serial killings have gone unsolved with no record of similar patterns in the future. Did these killers all die? Or did some possibly segue into another life stage? There is plenty of precedence that when organized killers hit a stage of frenzy, some of them simply approach what psychologists call a 'burnout stage.' At this point some have quietly surrendered to the police; others have committed suicide; and yes, some have apparently gone underground, never to be heard from again. I correlate the organized killers who go underground with the general psychopathic population."

"How so?" Willingham asks.

"A lot of people have never heard—and probably wouldn't believe it if they did—that psychopaths cure themselves as they age. Starting at age twenty-one, approximately two percent of all psychopaths go into remission every year. In other words, the older a psychopath lives the more likely he—or she—is to become a functional member of society."

I don't quite believe the "cure themselves" angle. How could I? I attend AA and am pretty well versed in the principle that you have to acknowledge a higher power. That, and the fact that I've gone to church all my life, means I believe we need the help of God and other people. Not sure I practice my belief system like I should but I do believe it.

AA meetings have really been interesting. I'm not an alcoholic, but it does seem kind of natural to be there. *Hi, I'm Kristen and I have an anger problem.* No, that's distancing the problem from myself. *Hi, I'm Kristen and I'm an anger-holic. Started small, but man I am all in, these last few months in particular.* When I talk about my anger, not by name of course, everyone in the groups I've attended perk up and think I'm talking about vodka or cocaine. I wonder if my anger will be cured with age. Gray, the guy from Internal Affairs, suggested I'm heading for a burnout stage. Me in a frenzy? That's a scary thought.

We're at the State Building on Wacker, just south of the Chicago River and on the north edge of the Loop. I like meeting at the FBI's place better than the Second Precinct. They have carpet; we have linoleum. Their conference room table is made of mahogany; ours Formica. Their chairs are covered in soft leather; ours might have had cloth covering foam at one time. We have quite a bit of wide plastic tape patching up slits in the fabric. They have art on the wall; we have rust-colored water stains. Their ceilings have geometric flourishes and trims. Half our ceiling tiles have at least one major chunk missing or some discoloring best not to investigate.

But what makes meetings at their place infinitely better than ours is that they have a cool space age machine that grinds coffee beans and brews an individual cup of the freshest joe in the world for you. Oh, and they have real half and half. As in liquid. We have wretched, stale sludge with a powdery cream substitute that never quite mixes all the way into the coffee without some floaters on the surface. The fresh bagels and lite cream cheese are a nice added touch.

An attractive young lady, young now being anyone that doesn't have three or higher as the first number of their age, walks in and stands at the FBI Deputy Director's left shoulder, waiting for him to acknowledge her. I wouldn't interrupt him either. I didn't refer to her in my mind as a girl, so maybe I am becoming more politically correct. I'm not sure that's a good thing.

"Thanks for the insights, Dr. Van Guten," Willingham says. "I think you might have thrown us all for a loop on that one. Bottom line, we've got to catch this guy. I hope it doesn't take our killer entering a period of frenzy to do so. But I sure as heck hope this guy doesn't go underground. As much pain and suffering as he has wrought on this world, I want us to be able to tell some families that we have apprehended the man who killed their son or daughter."

"He's killed men?" I ask.

That was for sure out loud. I blurt it out quickly, not considering that I am interrupting one of the most important men in our country. Robert Willingham is a legend. He was involved in the TWA Flight 847 hijacking in 1987 and I read about him in a case study in a class at NIU. He was the behind-the-scenes hero who did the legwork that led to the secret indictment of Hezbollah's Imad Mughiniyah. He was also the lone dissenter when Janet Reno sent the tanks in against the Branch Davidians in 1993. He got demoted and was out of the Bureau for a couple years. That was another case study I had to write about on "group think." Oh, Willingham is an American legend alright.

There's a pause in the room among the FBI personnel. Zaworski looks up at Willingham and then Reynolds sharply. Willingham makes a church steeple with his forefingers. He looks at me and I can't tell if he's mad or amused.

"What gives, Bob?" Zaworski asks.

"At least three instances," Willingham answers.

"That's not in any of the reports Virgil has generated," I say, my voice cracking.

How come everyone else can speak so poised and modulated and I sound like a blathering fool? A blurting fool. Van Guten and Willingham look at me puzzled.

"That's Detective Conner's nickname for PV; Project Vigilance," Reynolds answers for me.

Willingham narrows his eyes. Now I'm sure he's mad. Then he smiles at everyone in the room. He lets out a loud laugh and everyone joins him except Van Guten. She has the start of a smile on her lips. Not sure it's a friendly smile, though.

"There's a few things, uh, Virgil has expunged that I'll cover with you off line," Willingham says to Zaworski. "But now we're getting off topic. I'm bringing in another four street soldiers from Fairfax. We need more local investigators in the field. Captain Zaworski, you have an exemplary record and reputation in law enforcement, but this is as big a case as your city's had since the IRS shut down Al Capone. You've only got eight officers full time on this. I'm just going to be blunt and ask you: Are you taking this seriously enough?"

"We've got our best on the case," Zaworski responds, unruffled.

He barely glances in my direction. Other than Zaworski, I'm the only CPD present at this cozy little meeting. He's probably wondering how I ended up invited to this high level power breakfast. I get the feeling he's also wondering if I'm really one of his finest.

"And you're not factoring in that we have another hundred officers and staffers working the case, a minimum of twenty hours per week. All told, we're working the equivalent of sixty-one full timers every day since this thing started."

"When the Green River killer moved from Washington to Missouri, the Kansas City Police Department had the equivalent of fifty-nine full timers per week," Willingham quickly rattles off. "Boston had thirty-four officers, not counting background support, on Son of Sam for five straight years. Los Angeles created a whole unit that ran for a decade for the Zodiac Killer. Your Cutter Shark makes these guys look like amateurs."

"First of all," Zaworski says in a measured tone, "you keep saying he's 'your killer.' He's our killer. He's got a lot more history in your jurisdiction than mine."

"Good point and fair enough, Captain," Willingham says. "I'll watch my phraseology. In fact, I'm more than willing to take responsibility and say he's my killer. He's crossed state lines, which makes this a federal case, and he's done it on my watch. He's mine. But he's in your city now. So he's yours, too. He's mine but I guarantee you're better off assuming he's all yours. It will keep things in better perspective. What I want to know is what you're ready to do. Today. Forget tomorrow. I need you to step up to the plate in a big time way." He pauses and then slams a fist on the desk and yells, "Right now!"

"Hey, help us out with some leads and I'll put the whole damn force on this," Zaworski answers, his face red, his eyes flashing. "We have three murders and a very limited number of clues. We're sifting the same bag of dirt over and over and over—and there isn't any gold in it. I'd put more detectives on this if I had any real work to give them."

"Captain, I will repeat, I admire you and your track record," Willingham responds, "but I'll also echo what I've been suggesting for the past hour.

Whatever it is we're doing, isn't working. Let's do something different. Anything. Start there. There's something you could be doing that you haven't thought of yet."

"If Virgil hadn't left the 'guy' part out, we could have been hitting the gay bars," I snap out. I hope that Zaworski appreciates I have his back.

I look over at him. He has the same body language Don gets when he doesn't want to be associated with me.

"I don't know," Willingham counters, "you might stick out like a sore thumb."

He might be about to smile again—or not—but he pauses and looks at his aide.

"Yes, Megan?"

"Thought you should see this, sir."

He takes off his glasses and reads a print out she hands to him. It takes him about thirty seconds. He hands the sheet of paper back to Megan. He pinches the bridge of his nose as he looks at each of us around the table.

"Anyone here ever heard of the ChiTownBlogger?" he asks.

"A real hack," Zaworski answers. "Sees himself as defender of the people. Peddles every rumor and conspiracy theory associated with city government. He's got enough of a following we know he who is. In fact, if I'm remembering right, he came up with the Cutter Shark nickname. What's he done this time?"

"Let's just put it this way," Willingham says, "by this time tomorrow, ninety percent of Chicago is going to know that this guy he calls the Cutter Shark is a multi-theater phenomenon."

Doing anything fun today?" Zaworski asks me.

We're in the elevator going down to the parking garage, which starts two levels below the street entrance to the State Building.

"Not really," I answer.

"I was going out on Lake Michigan with my wife, daughter, son-in-law, and three grandkids."

"Sounds nice," I say. "What kind of boat you got?"

"I've got the Bayliner Buccaneer. Model 295. It's a thirty-five footer that can sleep all of us. My one indulgence through the years. Know anything about sailing?"

"Not a thing."

"I won't bore you anymore then."

"I wasn't bored a bit, sir. And I'm glad you get to go out with the family."

"Not going to happen for me," he says. "I'll call my wife on my way over to the mayor's office. She isn't going to like it but she'll understand. We've been married forty years and a good part of the reason is she understands a cop's life well enough not to complain or waste her time getting bitter and trying to lay guilt trips on me when plans get messed up."

"Bummer."

Bummer? I've got to get better at this professional interaction thing. I'm not looking for a promotion for a long time, if ever. My goal has been to be a detective. It's what I am and it's what I love doing. Some teachers teach their whole career. Others want to be principals. I think I'm the be-a-teacher kind of detective.

"The mayor and chief aren't going to like what I've got to tell them, either," he says, now with a preoccupied tone. "But I'm not positive they'll be as understanding as my wife."

Neither of us smiles. The car stops, a bell rings, the doors open, and we exit the elevator and give each other a nod as we go opposite directions for our cars.

"Conner," he says.

I stop and look back at him.

"Do something fun with your family today. Life is about to get miserable."

I nod awkwardly.

"In case you were wondering," he says, "that's not a suggestion. It's an order."

Chapter 52

I'll pick the kids up at six," I say to Kaylen for the sixth time. I'm ready to hang up. I've got a few more calls to make and I need to think. I'm driving from the State Building to my precinct. A whole lot of dynamics were going on this morning at FBI headquarters that I didn't understand. Beyond the weird vibe that Van Guten is projecting my way through her extra-terrestrial intellectual powers—and her far superior wardrobe—there's that disturbing little detail of why the FBI has been holding out past evidence from our killer's non-isolated crime streams. Their phrase, not mine. As proud as they are of Virgil and their connected stream theory, leaving out that the Cutter Shark has killed men is a significant omission. Huge. Unbelievable.

I was half joking about hanging out at gay bars but it might have been a great idea.

"Are you sure, Kristen?" Kaylen asks. "Danny and I were just talking about all you're going through right now. Life's been so crazy this past year for all of us. We haven't always been there for you. This Cutter Shark thing is so scary. What happens to people that they become monsters?"

"Hey Kaylen, I'm actually doing okay today and I want to take the kids out and have them spend the night. I miss them! You and Danny do something fun, you know, get out the old Scrabble board or maybe play some Parcheesi. Danny can pop popcorn over an open fire in the backyard and lead Mitch Miller choruses."

"Hah hah," she says with not even a scintilla of humor in her voice.

"Hey," I add, "if you've got other ideas, maybe even romantic ideas, you're adults and you're even married, so have at it."

"You are so dead when you get here, Kristen," she says. She pauses and says, "you know that's probably not the best choice of words right now."

Then she starts crying. I immediately swear to myself I'm not going to join her in crying. Kaylen cries when a fireman saves a kitten from a tree. Since I'm not sure that has ever actually happened except in storybooks and Norman Rockwell paintings, I'll go a step further and say that the thought of a fireman bringing a kitty down from a tree and handing it to an old lady, who I hope was not an organized killer in another life, makes her cry. But I start crying anyway, too. It's been a long time since tears have really flowed for me. Twice in a week. What's gotten into me?

We agree that life is going to get better for Mom and us girls. We tell each other how much we love each other. I sit in my car for five minutes, letting the tears dry. I crank up a classic rock station and listen to Chicago belt out "25 or 6 to 4." I once heard a deejay earnestly explain that the "25 or 6 to 4" phrase was just something nonsensical someone in the group came up with at the end of a studio session so they could go home. Nonsensical? Gee, do you think so?

Whether it was the peppy beat or a flare up of my sarcasm gene, I now have my game face on and head into the building. I nod at the officers working the front desk and sign in. I eschew the elevator and jog up four flights of loud, metal stairs. The floor is reasonably quiet but I can hear voices here and there. I get to my cubicle. There is another yellow sticky note stuck to the middle of my computer screen:

ROSES ARE RED
VIOLETS ARE BLUE
DOES THE FBI STUD
REALLY LOVE YOU??

Someone is dead meat. Someone is going to pay for this. Shandra, if it's you, leaving an apple on my desk is not going to get you out of this.

It takes me almost an hour to stop fuming about the Post-it Note and get my mind fully on task. In terms of progress on the case, no one would be able to tell the difference.

Dear God, please help me to control my anger.

Chapter 53
May 18, 2:00am

*G*oody goody. Word is getting out there.

His legend was growing.

I hate that CTB guy—he wants to own this plot when I, and only I, am supreme Author. Me doggone it. I'll tell you someone else who is way overrated. Truman Capote. One decent book. But he didn't even really write it. He just stole it from those kids. They're the ones who deserved the credit except for being so stupid they got caught. If he won awards for In Cold Blood, *think what they'll do for me.*

But I'll admit CTB is effective. And safe. Just like Preparation H! I took some risks setting up a chat room with him, but there's no way he's going to risk losing a source for the biggest story of the year. Well, not just a source. The source. This is the biggest story of the decade in Chicago and I will work to keep it that way. The only thing that could come close is if the Cubs made it to the World Series. Ha! Ain't going to happen. The FBI and Chicago Police Department will undoubtedly monitor his internet use, especially things like private chat rooms, going forward. So I'll have to stick to quick, down and dirty emails from now on.

The main thing is I'll be back on page one of mainstream media tomorrow. Man, it's hard to keep their attention. I keep flipping around radio and TV channels, and right now I'm getting decent air time locally—and I'm finally scoring some national play—but it should be more. I swear if Lindsay or Brittany get drunk and run over some paparazzi, I'm back to page three again.

There could be something new as early as tomorrow for all those stupid media lemmings—almost as dumb as cops.

Even in the midst of adversity, he'd once again brought order to his work. He'd practiced his trademark brand of discipline and self-denial for several particularly arduous weeks. His latest kill was a matter of putting things back on track.

Two weeks ago, Gigi was a perfect one month schedule behind Leslie. So why shouldn't I work this weekend? Some might think I'm early—but I'd actually be right on schedule with Candace. I like the way I'm thinking! Rules are the bomb. I can make and break them at will. Track that, FBI psychologist!

He wished the night sky would carry a full moon that night. Not for his needs, sophisticated and extensive as they were, but to perfect the ambience for his next intimate encounter.

It would be good to wait for a full moon, but man, the pressure is building. I know myself well enough. I can't. I've been a real bear to live with if I don't say so myself ... Grrrrrr! No time like the present. And my date tonight is a dream girl. This city is going to explode sometime in the next few days when they find out who she is. She's going to explode when she finds out who I am, too! Man. Brains and a sense of humor. Eat it up, ladies.

He amazed himself. The beauty of his work.

Can I really call this work? I'm having a blast. Now. Finally.

Yes. He really had created a story for the ages, filled with irony and subtle plot turns. Terrifying in its brilliance and simple violence.

I said I was smart, I didn't say I'd applied for sainthood!

Chapter 54

I told you why I can't go out tonight. I've already got a date with my adorable niece and fabulous nephew. Even if I hadn't made plans, I'm not sure I'm ready to go out two nights in a row."

"And why would that be?"

I shift into fifth gear and drop the phone off my shoulder. I've got to get a hands-free earpiece. Maybe that would help me start discerning when a stranger looking right at me is talking to me or their stock broker. I always start to respond and end up feeling like a fool. I fumble around with my right hand while keeping both eyes on the road. I'm doing seventy-five in a sixty-five zone and Saturday afternoon traffic is surprisingly heavy.

"Are you still there?" Reynolds is asking as I get the phone back up to my ear.

"I am."

"You haven't answered my question."

"Sorry, I dropped my phone. But you know what Austin; I don't think I'm going to answer anyway."

"That hurts. However, you did use my first name, I believe for the first time, so I'm not going to complain."

"I'm honored, Major."

"Listen, I think it's great that you've got your sister's kids tonight. But you've got three hours before you pick them up and knowing you, you haven't had anything to eat since you picked at that bagel this morning. Meet me for a late lunch on your way home."

"I've got to get cleaned up and do some housework."

"You've got to eat lunch sometime. We'll just sit down for an hour."

"I'm thinking."

"Keep thinking and see if this helps. There's a great little Philly Cheesesteak place near the corner of Clark and Belmont."

"After eating a pound of cow last night, for some reason the thought of a sandwich piled with meat is not helping my thinking process."

"There's vegetarian place a couple blocks away. The Chicago Diner."

"Okay, I'll meet you there, but two things."

"Name them."

"First, I buy my own meal. Strike that. I buy both meals. Just make sure it doesn't go over twenty bucks between us because they don't take credit cards and that's all the cash I've got."

"Sounds good. I like a strong, independent woman and I can eat on a budget. What's number two?"

"Forty-five minutes, tops, is all I've got. I have to have some down time at my place before I pick up the kids."

"Doesn't sound as good as number one, but you got it."

Lunch was great. Austin is a good conversationalist. He was wearing the same thing that he had on in the morning meeting, so he spent the day at work, too.

The Chicago Diner is vegetarian and organic, too, I think, but that's not the same thing as low calorie and small portions. I was in the mood for an omelet so I ordered up one with tofu bacon, caramelized onions, asparagus, olives, fresh basil, and feta cheese that's not really cheese. I get after Klarissa for never finishing her food, but I left half the omelet uneaten and didn't touch the potatoes or whole wheat toast. I did drink one of their juice mixes with carrots and apples and wheat germ. I may wear my love beads and Birkenstocks tonight.

Agreement number two was that I had to be out of there in forty-five minutes. I should have stuck to the plan. We went twenty-five minutes over. That's when things went downhill in a hurry. I went to pay the bill at the cash register and was a couple bucks short. Austin dropped my twenty back in my purse and pealed off a ten and a twenty from a pretty fat wallet. He told the cashier to give the change to our waitress.

As we turned toward the door, Austin put his hand lightly on the back of my shoulder, which shouldn't have taken me by surprise, but it did. I know I stiffened and reddened a little. But I went beet red when I looked up to see Dell standing ten feet from us. His mouth was slightly open in surprise and he was still as a statue. I froze, too. I hadn't talked to him in close to a month. He had called and left messages two or three times. I never returned any of them. This probably didn't take more than a second or two, but it felt like an hour. I finally snapped out of it and walked forward. He seemed to recover, too.

"Well, Kristen Conner, it's good to see you again," he said.

"Hi Dell."

I'm not good at awkward situations. Don says that that makes me excellent at interrogating suspects. Talking with me can be so painful that confessing seems like an ice cream cone in the park on a hot August day in comparison. Don also says I am terrible at making analogies and drawing word pictures. He's right, of course. That doesn't really bother me, but I do wish I could tell a better joke. I stuck out my hand and Dell and I shook. I know that's weird but like I said, I was feeling acutely awkward.

"Good to see you," I said to him. "I owe you a call."

"Anytime," he said with a forced smile.

"Dell, I'm Austin," Austin said to him and they shook hands.

"A pleasure to meet you."

"Yeah, you, too."

As we exited the restaurant, I looked back in and Dell was sitting down at the counter. Austin wanted to know who Dell was. I told him I didn't have time to get into that now and almost sprinted to my car.

I didn't feel good about myself the whole drive home. No one can make me reciprocate romantic interest and I have no qualms with that. But I should have returned one more phone call and had a final talk through. I was pretty abrupt when I told him it was over.

I used to think of myself as a very nice person. Christian. Caring. Have I always been this self-absorbed?

Chapter 55

I think you're supposed to vacuum before you dust. Vacuuming stirs up dust, so it undoes, at least in part, what you've just got done doing. That's what Mom always told me anyway. I always remember her words of wisdom after I've dusted first. I think about that as I wind up the cord on my vacuum cleaner and push it in the back corner of the small coat closet in my front hallway. The thought robs me of some of the satisfaction I feel for having a top-to-bottom clean apartment—even the cobwebs in the corners of the crown molding.

I still feel good. Clean bathroom; clean kitchen; clean everything. I got two loads of laundry done, which is all my laundry. I've got a pile of warm whites on my bed. Won't take me more than fifteen minutes to fold them and put them away. Even my desk is cleared in my second bedroom. Okay, the top right drawer will barely shut with all the junk mail and unpaid bills I've still got to sort through, but the clutter is out of sight. Fresh sheets are on the spare beds for the kids.

Kendra's seven now and won't want to sleep in the same room with Daniel. Daniel won't go to sleep by himself unless he's in his room at his house. I'll whisper in Kendra's ear to lie down beside him for twenty minutes until he falls asleep. Sometimes that even works and then she runs over to my room and jumps in bed with me. Once she fell asleep before

Daniel, and I left her to sleep in the guest room with him all night. She was so hurt and distraught, she wouldn't talk to me the whole drive back over to her house. So if she does fall asleep with Daniel now, I pick her up and carry her over to my bed before I drift off.

And sometimes neither kid can fall asleep. Then I let both of them come over to my bed. One of my few extravagances in life is I have a king size bed, which means there should be plenty of room for the three of us. It doesn't quite work out in real life, however. Daniel never stops moving. He wiggles. He tosses and turns. He gets sideways and starts using his feet to claim new territory. He is fundamentally a sprawler. I end up on the very edge of my bed, one arm draped over the side. Kendra ends up snuggled tight in my back, her breath on my neck. Sir Daniel ends up with two thirds of the bed.

Clothes put away, I lace up my Nikes and head out the door. I do a fairly hard 5K run in just a little under thirty minutes. Back in my college days I could run a 10K in thirty minutes. That's five minute miles. Back in my college days, I barely noticed my oft-repaired left knee either. I haven't run much this spring and it is barking at me.

I strip down and take a glorious fifteen minute shower. I'm not going to have time to dry my hair if I'm going to pick the kids up at six. Doesn't matter. It's in the upper seventies and I'll just pull it back in a ponytail and let the wind from an open convertible do whatever it wants to with it. I put on a jean skirt, just a little shorter than Mom and Kaylen approve of, but a couple inches longer than Klarissa, the weathergirl, wears. I pull a black cotton sleeveless shirt over my head and look in the mirror. It used to be half a size tighter than Mom's standards of modesty, which are pretty strict I'll add, but I notice that I really have lost weight, some of it in places I can ill afford to lose any size. I think looking for a serial killer for a couple months has been tougher than I thought. Major Reynolds is doing his part to try and put some meat back on my bones.

I grab my purse and phone and head down the stairs to my car. Two missed calls. One is from Don. That's unusual for a Saturday. He's a hard worker, but he is also able to separate the job from family time with Vanessa and his kids. The other is from a number that I don't recognize. It's not a Chicago area code. I'll listen on the drive over.

I thought the kids were spending the night. Maybe they're moving in with me for good. Both have suitcases on wheels.

"I'll have them to church on time," I say in response to Kaylen's admonition that I do so for the third or fourth time.

Danny slams the trunk shut. The kids share a seat belt on the passenger side. Kaylen looks worried. She always looks worried when the kids get in my car.

"I'll drive safe and slow," I say to Kaylen with a stern voice.

She laughs and bends over and hugs my neck.

"You're not eating," she says. "You're getting as thin as Klarissa."

I've never noticed Mom's tone of voice in her before. I hear it this time. I roll my eyes at her, blow her a kiss and we're off to Chucky Cheese for lukewarm pizza and a scary mechanical gorilla singing oldies.

I'm glad the top is still down. It's too noisy to talk to the kids and I still need to cool down. I'm hoping Danny and Kaylen didn't see how angry I am. I shouldn't have listened to my voice messages before picking up my angels.

Kristen, this is Don. Wanted to catch up with you before Monday. I hear you've figured out a way to get invited to the big boy meetings. I'm impressed—and a little surprised—by your strategy. Don't forget us little people on your way to the top."

What a jerk. I know he's joking. But sometimes when people tease, there's some real feelings packed into it. I get accused of being paranoid, but I feel a barb in his message. That is so unfair and it makes me mad. But not as mad as the next message makes me.

"Kristen, this is Dr. Van Guten. I stopped by your cube over at CPD. You were already gone." She paused as if to emphasize that I should have still been at work if she was. "I was talking to Director Willingham and at the risk of being rude, we wanted to make sure you know that we take this business with the ChiTownBlogger very seriously. We don't want anything that was said in today's meeting being repeated over at CPD outside of direct task force members—or with anyone in the media. That includes WCI-TV and family members. Just in case you are wondering, this isn't Reynolds' call. This is straight from the Deputy Director. Call me on my cell if this isn't clear or you have any questions. Have a nice evening with whatever your plans are."

She's accusing me of sharing secrets from our investigation with Klarissa?

God, I know that vengeance is yours, but I want to pop her in the mouth so bad. Amen.

Chapter 56
May 20, 7:30pm

*T*here's been a change of plans. I hate that. That's right, the Shark is not happy. Note to the wise: even if I smile and laugh, I'm not joking this time ... psyche!

There had been complications. He was not pleased.

This was my special night. Mine. What about me and my feelings? I hate country music, but I love that song that big buck Okie sings, "I want to talk about me." Me too. I want to talk about me. And I want everyone else to talk about me too! Now, is that too much to ask?

He had to find a new subject.

No, I'm always the subject.

He had to find a new object. He had to complete his work for the night. He would rise to the challenge.

I'm going with Occam's razor; when in doubt over two possible explanations, go with the simplest one. I'm in doubt as to whether I should cancel or press forward, so I'm going simple. Press on because I bet I have a desperate dirty thirty nibbling on my ear by ten. Girls are dumb with a capital D. Occam, of course, is smart. He has a razor! A fellow man of style.

He had been cheated of satisfaction.

By a freaking blonde. That's just insulting.

But he was determined and he would set it right.

Chapter 57

I wake up with a start, light streaming on my face. It's quarter to nine. The kids' Sunday School starts at nine twenty-five. I have no idea why it doesn't start at nine thirty or even better this particular morning, at ten or some other round number. I just know that it takes thirty minutes to get there and the kids are gone to the world. Kendra is one foot from the edge of the bed. She'd be all the way on the edge but that was the space afforded to me. Daniel is at a forty-five degree angle, his head in the direction of the foot of the bed. He looks very comfortable. He ought to; he worked hard to get the whole bed to himself.

I throw the bedroom curtains all the way back and start barking for the kids to get up and get ready in a hurry. Neither looks so inclined. I'm in big trouble.

We had a great time at Chucky's. Klarissa ended up joining us and that was a hoot. After winning close to a million tickets, most of them based on my mad skills at skeet ball, we were able to cash in and get both kids a prize worth at least one buck each.

We invited Klarissa to make it a slumber party but I think the mechanical gorilla was all the youthful frivolity she could handle so she booked it back to her place, winding her Carerra's engine into a loud whine before she exited the parking lot airborne. Kendra, Daniel, and I pulled up to Chez

Kristen at ten with yet another voice message waiting for me. This one on my landline. I didn't know anyone was aware of or called that number unless selling vacation packages or grocery services designed to save me a thousand bucks a month and provide me with the quality of nutritional food I and my large family deserve. I'm not sure why I have phone service at home anymore, but I think it might come at no extra charge with the cable package. I should check.

I hit the flashing red button and left it on speaker phone. It was Dell with a tone of voice the kids had never heard. Me either.

"Well, well, well … I guess you're really just not ready to see anyone at this phase in your life," he said, his voice dripping with sarcasm, loud enough for me, the kids, and my neighbors on either side to hear before I could snatch the headset and click it off speaker phone.

"Nice way to repay someone who treated you like a queen. That's right, a queen. Thanks for kicking me in the teeth. I didn't deserve to not be treated better and you sure as heck didn't deserve to be treated as good as I was to you. I knew you were going through a rough time and I never complained when you treated me like a dog. I gave you all the space you asked for and boy did you run with it. Hey Kristen, your day will come. You'll know how it feels to get hurt and abused by someone you care about. Payback is a killer. And princess? I know the world revolves around you and your whims, so good news, you won't be hearing from me again."

I didn't even bother putting the kids in the spare bedroom. We all climbed in my bed and watched half a Disney movie before the kids—actually all of us—finally succumbed to the call of sleep. I woke up an hour later to check all the locks on my door, so I ended up rewinding and then watching all of *Beauty and the Beast* by myself. I like to think of myself as Belle—the hair color's even right. But I wonder if I'm really the beast.

Klarissa was always Ariel from *Little Mermaid*. Kaylen was *Snow White*. She is old school after all.

Dell was absolutely unfair and out of line. I never led him on or promised him anything. I might have felt even worse but his self-serving words and scathing tone made me feel a lot less guilty about not calling him back a couple weeks ago. It was obvious he had a picture about us in his mind that was not going to allow this thing to end gracefully no matter how many times I called back and explained. I still felt more like a beast than a beauty when I finally fell asleep about an hour after the movie was over.

I think I dreamed that Lumiere, the candlestick with the heavy French accent, was scolding me for turning my back on true love. I don't think that little clock guy was very happy with me either.

Kaylen is waiting for us as I run in the door to the children's area of our church. We got out the door of my apartment in fifteen minutes flat. But the kid were starving and we stopped at Dunkin' Donuts. I'm obviously not a mom or I would have known not to let Daniel get a powdered sugar donut. His mouth and the front of his shirt are coated in white. I brushed Kendra's hair out and put it in pig tails. I now notice that the part is a jagged line and that the left pig tail has about twice as much hair in it as the right. So does Kaylen.

I give a sheepish smile. She just shakes her head. I want to say something smart but just walk up to her and hug her tight.

"I love you Sis," I whisper. "Sorry."

I then do the only thing I can think of under the circumstances because frankly, I've been scolded enough for one twenty-four hour period. I turn around and walk out the door.

Chapter 58

V anessa, this meal is unbelievable."
"I'm pleased you like it," she answers.

I drove south after my dramatic exit from Kaylen and went to Don and Vanessa's church. I read a sociology textbook back in college that had a highlighted sidebar noting that Sunday morning is the most segregated window of time in America. I'm not sure how much it bothers me that birds of a feather kind of flock together when they go to church, but nonetheless, even if I don't bow at the throne of diversity—something you don't say out loud when you work for the city of Chicago—I know it would be a good thing if people from all walks of life got together for worship. I don't know whether church is more segregated than other places in society, but I do know that I am a minority—maybe of one—at Don's church.

The sign out front indicated that it was a temple. It was a one story converted strip mall and wasn't very ornate so in my mind, it's a church. I got there at ten fifteen and no one seemed to care that I was late. *Hah* I say to Kaylen in my mind. A lot of people came in after me. I didn't blame them, either. The service didn't end until after one. I think we stood for more than an hour of singing. And dancing. And shouting. Don has invited me to attend church with him and Vanessa a bunch of times. I'm not sure he thought I'd actually follow through. I think I'm putting a damper on his freedom of expression. Vanessa feels no such inhibition. Not only can that girl sell real estate but she's got moves.

I liked the people, the music, and the preaching. Even the announcements were pretty good. I might have some helpful suggestions for Danny on livening things up at our church. I do have one problem with Don's church—and I know it makes me a Philistine to admit this—but I can't handle a three-plus hour service. Sometime after noon, I committed myself to working things out with Kaylen. I think Klarissa's been church hopping a little—this will be my sole excursion into discovering the diversity of worship experiences in my community.

Afterwards, Vanessa invited me to dinner at their place. I had never been to the Squires residence. I didn't know what to expect what with him being on a cop's salary and her being on quite a roll with real estate, but whatever my preconception was or wasn't, the place was nicer than I had imagined. Don and the kids showed me around while Vanessa finished pulling everything together in the kitchen.

It wasn't a new house, but it was big, at least four thousand square feet—probably more—with a whole lot of remodeling and upgrades like a marble foyer and everything granite and copper in the kitchen. Danny and Kaylen keep talking about some things they want to do with their place and Kaylen's lament is that it costs more per square foot to build out and remodel than what you pay per square foot if you just buy what you want new. I live in a two bedroom apartment and don't have to deal with things like that.

Vanessa may make the money but Don's the king. Both he and Vanessa have their own office, but his looks more like the lounge of a British private men's club, with leather chairs studded with brass and a lot of pheasant and fox hunting scenes on the wall. I'll have to ask Don at work if he's ever been pheasant hunting. Having never been to a private men's club in the British Isles — or to the British Isles to visit anything for that matter—I'm using my imagination here. Vanessa's office is nice but Spartan in comparison. I'm guessing a lot more real work takes place in her space than his.

The kids' rooms are way cooler than anything me or my sisters grew up with. Devon's nine. He has bunk beds, his own space age desk, a nicer media center than I have at age twenty-nine, a basketball goal over his laundry hamper, and a bunch of those oversized Fathead posters of sports stars on the walls. He likes Brian Urlacher. Everyone in Chicago likes Urlacher. There's also a whole collage of posters dedicated to Walter Payton. I'm guessing that was Don's idea. He has an informal shrine to the immortal #34 of the Bears on his desk.

Veronika is seven, same age as Kendra. Vanessa has had one of her walls painted by a local artist with a scene out of a fairy tale. It actually has a Beauty and the Beast look to it, though I don't remember Belle being quite that dark skinned, which makes me remember the lousy feeling I had all last night.

We spend ten minutes looking over things in the half-basement game room—pool table, foosball table, ping pong table, Xbox set up with a plasma screen TV, a couple of old arcade games—I had forgot about Space Invaders—a table that might be for Monopoly with the kids and poker night for Don and his heathen friends if Vanessa lets them in the house, and a wet bar. Then we walk up another flight of stairs and down a back hall into the formal dining room. The paintings look real. The china is something out of a Martha Stewart decorating special—and I'm not talking her prison phase.

I'm not sure Vanessa was expecting me to accept her lunch invite because she told me numerous times that the meal wouldn't be much. And she's absolutely right if salmon with dill sauce, creamed spinach, new potatoes baked with a fresh rosemary and garlic seasoning, fruit compote with the fattest blackberries I've ever seen in my life, steaming mini-loafs of sourdough bread, and some kind of sweet potato casserole that ends up tasting an awful lot like Mom's pumpkin pie, isn't much. The iced tea flavored with peach nectar was a particularly nice touch that I want to remember when hostessing. Hah.

We were almost through with dinner, the unbelievable aroma of an almost baked apple pie now wafting through the room, when my phone buzzed four times. I figured it was probably Kaylen so I decided to ignore it. It went off four more times. Good, she misses me, I figured. When it started a third round of buzzing, I looked at the tiny screen.

Zaworski.

I wish you didn't have to run."

"I know Vanessa. This was wonderful. I feel so bad inviting myself over and then bolting before dinner is even over. I would have helped with the dishes."

"You didn't invite yourself girlfriend, I invited you!"

Cool. I'm a girlfriend. Vanessa and I are in the doorway with Don and the kids dutifully in the background. He doesn't look happy. I went into the living room to talk with Zaworski but I know he knew who I was talking to. His phone hasn't made a peep. I know because he keeps glancing down at it.

"You know girlfriend," Vanessa says as I'm halfway through the door, "I bet we've said 'let's do lunch' a hundred times and we've never done it. We need to do it. Really."

"I'd love that," I say.

We hug, everyone calls goodbye at my back, and I'm on my way to St. Elizabeth's hospital.

Kathy, who I first met when she was going by the name of Bethany, is in intensive care and asking for me.

Chapter 59

"I don't know what I'm going to do. I love her so much."

Jeff is sobbing, his face in his hands. We're sitting at a forty-five degree angle in the family waiting room of the ICU at St. Elizabeth's. A 911 call came in at five in the morning. Kathy was found in an alley, just outside the backdoor of a biker bar. Raped—presumably—and beat to a bloody pulp. I can barely recognize her pretty features. Nose broken in three places. Broken jaw. The emergency room doctor wasn't sure, but he thought she might have a detached retina. Blood alcohol levels high enough to have drunk herself into a coma or even to death. She was in trouble even if some Neanderthal hadn't decided to make her his punching bag.

"I'm so sorry, Jeff."

He looks up at me, snot smeared in his neatly trimmed mustache and beard. His eyes are rimmed and red and puffy.

"What do I do?"

"I don't honestly know, but you're here right now and that's the best thing in the world a man can do for his wife in a moment like this."

"Do I stay with her?"

"You're here now, so I'm guessing the answer is yes. You're going to do all you can to hang in there with her."

"I screwed up driving you out of her life. You were so good for her."

"Jeff, I barely knew Kathy. For all intents and purposes, we had one major conversation in our entire lives—and you were there for most of it."

"Something about you rang true with her."

"Despite the fact that I was lying to her about why I was at AA?"

He actually laughed and snorted a snot bubble at that. He didn't look particularly lawyerly at that moment.

"Yeah, despite the fact that you helped her under false pretenses. I'll drop the lawsuit tomorrow," he says with a shake of his head. "But I need your help."

"Jeff, drop the suit if it's the right thing to do. But you can't attach strings to it. I don't know if I can be there for Kathy."

"I'll drop the suit against the church, the city, the police department, and you—because it's the right thing to do. I'll also keep tearing up the checks you send me for that bucket of bolts you drive because that's the right thing, too. All I'll ask is that you consider being a friend and sponsor to Kathy."

"Jeff, you do realize that I'm not really an alcoholic?"

"Yeah, but somehow, someway, you're a wonderful mess, too."

We both laugh. Then he starts to cry again.

"I met Kathy at Northwestern. I was a senior, she was a freshman. I was so ready to get married. Maybe she wasn't. But she came from modest means. My family's loaded, so she loved the life I offered her. I stuck around three years for law school. She got her English degree and a teaching minor. She never went into the classroom. Might have been good for her. Her background was strict and I think she'd had a total of three beers and one joint when I met her—don't arrest her for the joint. I was a party animal but I never had a problem compartmentalizing my weekends from my work week. I swear she didn't touch anything for the first couple years, but once she started drinking, it was different for her. I didn't pay much attention because I just figured she was finally getting to sew her wild oats.

"My folks slammed the booze pretty good, too, so I was used to it. They weren't bad people. Anyway, I moved up to associate partner in my firm pretty fast, so I wasn't going to risk that with anything illegal, although we did toke a few from time to time. I just thought we were having a great time. About the time I figured she was out of control ... well, she was out of control and there wasn't much I could do about it. And I know this sounds corny but I was just crazy in love with her and figured everything would work itself out.

"We hit it hard over the holidays and then she just went off the deep end in the spring. Like I said, I'd always thought we were just having a good time."

"You sure about that?"

"I know the answer is no, but really, we did have some fun."

"So what went wrong in the spring?"

"Things were probably never as right or good as I remember them in my head. But things definitely went south in a big way when her dad died. She was a daddy's girl growing up and then they drifted apart and when he passed on, I think she got hit with a wave of guilt and remorse. They hadn't got along for awhile and they never got things worked out."

I don't say anything. I just wait him out, just like they taught me in cop school. Most people can't handle silence, so they talk. As Don says, I'm the master of the awkward silence. But with Jeff right now, silence feels just fine. Comfortable.

"It's a tough thing losing a dad like that. My parents are both alive, so I can only imagine what she was feeling. I should have taken some time off just to be with her. I've always worked too much."

"You don't have to apologize for working hard," I say. "I've seen a lot worse habits from husbands in my time on the force. And that's just the cops. You should see the bad guys."

He gives a half-hearted laugh.

"I'm not sure I'm buying that your partying was as innocent as you say. Sounds like something you need to think about for yourself, too."

"I'm thinking, Detective, I'm thinking."

We talk some more. We motion for an investigating officer to come over and the three of us cover some incredibly uncomfortable questions that may or may not help with finding who messed Kathy up. My guess is Jeff won't be much help. Any answers will come from finding and talking to everyone who was in the Sexy Hog last night. No easy task.

I walk back into Kathy's room with Jeff. She wakes up and looks up at me. Her eyes are filled with tears as I hug her. I pull back and hug her again and kiss her forehead. I whisper the serenity prayer in her ear. She opens her eyes as I finish. I tell her I love her. I tell her that Jeff is here for her and to let him love her. I don't know if she hears me or not. Her eyes close and she is asleep again.

Jeff walks me outside the door and offers to escort me down to the lobby. I decline and tell him to stay close to Kathy.

"So what do I do?" he asks, dried tears streaking his face.

"Just do what you're doing now. Be here for her."

"Can she get better?"

"Yeah, I think so," I answer. "She's got a good man who loves her. That's a heck of a start."

It must be nice I think as my heels click down the long tiled hallway. I wonder how obvious it is to the rest of the world what a wonderful mess I am.

Chapter 60

I'm sorry, Klarissa, but I just can't break free tonight. You know how bad it is right now."

"You're there for the drunk."

"Klarissa, be nice and please don't call her that. She needs me right now."

"Who says I don't need you?"

"Do you?"

"Does it matter? Hey, I don't have to beg to get a dinner date. So please, don't go out of your way for your sister. I guess booze is thicker than blood."

"Is this still about Warren?"

I shouldn't have asked that but her calling Kathy 'the drunk' made me a little mad. There is a pregnant pause on the line.

"I cannot believe you just said that," she says, barely controlling her anger. "When have I once mentioned that my breakup with Warren is a problem? Give me one example. Now you and Kaylen and Mom talking about it is another issue. Behind my back I would add!"

"Don't bark at me, Klarissa. The fact that you haven't mentioned him has made me figure you're having a tougher time with the break up than you admit. I wasn't trying to make this into a big biggie."

"I am not barking," she barks at me. "You just don't listen. No wonder you're having a tough time being a detective these days."

"I'm not listening to that crap," I storm back.

"You don't listen to anything I've been trying to tell you for four months now."

I'm going to let her have it with both barrels, but she's hung up on me. I can't believe she just said that and that she just did that. What a week. It's Friday afternoon. I was in a hospital room last Sunday with Kathy. I made it home for fifteen minutes. I was at the scene of a murder half an hour later. Victim number four. Stefani Allen. Forty. Single. An attorney, specializing in intellectual property rights, specifically scientific patents. A very posh condo with a lake view.

Two more of Chicago's finest are on the case. Our team has interviewed all 737 people who live in the 412 condos in Stefani's building. Plus another 189 maids, security guards, salespersons, maintenance workers, delivery truck drivers, and anyone else who has consistent contact with her building. The city would shut down without our large illegal immigrant population, so getting to everyone who has access to the Marina Palace is impossible.

No one can remember seeing anything out of the ordinary. Stefani did use her ATM card the night the coroner says she was killed, and from that we have been able to trace, she was on a three bar crawl. Problem is that no one remembers her leaving the third bar. So she might have hit one more spot where she met the Cutter Shark or maybe she left from there with him. We've checked security cameras but they're limited to the back hall leading to the public restrooms. We've been working with the bar management to identify and visit everyone that showed up on the camera as well as everyone who used a credit card. We've also canvassed every bar in a three mile radius with her picture in hand. No luck so far.

The press is having a field day. The ChiTownBlogger is now officially a rock star. Zaworski rattled the cages of the powers that be after the Saturday morning meeting at FBI Command Center in the State Building. Our entire task force now has updated and notably unexpurgated notebooks from Virgil. The FBI didn't bother to highlight what they had taken out in the abridged editions they gave us, so it's almost like reading the notebooks for the first time. Willingham said that is probably a good thing. He would.

I went to lunch with Vanessa earlier today. We had a nice time. But there's a reason we've promised to get together and never done so until now. Both of us are swamped in our personal and professional lives—and we really don't have that girlfriend chemistry thing going on, no matter how many times she calls me girlfriend. We talked the whole ninety minutes, but it was hard work.

She made reservations at Oceanique—very chic and expensive. I felt out of place in my off the rack ensemble and comfortable Eccos. She insisted on picking up the bill because it was almost a hundred bucks for lunch. Good thing. Out of my price range. I'm not a big fish lover, but the sea bass with some kind of chutney relish was out of this world. I could get used to fine dining.

I've experienced it more in the past month than in the previous year, I think. I wasn't going to, but I did end up going out with Reynolds again—twice. Once for an early power breakfast in the lobby restaurant of the Hotel Intercontinental on Michigan Avenue, which is pretty close to the State Building where we had a meeting. The second was for dinner at Sushi Para II in Lincoln Park. Very nice. Very expensive. Again.

I've got to cancel dinner tonight."

It's four thirty and my eyes are bleary from looking through notebooks. Maybe I can call Klarissa and reschedule dinner with her. Other than the outburst a couple hours ago, we've been getting along so much better. I want to keep it going. I don't care that she trashed my ability as a detective. Okay, I do care.

"Hunkering down with Willingham and the Ice Queen?" I ask Austin.

"Funny how I know just who you're talking about," he says with a laugh. "Actually I've been hunkered down with those two for a couple hours over here. Something's come up from one of the other cases. I'm catching the seven o'clock United flight to Denver and a car is picking me up in twenty minutes."

"Do you keep a toothbrush packed?"

"Yes, I do. Plus clean underwear and a fresh dress shirt and tie."

"Let me guess on the shirt. White button down Oxford."

"Lucky guess."

"No guesswork. It's the only kind of shirt I've seen you wear and I am a detective you know. So what's up in Denver?"

"I sense you're detecting right now and you need to know that I've been trained to withstand torture, including time on the Chinese water board, so you're not getting any information out of me."

"Really? The FBI teaches you to withstand torture?"

"Not the FBI. I may have forgotten to mention that I was in Special Ops before I joined the Firm."

"I'm used to you and your colleagues leaving vital information out so this little bit of personal data shouldn't come as a surprise."

"Sorry. I've lived on a 'need to know' basis too long and it's permeated my entire life. If it makes you any happier, my mom isn't very happy with me either."

"So you have a mom? I thought to be in the FBI you had to be hatched."

"Believe me, if they get any better at this test tube cloning thing, all future agents will be."

"So what's going on in Denver?"

"Actually, I'm going to brief the whole task force when I get back. I'm not stopping in Denver. There's a private jet waiting for me at a small private airport on the other side of the city and I'm going to connect down to Durango."

"Isn't that where all the UFO sightings take place?"

"Yep. And there's a few things that suggest it might be the home base of our killer."

We hang up. My mind—and stomach—immediately start churning.

Single. Professional. Smart. Unconnected. No, that's just too bizarre. That could not be. I would never live it down if it was.

Klarissa is mad or on-air because she won't pick up. I should go over and see Mom. I'm thinking I'll make another stop on the way over to see her. I know one person who has a base of operations in Durango.

Chapter 61

"Absolutely not," Zaworski says to me.

"Boss, I was just giving you a heads up. It's probably nothing. If it's something, I can handle it myself or call the team then. I don't want to mess up everybody's Friday night plans on a whim."

"Let's be clear," he says. "This is a direct order. Stand down. Pick a location within a mile of the destination. Support personnel will be thirty minutes behind you. You can then make contact with appropriate backup."

"Can I at least drive by and see if his car is in the driveway?"

"Negative."

Oh boy. I called Zaworski to let him know about Reynolds' travel plans to Durango and the fact that Dell, a high end drifter with no family or social bonds, has a home near there in Colorado. I can't remember if his place is in Durango city limits or if it's in an unincorporated area outside of town. He told me one of those two things once but I can't remember now.

In this next hour, I can foresee two embarrassing scenarios playing out. One is if Dell is the Cutter Shark. How bad would that be for me? Ace detective dates the man she is supposed to be hunting. I can see the headlines: She Never Suspected a Thing

I just can't believe Dell is connected to this, but it is eerie how well he fits the profile of a serial killer—all the way to the fact that he is someone you would never suspect. And what about that harsh phone message he left? He sounded threatening and ominous that day.

But there's another embarrassing scenario. Just like the takedown of Jonathan at the St. Bart's AA meeting, what if Dell is innocent? I'm going to look like the boy who cried wolf all over again. That's why I'm trying not to cry wolf. I was going to just drop by and say hi and get a feel for things. Then I realized I better call the captain. I might as well have walked into a crowded theater and shouted, "Fire!"

Dell's car is parked on the street. It has a couple tickets on it, which is strange. I walk up the stairs to his first floor town home with street access on Lake Shore Drive. Overall, a very nice place in a very nice neighborhood. The only furniture Dell owns is in Durango—at least that's what he's told me—so he gets stuff from a rental center every time he moves to a new city. I shudder at the thought that he could be our killer.

I've got a wire on; Zaworski sent a techie over to outfit me. I politely demurred but rank has its privileges, one of which is to tell me what to do.

I pause on the landing before ringing Dell's doorbell. The tickets on his windshield jump out at me as very weird again. I get a wave of nausea. He wouldn't have done something to himself over my breaking up with him, would he? Surely my imagination is just running a little wild isn't it?

Don, the techie, Blackshear, and Martinez are in an unmarked sedan a couple houses away. If Dell so much as sneezes wrong, there are going to be three serious men breaking his door down, and a techie is going to be calling the Navy, Air Force, and Marines for support.

I can take care of myself though. I have the Beretta in a holster on the small of my back but also have a knife sheathed on the side of my ankle. I know Dell is not the Cutter Shark but a rough paraphrase crosses my mind: live by the knife; die by the knife.

Zaworski, I think sensing my unease that Dell probably isn't a real suspect, has decided not to call the FBI. He hasn't said anything out loud, but I think everyone in this little operation knows what the rules are. If we take down a bad guy, the techie will send an all points call out, and we'll just say we didn't have time to include anyone else before we got there. If Dell is the nice, God-fearing, church going, Amish-loving—though isolated— man that I think he is, no one says anything to anybody at any time. This will never have happened.

I ring the doorbell. I don't hear footsteps. My heart starts to race a little. I breathe deeply to get everything under control. If he's here and he's guilty or innocent, I need to look natural. I wait fifteen seconds—I know because I count them off with Mississippis in the middle—and ring it again. There are about ten newspapers on the stoop, some of them already turning yellow. Some sales flyers are crammed inside the screen door. Nothing. Ten seconds go by this time, and I open the screen and knock hard. The door creaks open. My heart is pounding.

"What's happening?" Don asks into my ear plug.

"Door was open. I'm going in."

"Don't do it," Don hisses. "Anything you find in there would be tainted evidence for a jury trial."

I ring the doorbell a couple more times and then retreat to the car. Martinez is on the phone with Zaworski.

"Yeah, car's here, but we don't think it's been moved for a while," he's saying. "It's got a couple tickets on it. Newspapers are piling up on the front porch. Conner just looked in the mail slot and the front hallway is filled with letters and junk mail."

He listens.

"No. She didn't do anything to open the door. She just knocked and it opened a little bit. No one's gone inside, Boss."

Another pause while Zaworski gives him orders.

"We'll sit tight Captain."

He explains that Zaworski is getting a search warrant from a judge. If Dell is the Cutter Shark—or is guilty of any other crimes—we aren't going to do anything to jeopardize a righteous conviction.

I'm sorry Mom. Honest, I was looking forward to coming over and being together, just you and me. It's this da—this darn case."

"Are you okay?"

"I am."

"I miss your smile."

"It's been a hard couple months. For all of us. It's getting better. I'm even getting along with Klarissa."

"That's not what she told me an hour ago."

"We had one little fight. It was nothing. I tried calling her back."

"Have you talked to Dell lately? I worry about him. He seems like a lost soul to me. I think our family was good for him."

"Believe it or not, I tried getting a hold of him tonight. He wasn't there. Look Mom, I'm pulling into my parking lot, I've got to get some things out of the car, so I'm going to sign off. But I'm coming by tomorrow for lunch. Just the two of us. We'll talk. I swear."

"Well, if you're not here by noon, I'm going to come find you wherever you are. I still have contacts on the force, you know."

We laugh.

"Love you, Mom."

"I love you Baby Girl. And Kristen … be careful."

"You got it."

"I mean it. Be careful. I couldn't stand the thought of something happening to you."

I hang up before she can start crying and pull into a good spot near the stairs to my walk up. I turn off the engine. I just sit and look at a brilliant full moon. I sigh and shake my head. I rub my temples. I can't believe it. Dell is gone. The furniture's still in his apartment and apparently everything from his car—rented, of course—to furniture and utilities, is paid for through the end of August. Does he plan to come back and have everything picked up? Otherwise, every stitch of clothing, every book, every knickknack, his toiletries, cleaning supplies, linens, plates—anything that was a personal item—has been cleared out. The place is dusty now, but when he left, he or someone cleaned the place thoroughly. Top to bottom. Everything. When the full tech crew got there, they weren't sure they were going to find any evidence of a human presence.

"This guy even vacuumed the traps in all the sinks," Jerome tells me. "That's a sure sign of someone with an obsessive compulsive disorder—or something to hide. I'm not a detective but I suspect the latter."

"Thanks for the tip, Jerome."

He and Bruce, who I've now been with at four murder scenes, were called in to maintain consistency on examining any evidence that might be tied to the Cutter Shark case. They are apparently on the same bowling team because they had matching shirts with their respective names stitched on the chest and both were still wearing bowling shoes. They must be good bowlers because those weren't rentals. As an ace detective, I detect things like this.

We knocked on every door up and down the street. We've discovered two things. First, Dell didn't know his neighbors. Second, his neighbors didn't know him. No one can definitively say whether they even saw him in the previous month, but some are quite certain they have never seen him. There's Chicago not being very neighborly again.

I supplied his work number and through some calls back at the office, we got the number of the person who issued a freelance contract to Dell and who is his project liaison at Goff & Duncan, the manufacturing company he is consulting for. Blackshear finally located the guy at an engagement party for his niece and he wasn't happy that two uniformed officers showed up and insisted that our investigation was a higher priority than a family celebration. They impressed on him the importance of being a good citizen and he got busy helping us understand Dell's business arrangement.

About a month ago, the guy's not sure the exact date and is on his way to the office tomorrow to check, Dell exercised his out clause. He handed the liaison a final invoice with instructions to send his last expense and fee payments to a drop box with a bank in Durango. He had cleared out his temporary office and was off premises two business days later. His work was exceptional from start to finish and the guy hated to see him go.

Why didn't I at least call Dell and talk things through a little more?

I unbuckle my seatbelt, push open my door, slide my legs outside the car and stand up and feel a gentle summer breeze, even though summer doesn't officially start until June 21 and this is the last day of May. It's now in the eighties during the day, but it's probably seventy-five degrees right now and it feels great. I push my door shut.

I feel an explosion on the left side of my body as someone slams a fist into my kidney. I throw up in my mouth as I go down like a rag doll.

Someone whispers, "don't even think you can get away messing with my life," in my ear before I pass out in a swirl of dark, all-encompassing pain.

The Month of June

It is dry, hazy June weather.
We are more of the earth,
farther from heaven these days.
Henry David Thoreau

Chapter 62

I lifted my head slowly. I was laying in a small bed but had no clue where I was at or what my situation was. A light shone through a crack under the door. My instinct was to call out and find out what I was up against. But I didn't want to alert my captor or captors that I was awake, so I kept my breathing as slow and quiet as possible.

I began taking stock. First, I moved my fingers and toes. Check. All present and accounted for, even if they felt slow and unresponsive. Drugged. I rolled my neck back and forth. Everything worked but there was a group of renegade dwarfs swinging pick axes on the inside of my cranium. I thought they were singing "Hi ho, hi ho, it's off to work we go," at the top of their lungs. Maybe not, but it sure felt like it.

I lifted one arm and then the other. I wasn't restrained. I knew that was a big mistake on someone's part. Just because some gorilla can punch like a heavyweight boxer when I'm not looking doesn't mean he is going to withstand a quick shot to the trachea if I get even half a chance. I clenched and unclenched my fists to get the blood circulating. I began practicing a couple of attack moves in my head.

I heard footsteps outside my door. I barely breathed. I was pretty sure there were at least two sets of shoes on hard flooring. Not what I wanted to hear. That was going to make escape more challenging than I was hoping for. I quickly started thinking of drills and strategies for neutralizing two opponents.

The door swung open. One of my assailants moved on me with a cat-like quickness while the other turned on the light to blind me. I was as ready as I was ever going to be. I was already moving before he reached the bed and drove the heel of my hand in the direction of his face with the simplest karate punch in the book. He twisted his head sideways and got his forearm up to partially block my punch in a trained move, but I knew I still landed a decent blow that did more than graze his cheek. I was hoping to catch him on the bridge of his nose, which would probably immobilize him.

I spun up and off the bed ready to kick and throw another punch. I aimed at his groin and throat. But I was lightheaded from the sudden change of positions—and something else, I realized I really had been drugged—and my movements were too slow. A pair of muscled arms from my second attacker wrapped me up tightly from behind. I kicked up and backward and heard a heavy grunt. I got him in the groin but not good enough because he held on, cursing in English and Spanish. He pushed me back down on the bed and brought his weight to bear on me. I snapped my head back and might have caught him on the eye but I couldn't get free.

I'm sitting up in bed drinking a glass of water. A tray with a bowl of untouched chicken noodle soup is on the tray next to me.

Don is sitting across from me, an icepack on his left cheekbone. Zaworski is standing by the door shaking his head and trying not to smile. If he keeps this up I'll think of him as Mr. Chuckles. Martinez is sitting on the other side of the bed. He has an icepack on his lap. Enough said.

"*No nos pagan lo suficiente paraeste tipo de trabajo,*" Antonio says to me with a weak smile.

"What's that mean?" I ask him.

"I can answer that," Don interrupts. "'We don't get paid enough to do this job,' and for the record, I think I agree with him on this one."

Zaworski walks back over to my bedside.

"Kristen, now that your head is clearing a little, you're sure you don't know who it was then?" he asks again. He for sure is suppressing a smile now.

"I can't say with any degree of confidence, sir," I answer.

"You didn't get a look at his face? Not even a glimpse?" Martinez asks.

"I never saw him coming."

"You didn't recognize his voice?" Don asks.

"I didn't."

"Was he disguising it?" Zaworski asks.

"Possibly, but I'm not sure it mattered. I was fading fast when he spoke. And he whispered."

"What did he say again?" Don asks.

"Something about not getting away with messing up his life."

"So it's possible it's this Dell guy?" Zaworski asks.

"I know he was angry with me. We dated off and on for almost six months. He did all the work and all the pursuing. He just wasn't going to accept that I didn't have feelings for him. Then he saw me out with Reynolds last Saturday."

The three men say nothing and try not to look surprised by my admission about Reynolds.

"He's got to be the guy," Martinez says with enthusiasm and then immediately winces from the movement.

"I don't know," I say. "First of all, I have never seen any evidence of violence in Dell. Really, he's a gentle soul."

"But you said yourself you never really got to know him," Don says. "Heck, I'm your partner and I don't remember you talking about him more than two or three times."

"Yeah," I agree, "but you know my family. They were great to him. I think he was in love with them and I just happened to be his access."

"So why don't you like him for doing this?" Zaworski asks, puzzled. "He seems perfect. He was a little obsessed with you it sounds like, so he definitely has the motive."

"Well, for one thing," I answer, "I'm just not sure Dell could hit as hard as this guy did. I've never been punched like that. I'm not saying Dell didn't work out and was weak or anything. I'm saying this guy knew how to punch."

"But you don't got no meat on you, girl," Martinez says. "And who stands up to a well placed kidney shot?"

"I could have had a spare tire and the result would have been the same.

Martinez, you would have gone down same as me."

"That's not saying much," Don says with a wicked smile.

"You want see how easy it is to take me down, amigo?" Martinez challenges back at Don.

"Ladies, not now," Zaworski says, cutting them off. "Kristen, can you think of anyone else? No other enemies or scorned lovers?"

"He wasn't a lover," I say with a sternness that backs off even the captain. "If you don't count my family or Internal Affairs and someone in the office who writes me nasty Post-it Notes, I really can't think of anyone else that is mad at me right now. If things hadn't got fixed with Jeff and Kathy that might have been a lead. But no, I'm flying below the radar these days."

"Think, Kristen," Zaworski says. "Because if you can't come up with somebody else, I'm going to assume it's this Woods guy."

"What about the punk we collared a couple months back?" Don asks, looking at me. "Hard last name, Polish or Russian or maybe even Italian. Pepperoni. Something like that."

"The punk?" Zaworski says.

"Oh, the punk," I say. Then I think and continue, "couldn't be him. He's locked up."

Zaworski and Squires look at each other.

"What?" I ask.

Don smacks his hand on his forehead and says, "he got cut loose. I was supposed to tell you. A big bureaucratic snafu. He got in line and gave somebody else's name and walked out of Cook County Jail."

Zaworski gives him a hard look. Don is not happy with himself for forgetting to forewarn me. I'm not happy with him either.

"You're telling me a murderer just walked out the front gates of our judicial system?" I ask. I'm stunned. I feel sick to my stomach.

Don is picking at imaginary lint again. I've never seen Zaworski look so uncomfortable. I am suddenly mad and want to let someone have it. I count to ten and take a couple deep breaths. I begin to feel incredibly tired. Too tired to stay angry.

"Guys, I can barely keep my eyes open," I say. "But I don't think it was Jared Incaviglia. Now he was tough I'll admit. But I don't think he weighed 170 pounds. I don't think he could generate the power this guy had."

"Well, we're going to let you catch some sleep and get rested up. You think of anything or anybody, you call me directly," Zaworski, orders.

Before they have a chance to exit, Big Tony Scalia comes through the door and beelines over to my side.

"I promised your daddy I'd look after you and I'm doing a crummy job of it," he says, giving me a gentle hug around the neck and smoothing my hair down.

He turns to look at Don and then at Martinez and starts roaring in laughter. Zaworski, who I've seen smile maybe two or three times in the couple years I've worked under him, joins Tony. Don rolls his eyes. Martinez still looks a little glazed.

"I guess you can take pretty good care of yourself," Scalia says, fighting back laughter.

Don and Martinez are not amused.

"You all got anything on the attacker?" he says to the three men present.

"Well, maybe this Woods guy or maybe the purse snatcher with a knife Kristen put down a couple months back," Zaworski says. "But she doesn't think either could punch like the guy who got her."

"Hey, I got a call from Soto," Tony says to me. "He wondered about that guy he had working for him in the training room. Says he really had it in for you."

"Timmy," I respond with my eyes half open. "In fact, a lot more likely than Dell."

"We got a name?" Zaworski asks Scalia. "If so, let's get an APB out and bring him in for questioning."

"Already done. We used his last known alias, Timmy Sullivan. Sure would help to have his real name but we've got some investigators working on it." He turns toward me and continues, "by the way, Soto is on his way down here. He swears he's going to kill Timmy or whoever it is that did this with his bare hands. He's also not happy with someone in this room. He thinks she's not taking the personal threat of the Cutter Shark case seriously enough and is being way too careless in how she moves so freely in our fair city."

"Any truth to that?" Zaworski asks.

Before I can answer more visitors arrive. Konkade and Blackshear enter the room first. Both come over and give me a pat on the shoulder. I'm waking up a little. Both look at Don and Martinez with incredulity. Konkade whispers something in the captain's ear. Zaworski looks up toward the door sharply. On cue, Willingham and Van Guten enter. This is getting interesting. I'm wide awake now.

Willingham ignores Zaworski and walks over to the side of my bed. He takes my hand and looks at me kindly. If Willingham hadn't decided to be an FBI bigwig, he would have made a great doctor. His bedside manner is impeccable.

"How are you doing Detective Conner?"

"Great, Sir, thank you for asking. In fact, I'm ready to go home now. All we're waiting for is the doctor's clearance."

Despite the ice packs—sure hope their ice machine is industrial strength—my side still aches dully. I was also still pissing a little blood as of fifteen minutes ago. Until there's no blood in the urine Dr. Singh is not letting me go home.

"Good," he says, giving my hand a reassuring squeeze.

He turns toward Zaworski. The two men lock eyes. I don't think either is willing to blink first. Van Guten breaks the impasse.

"Why don't you gentlemen clear the room and let our intrepid detective have some privacy. You can run your task force meeting out in the hall."

"Good counsel, Leslie," Willingham says. "However, I think Captain Zaworski and I might have a private conversation in my car. Can you get a ride home?"

"No problem. I'll catch a cab, Sir," she says.

She gives Don, who is now standing, a playful but firm nudge toward the door. Everyone but Leslie begins to shuffle out. I notice that Don has ditched his ice pack, probably in the foolish hope that everyone will forget I got a pretty clean shot on his face. His dark skin might hide discoloration—but he's already got a golf ball sized swelling on the side of his face.

Martinez isn't letting go of his ice pack. He seems to be taking what I thought was a counterattack more in stride than Don. He moves gingerly as he follows the others out of the room. With the men gone, Dr. Leslie Van Guten closes the door and walks over to me. She looks at me without saying anything for a moment. I feel like a bug under a microscope.

"So what was my ex-husband working on tonight?"

"Come again," I answer, confused.

"In Durango."

"I have no idea what you're …"

The words come out of my mouth and then my voice just stops as realization dawns. My head is spinning. I'm sure it's the reaction she was hoping for. She is now looking at me with detached amusement.

"I guess he didn't mention that to you. Typical Austin. What I want to know is why he's in Colorado?"

"You're the Mensa member, why are you asking me?"

"Clever," she deadpans. "Let's just say the director and I are not absolutely sold on the way Major Reynolds is conducting this entire investigation and he's not keeping the chain of command as appraised to everything as he should."

I say nothing. She just looks at me, I guess to see if the uncomfortable pause will coax me into blabbing. Not going to happen. Everyone's been trying that one on me lately. Plus I'm mad and I'm not saying anything. My eyes are also fluttering a little from fatigue. I'm basically shut down and she realizes it. She turns and leaves without another word.

She could learn something from Willingham's bedside manner.

Chapter 63

Y ou're staying with us," Kaylen says. "There is no way you're staying here by yourself."

Kaylen, Klarissa, my mom, and me are at my kitchen table. It's eleven on Saturday morning. I got cleared by the hospital to leave two hours ago. Don and Martinez, fortunately two good sports who don't hold grudges, drove me home. Vanessa was already at my place when we arrived and had brought flowers, stocked my fridge, and done some clean up, including a couple loads of laundry. I was thankful beyond belief that the place was fairly clean before she got there, though I don't think I've ever vacuumed the traps on my sinks.

Vanessa also whipped up the most unbelievable coffee cake that she popped into the oven half an hour before I arrived home. Don called ahead. I am currently on my second piece with my mom and sisters. Even Klarissa, who eats less than any other human being not living in a famine stricken country has cleaned her plate. Granted, it was a small piece to begin with, but this still represents a breakthrough in my mind. I may have even caught her looking at the half eaten second piece on my plate with something other than disdain. Interest?

"She can come home and stay in her old room," Mom says.

Referring to me as "she" implies that perhaps she is not aware that I am in the room, three feet away from her. I've been up an hour and still have a summer weight nightgown on. My hair is pulled back in the default ponytail I wear when I'm out of time or too lazy to fix it otherwise. That would be almost all the time.

"Hey guys," I say, "I have two of Chicago's finest as my body guards. They're sitting in the parking lot right now. I'll be fine."

"Body guards? Are they cute?" Klarissa asks.

"Think they want something to eat?" Mom asks. "We could take them a piece of Vanessa's breakfast cake and a cup of coffee."

"I'm not sure we're supposed to do that, Mom," I say, trying not to roll my eyes. "I think they want them to be as unobtrusive as possible. And Klarissa, we can go on a double date with them after this case is solved."

"And you're sure it wasn't the Cutter Shark who attacked you?" Kaylen interrupts with a shudder.

"Well, there's just no way to answer that," I answer, "because we have no way of knowing who he is. I think my attacker might be a guy named Timmy—at least that's what we think his name is—who was one of the trainers at CPD for a month or two. He was working for Barry Soto."

"And Barry didn't know this guy was trouble?" Mom asked. "I always thought Barry was sharp. He must be slipping if he let a murderer work for him."

"Mom, I didn't say that this Timmy is the Cutter Shark or even that he attacked me. This could be a random attack, which is doubtful, but there's at least a couple options we're exploring."

"If you've got colleagues attacking you," Klarissa says, "you must be a real bear to work with."

"Thanks Baby Sis," I say. "You know how to brighten my day."

She laughs and gives me a punch on the shoulder. I wince. Every movement still hurts. Even Klarissa's girl punch.

"Sorry," Klarissa says and then asks, "who else is an option?"

"I just can't say," I say. "Honestly, I'm not even going to speculate. I got no look at his face and he whispered when he spoke to me."

"That gives me the creeps," Klarissa says with a shudder.

I haven't been up long but am already ready for a nap. My family is wearing me out and it's obvious they are not going to leave me alone any time soon. That's sweet, I think. It's been tough sledding this spring and early summer—really the whole past year—so it's nice to have everyone close.

We finish the coffee and Kaylen pulls Scrabble out of her overnight bag. Okay. She sets up the board deliberately and wordlessly—I think to make sure I know that this is what we're going to do and there's not going to be any debates or jokes about it. Mom pours refills and when I get back from using the bathroom, I take the fourth chair at my kitchen table. Kaylen draws the A tile and gets to go first, which means an automatic double word score. She gets a cute little smile on her face and plays all seven tiles first move. Not only does she get a double score on a word with a Q in it, but she gets fifty points for playing all seven letters in one turn. Basically, none of us have a snowball's chance in Death Valley to win after she adds up 139 points. I think about suggesting that this is a sign that maybe we should watch a video or that everyone should go home and I should go to bed.

"Oh dear," Mom says. I think she's figured out that resistance is futile.

I open the little drawstring game bag and make everyone put their tiles back in. This time I shake it up extra good and we start over. I pull out a Y. Guess who gets her first turn last? Talk about a blast from the past. Scrabble with Mom and my sisters. Beats getting grilled about who my attacker might be.

I look at my wall clock. It's four in the afternoon. I couldn't take any more excitement from Scrabble—and yes, Kaylen won again and again—so I fell asleep on my couch at about one o'clock. I feel groggy. But the vibration of my cell phone has wakened me.

"Feeling better, honey?" Mom asks. "What can I get you?"

I look around. Kaylen and Klarissa are gone. It's just the two of us now.

"I could use a glass of water and another pain pill," I say.

Percocet—a witch's brew of oxycodone and acetaminophen—definitely makes pain management easy. When I was a uniformed officer, Percocet was becoming a real problem on our college campuses. I guess all you have to do is take one and chase it with Jack and you've got a major buzz for the whole evening. Kids were paying thirty or forty bucks per tablet.

"Is it time for your antibiotic, too?" she asks as she puts down a crossword puzzle book and gets up from the recliner to head for the kitchen.

I'm no longer thinking about pain pills. The vibration isn't from a call. Two text messages have popped up. The first is from Reynolds:

On my way back. Lots happening in Durango. Late dinner tonight? Carmines on Rush? I'm starved! I want 2c u!

I want to text back that he is no longer on a "need to know" basis with my dinner plans and that he probably needs to touch bases on developments in Chicago with his ex-wife when he lands. I delete it and go to the next message instead. It's from Don. I'm surprised. I didn't think he could text with his fat thumbs. I read it and my heart sinks:

Our friend strikes again. Another body found. Sit tight and get better. I'll call u later w the details.

In your dreams, I say to Don in my mind.

"Mom, can you make me a sandwich?"

"Sure honey. Go sit down and I'll bring it over to you."

"Better wrap it. I've got to take a shower and get rolling."

"What? Tell me you're not serious. Kristen, no."

I poke my head out my bedroom door and look her in the eyes. "Our guy has struck again."

She shakes her head and sits down on one of the kitchen chairs, tears in her eyes.

"Why do people have to be so hurtful?"

I walk over and give her a careful hug. Not for her benefit—she's fine—but I'm still aching from the punch to my kidneys and then hitting the ground like a rag doll. I gently touch a scrape on my forehead that has scabbed over. It's in the same spot where Daniel whapped me in the head with an oversized whiffle ball. I've been known to pick scabs in days gone by so I've got to leave this alone or I'm going to make a permanent red mark on the top center of my forehead.

"I don't know, Mom. But I'm going to put this guy in a place where he can't do any more harm. I promise."

She cries and I give her another quick hug and a kiss on the top of her head. Then I break away and head for the shower. I call Dispatch first, identify myself, and tell them I need the address of the latest murder repeated.

I wipe mayonnaise off the corner of my mouth with my sleeve. Glad Mom didn't see that. She's already very unhappy with me. I walk straight to the unmarked police car where the two officers assigned to guard detail are sitting. They're out of the car before I get there.

"Yes ma'am?" a kid with a buzz cut and acne says.

Ma'am? That hurts worse than a kidney punch.

"I'm heading over to the crime scene. You all going to stay here and watch my apartment or come along and keep an eye me?"

The two officers look at each other, both hoping the other knows the right answer. Their instructions are that no one enters or even gets near my place without clearance. They're not sure if that includes me since the assumption was I wouldn't be going anywhere anytime soon.

"I think we need to call it in, ma'am," the buzz cut says.

"Well, while you do, I'm going to be driving over there. Stay or come. Your call. But if you do stay, my mom will be leaving in few minutes and she is authorized to move freely."

The young men look at each other and shrug. The second one speaks for both of them and says, "we'll follow you."

I nearly go airborne over the speed bump halfway around the circle drive in front of my apartment. Ouch. Bad move. That hurt. They follow close and bounce out of the parking lot right behind me. I pound through the gears and drive fast through city traffic on my way to the toll road. I run at least four yellow lights, so I don't know how the heck they keep up with me.

I've got an EZ-Pass on my windshield for the toll booths, but as I enter the highway, already doing sixty-five, I think I pass through the automated lane too fast for the camera to scan the barcode on it. I hear a loud buzzer behind me as I immediately cut across three open lanes, downshift into third and push the pedal hard with my foot to zip around two cars that are poking along, and then zip back across two of the lanes going the other direction while shifting into fourth and fifth in rapid succession. I am not going to let slow drivers get in my way as I head for the crime scene. I look in the rearview mirror. Buzz cut is doing a nice job of not losing me. He's kind of got that NASCAR look about him.

There's a rumble in my brain that's about as loud as the buzzer at the toll booth. Everything on me hurts, particularly at my temples and on the lower left side of my back. I should have taken two Percocets. I look down at my phone and see the red light is still flashing. I got to my text messages before hopping in the shower but didn't check to see if anyone had called. I scroll down and see that I have a missed call from a private number and that I have a voice message. I press down on the one key and listen. It's Dell.

"Kristen. I need to talk to you. You can't reach me so I'll call back later. I know I got out of town in a hurry and I'm sure my last message on your home phone freaked you out. I apologize. Sincerely. There's a few things about my life I never mentioned to you that have come up and that I have to deal with. I'm in a little bit of trouble right now. I know you probably hate me, but you're still the only one I can talk to. Keep your phone close, would you?"

Chapter 64
May 26, 4:30pm

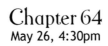

*A*bout time they showed up. *Slow pokes. Stupid slow pokes.*

He was not pleased. His recent work had not been up to his exacting standards.

I couldn't wait the whole month. Again. Things got messed up because of her and I had to hurry and find someone new. She does have a way of screwing things up. I don't like hurrying. This moment just doesn't feel as good as it should and that's not fair to me. Now I'm going to want to start early to get things right. Again. Totally not my fault. People mess with my plans and I mess with them.

He decided to make an exception. To start early.

Again.

The psychologist from the FBI would receive acclaim for her work on his story. He knew there might even be a Pulitzer awaiting her after she had analyzed this part of his career with all sorts of pejorative adjectives—

hurried, desperate, frantic, and the like. But she didn't know the truth. She relied on a pseudo-sophisticated veneer of academia rather than simple observation and understanding. He was too complex for her to put under her flawed microscope and understand. She couldn't possibly know how calm, cool, and collected he was. No, there was no sense of desperation or hurry to his measured movements.

She's probably telling the gang that I'm going too fast and that I'm on the verge of a mistake. She doesn't know me. But I know her. Not the FBI geek. I know my new object. I just hope nobody messes things up between us again or I'm going to get really mad this time.

Please note my use of the word, pejorative. Clothes and vocabulary make the man!

Chapter 65

Zaworski is waiting for me as I drive up. My babysitters called ahead, which I knew they would do.

"Who told you where we are?"

"I am a detective, Captain," I answer. "I detect for a living."

"Don't be a smart alec, Conner. I know it was Squires and I'm going to kick his ass on this. Plus him forgetting to tell you Incaviglia was out. Everyone had strict orders to leave you out of this one. I want you to get back in your car and drive home right now. You don't need to be here."

"Sorry, Captain, I'm not going to do it … And before you say it, I'm not leaving even if you give me a direct order."

We stare each other down, hands on hips, jaws set. Out of the corner of my eye I see a mob of journalists, photographers, and video cameramen hustling our way and clicking cameras. Zaworski does too, and backs down quickly to get us out of that particular line of fire.

"I knew you were going to be a pain in the ass," he says with a dull tone. "Let's move it."

He looks at my two bodyguards who have just walked up and says, "You have a new job. No one gets past the tape. And you don't leave until we do."

He lifts the crime scene barrier himself and nods for me to follow him.

I'm an hour behind Blackshear, Martinez, Konkade, Don, Big Tony, and a host of new FBI faces. Everyone on the perimeter—reporters, uniformed cops, spectators—follows Zaworski and me with their eyes and shouts questions as we walk up to the front door of a small ranch house with beat up aluminum siding. There are brown patches all over the yard and the shrubbery, which looks like it hasn't been trimmed in years, is growing in wild and grotesque shapes. The sidewalk is uneven and cracked and missing whole chunks of concrete. One of the downspouts broke free of its moorings and is hanging away from the eaves of the house, ready to fall in a twist of metal any day. One pane is missing an entire corner in one of the front windows. Tar paper shows through some areas of the roof with missing shingles. I take it all in.

Without turning my head, I say to Zaworski, "Dell Woods called and left me a message while I was sleeping."

He stops in his tracks in the doorway and looks at me.

"He says he's calling back. I figure you'll want to huddle the team and let them listen to his message."

"You got that right."

"And I'm guessing the FBI is going to patch into my cell line so they can triangulate his location when he calls back."

"How do you know he'll call back?"

"He said so in the message."

I hold up my hand before he can say anything else.

"I'm going to hand you my phone. If my mom or one of my sisters call, hit the green button to switch lines and tell them I'm fine so they won't worry. To listen to Dell's message all you have to do is hit and hold one and then hit one-one on the prompt. I don't use a pass code. Dell's is the only message saved. Push this button over here to put it on speaker phone. You gather the team to listen in together and give me thirty minutes to walk this crime scene alone. You all will know as much about Dell's most recent contact with me as I do at that point."

"Anything else Conner?"

"No sir, that will be it."

I know everyone is enthralled with crime scene investigation dramas. That's because they've never been to a crime scene. A quick camera shot of a dead body is one thing, but when you're actually there and have to take in real flesh and blood that has been traumatized with a knife or blunt force, the sights and smells of decomposition, then it's not so glamorous. I've watched the show set in Miami a couple times. Sure they put plenty of blue makeup on the corpses, but victims still tend to be beautiful. They're not at a real crime scene.

I don't know how Jerome and Bruce do it. Our two techies are working murder number five for us. They are putting items into clear bags and then writing notes on the bags with Sharpies. The Medical Examiner is leaving as I arrive. Once we give the green light, the body will go into a big black bag, which will be zipped up and taken to the morgue so the body can be seriously studied.

Grace Mills is the victim. Her background is a little different than the others. She doesn't have a professional job—she is waitressing at a cocktail lounge about ten minutes from her less than nine-hundred square foot house—and obviously, her place isn't nearly as nice inside or out as what the others lived in. Not the same zip code—literally.

I cover all the rooms in a slow and methodical walk through. When I get to her bedroom, I just stand at the door and watch the workers preparing to move her, trying to imagine the place with just her and him. I breathe slowly. I say a prayer. I have an impression. Of what? Frustration. Disappointment. Hurry. Resentmet. I try to hold onto the soft blurred image in my mind but then it's gone.

We met back at the State Building at seven p.m. Fifteen of us sat around a long conference table. Willingham was head of the family, with Zaworski right next to him. Reynolds arrived a few minutes late by helicopter. He sat at Willingham's left hand. I look at them. The holy trinity of the Cutter Shark murder investigation.

Van Guten had been sitting in the seat next to Willingham when the meeting started but left the room to answer a phone call. When she got back in, Reynolds had taken her chair. She gave him a decidedly dirty look and appeared less than thrilled to get stuck down at the other end of the table next to me. I glance at her several times out of the corner of my eye. How can anyone have such perfect finger nails? I can't stop stealing looks at them—honestly I don't think they're fake. I'm not sure if that's true of her chest but I'm going to stop being catty so I refuse to speculate on that matter any further. Her hair is perfect—she could walk away from this place and into any restaurant in the city fifteen minutes later—without stopping in the powder room—and fit right in. I've never wanted to win a beauty contest but I feel just a little self-conscious looking at my short-clipped nails. No polish. Maybe I'll get a manicure tomorrow.

We'd been going at it hard for ninety minutes. We spent the first thirty minutes on Dell. I got my phone back and was given explicit instructions to pick the thing up the second a private number calls in, no matter what time of day or night, whether awake or asleep. Three hours before I was being ordered to stay in my apartment and not move all weekend.

Reynolds confirmed that Dell's home has been linked to Cutter Shark activity. There's no sign of him being there recently and even though they've been tossing the place for almost twenty-four hours, they've found no direct evidence explicitly linking him to any of the crimes. Does that mean he might be innocent? Probably wishful thinking on my part.

I feel incredibly sad for him. And I'm very bothered by the fact that I could hang around with someone off and on for most of six months and never have a clue that there was something terribly wrong with him. Did I sense something? Anything? I did think his approach to me was off but never gave it extra thought. He isn't the first guy to get things all wrong with me. But is that why I never opened up to him? Or does it just mean I'm a lousy detective?

Right before we transitioned to the post mortem of the Grace Mills crime scene, my cell buzzed and sure enough it was a private number. Everyone in the room froze and my heart was racing as I hit the green answer button on my Nokia. It was my credit card company wanting to know if I wanted to try their identity theft protection plan free for a month with no obligation to buy. I thought it might be funny to ask a few questions about costs and benefits with everyone listening in, but Don's audible sighs and angst-ridden expression were helpful deterrents.

Willingham looked irritated. Not my fault, I wanted to say to him. Any thought of actually voicing such sentiment and defending myself was cut off by Zaworski's stern gaze. Has he been talking to Don? Reynolds was trying to make eye contact with me the whole time. It wasn't going to happen.

I've kept my mouth shut since explaining for the seventh time everything I know about Dell's call. How many times can you say you were asleep, he called, you didn't pick up, he left a message, and you listened to the message while driving over to a murder site?

A number of theories were espoused as to why the Cutter Shark picked Grace Mills. She wasn't really that less attractive than the other women and yes, she met the qualification of being single, but she definitely stood apart from the rest in her occupation and residence. She didn't show signs of illegal drug abuse but she definitely liked her alcohol. There were empty beer and whiskey bottles everywhere. Pabst Blue Ribbon and Jim Beam were her poisons of choice. There were enough cases of PBR stacked on one side of her garage that she could weather a couple years of famine, pestilence, and nuclear fallout without having to drive to the corner convenience store for a six pack. My guess was that the guy who owns the bar she works at, downstairs for questioning even as we spoke, is going to have a lot less beer missing from his inventory in the years ahead.

Don started things off by asking if Grace's murderer was even the Cutter Shark or maybe a copycat killer instead. One of the FBI forensics experts got Bruce on the speaker phone and after about ten minutes of question and answer, the group was reasonably certain that this was the work of the original and only known serial killer currently at large and active in Chicago land.

Konkade chalked up the Cutter Shark going for a drunk slob—his phrase, not mine—rather than a sophisticated lady to the law of averages. If you go out with enough people, some of them are going to look better, have better habits, and generally be better off than others. Grace just happened to be on the very right edge of the murderer's Bell Curve as applied to victim selection.

That didn't really fuel a lot of discussion. Reynolds was flipping through notebooks the whole time to see if there was precedence. He was sure he remembered another woman who might be a little like Grace. He found the page he was looking for and it ended up that one of the Cutter Shark victims in Charleston, South Carolina, was almost as messy as Grace. But then the comparison broke down. She was actually a very successful artist who kept her studio in her home, which was on the U.S. Historical Register and worth a couple million dollars. She was also beautiful and from the pictures had good personal hygiene. She just kept a messy house.

Konkade argued that that just might prove his point; over time not only would the killer find women who were more or less messy, but he would also find some women who were richer and some women who were poorer. He still didn't have anyone convinced. He looked deflated.

Van Guten took over the conversation and discussed the Cutter Shark as a man in and out of a killing frenzy, not quite on top of his game, showing cracks in his veneer, and making mistakes. The only problem Willingham pointed out was that the guy really hadn't made any mistakes; at least none were immediately identifiable at his latest killing ground. He still hadn't left the proverbial calling card with his current address. Van Guten didn't like this response. I could see her swinging the toe on her high heeled right foot, higher and higher over her left-crossed leg.

The conversation ground to a halt and it looked like things were done for a Saturday night. I started organizing my papers into a neat pile.

"Conner, you haven't said anything. Why Grace?"

Willingham was looking at me intently. I snapped out of my reverie.

"Why Grace?" I asked rhetorically. "Why not another accountant or attorney or human resources director or media personality or studio artist? Why someone in a filthy little hovel when every other person had a ritzy place that was clean as a whistle?"

I wondered where that phrase came from. Why would anyone think a whistle was clean? I would think a whistle would be full of germs. I pinched myself because I had an idea and I'm usually not very good at responding on the spur of the moment. I forced myself to focus.

"I think his plans got messed up at the last minute," I said, "and he had to improvise. I think Grace was Plan B."

There was a silence in the room. Every eye was focused on me. I like creating awkward pauses for others, but hate them for myself. I wanted to explain my thought further or apologize for wasting everyone's time with such a stupid idea or let the group know that I had to get home and go to bed because I didn't feel well. Using all my willpower, I held my tongue and said nothing.

"Ding, ding, ding, ding, ding … I think we've got a winner," Willingham said, breaking the silence.

He dismissed us and set another meeting for ten the next morning. I looked at my watch. If I'm in bed in an hour, I thought, I can cop a whole twelve hours of recovery sleep. I need every second of it. I walked out of the conference room. My body guards were drinking coffee and looking at magazines in the reception area. I suddenly loved my body guards because they meant I could leave my car in the parking garage and get a ride home from them and then a ride back over here in the morning. I headed their way.

"Nice job, hot shot," Martinez said as he held the door for me.

"I've learned from the best," I answered him.

"And that would be me?" Don said, walking into the conversation.

Konkade, Blackshear, Big Tony, Zaworski, and Van Guten overheard and joined the circle to see how this would turn out. Reynolds was still back with Director Willingham.

"Tell them," I said to Tony.

"That's easy," he said to an interested audience. "Her daddy."

Good answer. We head our separate ways. One of these days I'm going to ask Scalia about his AA story and whether he really broke my dad's jaw.

Chapter 66

I call my mom from the back of the squad car on my way home. At the moment I like being chauffeured but I'm guessing it would drive me crazy over time. I can't stand when Don drives and I get shotgun. Mom went back to her house for a couple hours to pack some more things and feed the cat and is already back at my place. I tell her she doesn't have to spend the night, which makes her indignant and defensive. How dare I accuse her of not being a good and loving mother!

Kaylen is at my apartment, too. Mom tells me they've made my favorite chicken salad for me. Mom made me a quick ham and cheese sandwich earlier but I suddenly realize I am starving and chicken salad with golden raisins, fresh dill, walnuts, grapes, celery, and a little mayonnaise sounds wonderful. I ask about Danny and the kids and Kaylen gets on the phone to tell me that he is on his own. All he has to do is finish a sermon and get Daniel and Kendra to bed. I wonder how long it takes to write a sermon and practice it. I know how long it takes to get those two kids into bed. Kaylen tells me she isn't planning to go to church in the morning but is going to stay at my place and make sure I don't go anywhere for the rest of the weekend, even if she and Mom have to form a human barricade in front of my door. I decide not to tell her that I'll be back in the office at ten just yet. I now wish I had one of those rope ladders so I could make an easy escape in the morning.

As far as Kaylen asserting that she is going to miss church, I think I'm going to pass out from shock. I'm not sure she's ever missed church. When we were little kids, our Baptist church had a perfect attendance award system. You got a medallion for your first year with no Sunday misses, and then you got a gold bar that hung on tiny hooks from the medallion for subsequent years. She looked like a five star general when she wore hers. I never made buck private.

My cell does a sequence of beeps twice while we talk. I pull the phone from my ear and look each time to see if it is a private number that will end up going live with me and about a hundred FBI agents at the same time. It is Reynolds both times. I'm not taking his call. But if I do, it will be to let him make a fool of himself within earshot of his colleagues.

My cell starts beeping again. It's Don. I tell Kaylen I have to take it and that I'll see her in a few minutes.

"What's up, Don?"

"Just talked to Vanessa. Need a roommate tonight? She's already packed if you need her. She says I can get the kids ready for church all by myself tomorrow."

"I was going to say no, but the thought of you being a mommy makes me want to reconsider my first response."

"Hah hah. KC, consider it done. She'll be there in less than hour."

"Just kidding, Don. Tell her to sit tight. My mom and Kaylen already have dibs on the beds in my guest room. I'm calling Klarissa next and if she comes over she'll get half my bed. That would leave the couch for Vanessa. I wouldn't wish my couch on an enemy and I think Vanessa is wonderful."

"She's made dinner to bring over," he says. "Wouldn't have to spend the night."

"Tell her to leave now," I say with a laugh. "And tell her to bring her pajamas and a sleeping bag just in case."

"Done."

I love Kaylen's chicken salad. But Vanessa is a gourmet and I am taking a liking to fine dining. Don hangs up in a flash. I hold down the number four and Klarissa's cell starts chirping Beethoven's *Ode to Joy.* Her voice message comes up:

"You've reached Klarissa Conner, weather anchor at WCI-TV, Chicago's number one source for news. I can't come to the phone right now, but your call is important to me. Please leave your name, a detailed message, and the time you called. I will get back to you as soon as I can."

"Hey Klarissa, this is Kristen. Call when you get this. Better yet, just come over. It's slumber party night."

She wasn't very talkative at my apartment today, which now feels like a couple weeks ago. She's probably jealous of the attention I'm getting from Mom and Kaylen. She probably feels left out and she for sure feels I'm not listening to her. Okay, cool it, I tell myself. You two have been getting along fine. Better than fine. Better than ever. Don't get pissy now.

Dear God, help me keep positive momentum going with my sister. And please, please, please help us find this killer soon.

Chapter 67
June 6, 8:40pm

BOTTLE WASHED UP ON SHORE OF LAKE MICHIGAN...
...and told me the Cutter Shark Has Been a Bad
Bad Boy ... AGAIN!!!!
By ChiTownBlogger

> We're not even America's 2nd City anymore ... that honor goes 2 Los
Spangeles ... but ur ever vigilant, ever listening ChiTownBlogger—CTB
Numero Uno 2my throng of fans that make CTB-mania the only place 2b
in town—hears through the beat of the drum and the smoke of hilltop
fires that we r now the U.S. of Americos's official FBI Headquarters,
including a posh, contemporary yet classic new office 4a certain dashing
Deputy Director ... at an expense 2tax payers of one hundred and fifty
thousand clams. If ur gonna sit on ur ASS all day, Citizen Willingham,
u might as well b comfortable. How's the coffee service? Did u bring
a grinder along 4those fresh Jamaican Blue Mountain Coffee beans u
can't live without—or do u just use sharp utensils from the evidence
room ... LOL! (I so naughty! But u likey-likey-likey me!)

Now why would the Deputy Director of the FBI—and the world's #1 superhero in the war on terror—take up residence in our fair city ... why not just a hot shot Special Agent? Oh, u mean u've already got a couple of them here and they haven't found Jack? 2b fair Mr. Willingham, and Special Agent Reynolds (I know ur name ... I know ur name !!!) and Dr. Von Good One, it's not like ur gonna get a lot of help from the CPD, though our transit workers can probably slow the Cutter Shark down just like they do the rest of us if u get him in ur sights. Not likely. I heard he's been dating one of the lead officers. I hear she would have married him by now but she thinks he cuts up 2much! Hey, jk jk. LOL!

Who wrote a note and put it in bottle 4 little old CTB Numero Uno 2read? Was it Nicholas Sparks? If only it were so, I would b featured in a Hallmark Hall of Fame film destined 4the four dollar bin at Wal-Mart! My adoring Mongolian hordes would go crazy with glee! Alas, twasn't Literary Marvel Sparks. But still, wouldn't u like 2know, Mayor Daniels? Well whoever it was left a clue ... Even though I am not a trained law enforcement officer, I actually think I know what it means. He says and I quote: "Seasons change soon ... only time 4one more date ... maybe 2if the weather stays cool!"

ChiTownBlogger Hint of the Day: I think that means he's gonna kill a couple more people b4 the first day of summer. (Was i2 subtle 4our befuddled CPD keepers of the status quo? Probably. LOL!!!) Gee Deputy Director Willingham ... that's worth pouring another cup of coffee just 2sit back and consider things 4awhile! I bet the Queen Bee Shrink can write another meaningless journal article. Suggested title: cuts like a knife ... but it feels so right! Why? She has no feelings! LOL

Bon voyage and XOXOXO from ur favorite blogger! ChiTownBlogger is out! Can't wait 2read ur ever-cleaver responses. Oops! I've gotta start using spellcheck! I mean ever-clever responses, of course. The CTB board is open 4business like 7-11 ... 24hrs a day!

POSTERUNO gets a FIVE BUCK coupon @ MacDonalds. I'd go w the value menu. With Washington FAT CATS prowling our city, taxes r gonna go up up up and away. Sorry Ms. McCoo ... no beautiful balloon :o(

SHAZAM!
>

Chapter 68

"More company. Says she knows you. Want to come to the front door and verify?"

I hit the red button and put down my cell phone on the coffee table. I've got two new babysitters guarding me outside and Randy, at least I think his name is Randy, has just called. Mom, Kaylen, Klarissa, and Vanessa are in my living room to make sure I'm okay. I think they're spending the night. Mom's in my recliner, I'm laying on the couch, and my sisters and Vanessa are leaning against big cushions on the floor. I get up with a groan.

"I can go to the door for you, honey," Mom says.

"But you might not be able to identify who is there," I say to her.

I walk slowly to the front door and look out past a kid with a shaved head, not Randy—is this one's name Kirk?—in a neatly pressed dark blue uniform and shiny black shoes. He's got to be ex-military. You can usually tell. He can't be twenty years old, can he? Did he do Iraq? I'm still almost a year from turning thirty but I suddenly feel old. I look past him. It's Kathy. She has a splint on her nose and her face is bandaged. She looks worse than me by a long shot. I don't quite know what to do but she just gives me a hug and walks in boldly. Jeff hands me her small carrying bag with a shrug, a smile, and a quick about face. Now the party is getting interesting.

I can't keep my eyes open but for once, the party is at my house and I don't want to be left out. So I'm sort of in and out of sleep on my couch. Every time I lift my head, I see Mom and Kaylen talking with Kathy at my kitchen table. They're laughing, crying, hugging, praying, and heaven knows what else. I wish I would have thought of them earlier with Kathy. Maybe we could have kept her out of the hospital.

Klarissa and Vanessa are sipping Chardonnay and sitting on the floor talking about the contemporary furniture exhibit coming up at McCormick Place. Mom keeps giving them dirty looks. I can't quite follow the conversation but I think matte pastels are still in. And it doesn't sound like pink and brown are going anywhere soon. I'm not sure if they said chrome and painted concrete are making a serious comeback or not. Might have been the other way. But I'm pretty certain that the rich grained mahoganies and other dark woods have got to be on a cusp of a breakthrough. Finally. Cool. I drift back to sleep. Again.

Vanessa brought a chicken casserole that was to die for. Even better than my favorite chicken salad. Rosemary and thyme, straight from her garden, she explained. I tried to make a joke about a song from the '60s but couldn't quite get it out. Wouldn't have been very funny away.

I wake up with a start. I look at the clock on my nightstand. It's 2:55. I don't know how I got into my bed and under the covers. I just know I was dreaming. I was being chased. I was sure it was Timmy but when I looked back it was Dell. When he caught me and knocked me to the ground it was the punk. He is leering and slowly moving a blade side to side, inches from my face. My head clears a little. I had forgotten about him and Tom Gray from Internal Affairs and what Don forgot to tell me. I wonder where the punk is and fall back to sleep.

I swing my legs over the side of the bed at quarter past four. I really have to go to the bathroom. I finish and look down before flushing. I am relieved that there is no pink blood in my urine. I pad out to my kitchen, pour a glass of water from the dispenser on the door of my Frigidaire and pop a pain pill in my mouth. Last one, I think. I don't trust pharmaceutical companies. If something hurts, I still take an aspirin. I creep around my apartment. I look in the door of the guest room. Mom and Kaylen are asleep in the twin beds. I think of Daniel and Kendra and miss them.

I walk into my living area. Klarissa is asleep on the floor. She has made a nice pallet with blankets I inherited from Grandma. I look at her face. She is so beautiful my breath catches. She is an angel. She can be so hard and tough from being in a hard and tough business, but right now she is childlike and elfin.

Kathy has made a little bed on the floor, too, and is at a ninety degree angle from Klarissa. Her face is about an inch from Klarissa's feet. She's going to end up with a toe in her ear. I want to laugh but my side and back still hurt too bad. She called Jeff earlier in the evening and he spent an hour on the phone with my mom. He is going to go with the kids to Danny's church in the morning. We're all meeting at Danny and Kaylen's for lunch. They think I'll be there and I'm not lying, but I'm just not telling them that I have to be at the office at ten.

Kathy is a mess but I somehow think things are going to work out for her and Jeff now that they have real sponsors. I think I'm good for a shot of adrenaline to kick your butt in the right direction—Red Bull for the soul—but it's the saints of the world like Kaylen that can help you make it over the long haul.

Vanessa is asleep on the couch. She is on her back with one arm hanging over the side at a weird angle. She's going to be sore in the morning, I think. Probably not as sore as Don when he actually has to get the kids ready for church by himself. I bet they get there late. I bet it doesn't matter. I walk back through the little place I call home and look out my front kitchen window. An unmarked Chevy Impala is in the parking lot with an interior light on. One guy is obviously asleep and the other is reading. Some body guards. But I'm not worried. I feel very safe surrounded by my friends.

I go back to my room and climb into my huge king size bed. I feel guilty for having all this space to myself, but only for an instant. I feel myself falling back asleep while rubbing my feet together. A professor in one of my psych courses said that we rub our feet together to comfort ourselves. A punch to the kidneys always demands a little comforting.

My phone chirps on the nightstand. I fumble for it so I can turn off the alarm. Then I realize it is not the wake up signal but a phone call. I look

at the small display. It's only 4:58. It is a call from a private number. I pick
up at the very end of the fourth ring, hoping that whoever is calling hasn't
already been transferred over to voicemail.

"Dell?"

"Yeah, it's me. How are you Kristen?"

"Just so so."

"What's the matter?"

"Other than getting attacked in the parking lot two nights ago I'm still
in the middle of the city's biggest homicide case in decades."

"Are you serious? Someone attacked you?"

"Very serious. Imagine that. Someone not liking me enough to get
violent."

He laughs. And then he starts to cry.

"Dell?"

"Yeah."

"What's wrong? What's going on?"

"I can't tell you."

"Yes you can. That's why you called."

"I can't. You wouldn't understand."

"Probably not. But I think you're in a lot of trouble and you're going to
have to start talking to someone, sometime. Why not now? To me?"

"This call is probably being recorded isn't it?"

"It is."

"So I wouldn't really be talking just to you, would I?"

"No."

"You've probably been told to keep me on the phone as long as possible,
haven't you?"

"Yes."

"They probably already know what city I'm in right now, don't they?"

"I don't know," I answer truthfully, though I suspect they do.

"It's funny but you were always afraid of hurting me ... that's why you
didn't just break things off even though I knew that's what you wanted to
do ... but you went ahead and kicked me in the stomach anyway. But you
know something that might surprise you?"

"What?"

"I was always afraid of hurting you, too. I have a secret, you know."

"I know."

"You do?"

"Yeah."

"Know what it is?"

"I think so."

"I'm not sure you do, but you are relentless, so maybe so."

"Come meet me, Dell, and let's talk this through."

"Alone?"

"Absolutely."

"I always respected that you were honest with me—even when you were a little too honest for my state of being. But I somehow suspect you aren't telling the truth right now."

"Dell, I promise, if it is within my power to make it so, we can meet alone."

"Empty words. You know it's not within your power. And it's too late for that. I need to hang up now. But I'll call you again in the next couple days."

"Dell? Dell … don't hang up."

He's already gone.

It's seven. I'm showered and dressed. I actually feel pretty decent, despite having had my sleep interrupted a couple times. I have two hours before the task force meets down in the dingy, gray conference room at our CPD precinct. My plan is to sneak out without anyone hearing me. I never told Mom or Kaylen that I was heading back to work today. I am about to pull the door open when I hear footsteps behind me.

"You never told me," Kathy whispers.

"Told you what?"

"That your dad was shot in the line of duty. That he's dead."

I say nothing. I just look in her tear filled eyes that peer out from the bandages.

"Did you know your dad died the same date my dad died. I told you the exact date the night you were over at the house with Jeff and me."

"Yeah. I did. I do."

"Why didn't you say something? I knew you were dying inside, just like me. I could tell."

"I couldn't. I still can't talk about it."

"You're going to have to sometime. Why not to me? I could have helped you. A year is a long time to hold things in."

"Because … I don't know. It still feels too raw."

"That I understand," she says. "But my dad only died a couple months ago. Is this something that doesn't go away?"

"I'm guessing part of it never does," I answer. "I'm sure the timetable is individual."

"So why a year later are you still not talking?"

"You wouldn't understand, Kathy."

"Thanks for the vote of the confidence, Kristen."

"I didn't mean it like that."

"Then try me."

I start to speak and then pause. The words won't come out. I try again, still no words.

"Just say it," Kathy says.

"Your dad died of a sudden stroke, Kathy. That's awful. You didn't have time to work out the things that came between you and that makes it even awfuller. You say he's a religious man and that he's in heaven, so you're going to feel some regrets, but you'll work through them. He's in heaven. Right?"

"I think so," she says. "I've been too drunk to think about things like heaven." She pauses and looks back up. "But what are your regrets? You had a great relationship with your dad. Your mom says he was your hero. Kaylen says you two were as close as a father and daughter could be. And she wasn't complaining. She thought it was great. He died a hero in the line of duty, doesn't that help a little?"

"He didn't die in the line of duty," I answer dully. I can feel a deep-seated wave of emotions rising in me—grief and then anger—ready to spill over and cover everything in my path. She just looks at me, confusion on her face. She doesn't get it.

"I don't understand."

"I'm angry because someone shot my dad—he died later—and we don't know who he is and I can't do a darn thing about it. They closed the case on March 15 of this year. Even though it wasn't a homicide, I could poke around and do leg work when it was still an active file. Now I can't do that even on my own time without permission from the Commander's office. I don't feel at peace and I don't want to feel at peace until someone finds the guy who shot him and puts him away."

We look at each other in my little hallway, neither knowing what to say.

"I'm so sorry, Kristen," she finally says.

I nearly flinch because I just can't handle sympathy right now. I don't pull away but start talking fast.

"My family is worried about me and how my anger seems to be out of control. They seem to be coping okay, but I think they're still struggling. Klarissa's always been a twig but I don't think she's eating enough to feed a cat—although she's doing a little better since we've started going out to eat together. Kaylen has Danny and she's a rock, but primarily because he's a rock, because I don't hear her talking the dad thing out either. But I've been borderline out of control since the day of the funeral and they just don't get it. Working the case, even when it wasn't mine, helped. When CPD made the file inactive, I felt so helpless all of a sudden. I've grown up with the CPD. The CPD helped raise me. My dad worked for the guy who made his file inactive. Czaka. The CPD I know and love would never close the file on a cop shooter. And Mom and the girls just don't understand. They can't understand."

"Because they aren't on the force?"

"Yeah," I answer.

"So are you dealing with the loss of your dad or the fact that his killer is free or a feeling of betrayal from the CPD?"

"Yes. Doesn't have to be just one does it?"

"I agree. But which one is driving your anger?"

"I've always had a temper," I answer. "But a burning anger that has me ready to fight anybody, anyplace, anytime, took off when Czaka moved my dad's case to the back burner."

"So you feel betrayed. What are you going to do about it?"

"Same thing as before. Keep investigating on my own time. Hope I catch the guy and wake up one day not feeling betrayed. Sometimes things just go away with time. If we had time, I'd tell you about the number of psychopaths who return to normalcy every year."

"Do you think I'm a psychopath?"

I almost laugh. "No Kathy I don't think you're a psychopath. I was just thinking of something somebody said on this Cutter Shark case."

She looks relieved and says, "I hope it works exactly that way for you. Not because I think you're a psychopath either," she laughs. "I just hope your bad feelings go away, but in the meantime, listen to someone who has screwed up enough that she's holding onto her world by a thread. Deal with your anger somehow, someway positively. Right now. I know you don't want to hear this but it's possible to end up in a hospital even if you're not drunk."

I close my eyes at the memory of Kathy in ICU. Was it just a week ago?

"Kathy, I am dealing with things right now. The funny thing is AA has actually helped me. A lot. That was the farthest thing from my mind when I showed up at that first meeting, same as you. Over time I kept trying to come up with a drinking story and I finally just started substituting the thought of 'anger' whenever I said the word 'alcohol' and you all ate it up."

She has a hurt look on her face.

"I'm sorry. I didn't mean it that way. Well, I guess I did, but my point is that I was finally one of you—one of the group and I fit in and could relate and could get help. That's the reason you and I connected that night."

"Okay," she says. "But one of these days you're going to have to talk about your dad—not just anger."

"I agree."

"I can tell you're already out the door in your mind and you'd agree with anything I say to get away from here, but it would mean an awful lot to me if you'd let me be there for you."

In an instant of absolute honesty I answer, "maybe."

"Good enough," she says. She pauses and continues, "I'll tell you something else funny, I definitely did not like you the first time I laid eyes on you." She pauses. "And before you pretend it was otherwise, I know you absolutely despised me, too."

"Was it that obvious, Bethany?"

"Oh yeah," she says with a laugh.

"Kathy," I say hesitantly. "I know we've got a lot more to say to each other, but I've got to get out of here. If I don't move and do something I'm going to explode. See? I'm dealing with my anger."

She smiles and retorts, "and you don't want the others to know you're sneaking out?"

"Maybe."

"I'm pretty sure it's a for sure, not a maybe. So get out of here and go save the city from the Cutter Shark before I wake everybody up."

"Kathy, you're an angel."

Kathy gives me a hug and I accept it. But only for a second. I pull away and walk out the door. I fight like crazy to not let even one tear form in the corner of each eye and almost succeed. A few small drops well up but none escape from the corners of my eyes. I just breathe in and out with my game face on as I stride purposely into the parking lot.

Everything I said to Kathy was true. I just didn't tell her everything. And of course Mom and Kaylen didn't tell her because they don't know. Lying by omission. I still have to ask Danny about that.

My world didn't stop the day my dad was shot or the day the case file was closed. My dad wasn't killed in the line of duty. Oh he was mortally wounded all right, but despite little things like paralyzed legs and his bladder not working, his body wouldn't die. But over time his spirit did. So the man who was God to me died. He and I had a lunch date planned so I found him. Let's just say I'm not convinced he stopped breathing due to natural causes. Cops don't leave their wives much to live on without the life insurance, so it wasn't hard for me to declare "respiratory complications" to the EMT who got there first. I didn't hide or destroy anything. But I didn't really look. I was afraid to. It wasn't my job to investigate but I still feel a perverse sense of guilt.

I'm alone in this. I'm glad Kathy knows her dad is in heaven. I can't get Danny to finish a conversation with me on eternal security so I don't know where my dad is.

Dear God, where is my daddy?

Chapter 69

I drop my change from four crumpled dollar bills into the tip box at the drive-through window. I greedily snatch my steaming grande Americano with an extra espresso shot and one Splenda. I am sitting in the back of a police cruiser. My two babysitters have been sipping coffee all night and aren't interested in any more caffeine. Their shift ends in an hour and I'm guessing they'll be asleep within five minutes of getting home and putting head to pillow.

Randy is driving and Kirk is riding shotgun. I'm separated from them by a metal mesh protective screen. It's not a fancy limo but it's a ride. Randy wheels out of the drive-through lane as I take my first sip. My friend with the tongue stud and green apron has put hazelnut syrup in my drink. I hate any flavoring other than artificial sweetener in my coffee.

"Hit the breaks," I order. "Pull into that parking spot by the front door and let me out."

"Everything okay?" Kirk asks.

"Definitely not."

They look very concerned. I fumble to open the door but realize there are no handles in the back of a cruiser.

"Can you let me out?" I demand.

"Sure," Randy says glancing nervously at Kirk.

He kills the engine, gets out, and opens my car door for me, quickly stepping aside. I head through the entrance of JavaStar with two very worried body guards on my tail. They read and slept last night. They look professional now. Their heads are on swivels as they look left and right for possible threats against my person. It's not me they need to be worried about.

Can I not speak clearly? Do I stutter? Mumble? I have never in my life heard anyone else mention that they get the wrong drink at JavaStar on a regular basis. Maybe never. It's got to be me. I step to the front of the line right in front of a guy who is about to order and who turns to let me have it for cutting. He sees my expression and my bodyguards and backs down. I explain to a cheerful young blonde that I didn't get the drink I ordered. The girl at the counter assures me that it is no problem if I changed my mind. They want me to be happy. That's not what I want to hear. I tell her that I will only be happy if she or someone else from the establishment admits that they are the ones that made the mistake.

"Uh, sure," she says. "My mistake."

Since she's not the one who took my order, her mea culpa doesn't feel very satisfying. I look over at Kirk and Randy while tapping my fingers on the high amoeba shaped counter where my replacement drink will be delivered. They look worried. Smart boys.

On the freeway I hear the sound of a submarine's sonar system. I look at my cell and see that a text from Reynolds just came in.

I was going 2 tell u. U have every right 2b mad. Let me explain. Let's talk. Please?

I hit delete and lean my head against the seat. I close my eyes and take inventory. I'm feeling much better physically, all things considered, but am just queasy enough to keep moving at a slow pace.

Randy and Kirk weren't quite sure what to do when I came out into the parking lot earlier this morning. They had explicit orders to watch over me and anyone else at my apartment. No one added a note that they were to drive me down to precinct on their assignment report. They called Dispatch and another car was sent over to take their place on guard duty so they could drive me to CPD.

*I'*m in my cubicle before eight. I attack everything relating to the Cutter Shark case on my desk with a passion. I bury my head in notebooks, documents, photographs, profiles, and everything else that is in the mountain of paperwork we are generating. I worry about the trees in the Rain Forest for just a second.

A half hour before our meeting is to start, I find something in one of the notebooks. Another thing that the FBI didn't feel free to share with us and maybe didn't want us to discover. I jot a note on a blank sheet of paper and start skimming through the other notebooks as fast as my fingers and eyes will work. I scribble more notes furiously for the next hour and when I look up I realize I am already half an hour late. I know something new for sure now. I grab my notepad and run for the conference room.

I am last one in the room. Everyone looks up at me.

"You didn't have to come," Director Willingham says. "We would have understood."

"No problem, sir," I answer, "I'm feeling great. I wouldn't miss this for the world."

As I make my way around to the only open seat, between Blackshear and Don, I remember that Vanessa is snoring at my house and wonder who is watching Devon and Veronika and getting them ready for church.

Don reads my mind and whispers, "My sister came over," as I sit down next to him. I didn't know he had a sister. He's never mentioned her. Weird.

Van Guten looks at me with disdain and gives Don a dirty look. I guess students are not supposed to speak without teacher's permission.

*A*ny more ideas?" Reynolds asks.

He reported at length on his trip to Durango. About the time Zaworski was getting a search warrant for us to crash into Dell's rented townhome here, an FBI numbers cruncher created a graphic model and plotted southwest Colorado as the likely geographic home base for our murderer.

The FBI then rented one of the U.S. Army's supercomputers—at a cost of more than $875, 000 per hour we were informed—and cross-tabulated calls and financial transactions between that area of the country and the target cities during corresponding dates.

To the FBI analyst's amazement, the computer was able to narrow the search down to a list of fewer than seven potential residents. They called a small army of financial and logistical analysts in Washington, D.C., to work a graveyard shift in order to understand everything about the movements and patterns of members of these households. Dell's home and a few select accounts came out as the winner. So now we have a name, a face, and a base of operations. We don't know where Dell is but that's just a matter of time. The plan is to put his face on every news outlet in America starting at five o'clock Eastern Time Zone. Government lawyers are getting Federal warrants and vetting the entire process to make sure nothing is done that will let a bad guy off the hook based on inadmissible evidence and that there won't be a civil rights lawsuit a year from now if a mistake is made.

It's been well over a decade but the memory of the FBI announcing Richard Jewell as the prime suspect in the '96 bombing outside the Atlanta Olympics venue and how the press subsequently crucified him is still a textbook case of what not to do—and how not to do what you shouldn't have done in the first place. Putting a man's face on a couple hundred million TV screens is no small decision. In Jewell's case it probably killed him.

Dell. A bad guy? Wow. Could this be a mistake? Other than the fact that they keep leaving out relevant information—like this Durango operation—I look at the feds and see a lot of competence. And dedication. I don't see them as mistake prone. But it wouldn't be the first time. Hey, Willingham went through a purgatory of sorts due to others' mistakes. There's no way he could get something like this wrong is there?

Willingham looks around one more time. He's very relaxed. He even laughed when he read the ChiTownBlogger's latest story that included the cost of his furniture. Everybody's ready to leave. I start to lift my hand, put it down, and then just blurt out what's on my mind.

"Sir."

"Yes, Conner."

There is a near audible sigh in the room. Task force members who were halfway out of their chairs settle back in.

"It may not have made a difference but I just need to say that the expunged material in Virgil's reports might have helped."

"We got that to you two weeks ago.".

"The fact that there were male victims, yes," I say, "But not everything."

"Oh?"

He says it with a definite note of challenge. Now everyone in the room is awake and interested and not in such a big hurry to get out the door. They shift their gaze from me to him and back again.

"I found at least one other place our perpetrator goes to find his victims."

"Really?"

"Do we have time for this?" Van Guten demands impatiently.

"Damn right, we do," Zaworski says with a glare her direction.

Thanks Captain, I think.

"Let's hear it," Willingham says. He is trying to look amused but the normal twinkle is missing from his eyes.

"Church," I say.

Chapter 70

"Conner, you are the man," Martinez says again, his mouth stuffed with a jumbo hot dog with more trimmings than the bun or any mouth should be able to hold. He has mustard dripping down his chin along with half cucumber slice that just won't fit in the door. Yuck.

He, Blackshear, Konkade, Don, Big Tony and I are at a hole in the wall a mile from HQ called the Devil Dog. Reynolds asked me to go to lunch with him. I politely declined. He kept trying to make eye contact while asking. I finally did. That helped him understand I wasn't going out with him.

What do I think of Reynolds? I'm not too hung up on looks but he is attractive and he caught my eye in that regard from the first time I saw him. I do like a confident and fun personality and he has that going for him, too. He can be a little self-deprecating with his humor but you can easily tell that underneath he's comfortable with himself. I like guys who like their work—I was a daddy's girl after all—and that was another checkmark in his favor. I don't like needy. And Reynolds, despite trying to give me a hangdog look for sympathy the last two times I've seen him, really isn't. I know some women want tears and sensitivity from a man. Not me. Doesn't mean I want a Neanderthal. I do want caring and considerate. I just don't want wimpy. I'm sorry if that means I lose my official Gen-X membership card. Hey, I like old fashioned hymns and sitting down in church every once in a while, too.

"Nice job, Kristen," Big Tony adds. "Your dad would have been proud."

I'm only halfway through a grilled cheese and I've barely touched the fries. I had just poured a major puddle of ketchup on the wax paper liner in my red thatched food basket. I'm not hungry anymore. I want to go home, take a bath, and cry. I loved having a slumber party at my place last night, but now I feel like going home to an empty apartment and just feeling my space.

Why didn't I tell Kathy that my dad died the same date hers did when she first mentioned her dad's death? Did I think I was better than her and not want her to know that I've been in a tailspin of my own since we lost him? Even as I ask myself that question I note that my tailspin has been a lot slower than hers. Pretty smug of me I realize. Yeah, part of my reticence in opening up to Kathy or anyone else has been my wanting to be above things like being depressed and mad over a situation outside my control.

Then I wonder why my family hasn't been able to talk about him—that'd be Dad—at Sunday dinners? I know why I don't, but heaven knows Danny can talk about anything, anywhere, to anybody. Are they each protecting their own sense of private loss? All the while never knowing the whole story? Maybe we're protecting what feels like a tenuous faith in God. Nah. I know Van Guten and other shrinks would have a field day putting me under a microscope on this one and analyzing the cognitive dissonance that comes when the person who imparted faith to you seems to have lost or forsaken his. But I'm simple. I'm practical. I believe in God and love Him even when it's not convenient or I don't feel things emotionally.

I think of Kathy's dependence on me. Maybe I have a protective complex. Why haven't I been there in the same way to console Klarissa when I just know she is dying to talk about things with me? I wonder what she's been feeling this past year and these past few months with Warren and other things not going her way. Me; I've wanted to punch somebody in the face. What about her? Mom and Kaylen can take care of themselves and Kathy. I've got to get there, be there for Klarissa. Princess Klarissa.

I look up, a tear or two pooling in my eyes. I will them to stay in place. I'm not going to cry in front of the guys. Five sets of eyes are on me. I put my head back down and when I look up again they have all politely looked away. Not even Blackshear is eating, though.

"Hey Tiger," Big Tony continues, "You really have done a great job holding things together and a great job on this case. I'm proud of you."

He places his hand on mine and I look back down.

"*Esto tipo es un loco bastardo*—and we're gonna catch him," Martinez says with his flair for words—even when we don't understand all of them. "When we do, we're going to make sure you get taken care of. First you're going to get your medal. Then you're going to get some time off and go on a vacation like everybody told you to do when lost your pops and that son of a bitch Czaka closed his file to save budget money. We're brothers here and we don't let no cop killer walk free."

I look up at Martinez with gratitude. I think he might suspect the whole story. Maybe everyone in the whole department does. And cops feel things like this stronger than others because one of the occupational hazards of the job is being on top of the leader board for suicide rates. We're pretending a little but it's all still real. It honestly just feels so good to hear someone else say out loud, even if they're skating around the issue a little, exactly what's been eating my insides away.

"That file will never be closed until we get him," Scalia says. He looks at me, "The big brass might be keeping you away from things for awhile but that's just so you can cool down. There's other ways to keep knocking on doors. As long as I'm alive, we won't forget your dad, Kristen. And yes, the story you heard me tell at the basilica is true."

I brush away my tears before gravity starts them rolling and look up at him. I've just got some medicine for my soul.

"Ah, who needs a vacation?" I ask, recovering myself and talking tough again. "I thought about going on one the first week of April. Just think of all the fun I'd have missed hanging out with you guys. Without me, you guys wouldn't have gotten anything done. And I'll admit it. I'd be one lonely girl."

"*La próxima vez que estés sola, ya sabes a quién llamar!*" Martinez says to me with a big wink and his hand over his heart.

Big Tony gives him a dirty look and Martinez holds up his hands in surrender.

"I'm just kidding," he says laughing. "I keeed. I keeed."

Everyone at the table except for me and Scalia join him. I don't have the energy to bust on anyone right now. Doesn't mean I won't feel good enough to do so tomorrow.

"We do need to do something first," Scalia says. "Catch a serial killer."

"Woods can run but he cannot hide," says Don, invoking one of the most tired and trite clichés in law enforcement.

Even as he says it, something strikes me wrong. Again. I can't put my finger on it. We all know Dell is the Cutter Shark—has to be based on what the FBI has discovered in the last forty-eight hours—and that's going public in less than four hours, but something keeps gnawing at me.

Dear God, help me find a serial killer.

I enter my apartment and immediately know something's wrong. It's absolutely spic and span with everything in its place. I'm sure Mom saw to that. I always keep a clean place but that doesn't mean it's always tidy. But the order and stillness isn't what's got my antennae up. I haven't been as careful as I should in recent days and even though I still have police protection less than a hundred feet from my front door, I carefully and quietly de-holster my Beretta. I ease off the safety and bring it up to chest level with both hands.

I poke my head in and out of my kitchen and eating area. Nothing there. I walk in slowly and look under the table and in the broom closet anyway. I step back into my front hall. I creep up to the coat closet. I pull it open quickly and step back with drawn gun. Nothing. I repeat the process in my living room, my common bathroom, and my guest room. Still nothing.

My bedroom door is shut. I almost always leave it open. Maybe that's all that's bothering me. Of course, I wasn't the last one in the apartment. Maybe Mom or Kaylen pulled it shut before they left.

I now ponder my options. Continue searching my apartment so I can confirm nothing is wrong or go outside, ask two officers to come inside to help me finish checking everything out and when we don't find anything, let out a little embarrassed laugh and explain to them that I'm just a little jittery since getting punched in the kidneys and finding out my kind-of ex-boyfriend is a serial killer?

I turn the knob soundlessly and then push open the door hard enough that it slams into the wall stop. No one was hiding behind it. I keep my head on a swivel and check under the bed, in my small walk-in closet, in my tiny master bathroom, and even in the wardrobe that is probably just big enough to hold a person. Nothing. I look at my nightstand. The framed picture of me standing with Dad on the day I graduated from police academy, my uniform so neat and pressed, him in his dress blues and cap with braids on the bill, is missing. Weird.

Klarissa has said several times that she wants to come by and pick up some of my pictures and photo albums so she can have them scanned and saved electronically. Would she have just picked up that one picture and frame? I walk back into the living room. All my growing up photo albums are still lined up on the bottom row of my bookcase.

I walk back in my bedroom. I feel a chill and shudder. It has nothing to do with the weather. It's a gorgeous June afternoon, with temperatures in the low eighties. But something has caught my attention. My window is open a couple inches.

Sure enough, someone came up that outside wall with a ladder and through your window," Konkade says.

It's a few minutes after four. Willingham and Reynolds are holding a press conference in fifty-five minutes at City Hall. The mayor, police chief, and a whole lot of other muckety mucks will be on the podium. Zaworski has been allotted two minutes—and not a second longer—for opening remarks. I heard Commander Czaka was expecting to speak and is not happy that it's Zaworski slated to be in front of the press.

Don and Martinez have the TV on WCI-TV in the living room. It's a house rule. Have to be loyal to family. Big Tony is directing operations with some uniformed officers outside. My security detail is about to be increased. The consensus is that I represent our best chance of bringing Dell in, whether it be taking his calls and talking him into turning himself in or staying on the phone long enough for them to triangulate his location—or by serving as bait. They don't think he's through with me either way.

My phone rings. Private number.

"Hi Dell."

"Hi Kristen."

"Where are you?"

"I can't tell you. You know I'm in big trouble."

"I know you are, so why don't you come over and let's talk. Are you in Chicago, Dell?"

"C'mon Kristen, I'm not that dumb."

"Well, not coming in is not smart and you are a smart guy."

"It's interesting that now that you want something from me, you're incredibly attentive," he says with sadness. "I wish we could have talked like this before. You were always too preoccupied to really be there. Always multi-tasking and never doing any one thing all the way."

"It's been a tough couple months, Dell."

"I'm not just talking about this Cutter Shark thing or the anniversary of when your dad was killed or CPD shut down the investigation for his murderer. You were like this from day one"

"Well, I'm sorry and I'm listening now."

"I'm thirty-four years old and have never had a girlfriend for more than two or three months in my life. A lot of women think I'm great because I have a fair amount of money to spend on them. But I was never good at relationships. Too many problems growing up. You were the first woman I really thought I could get to know. Do you know you were my significant other longer than any other woman in my life? Even if you didn't think of me the same way that's still what you were to me."

"I'm sorry Dell."

"Don't apologize."

"Well, I do feel bad. Is it possible that some of the women from your past feel the same way about you that you feel about me? Like you weren't ever really there?"

"Good point, Kristen, and I concede that's possible. But that still doesn't absolve you. It just means that maybe I'm as bad as you."

"So when can we get this trouble you're in on the table and sorted out? When are you going to come in and talk to me?"

"I don't know. You don't understand. Your family is perfect. And I wanted to be perfect for you. My parents died when we were young."

I pause on the word "we".

"Who is 'we,' Dell? I thought you were an only child?"

"How would you know? You never asked. But to be fair, if you did, I might have lied. I have a brother. We got separated for awhile and grew up in different foster homes. I made out pretty good; he didn't. When I finally found him, he was only seventeen but he'd been in jail three times and countless juvenile homes. I put him in a nice place for troubled youth run by a church I attended and that seemed to help for awhile, but when I tried to move him in with me and get him back in school or at least help him find a job, he started disappearing for months at a time."

"When was the last time you saw him, Dell?"

"Six, I don't know, maybe seven months ago."

"Tell me right now; has he done something bad?"

"I just don't know. I do know that he emptied a bank account I keep for rainy days. Not the first time, of course. He went back to my place in Durango and stole some other stuff, too. He might not have thought of it as stealing, though. I've never really rented the place out. I've always kept it open so he could have a place to come home to. I'm not worried about the money; he's taken plenty of that through the years and I'm not hurting. I just found some things on the computer I keep in my office there that are disturbing. I need to talk to someone without getting him in trouble. I'm also worried because I can't get hold of him."

"You haven't done anything bad or criminal yourself?" I ask him.

"Of course not. What are you talking about?" I can feel his pause. "Oh, I get it. So you think I . . ."

"You need to come in and help us right now, Dell."

"Unbelievable. Thanks for giving me the benefit of the doubt. Let me think about it and call you back."

"Don't hang up Dell."

"Kristen, I've got to. And you've got to understand. You have sisters. This is my brother we're talking about. I don't know if he's done anything wrong."

"Promise me you'll call back in the next hour. This is getting worse than you may know, Dell."

He's hung up. I whirl to Don and Martinez who are looking at me with concern.

"We got to get hold of Willingham and Reynolds," I nearly shout. "They can't give Dell's name and picture to the press."

Chapter 71

The meeting was supposed to start a half hour ago. We're waiting for Willingham and Zaworski to arrive. Blackshear and Don are talking about the Cubs. Some kid up from the Des Moines farm club—a big right hander with a hundred mile an hour fastball and a wicked curve ball—threw a one hitter in his first major league start. Milton Bradley, who I thought was a game manufacturer, but actually plays outfield for the Dodgers, hit a single with one out in the ninth to spoil the kid's no-hitter. It's the second week of June and I haven't been to a game yet. When this is over I'm going to take Daniel and Kendra to an afternoon game at Wrigley and then out to Devil Dog for a fancy dinner, featuring lots of grease and mustard. I won't tell Mom. She doesn't like Devil Dog because of the name.

Konkade and Martinez are arguing about Virgil. Konkade thinks that Operation Vigilance provided a lot of help. Martinez says we didn't get squat, his word not mine, but a lot of wasted time at Alcoholics Anonymous meetings. I think of Kathy. My time at AA was a roller coaster ride but ended up doing me some good with my anger and just may have saved her life. Providence or coincidence? I'll leave that for the theologians and Danny to explain.

Van Guten is nearly pounding the keys on her laptop. Maybe she is working on a new article for a scholarly journal like the ChiTownBlogger suggested. The three newest members of our team, all from the FBI, two male and one female, are holding a half-hearted conversation in low tones, but seem more interested in typing emails on their tiny Blackberry keypads.

Big Tony is leaning back in his chair as far as it will go. His eyes are closed. The FBI agents have looked at him with a mixture of curiosity and maybe a little pity a couple times. I hope they don't take Lieutenant Scalia too lightly because he is formidable both on the street and in the board room when so inclined.

We're at City Hall in a conference room a couple doors away from the mayor's office. It's even nicer than the one we use at the regional office of the FBI in the State Building. An assistant to the mayor has brought in a tray of glasses—they look like real crystal—with the city's seal etched on the side. There's an ice bucket and a full assortment of soft drinks. She came back a few minutes later pushing a cart with full coffee service. That's where most of us headed. Van Guten never moved but nodded in the direction of the new group in from D.C., and one of the FBI guys got her a small green bottle of San Pellegrino and a glass filled with ice cubes. Must be nice.

I'm sitting by myself, tired and a little bored. How can you be bored at a time like this I wonder. Of course, a lot of police work is boring and routine. Chasing down a punk and having him wave a knife at you or getting punched in the kidneys are exceptions to the rule. Nothing sounds more fascinating and exhilarating than tracking down a serial killer or, as Van Guten likes to call them, organized killers. But in this case, our case, we've really not done much tracking. We've read a couple thousand pages of reports more than a couple times. We've interviewed hundreds—maybe thousands—of people who were in the slightest way associated with our five Chicago area crime scenes just to have them tell us for a fourth or fifth time that they know nothing and saw nothing.

I'm actually in the mood to do a crossword puzzle. I like the *NY Times*. The problem is I can breeze through the Monday and Tuesday puzzles, but they get progressively harder as the week progresses. Wednesday is a perfect level of challenge for me. Doable but not too easy. I blow hot or cold on Thursdays. Friday and Saturday usually beat me like a drum. I used to do a crossword at least three or four times a week. I haven't done one since we buried Daddy. They say doing puzzles keeps your brain fresh and strong. Maybe I'll curl up on the couch tonight after a bath and do the puzzle from last Monday. That'll be my speed.

I doodle on a notepad. I look over at Van Guten who continues to furiously break new intellectual ground with her description of a serial killer. I'm drawing pictures of flowers and soccer balls. And I wonder why she has so much nicer nails than me.

I had troubles getting online tonight so I couldn't download and print a copy of the *NY Times Crossword Puzzle.* I did find a copy of the large print edition of *TV Guide* that my mom brought over earlier in the week. They publish a crossword every week. The clues that didn't have anything to do with TV were way too easy. But most of the clues did have to do with TV and since I don't watch much, I was in trouble. I did get the three letter word for a fuzzy extraterrestrial sitcom character right away though. *Alf.*

At least I think so, even though I never connected any of the three letters with another word.

Our task force meeting went pretty quick. Reynolds confirmed that Dell does have a brother who has been in and out of prison and mental institutions from an early age. Van Guten wasn't writing a research paper but rather was running Dean Woods' data through a series of psychological corollary tests she uses. She thinks he fits the bill for our Cutter Shark. I've got to stop being so judgmental.

Finding him is priority one and agents are being dispatched to and law enforcement officials notified at places he has frequented. His picture will be on every police bulletin board as well. Every cop in Chicago will be distributing his picture to shop owners, bartenders, waitresses, bank tellers, and anyone else who might remember seeing his face in the past year. The decision has been made to not put his face on TV or the newspapers yet. Even though Van Guten likes his profile for the crimes committed, she can't be 100 percent certain. Lead investigators from the six other known cities he hit are receiving a dossier on Dean Woods as well.

Priority number two is Dell. Instructions to all law enforcement agencies are that it should be assumed that both he and Dean are armed and dangerous. I don't think Dell is a threat to anyone but himself, but I understand that intentionally or not, he is aiding and abetting a potential killer and he, too, must be approached with extreme caution. I feel bad for him.

I am the obvious link to Dell so my cell and home phones are live with federal agents both in D.C., and here in Chicago. After my parking lot incident, which I am now certain was not Dell but rather Dean—or Timmy—they are still going to keep a security detail assigned to me until the case is resolved. As boring as my life can be, I don't envy the mind-numbing nothingness that my babysitters have ahead of them.

The big item was a reread of the ChiTownBlogger's latest post on the Cutter Shark. Our killer is obviously using him to send us a message and the message is quite clear: the next murder will happen by June 21, the first official day of summer. Does that indicate that his work is coming to a close in Chicago, even if a little earlier than his usual pattern? And if so, what then? How will we know he is gone? How long will I need to watch my back if he's put a target on it?

I brush my teeth for the second time tonight. I shouldn't have eaten that oatmeal cookie from the batch Vanessa made for us. I use the bathroom, wash my hands, and pad to my bedroom. I check the windows and then walk through my entire apartment to make sure everything is closed and locked up. I pull back the covers on my bed and there is an envelope sitting on my pillow. How in the heck did we miss that?

Chapter 72

I put the call in to Konkade. Reynolds is the task force commander but
Konkade handles the details.

"Konkade here."

"Yes, Sergeant, this is Detective Conner."

"Good evening Kristen. I'm so pleased you are calling me to wish me a
good night's sleep. That is why you're calling isn't it?"

I sigh. He laughs.

"Didn't think so," he says. "My wife is going to have to watch *Desperate
Housewives* by herself tonight. What have we got?"

Mom can't come to my apartment without doing some cleaning. Thank
you, Mom, I think, now that my place has become the new task force
headquarters. Zaworski, Reynolds, Willingham, and Van Guten are in the
kitchen—obviously the command center.

Konkade's last instructions to me were to not touch anything. I was
too tired to exercise my incredible powers of levitation—I didn't bend any
spoons or move Coke cans with my thoughts either—so I disobeyed his
orders and put my tired rear end on the kitchen counter to wait.

Konkade called Bruce, the techie, but he was down at his mom's house
in Kankakee, at least an hour and twenty minutes from my place, even with

no traffic on a Sunday night, so he called Jerome next. Jerome showed up to handle the evidence. I'm praying it's not a mushy card from my mom that she left on my pillow. I've never seen her use block letters to write my name and I've also never seen her misspell it. Maybe it's the barista from JavaStar. He calls me Kirsten every time.

Jerome is first on the scene—you know you're having a great week when your apartment is officially the center of a serial murder investigation not just once, but twice within forty-eight hours—and he lets me know he lives less than two minutes away. I let him know that my mom had vacuumed and dusted subsequent to his last visit here so he sure as heck won't find much in the way of evidence—or dirt. But he still puts on his miner's hardhat with a blue light and spends thirty minutes examining every square inch of my bed and bedroom.

By the time he comes out with the envelope held between a pair of rubber-tipped tweezers the whole gang has arrived. Konkade, Don, Blackshear, Martinez, and I are sitting in my living area and the top brass is in the kitchen. I edge in to start a pot of fresh ground JavaStar and put out the last of the cookies Vanessa made. It takes me two minutes and they don't say anything until I'm safely in the living room again. The only ones eating are in the living room or outdoors in squad cars. My mom would have been proud when I took a plate of cookies out to the uniforms.

Jerome sets up a light box on the Formica counter between my living room and kitchen. He carefully lays the red envelope on it. Everyone moves in close but I manage to muscle my way to Jerome's immediate right. Hey, it is my letter.

Actually it's a Hallmark card. Somebody cared enough to give the best. There's a picture of a red rose on the front panel. The inside has no printed message, just a juvenile poem written in the same crooked letters that were on the envelope.

Roses are red,
Violets are blue,
You kicked me out of town,
But I'll get you!

"Someone find me a sample of Dean Woods' handwriting," Reynolds orders.

Chapter 73
June 20, 3:08am

I'm going to miss this city. The media really hasn't been up to snuff and I hate that Blogger guy but I've done good work here. The CTB dude always tries to make it about him, not me. I don't think I'm going to send him any more emails. If he brags about that retarded name he gave me one more time, I think I'll pay him a visit in person before I blow town. He'll find out who's really cleaver.

I must admit I've never seen so much activity from law enforcement. The FBI—Federal Bureau of Idiots—got lucky somehow and know something about me and my ways. Doesn't matter. They aren't going to catch me. They're not smart enough. Maybe I'll go on a cruise before picking my next location. I'd kind of like to visit Paris but the currency exchange is murder. Hah. Maybe that's a good sign.
I hadn't really thought of that before, but it could be kind of cool to be the first international serial killer.

Our young hero felt a pang of guilt over leaving the city with so little fuss. The mayor should have thrown him a parade in gratitude, he thought with a chuckle. He had never before had to move to a new chapter with only five conquests under his belt. He was calm and philosophical.

Well the heat is on and I probably got to switch kitchens, but there is one more person I need to take care of. Thinks she can just cut things off with me. Don't think so, honey bunny sweetie pie … you're all mine. You mess with the bull, you get the horns.

I am going to have to figure out a new revenue source. Big Brother has taken good care of me. I love manipulating his complex set of guilt inducers to get what I need. But if he suspects my special lifestyle that well will dry up. I bet I can hit a couple of his accounts I've hacked one more time. That'll hack him off.

Chapter 74

Left cross! Left cross! Right straight! Again! Again! Again! Harder! Hands up and keep hitting. I said hands up. You're about to get popped in the nose. Move and hit!"

I keep my hands up and keep hitting. Soto still doesn't seem to think my hands are up high enough.

"Don't stop. Hit! Hit! On your toes. On your toes. Dance, Kristen. Get off your heels and move. Get your hands up! If you're tired, quit and go home! Now hit!"

The only piece of exercise equipment that Soto likes better than a floor is the heavy punching bag. He likes the small speed bag, too, but he loves the big bag for building strength and upper body endurance. Go punch a bag for five minutes and you'll experience a profound and newfound wonder and appreciation for boxers. My arms are screaming for mercy and turning to Jell-O. I can taste bile in the back of my throat. My calves are burning. Even my butt feels like it's on fire.

"Don't quit! Don't quit! Kristen, get your hands up! This guy is going to break your nose. Hit! Mix it up. Cross, cross, straight, straight, left, right, right, left! Mix it up!"

Hearing him tell me to mix it up is a blast from the past. Dad kept a heavy bag hanging from the first story floor supports that were open in the basement and he was always after me to change up my rhythm and sequence of punches. "Mix it up" was also a favorite of his from the sideline when I played travel soccer. About the time I really mastered my scissor step he was after me to work the helicopter spin. Dad was an interesting combination of laid back and intense; of encouraging and in-your-face challenging.

I was running so late for work this morning that I figured once I hit my cube and started working I'd never be able to break free to get a work out in. At first Soto wasn't going to let me into his gym because of my brief stay in the hospital over the weekend but when I told him I wanted to work the light and heavy punching bags he relented. All I really waned to do was a soft spin on the recumbent bike but that was never going to get me in the doors.

"Maybe you're going to start paying attention and figure out how to defend yourself," he said while taping my hands. "You get yourself killed over this 'Cutter' mess and I'm going to be so mad I ain't coming to your funeral."

I looked up at him sharply. He crossed himself.

"Sorry Kristen. May your dad's soul rest in peace. Good man. He had a heck of a punch, too. If I could have ever got him to mix up his combinations he could have been a real fighter. As it was, he could handle himself just fine when the rough stuff came up. He and Big Tony. That was a team you didn't want breaking up your party. They could do the heavy lifting."

I laughed and gave him a hug and he dropped everything to personally put me through the paces.

As I walk toward the shower rooms, my legs and arms a little wobbly from a "light" workout, Martinez exits the men's door, takes one look at me in a loose fitting tee shirt and baggy running shorts, soaked through from perspiration, my hair a shiny tangled mess, and whistls.

"*Te ves bien. Aquién tratas de impresionar … además de mi?*"

I poke him in the chest with a forefinger and ask, "what'd you just say?"

Unfazed, he answers, "what do you think I said? I just wished you a lovely day. You've got to learn some Español if you want to live in this country."

I roll my eyes and laugh as he flexes for me. I head for the shower and he heads for the workout room. I'm pretty sure he didn't wish me a lovely day.

There's another sticky note on my computer screen.

DEAR DETECTIVE KRISTEN—SOME GIRLS HAVE A WAY WITH THE GUYS. HOW MANY BOYFRIENDS CAN ONE DETECTIVE HAVE? I NEVER KNEW YOU WERE SO ROMANTIC. I GUESS THE LAST GUY WAS A REAL KILLER. PLEASE MAKE A LIST OF WHO'S LEFT FOR THE REST OF US!

The signature is a smiley face. I've had enough of the notes. I pluck it off the screen and stride out front to Shandra's desk.

"Did you put this on my screen?"

"What are you talking about?" she asks with a coy smile.

She looks over at Connie Davis, Zaworski's personal secretary, and winks. I'm mad and I'm glaring at her and I can see some of her smug confidence starting to erode. She looks over at Davis for support but Davis is suddenly very interested in her computer screen. Some of the other support staff and a few of the detectives peak over and around cubicles in our direction, suddenly curious and not doing a very good job of being discrete.

"You have no right to accuse me of anything," she says, her cheeks turning a crimson red.

"You know what, Shandra," I respond, "your job is to make this place run smooth. Maybe you're the one posting the notes, maybe you're not. But if it's you, you better stop. If it's not you, you better find out who it is and make it stop. And I'm not jacking around with you. This stopped being funny the first time and it is a distraction on a case that is very important to the big boss. When the next note shows up on my screen, he's going to hear about how funny you think this is, and I don't care if anyone thinks I'm a snitch. Another thing, you want to write me up, go ahead and do it. In fact I hope you do. Because I promise I'm bringing your call logs during office hours with me to any hearing and it's going to get ugly."

Her mouth is wide open as I storm off and return to my cubicle.

I log on and start working through emails. I send quick answers back, make notes with little boxes for check marks once the task is completed on a separate sheet of paper to let me know what I have to work on that's going to take more than two minutes. I delete everything else in my inbox that isn't a crisis. If it's important, they'll send me another email.

I get to a message from Reynolds. Quick and to the point:

I'll be by your offices late afternoon. Let's go to dinner and talk.

Hmmm. Explaining to Van Guten's ex that I won't be having dinner with him tonight could take more than two minutes, so I just hit delete.

The next email is from Klarissa. She lets me know she's going out with Warren tonight to talk through all the reasons they're not together. She goes on to say that she has a corporate dinner on Tuesday but that she wants to have dinner with me on Wednesday or Thursday. I'm glad she can fit me in. I send back a quick, terse response.

You bet.

Don cuts across the aisle and asks if I'm ready.

"You bet," I answer. "For what?"

Willingham and Zaworski set up an appointment for Detective Squires and myself to meet with a group of clergy to discuss the Cutter Shark case and the fact that to date, based on the evidence we have from six cities, seven including us, our killer finds his victims in either AA or church meetings. We covered this during the task force meeting at my apartment last night. I was so tired I'm pretty sure I was delirious a few times, but I think I caught all the main points of this new area of investigation.

We were reminded repeatedly that we aren't going to explicitly tell the twenty-three priests, pastors, and rabbis that we have any certain knowledge, but we are going to simply let them know in so many words that we're working on a theory. We're to see if they have any ideas on how and why a serial killer might theoretically hide out in a place of worship. Van Guten has drawn up a list of questions we are to ask. I somehow suspect this meeting is going to do more for Virgil and Van Guten's writing career than it is for finding our killer. We're already 99 percent sure we know who he is. My ex-boyfriend's brother.

Willingham had Reynolds explain the reason information from Operation Vigilance was suppressed and expunged from our first briefings and the first set of notebooks we received. I pointed out that it was actually the first two sets of briefings and notebooks. The major stumbled through this part of the presentation and kept looking at Willingham who steadfastly kept his head down. Amazingly, Reynolds reported that the decision went all the way back to the President of the United States. They called him by the acronym of POTUS. I was glad to see that I'm not the only one that comes up with witty nicknames. I wasn't quite sure why we were hearing all this. I somehow suspect politics is involved. I am a detective after all.

It's very unusual for a murder investigation to make it all the way to the oval office, Reynolds stammered, but this one was so unusual in scope and sequence that Deputy Director Willingham felt compelled to let POTUS know that a serial killer of a magnitude unknown in the history of the United States was at work on his watch. The president requested—not commanded, Reynolds clarified about five times—that information be controlled for a couple reasons.

One, church attendees make up a big part of the president's base of political support and he didn't want to single them out for bad publicity if such knowledge was not going to help apprehend the murderer or actually protect any potential victims. The FBI felt that the information would, in fact, just send our killer in new directions of victim recruitment, their phrase not mine, so they concurred with POTUS on that point.

Second, it was POTUS' strong feeling that people are better off for attending church and AA, so he didn't want a mass exodus of citizens from important interactions where there was a good chance they were going to get significant help. After all, according to Reynolds, the president said it was John Adams himself who said good government is made up of good citizens and good citizens get that way because of faith and moral instruction. The FBI again agreed that if the word was made public, it would do nothing to catch a killer and based on psychological demographic test results, probably affect the attendance patterns by as much as ten percent of those attending worship services or recovery meetings.

Third, one of the planks of the president's national security program was naturally helping people feel more secure. Serial killers don't make people feel secure. Listening in on conversations of the fine people of my city in coffee shops and other public places I occasionally frequent, I have no argument with POTUS on that point. Neither did the FBI. So this aspect of our perpetrator's profile was kept mostly in the background, even with law enforcement agents. Of course, we were the first city where independent incident streams were brought together into a cohesive picture and the information was available to help.

We debated whether POTUS was putting people in harm's way for the sake of politics. I think Van Guten is a democrat because she was holding him responsible for all five of the murders in Chicago. It's an election year so there's going to be a new president anyway.

Willingham reminded all of us that we had signed a non-disclosure contract with the FBI back in April and that this conversation was covered in it. Any violation would be prosecuted to the full extent of the law.

"This conversation never took place," ended his closing remarks.

Everyone had left but Zaworski, Don, and myself. The last thing Zaworski said before heading out the door was:

"Willingham is full of himself. I don't believe he ever talked to the president. He just told us what he believed and blamed it on someone else."

Don and I looked at each other out of the corners of our eyes. We had never heard Zaworski criticize a government official. Willingham was definitely driving him crazy. We agreed that the topic of the meeting was interesting but probably didn't yield any new avenues of finding the Cutter Shark. Dell's brother. Dean. I'm pretty sure.

Don headed home immediately after Zaworski left. I went home to bed too but was weirded out by the thought that someone who meant me harm had pulled back my covers and put an envelope on my pillow.

Chapter 75

It's Friday night and I'm driving over to Danny and Kaylen's house. I miss Daniel and Kendra terribly. I've barely seen them in the last month. I've now missed church and Sunday dinner with the family three of the last four weeks. Or is it four of the last five? Time is blurring.

I'm still irritated. Klarissa stood me up for dinner earlier. She wanted to meet at Le Lan on Clark Street. I wasn't in the mood to head into the city in the first place and I was definitely not looking forward to spending fifty bucks on a meal. She's a weathergirl and I'm a public servant—there is a difference in what we can afford. I don't begrudge her any lifestyle or cuisine that she wants—and she loves going to trendy restaurants that serve a French-Asian hybrid like Le Lan or something equally exotic—but she should be sensitive to my budget constraints.

I said yes because Klarissa is right, I've not been there for her during a particularly tough stretch. I have finally come to believe her that the Warren break up isn't what's eating at her. I did get her to admit that a job interview she scored with CNN's national desk in Atlanta turned out to be a disaster. She's pretty prideful—a family trait—and I know that killed her to spit out. But something else is at the root of her discontent.

Obviously, she lost Dad, too. I've always felt like I was his little girl. After all, we spent more time together because of our bond over sports.

I've never got around to figuring it all out, but I suspect Dad had a way of making Klarissa and Kaylen feel the same way. I'm glad those memories aren't tainted for them.

I sat at a table in the bar area of Le Lan, looking up every time the door opened. I wondered several times why I hadn't just gone out and bought a large letter "L" to put on my forehead. Why not be up front with the world and let them know that I, too, know that I'm a loser. A guy in his fifties with a wedding ring on tried to chat me up for almost an hour. I think he told me he was from out of town and sure gets lonely in a big city at least five times.

"Hey pal, this just isn't going to happen," I finally said straight up to put him, and me, out of the misery of his trying to get a conversation rolling.

I hit redial for Klarissa every five minutes and after twelve times paid for my Diet Coke and left. Two dollars and fifty cents for a Diet Coke is outrageous. I didn't ask for change from the three bucks I laid down. Don would be mortified with my fifty cents tip. I hate to pay for parking in downtown Chicago so I walked the mile to the neighborhood west of the Magnificent Mile where I had found a spot on the street for my Miata.

Danny picked up a couple deep dish pizzas from Giordanno's and I ate three full pieces, no small feat for a man of any size, and simply amazing for a delicate young lady like myself. At least that's what Kaylen said. I'm going to run five miles in the morning. I notice Kaylen's face is thinner and she wasn't heavy to begin with and should be eating for two. None of the three Conner girls are quite right since March, the Ides of March to be exact, when Dad's case was taken off active status. I still can't believe it.

I plop between Daniel and Kendra to watch the Shrek 2 DVD. They don't go to movies so Daniel and Kendra are two of the thirty-seven kids between the ages of three and eleven in a metropolitan of five million people who haven't seen the latest adventures of the green ogre. I like the music. I love the tickling and cuddling but Daniel really does have a weird thing about sticking his feet in my face that gets irritating after awhile.

I check my phone to see if I've missed Klarissa's call back. Despite a piece of cheesecake from Eli's to wash down the pizza, I am seriously getting mad at her. What's the deal? I'm guessing Warren or the new guy, whoever he is, called and she got better offered.

Danny is sitting on the floor in front of Kaylen and is rubbing her feet. I am suddenly jealous of her for the relationship she has. Daniel is sticking his feet in my face again and asking if they stink. Kendra is clutching her Kristen doll, the one with a little bit different figure than the real life model, and stroking my hair. I sigh. Life's not too bad. Not too bad at all.

Earlier Kaylen asked if I was up to coaching Kendra's soccer team in the fall.

"Please, Aunt Kristen," Kendra immediately chimed in.

How do you say no to that? I think the Yellow Snowflakes are going to take some people by surprise. Especially Attila the Hun.

The phone rings. Danny gets up to answer while Shrek and the donkey, whatever its name is, fight some bad guys made up of fairy tale characters. There's no blood. Must be nice.

"Who was it?" Kaylen asks as Danny plops down on the couch beside her and kisses her on the head.

"Your mom. She's coming over."

Mom, Danny, Kaylen, and I are sitting at the table drinking coffee. The kids have gone upstairs to go to bed. They're not very happy.

Mom watched the end of the movie with us but kept asking questions about what things meant and what she had missed and kind of ruined the mood. How do you explain that Captain Hook wasn't really part of the story of the Three Pigs but that it kind of works together in this movie. It's about ten now and she looks up at me as if she just remembered something.

"Why didn't you go to dinner at Klarissa's house tonight?"

"Hah hah," I answer. "Very funny. I'm not the one in trouble for once, Mom. She's the one who skipped dinner with me."

"That's not what she said. She was very upset."

"And when would this be?"

"Before I left to come over here. Maybe eight. I called and she told me you hadn't come over to her place for dinner like you said you were and that she had fixed a big dinner."

I pull my cell phone out of my purse, hit the call log button, and hold it up for Mom to see.

"I don't have my glasses on," she says. "What is that?"

"I'm showing you proof that I called Klarissa fifteen times tonight," I say, exasperated, "and she never picked up once. Must be nice to have your calls answered."

"She picked up my call fast," Mom says. "She was all out of breath."

"Well that explains it then," I say. "She was supposed to meet me at Le Lan over on Clark and went to Planet Fitness instead."

We chit chat another thirty minutes. I look at my watch, and realize I am still exhausted. I yawn and tell them I'm going to hit it. I go upstairs to say goodnight to Daniel and Kendra. Daniel is fast asleep. Kendra is right on the edge. She still has her Kristen doll held close in one arm. Her purple hippo that Dad gave her is in the other. I tell her I love her. I think she tells me she loves me back but her words aren't clear.

I go back downstairs and give everyone a hug and kiss and head out the door. I press in the clutch with my left foot and fire up my Miata and shift into reverse. I back out of the driveway and shift into first to head up Oakmont Lane, across Belmont and up Clark toward my apartment.

I look in my rearview mirror and see headlights. I'm comforted. My police escort is still on the job. I shake my head. What in the world is going on with Klarissa? She's never cooked dinner for me.

Chapter 76
June 19, 8:55pm

*R*ock, paper, scissors. Rock, paper, scissors. Rock, paper, scissors.

I'm losing the plot. Literally. I have to focus.

He contemplated his options.

> *Where should we go? Rock means paying for a hotel room. I've got plenty of cash so that's no big deal. But how do I get her to the room without a lot of people noticing? I can tell them that she had too much to drink but it's still a problem because people will remember. I've already got a motel room with parking right by my door, but it's not very nice. A bit messy what with little Carrie all cut up over our date.*
>
> *No. Motels are so impersonal. I want this to be special.*
>
> *Scissors means Carrie's house. But that's a little tricky. Someone is going to start looking for her sometime and it could be tonight. Poor girl. Pretty young thing comes to the big city*

and no one knows her well enough to even know she's missing. Now that sounds like the perfect girl for me! She practically begged me to be her special friend after Dell dumped her for his hot shot detective. Kids and their problems!

Paper. Her place. Very nice. Very posh. But I'm not sure I can trust her family not to meddle. They may be slow and dense but they are a persistent lot. If her sister call one more time I may have to answer and tell her to mind her own business. What do I do? If that's not enough to deal with, I have an even bigger problem.

I'm playing rock, paper, scissors, and I'm not sure which hand to let win! With all the work I make them do, I don't want hurt feelings among the boys, after all.

Scissors!

Chapter 77

I pull into the parking lot of my apartment, find a spot close to my place, and turn off the engine. The sound of a submarine's sonar system probing the depths of the continental shelf pings to let me know I have a text.

> U can't go upstairs yet. Some1 put a nail in our tire. 15min b4 we get there. Drive around awhile. Capt's orders!

But they were right behind me, I thought. I saw their headlights turn into the parking lot behind me.

My senses are suddenly cranked up a couple notches. I begin to breathe very slowly and carefully. I take stock of my situation. I didn't see where the car behind me parked. If the Cutter Shark is already out of his car and close, I'm at a huge disadvantage. My Miata sits low to the ground and I know I don't want to have to fend off an attacker while moving to a standing position. Fight or flight?

No way am I going to have this monster this close and let him get away. I'm asking God to help me over and over in my mind.

Then I realize if he has a gun—we don't have evidence that he's employed one in coercing his victims, but it's definitely a possibility—it doesn't matter what position I am in. He's got me. Maybe flight is the way to go and live to fight another day. But the creep is so close. I can feel it. I put my hand on my key to restart the ignition. I look in my rearview mirror. Someone has ducked behind the bumper of the car next to mine. Okay, the decision is made for me.

I'm not letting him get away. It's fight time.

Chapter 78

I glance quickly at my phone. Mom's calling. I'm sorry Mom, this is going to have to wait. It's just not a good time. I hit the red button without answering while keeping my eyes glued on the side view mirror for movement.

I open my car door slowly. He's going to let me step out of my car, shut the door, and turn my back to him as I head up to my apartment. Then he's going to come at me from behind. Again. Dell's brother? Is he really the Cutter Shark?

I follow his script and throw in a big exaggerated stretch for extra effect. My heart is banging in my chest. I do the stretch to help focus my energies, too. I'm listening for his first step, his first move, any sound preceding his rush harder than I've ever listened for anything in my life. Even as the door bangs shut his shoes are scuffing the pavement as he moves around the parked car toward what he thinks will be my back. I'm so ready.

I wheel around in a crouch, my gun already at face level and do my best imitation of a Don snarl.

"Freeze right there! Freeze, now! Hands up where I can see them."

His eyes are wide in shock. His hands are in the air. I'm in shock, too.

It's not Dean Woods. It's Timmy who used to work for Soto. Is he the Cutter Shark? Then what the heck is all the drama going on with Dean?

I'm not going to lower the gun to give him any opportunity to attack or flee. I'm more than happy to shoot him with deadly intent but also want this guy alive. I reach slowly, carefully, with my left hand across the front of my body and pull my cell phone off the clip on my right side. I'll have the entire CPD and FBI back at my house in five minutes. I don't have to make the call. My guard detail is slowly pulling into my parking lot, the kid in the passenger seat, buzz cut is back, sees what's going on and yells at the driver who accelerates and then hits the brakes hard right behind my car. Two fresh-faced uniforms pop out, guns drawn and put Timmy face down, cuff him, frisk him and pull a gun and knife off his body, and start a sequence that soon fills the night air with sirens.

Something is so wrong with Timmy as the Cutter Shark but I can't figure it out. When did we determine that my attacker was the Cutter Shark? I'm standing in a circle with the usual list of suspects: Blackshear, Martinez, Don, Konkade, and Reynolds.

I look at my phone. Mom's missed call is all that's on it. I excuse myself and step aside to listen to her message. I hold down the number one and at the prompt, hit one-one.

"Hi Kristen, hope I'm not waking you, but would you call me tonight? Something's bothering me about Klarissa. I think she was lying to me."

There's a lot I don't see eye to eye on with Klarissa. Even though we're sisters, we really do seem to be more different than alike. But there's one area where we're pretty similar. Blunt, brutal honesty.

Chapter 79

Where in the world are you, Conner?"
I'm downshifting into second to slow down for a red light on Kenzie. Everything was under control with Timmy but that didn't matter. I'm driving like a winged nocturnal mammal out of Hades to check on Klarissa. Something's wrong and I'm worried about Little Sis. There's a terrifying thought that keeps trying to enter the conscious part of my brain but I won't let it.

I called Mom back and she was beside herself about Klarissa to the point of tears. Mom can be fairly dramatic but she's never been the crier in the family—that was Dad.

The words had tumbled out of Mom's mouth. Klarissa's been depressed more than she's let on to Kaylen or me. It didn't just start with Dad's death or his case file being closed but things got a lot worse in the spring. Mom then went on to tell me that Klarissa has been having a major drinking problem. Okay. That was unexpected. I wasn't sure what it meant since Mom doesn't believe in drinking at all. Dad having a beer on a hot summer night or Klarissa sipping a glass of white wine over the course of an evening was always one step away from raging alcoholism in her book. Instead of dismissing her concerns this time, I asked how she knew Klarissa was having a drinking problem.

"That's why she and Warren broke up. She's been going to Alcoholic's Anonymous," she told me as chills ran up and down my spine. That was a lot more than unexpected. That was shocking. That's when I bolted from my front porch and jumped into my car, burning rubber on the way out of the parking lot.

"I'm checking on my sister," I answer Konkade.

"This is not the right time to be gone," he answers. "Willingham and Captain are looking for you."

"They can question me in the morning about Timmy," I say. "Although he isn't their man."

"They already knew. They don't want to talk to you," Konkade says. "They want to use your apartment for a quick meeting and need your key. Someone let the door shut and lock."

Sorry boys. I hang up and drive. And think. Why was I so slow to realize Timmy wasn't the Shark? According to Virgil, this is crime stream number seven for the Cutter Shark. Virgil's never actually called him the Cutter Shark. But the name has stuck.

Each crime stream lasts around a year. He kills his victims over the course of six or seven months, almost always one a month with a few extras thrown in through the years. He then goes to a new city and sets up shop for six months. We don't know if he heads straight there to start chasing things or goes on vacation to the Bahamas ahead of time.

The Cutter Shark has been at this at least eight years according to Virgil. Based on the ages of his victims, who get older by a year on average with each progressive city, he goes after women who are roughly his age. Van Guten has extrapolated this to put him somewhere between thirty-two to thirty-six years old.

I'm no expert at telling someone's age, but I doubt Timmy is a day over twenty-five. If he's the Cutter Shark, he started a sophisticated series of crimes before graduating from high school.

Timmy's a tough customer with a mean streak—and can throw one heck of a kidney punch—but I don't think he's sophisticated or precocious. He's not the Shark. He just doesn't like me. Get in line, Timmy.

But if Timmy isn't the Shark, who is the Shark—and who is he with? I won't let my mind say it.

*L*ights are on all over the place at Klarissa's town home. But she's still not answering her phone or the doorbell. I remember where she hides her spare key and jump the wrought iron fence on the left side of her postage stamp front yard and head down the narrow brick walkway—nice touch—that separates her home from her neighbor's. I decide to take a quick look in her garage. The door is wide open and her car is gone. A strange night is getting stranger. I will not let myself think certain thoughts so I go through the mental motions of wondering if I should invade her home if she's not even there.

There's a drumbeat of denial that tells me if I call this off, everything will be fine; she'll call me in the morning and say that she and Warren argued until four a.m. I force myself to realize my mind is playing tricks on me to quell a fear that is growing in the pit of my stomach and wanting to suffocate me. I'm reminded of standing on the ledge of a thirty foot jump in the Rocky Mountains on family vacation when I was about fifteen years old. I was frozen in place on a small rocky perch for almost five minutes before absolutely forcing myself to dive into air and the deep cool waters below.

God, let Klarissa be alive. Please.

I force myself to move. I push the edge of the large molded concrete flower pot on her back stoop, feel around underneath, and find the key before letting the pot thud back to the ground. I go in through the backdoor.

I call Klarissa's name several times and start looking around in the back two rooms on the first floor of her three story brownstone, the kitchen and a small office. She's not in either room and there's nothing out of place at quick glance.

I quietly tread up the back stairs and poke a head in the common bathroom and three bedrooms. Instead of going on up to the third floor, which she only uses for storage, I go down the front stair case into the hall and look into her dining room. Nothing. I cross the hall and walk into the living room.

That's where I find Dell.

Chapter 80

He's lost a lot of blood but he's alive.

He groans and tries to lift his head. I carefully cup a hand behind his neck and lower him to the ground and tell him to be still. His eyes are unfocused. He has a gaping gunshot wound to the shoulder. The flow of blood is steady—the shooter got an artery. I pull off my Under Armour sweat top and tie it around the wound area as tight as I can. I click onto my call log, find Konkade's number, and hit speed dial. He'll make things happen faster than anyone else on the CPD.

I sit down and cradle Dell's head on my lap. The left temple is matted with blood, swollen, and turning an angry purple shade. I look around and don't see a likely blunt object. Either Dell's attacker took it with him or more likely, he shot Dell, saw that Dell was still coherent, so he calmly walked over and kicked him in the head. I look at Dell's side and see an empty phone clip. Someone took his phone.

Nothing makes sense. Would Dean Woods shoot his own brother? And what does Klarissa have to do with this? She knows Dell but they've never talked outside of church or Kaylen's house. At least I don't think they have. How in the heck would she know Dean?

I finally own the truth in my mind. She's been attending AA. Dean is the Cutter Shark. Oh my God. Things are growing suddenly clearer. How could I be so slow and dense? Why has it taken so long for the fog to lift? Why haven't I made time to listen to my sister? Am I as bad a detective, as bad a judge of human character and dynamics, as I think I might be right now?

Suddenly Dell clutches my hand.

"Kristen."

His eyes bore into me. His lips move but no words come out. A red bubble pops from his lips. His eyes now seem to plead for me to understand something important. He knows something I need to know right now, something that might save my sister's life, but I'm not sure he has enough life left in him to get the words out.

"Dell, just relax. Don't talk. Help is on the way."

"Kristen," he gurgles. "I'm sorry. I didn't know."

"I know you didn't, Dell."

"I didn't know."

His eyes close from the exertion and his breathing slows way down. For a second I think he might be dying in my arms but then he opens his eyes again.

"My brother."

"You didn't know, Dell."

"He has Klarissa."

The words I dreaded to hear but already knew. I can't let him rest. I have to coax just a little more out of him.

"Where does he have her, Dell?"

"I didn't know … I swear I didn't know he's the Cutter …"

Dell's head lolls to the side. His eyes shut again. Is this the final fade? I know I can't push him, but every fiber in my being is screaming for him to tell me something that will help. I've got to get to my sister. My sister who was trying to talk to me and who I just wasn't listening to. My sister who had a secret drinking problem. My sister who went for help and met the Cutter Shark instead.

"Dell …. Dell … help is coming, but you've got to help me. Where has he taken her?"

His eyes focus again and he is absolutely battling to get words out but they can't seem to escape his lips. One corner of his mouth is turned up. Has he had a stroke? He turns from me and looks at the ground. I think I've lost him, but then he starts moving his forefinger through the thin puddle of blood at his side. I watch as he writes one letter: C. Then another: A. And another: R.

"Car?" I whisper to Dell. "Has Dean got Klarissa in a car? What car? And where?"

Dell gasps for breath. His finger is trembling. I've got to let him rest but I've got to have whatever is left inside of him. I pause, holding my breath. His eyes flicker and he writes two more letters, another R and an I, and then passes out. I lay him down gently and look closer to be sure of what he's written. I can make no more mistakes. He's only missing one letter and I know what he's trying to say. Nothing to do with a car.

A siren roars up and two EMTs jump out of an ambulance. One of them is Lloyd. Not as easy to recognize as he was a month ago. He's losing weight. Maybe it was my prayer. I doubt it.

"Lloyd!" I bark.

He looks up at me in surprise. I'm wearing sweat pants and a sports bra and I'm covered in blood.

"Keep him alive."

I dash down the steps before he can answer. I already have the phone to my ear when I turn the key on my ignition. It takes about eleven rings but someone from the Night Desk finally answers.

"I need an address right now," I nearly shout.

"Hold on a second," a tired voice answers.

"This is Detective Conner, one of the lead investigators on the Cutter Shark case, and I have reason to believe I know the perpetrator's 'twenty' right now. Jack me around and I'll make sure you get fired. You ready now?"

"Name?"

"Carrie … Carrie Frazier with a 'Z'—I'm almost positive."

"Lives alone or is there another name with her?"

"I believe alone. Something close to Lincoln Park. She's a DePaul grad student."

"I've got their database, too," she says. "That might help."

I hear her fingernails clicking away on her key pad—she's giving Van Guten a run for her money. After what feels like an eternity, she gives me an address. I give her my general location and tell her to stay on the line and use Google or Yahoo or Mapquest or a satellite from outer space for all I care, but to find the best route for me once I get back on Cicero. She doesn't argue. Once she gives me my optimum route, I'll get off the phone with her and call for the cavalry to follow.

Megan who is working the Info desk tonight zips me across Wicker Park and north through Old Town. I'm darting through traffic on Clark trying not to kill any drunks and she's going to have me cut back west a few blocks on Addison to avoid a traffic jam that is due to an accident. I'm at Wrigley Field, on the far east edge of DePaul, in record time—I was only over the curb and on the sidewalk once—by the time we sign off. I thought I'd be able to call for support while in route.

I hit redial for Konkade. It goes into voicemail. I hit one and give him Carrie's address and tell him that I need back up right now. Right now, dammit. Either way I'm going in for my sister.

I call Don next. He picks up on the fourth ring.

"It's not this Timothy guy," he says before I can speak. "It's Dean, Dell's brother, just like we thought."

"You don't have to tell me, Don, I know who it is."

"Even when I got here, I just knew it still had to be Dean."

"That's great, Don. But shut up and listen right now. I need help."

"What?"

"Don, no questions. Just listen. He's got Klarissa. The address is 356 Washington Irving in Lincoln Park. I left Konkade a message. Central Data has the info, too. I need you rolling right now. Bring in the heavy artillery."

I hear a sharp crack in my ear and pull my phone away. After hearing some fumbling Don gets his phone back to his ear.

"Sorry, I dropped it. Kristen, listen. Martinez, Blackshear, and I are jumping in a car this second. We can be there in fifteen minutes. If possible, in less time. Don't—and I repeat, don't—move in without us. I'm pulling out of your parking lot right now. We're calling in for local cruisers with no lights or sirens to be there in less time than it takes us. Sit tight and we'll be there as fast as we can. We won't slow down until we're a mile away and need to cut some noise. Sit tight. Stand down. You better be listening to me."

"Don, I'm here now. I'm parked. I'm going in for Klarissa."

"Conner!"

I hang up, shut my door quietly, and jam a fresh magazine into my Beretta. Twenty rounds that will shoot almost as fast as any automatic. My scores on the shooting range are below average but if there's half a shot and my sister is still in harm's way I'm going to shoot the mad dog right between his eyes. I swear to God I will.

I move forward. My phone rings. Don. I hit the ignore button immediately. I'm close to the front steps now and my phone emits the sonar ping. I look at the text message.

Do not go in alone. Direct orders. Zaworski!

Zaworski doesn't know how to text so he had Don do it with his fat thumbs for him. As Mom used to say to the three Conner girls, it's quiet time. I pop the battery out and throw my phone in the bushes.

Dear God, help me save my sister!

Chapter 81
June 19, 11:15pm

*M*an, *this girl can't handle her booze.*

She slumped against him. A beautiful doll-like silhouette in the night. A play thing.

She only had one cocktail. But I may have helped knock her out a little bit. Fifteen cc's of Pentium Barbodol straight from a needle and into the carotid artery has a tendency to do that. It works on horses so I thought it might tame this filly. Maybe just a little too much though.

He was ready.

But she needs to wake up.

He patiently waited for her to open her eyes so she could watch him work. So she could understand just a little bit.

Wake up I said!

Chapter 82

I'm on the front stoop next to the front door of an ugly three story pure rectangular apartment building from the 1940s or 1950s. There are twelve white buttons with names etched on black plastic strips next to them. Carrie Frazier is on the third floor. Some of the name plates are blank. I need to get buzzed in fast, but a lot of these places sit empty once DePaul is out for the summer and a lot of other residents are out painting the town on a Friday night.

A light is on in the front left apartment, which I assume is one, two, three, or four. I hit all four buttons in succession. Someone's got to answer … but no one does. My heart is racing and I am now wondering how loud it will be if I kick in the plate glass on the front door. I hit the first four buzzers again and add numbers five through eight, the second floor. I'm not sure I want anyone moving around on the third floor and making the Shark wary.

I wait ten more seconds and hit all eight buttons again. Nothing. Can I get a freaking break? My sister is in there.

Chapter 83
June 19, 11:43pm

I'm kind of a high tech guy, but sometimes you've got to go old school to get the job done. It's amazing what a glass of ice water to the face does to one's sleep.

The angel awakened at last.

And says a curse word.

Her delicate voice crooned out a name. A common name. A dirty name. And he deserved far better.

Sticks and stones sweetheart.

The angel had fallen. She hadn't been a good girl.

I love the way a metal edge looks against skin like hers.

She needed to be punished.

Nice and shiny. Nice and sharp.

Chapter 84

I am so damn frustrated I literally have a couple tears pop, not fall—pop—from the corners of my eyes.

First of all it's possible Klarissa is not even in this building with the Cutter Shark. If that's the case, I can't save her. I'm believing that Dell has pointed me in the right direction. I have no choice but to believe him. Because I can't believe I'm going to lose my sister.

But secondly, if I don't get through this first door, knowing where Klarissa is isn't going to matter. If I can get to the third floor, I can blow Carrie's—and everyone else's—door off the hinges with a round of bullets. I wonder what's happened to Carrie and whether Dell is going to live and how in the world such a nice guy has a brother who is a serial killer and how he has my sister and whether Dell is really as innocent as he seems.

I stop thinking. There's a large rock on the front stoop with a blue devil painted on it. The DePaul logo. I push it up to see if there's a key. There isn't. I bend my knees and straighten my back and get the thing cradled in my hands. I don't want to go through the front door. Too much risk of noise. But all the first floor windows have ugly wrought iron bars. They are definitely not there for decoration. I have no choice.

Front door it is. I take two deep breaths, torque my body so I am facing the street, get my body weight moving toward the building, rotate my torso, and swing the rock through the front door with a crash.

I feel a pop in my right knee and pain shoots up and down my leg in a slow motion moment of déjà vu that takes me back nine years to my last competitive soccer game for NIU when I tore my ACL for the then final time.

Chapter 85
June 19, 11:55pm

He gently began to move the blade and—

It sounds like we have visitors, darling Klarissa. Just when I thought I had you all to myself. This isn't good. Let's hope no one is out back watching the fire escape.

Regardless of the outcome of this unexpected disruption, he knew he had done good work. All his life.

The stupidity of cops never ceases to amaze me. The stupidity of all people really. My brother. The shrinks who understood me about as much as they understand themselves. The FBI. The media. That blogger guy.

Even when no one else appreciated his aspirations, he had always known he was a superior being. And he would not fail. He would see his work to completion.

Chapter 86

Adrenaline is an amazing gift from God. My knee feels no pain. I am sprinting up the first flight, taking four stairs at a time. I keep my weight on my toes for speed and silence. I know he's upstairs. I know he's heard me. I just know it. I also know that Klarissa is poised on the precipice. She is facing the moment between life and death.

Chapter 87
June 19, 11:59pm

*T*hat's going to leave a bruise. Why not just hold still and make this easier for both of us?

She had to be a good girl for him. He demanded it. He deserved it.

You're interrupting me. You told me you were a believer. Now act like one and get ready to meat your Maker! And it wouldn't hurt for you to be a little more considerate of my needs. You may not have plans this evening, but I've got to run! Hah hah!

Hey! Watch it. That hurt you stupid bitch. Look what you did! Just look! Made me use a swear word. Mommy didn't like that. And I don't either. You just aren't going to cooperate are you? Maybe this will help. I have a pretty good idea how proud you are of that pretty face of yours.

Incidentally, people don't watch you do the weather because of your brains and articulation. If you were going to be around for awhile, you'd have to hire a career counselor! People like their weathergirls without facial scarring.

Now hold still!

Chapter 88

I'm on the third flight of stairs. In the back of my mind I know that my knee is shredded and will soon be screaming in agony. That doesn't worry me. It's the little voice telling me that if this gets to hand to hand combat, I won't be able to kick effectively, if at all. I give the brushed metal butt of the 9 millimeter cannon in my right hand a squeeze but don't feel a lot of comfort.

I'm on the final landing still sprinting, with just one rise of steps to go. The key for me now is to not think but to just keep moving. There is no plan available other than a full assault on the front door. Start blasting. Kick it in and be ready to shoot anything that moves. Other than Klarissa.

Has not waiting for backup, for a full blown SWAT team, encouraged the Shark to move faster? Maybe. But in the depths of my spirit I know that this was the only possible course of action if I am to save Klarissa.

The mind is a funny thing. A million events can flash before one's eyes in a second. A second can take what feels like an hour. I think Einstein had some of this in mind when he did his $E = MC^2$ thing. Or maybe it was his theory of relativity. I am amazed that I am thinking about this because I've never stopped sprinting and I'm at the door and my gun is up and I've discharged seven rounds between the handle and the jamb and the door is already buckling inward as I give it high velocity assistance with an excruciating kick.

I can only hope that my relative quiet on the stairs followed by my explosive and ear shattering entrance has confused the man with a knife to my sister's chest. Because I know that's where it's at.

Hold on Klarissa. I'm here. Just for once, listen to me.

Chapter 89
June 20, 12:00am

*S*isters. *A two-for-one bargain. Awesome.*

    He knew someone was approaching the door. He knew it was her. Maybe the one person in this story he could almost respect. He stood ready, anticipating...

> *Come in, come in. I've been waiting for you, too. You weren't nice to Dell. I may not like the toad that much myself, but I have a rule. Mess with the Woods boys and you're going to get hurt.*

Chapter 90

The apartment is tiny; one step up from a one room studio. The entry goes right into the living room. The kitchen and eating areas are immediately to the left. The bedroom and bathroom are accessed by an alcove that functions as a privacy hallway.

I don't have to guess where the Cutter Shark is. He is on top of me as I come through the door. I have a split second to see his face and an eternity to take everything in. I even have time to agree that it must be possible to see your entire life pass before your eyes in the instant before death. Except for blond hair instead of brown and maybe an extra inch or two of height, if I didn't know that Dell was in critical condition and being rushed to a hospital in an ambulance with Lloyd at his side, I'd testify under oath that he was the Shark. Was the hair color enough for Klarissa not to see the resemblance? I guess we really do tend to see what we're looking for and ignore the rest. Does it seem just a little bit too strange to confess that when you come face to face with death, you have to admit he's actually pretty good looking?

Robert Frost's road poem flashes in my mind. Two roads diverged in the woods or snow or something. That seems quite apt for Dell and Dean. Whatever happened to them as boys, they definitely went different directions. I'm not sure the forked road image works for Dell and me.

We were never on the same path. For Dean and me, our roads have now converged.

The instant I kicked the door in, it bounced off the rubber stopper and he used the momentum to drive it at me and try to sandwich me in the doorway and knock me out of the fight before it started. No more time for thoughts, even if they are compressed in two heart beats or less. I spin in agony and elude the full punch he throws at me. But the door still whacks the right side of my body and my right arm, sending my Beretta sliding across the room and I'm pretty sure breaking my wrist. I'm incredibly right handed and right footed. The attack side of my body is now nearly out of commission. I think of my dad taking me to the soccer field and having me kick left footed goals over and over to build my power and aim. I hope there is some physical memory trace to help me now.

Hey tough girl, you weren't very nice to Big Brother. He's been such a mope since you dumped him that I've actually had feelings of fondness for him. Plus you made me hurt Big D. He was never hard to trick so don't get a big head about things. I'm going to show you what happens to girls who mess with the Woods boys.

As he tackles me in a bear hug, with both of us falling over a cheap end table and lamp and then falling into the center of the room, I have a glimpse of Klarissa. She is tied to a chair with duct tape and there is blood everywhere. Is she dead already? Am I too late? I want to scream. I want to cry. I focus and feel a supernatural energy to fight kick in.

Okay, what do they teach you guys on the police force these days? I think your anorexic sister put up more of a fight than you.

He is trying to pin me on my back and bring a knife from his belt. I suddenly wonder where the gun he used to shoot Dell is. Desperate, I spit in his face. He recoils and gives me just enough room to really arch my spine and put everything I have into a head butt. I catch him right on the bridge of the nose. It is with great satisfaction that I hear the cartilage splinter and see blood explode from his face. He instinctively shoots both hands to cover his wounds and now I am able to twist away on all fours and thrust a donkey kick in the direction of his head. I feel a nice solid thud on his jawbone with my left foot. Some kids thank their parents for making them stay with piano lessons. I want to tell my dad thanks for making me use both feet.

You're a damn cheater. A damned damn cheater. And cheaters never prosper. I hate spitters. Spitting is cheating. You damned spitter. Damn you. Have you ever heard of seeing red? You are about to experience it, baby.

Enraged and bleeding he lunges at me, the blade arcing toward the center of my body. I get my right hand out to help deflect his thrust while rolling away as hard as I possibly can. My wrist is definitely broken and I can hear more bones grinding from the force. I feel the knife cutting flesh in my obliques, but I actually feel a surge of relief, knowing he missed my vitals and that the gash is going to be mostly superficial. Mom always tells me I should wear one piece bathing suits. It crosses my mind she is going to get her wish.

Hold still! I mean it. Right now. You just love screwing things up, don't you? Is there anything you don't screw up?

The momentum of his attack continues the trajectory of the knife into a solid wood floor where the point sticks. His eyes are on fire as he pulls up on the hilt to get it free. He clears the knife and raises over his head. But time has slowed down even more for me and even though I hear an army of sirens drawing close I know this is my last real opportunity to save Klarissa and stay alive myself. Now it's me on the precipice between life and death.

I spin into a crouch and drive my left fist into his solar plexus with every ounce of power I have—Barry Soto would be proud. He was looking for a right and I mixed it up. I won't tell Barry it was from necessity.

This is not happening. I will not let a girl screw with me. I swear on a stack of Bibles and my mama's grave, this girl will not screw with my life any longer.

The Shark grunts and I hear a raspy wheeze as the air is knocked from his lungs. I keep moving and get a finger in his eye socket and my thumb leveraged on the base of his already fractured nose. He screams and drops his knife but I don't want to give him a chance to get his bearings. I am in front of him in a crouch. I get both of my hands behind his head and pull forward as I drive my left knee forward into his already severely damaged face. He drives his knee up and hits me in the crotch. Even as I bend forward in pain I pray that nothing's broken. I may not want a husband just yet, but I know I want children someday.

You are not going to take the wonderful life I've created away from me. You will not ruin my story. You want to but you can't. I'm better than you. I am going to kill you, bitch, and then I am going to a new city and starting over again. If you've messed with my face, I swear I will never forgive you. Never. You will rot in Hell knowing that I never forgave you.

I'm definitely not going to forgive her for making me use curse words.

He grabs my hair to push me down again and drives a sharp elbow into the middle of my upper back. The momentum is his but I'm not through. I throw my head back and up, hoping to catch him in the chin. I know it will hurt me as much as it does him but I've got to get upright. I connect with his chin and from the sound of grinding and twisting bone, I'm sure I've busted his jaw. I hope so because I am really seeing stars and wobbling on my feet. We are both upright now and look in each other's eyes. How am I going to attack him next? What do I have left that works?

I've got to get down that fire escape before company arrives. But I've got her where I want her. Look at those green eyes. She's scared. She better be. I just have to keep breathing. I am going to pound her to death. Not my style but sometimes you've got to do what you've got to do. I'd give her a whole chapter in my new book but I bet she'd like that. I may leave her out completely. Now that would piss her off. She wouldn't even get to be famous. That's it. I'm writing her out entirely.

He takes a faltering step forward, fists up, sneering—and falls backward with a small grunt, out for the count. I barely stay on two feet and stare at his hands for any sign of movement. I kick him as hard as I can in the side with my left foot just in case he's playing possum. A couple broken ribs will make any sudden motion just about impossible. I'm still not satisfied. I aim the toe of my foot at his temple and kick—not to kill him, though the thought is in my mind, but to make sure he's not coming back like Arnold in *The Terminator*. My eyes never leave him as I back toward the corner of the room where my Beretta landed. I grope around and pick it up with a shaking left hand.

Handgun firmly gripped and a million nerve endings in various parts of my body screaming, I stumble over to my sister. She is sobbing but no tears are falling down her cheeks and she is not making a sound. She could be doing a pantomime in an old silent movie or posing for Edvard Munch's "Silent Scream" painting. I look her in the eyes and they are absolutely empty. But she's alive. We can worry about empty eyes tomorrow.

I pull her close and feel the pulse on her neck, which is strong and true. Now it's me who is sobbing as I rip the duct tape off her. I free her and fall on my butt, pulling her off the chair. She lands beside me with her head cradled in my arms. I can hear heavy footfalls pounding up the steps.

Don, Martinez, Blackshear, Reynolds, and a beat red Konkade—he's going to have a heart attack along with Lloyd if he doesn't lose a few pounds—rush through the door, guns in two hands and safeties off, their eyes racing in every direction. The cavalry has arrived. My heroes. It's about time, you slackers, I think. I don't even have enough energy for sarcasm. The battle's already won. I can relax now.

I pass out.

Chapter 91

June 27, Obituary Page, *Chicago Sentinel*

Charles (Chuck) T. Bellamy, 34, died at his home in Lombard, Illinois last week. The cause of death was internal bleeding from knife wounds. Bellamy was the only child of Frank and Mary Bellamy. He is a graduate of St. Michael the Archangel High School. He attended Lombard Junior College and Harold Washington University where he studied public policy and journalism. While at HWU, he started an online magazine that featured his unique and iconoclastic views of Chicago. It is estimated that his ChiTownBlogger site received more than half a million hits every week. He was the final victim of serial killer Dean Woods, the man that Bellamy dubbed the "Cutter Shark."

Bellamy was a particularly vocal critic of Mayor Michael T. Daniels, Jr. The mayor issued the following comment in a press release from City Hall: "Many people assumed that I disliked the ChiTownBlogger. Honestly, I found him entertaining. I always respected his willingness to engage in the issues confronting our city. We will miss his sense of humor."

According to Allen Bowker, Professor Emeritus at the McGill School of Journalism, Northwestern University: "The mainstream press dismissed the ChiTownBlogger for his brand of 'yellow journalism' yet he was both admired and feared. His popularity with Gen-X and younger residents of Chicago far outpaced the major newspapers. His death will leave a hole in the fabric of Chicago's information and entertainment network."

Bellamy was preceded in death by his father, Frank. He is survived by his mother, Mary. He lived in one home his entire life. His body was found in his basement apartment by his mother. Police are still investigating how his murderer located and gained access to his residence, which was a closely held secret.

Bellamy was a member of the Chicago Direct Marketing Association, the Lombard Junior College Alumni Association, and St. Michael the Archangel parish.
His family will receive friends at O'Flarrety's Funeral Home in Lombard from four to eight p.m. Wednesday, June 24. In lieu of flowers the family requests that donations be made to St. Michael the Archangel High School Fund for Disadvantaged Students. Father Ian McKellips, assistant rector of St. Michael the Archangel, will officiate. Bellamy's body, at his request, will be cremated in a private non-Catholic ceremony.

Chapter 92

I roomed with Kaylen until I was five years old. She turned ten that year and was awarded her very own room, including her own desk, which I thought was so cool and grown up. She moved into what had previously been Klarissa's baby room. My dad wasn't the greatest at doing household projects so Kaylen had to whine close to a year before he painted over Klarissa's bright pink baby room with a sunflower yellow. Yuk. Klarissa turned three that year and moved into the twin bed next to mine. She never complained about losing her individual room status. I complained plenty.

"Kristen," Mom would say when my friends were over and she wouldn't leave us alone, "she just wants to be included. Can't you let her play with you?"

It feels like old times right now. We're in day two of our hospital stay together at Northwestern Medical Center off Michigan Avenue. My right wrist is in a cast. They had to put titanium pins in there. They've put a brace on my right knee. MRIs confirmed that I have torn the same ACL that I did almost a decade ago playing soccer—and for good measure I got the MCL, too. The patella is broken, too, but it's more or less in one piece—a little more than a stress fracture. The orthopedic surgeon has assured me that rehab is going to be a lot worse this time around due to the interior tear and my age.

I'm not thirty yet. What's the deal with everyone mentioning my age? If Mom and Kaylen don't stop rounding up to thirty I'm going to kick some butt. If I can catch anybody that is.

I would have gone home the morning after we—after I—nailed the Cutter Shark, but after the trauma of two attacks in one week the doctors insisted I stay in for observation. Wouldn't have mattered, Klarissa has always been afraid of the dark, so I would have stayed in the hospital room with her, with or without a bed.

I look over at her sleeping like an angel. How could anyone not want to include her? I reach over to give her hand a squeeze but they couldn't get our beds quite close enough for that. Both of us have to reach out to make contact. I guess that's what we've been trying to do these past four months. Really our whole lives.

She is heavily bandaged. They brought a plastic surgeon into the emergency room. The Shark slashed her three times and the doctor spent five hours in the middle of the night and into the early morning sewing her up. I live in America and that means I love numbers. I asked how many stitches. He explained that they really don't do individual stitches anymore. Just one long thread per wound. I guess I looked disappointed so he said that in the old days it would have been close to hundred of them. Maybe a hundred-fifty.

I blink back tears from the corners of each eye. It's official. I've cried more in the past week than in the previous decade.

Chapter 93

"You're a hero."

"Thanks, Don. You're a hero, too. Well, at least my hero. Against all instincts, you didn't shoot me when you *finally* showed up."

"You never let up, do you?" he asks.

"Would you still want to be my partner if I did?"

"I'm going to get back to you on that one."

I glare at him in mock anger.

"Good point," he corrects himself thanks to a sharp elbow to the ribs by Vanessa. "What would life be like without you as my partner?"

I start to answer but he holds up his hand to stop me and says, "that was a rhetorical question."

Vanessa rolls her eyes, pushes him to the side and comes over and hugs me. I'm in my recliner with an ice pack wrapped around my right knee. They didn't want to do my arthroscopic surgery within a few days of my night with the Cutter Shark because I would need both hands for crutches. I insisted. I won't get to play adult fall soccer league this year, but I do want to be ready to coach my Snowflakes. They rigged an extra metal splint in the cast on my right wrist that allows me to put more weight on the crutches. I had to sign a waiver promising I wouldn't sue the doctor and hospital if I have future troubles with my wrist. When Jeff and Kathy came by he said not to worry about; in America you can't sign away your rights and he'd represent me for free. I guess we're friends again. Okay.

Kendra comes out of the spare bedroom where she's been playing with her Kristen doll. She wrapped the doll's wrist and knee in white medical tape. I think that's sweet. She motions for Veronika to come back and play with her. I guess Vanessa told Veronika that she had to hug me and say something nice before doing anything else so she pushes in front of Don and Vanessa and gives me a hesitant and just a little bit frightened hug and tells me she hopes I feel better soon. She scurries back to play dolls with Kendra.

I love my work but I have to admit, it's pretty nice just hanging out for a couple weeks while getting paid. I've always felt guilty when not doing something, but my various aches and pains and medical accessories have assuaged all such feelings. I've had plenty of visitors though, including the mayor, the Chief of Police, the Deputy Director of the FBI, and my local congressman—all at the same time. I'm guessing that allowed them to split costs on security. I've got a couple awards coming my way. Very cool.

Czaka never showed up.

I'm pretty sure Don is jealous. Extremely cool.

Danny and Kaylen are coming over later with Klarissa. She's going to move in with me indefinitely. She can't sleep. She needs her sister. I offered to move into her place, which is a whole lot bigger and nicer than mine. But it's not just being afraid of being alone that has Klarissa spooked. The Cutter Shark, Dell's brother, spent time in her town home. I think we're going to have to pack up the whole place for her because I don't think she'll ever step foot in there again.

There's a good chance Vanessa is going to get a new listing as a real estate agent. Once she makes the sell I'm guessing Don is going to get a new watch—he's had a picture of a Breitling model that costs a couple thousand bucks tacked to the wall of his cubicle—and the cashmere fall weight blazer he's been yammering about. He isn't going to stay jealous about anything shiny I get from the city for very long.

Dell is alive and got moved out of ICU yesterday. They've questioned him as hard as the doctors would allow. The long and short of it is that barring any new information, he will not be charged with any crimes. Everything in his story of trying to be a good brother and not being aware of what Dean, the Cutter Shark, was really into has checked out.

I believe him, almost, I still wonder how there would be no tell-tale signs—like every time you move to a new city, a series of murders of young ladies take place. Dean followed Dell around the country. Maybe he assumed that it's like that everywhere. Murder is common. Serial killings are not. I guess some of the cities didn't know they had a serial killer, so the press coverage wasn't intense. I need to let this thought go.

I haven't visited him. I feel very awkward. However unconsciously, he put Klarissa in harm's way. Of course, then he almost died trying to save her life. My family visits him every day. I don't know how to sort that all out.

Mom, Klarissa, Kaylen, and I are talking about taking a girls trip to Florida or California for some recovery time. Kaylen doesn't believe that girls' trips are right for married women who are seven months pregnant, but she is thinking maybe she'll make an exception.

The Beginning of August

Dictionary: dog days of summer
pl.n.

1. The hot, sultry period of summer between early July and early September, when Sirius, the dog star, sets and rises with the sun.

2. A period of stagnation.

Chapter 94

"Aunt Kristen, can I see your scars?"

If it was anyone asking but Daniel, I'd be tempted to shoot first and ask questions later. That's not really a threat with my shooting scores, which are on a downward trajectory if that's possible.

Chicago is having a record setting heat wave with the calendar page turning to August. I'm off my crutches and even though I'm still moving slow, I feel wonderful. Even without Percocet. It doesn't mean my life isn't as surreal as ever.

I'm at Danny and Kaylen's for Sunday dinner with Mom, Klarissa, and the kids. There's always extra company and this week it is Jeff and Kathy, my AA friend, who I met as Bethany and who is sober and apparently mad crazy in love with her husband. If she hugs and kisses him anymore at the dinner table, I'm going to projectile spew the delicious barbecued brisket that Kaylen has prepared. I'm on my third helping. I may puke anyway.

Warren, the sports guy, is here for the second or maybe third Sunday in a row. I think this has got to be killing him because Sunday afternoons are a big work day for him—if you call watching baseball games and then reading what others feed into a teleprompter work. He goes on air at 5:20 tonight. But he seems relaxed and is laughing and interacting with everyone. Might have something to do with the fact that he has asked Klarissa to marry him.

Klarissa hasn't said yes yet but she has agreed to wear the biggest diamond ring I have ever seen in my life. She's been my roommate for a little more than a month but we still haven't talked about the break up with Warren and what she saw in Dean in the first place. If I was her, I wouldn't want to talk about it either.

I am officially the only Conner girl with the letter L on my forehead. Loser. I'm actually not resentful or jealous of anyone else's happiness. At least not today.

Lloyd the EMT, who has lost more than fifty pounds in the past two months eating at Subway twice a day, every day—you can't make this stuff up—is here. We're not fighting anymore. I still never heard an adequate explanation of how he had my cell number in the first place. I don't believe Shandra gave it out at the office. But live and let live. Daniel keeps poking a finger in Lloyd's belly and asking where the baby went. Good thing Lloyd is a good sport. At least no one's sticking toes in his face and asking him to smell them.

Dell's at the other end of the table from me talking to my mom. Dad didn't get the son he always wanted but apparently Mom has. Heaven knows Dell needs all the help he can get. His brother was killed in the Cook County jail before his arraignment. Criminals often don't approve of criminals worse than themselves. Dell's pale and thin. He doesn't have much of the quiet confidence and suave demeanor he exhibited before all this happened. How could you?

I still haven't had a conversation with him. I've listened to him for hours live and on tape during police questioning. He is now a permanent resident of Chicago. I guess we're a big enough city that no one thinks they are going to run into a participant in that macabre Cutter Shark business, so he's been left alone. He's a good looking guy but there are a lot of good looking guys and he blends in. He has taken a full time position as Vice President of Inventory Management for Goff & Duncan so he's obviously doing well. Danny and he have become close. I'm glad. I'm not ready to talk to him and Danny's participation belies any guilt I might feel to reach out.

There are a few mysteries outstanding on this case. Timmy admitted he left the card on my pillow but maintains he didn't steal the picture of me and my dad. No one else says they touched it either. Why would Timmy lie about that? Did someone else get into my place? The case of the yellow Post-it Notes is still open, too. Shandra swears it wasn't her. She brought flowers from the department to me when I was in the hospital and did a sticky note to prove she has a different handwriting than whoever really did it. She's also saying that she saw Van Guten in my work area a couple of times.

Would a doctor in psychology plant harassing Post-it Notes in my cubicle? I've heard that on the average psychologists and psychiatrists have more psychological problems than the general population. I guess people with psychological problems go into psychology to help themselves. I don't know if any of this applies to Van Guten or whether she doesn't want her ex-husband for herself but doesn't want anyone else close to him, either. Who knows?

Maybe I was born to have doubts. Maybe doubt is an occupational hazard—or a prerequisite for employment as a detective. Maybe I just haven't cared for my spiritual life as much as I should. Having Mom and Kaylen around I almost have the feeling that they will take care of my spirituality for me.

I've always believed God is real. But on emotional and functional levels, I have to be honest, I haven't always really believed, much less acted like He actually meant anything in my world or in my life. I'm not thirty yet, but I've seen a lot of ugly things already. I'm not complaining or painting a sob story. My life has been pretty blessed, but I've experienced a few bad things, too. One or two of them worse than most.

Watching a recovering alcoholic, an ex-jock, a proud and grieving widow, a scarred beauty queen, a preacher, a businessman with no family left in the world, an overweight but shrinking EMT, a mother with two adorable children and pregnant again, talking and laughing and happy to be together, I almost believe like I did back when I went to Baptist church camp as a schoolgirl. Doesn't mean I don't have a question or two I want to ask him.

My phone buzzes on my hip. I don't plan to answer but look down and see it is from good old Austin Reynolds. I haven't talked to him either. Not even after he brought flowers to the hospital and camped out at my bedside. I pretended to be asleep every time he stopped in. I think there's a non-isolated activity stream in my life when it comes to guys. I push my chair back, stand up, push the green button, and walk into the kitchen before answering.

"Conner."

"Hold on a second," he says. "I have to sit down. I think I might faint. I can't believe Chicago's most beautiful detective picked up my call."

"Hah hah."

"Let me guess; it's Sunday dinner at Kaylen's house and there's a big crowd."

"You have me under surveillance again?"

"Believe it or not, I've considered it."

"Yeah?"

"Just kidding. Don't hang up on me."

"Listen Austin, if you want to talk about us and what happened, I'm going to be honest and tell you I don't see the point."

"You never do waste time getting to the heart of the matter."

"Dad said our strengths are our weaknesses, so I guess this is one of those double-edged swords for me."

"No doubt," he says, "but hey, I didn't call about us."

"Okay." Did I sound disappointed? Am I disappointed?

"I'm actually calling for Willingham. He thinks you are the 'bomb'— his word, not mine. He wants you in D.C. tonight and working with us on a new case Virgil came up with. Starting tomorrow."

"Did you remind him that number one, I already have a job and number two, I'm still on paid leave?"

"I did. But he's pretty direct himself. He's already called your mayor and chief of police and they said if you agree, you're free to work with us on a temporary assignment—and still keep your temporary disability pay. Double dipping wouldn't be too bad for your finances I bet."

My head is spinning as he tells me to get packed, head for the United counter where a first class ticket will be waiting with my name on it to whisk me to Washington Reagan, and that I should just get a cab and head for the Marriott Marquis by the White House where there's a room reserved for me. I'll get more instructions in the morning at the JavaStar on K Street.

I hang up and wander back into the dining room in a daze. Mom is holding court as I bend over and hug Kendra and Daniel close to me, planting a big kiss on their cheeks. Daniel protests and makes some retching sounds. Danny gives him the look and he stops immediately.

"I was just telling everyone about how us girls are going to drive down to Destin, Florida," she says cheerfully, leaning forward so she can see around Dell and smile up at me. "Tell them some of the activities we've got planned, Kristen."

"Mom, this isn't a good time for me to go into things right now," I say as I grab my purse, slow down to give quick hugs to her, Klarissa, and Kaylen, and head for the door. Klarissa has been spending some nights with Mom lately, so I'll call her on my way to the airport and tell her to sit tight there for a week or two.

Chapter 95

Packed and ready to head for the airport, I notice a familiar looking red card on top of a stack of unopened mail for the first time. Being an ace detective I notice there's no stamp on it. Someone was in my apartment. The hair on the back of my neck is up and a tingle runs up and down my spine. I look at my watch. My cab will be here any minute so I'm not calling anyone. I break the seal on the back of the envelope with my name spelled wrong again. Has to be the barista at Javastar. I carefully slide out the card and look at the back. Hallmark. Someone cares enough to give the best. Again. I open it expecting another poem but someone isn't quite as creative this time.

Too bad you never visited before my escape. Too bad for you. I was getting ready to request a visit from you. I know something you want to know. I was ready to start dealing. Looks like I don't have to deal now. I know a little something about a certain cop who got shot. Imagine that. Next time we meet, maybe your partner doesn't show up.

Dee Dee Apple

Turn the page for the opening chapters of the new
Dee Dee Apple novel, featuring Kristen Conner.

Ride Like the Wind

Available Soon

Chicago, Illinois

Accidents happen.
Phineas Fogg

CHAPTER 1

September 29 / 9:59 p.m.

Oh my gosh … how did that just happen? No way. That didn't just happen. I didn't just do that. I wouldn't do that. I couldn't do that.

I just wanted to scare him. He deserved that and more. But I never meant to really hurt him. Not physically.

But he said horrible things. I didn't think it could get worse than what he wrote to me. But it did. He did. How could anybody be so cruel and laugh about it? Did he do this to other girls?

And then he charged me like a wild animal. That's what he is. A wild animal. I just need to call the police and explain what happened.

But how do I explain why I was here? And how I got in? They'll take one look at me and know I'm not his kind of girl.

But I can't just leave. What if he's not dead? I'm sure he is but what if he isn't?

I can't just leave can I?

Arlington, Virginia

In Washington, success is just
the training course for failure.
Simon Hoggart

CHAPTER 2

The Marines have a saying that seems quite apt right now. Hurry up and wait. Maybe it's the Army that says that. Maybe it's the entire frigging military. I'm living it right now.

I'm wearing black from head to toe, including head gear that covers everything but the oval of my face. Lightweight night goggles and high-tech grease paint make me almost invisible. The black synthetic material—looks and feels like Under Armour to me—is designed for summer operations the quartermaster told me. It was ninety-eight degrees in the shade all day here in D.C. The sun has nearly set so the temperature has dropped, mercifully. Can't be more than ninety-five now. There is no fabric that can make this sweltering humidity bearable.

The thin panels of Kevlar protecting most of my torso don't make things any cooler. I was told they are bullet resistant. That word, resistant, is bugging me. Why can't they be bullet proof?

Drops of sweat bead and then fall in rivulets down my forehead over and around my goggles, some seeping through the rubber ring that fits snug to my face. When Austin Reynolds called me, this wasn't the type of assignment I was expecting. Sure, I'm way ahead of my rehab schedule. But still, I had a torn ACL and MCL repaired just six weeks ago. The three weeks I've spent running the rolling hills of the FBI Training Grounds in Quantico, Virginia, every morning have been nothing but wonderful for my recovery. Still, am I ready for this?

We've been poised for the strike for forty-five minutes now. A terrorist cell has been operating within thirty minutes of our nation's capital. The FBI, in its infinite wisdom, has moved cautiously on this one, letting the group move freely for more than a year in the hopes that members of Allah's Fatwa would make a mistake in their overconfidence. It wasn't cell chatter intercepted by the supercomputers at NEA that made Deputy Director Willingham issue the order for immediate and terminal action. It was the lack of chatter. Change may be good for personal growth and corporate survival—that's what Dell told me in a recent letter—but when it's a homicidal cadre of mad dogs, change should always make you nervous. Sorry Oprah.

Another bit of data came in from Virgil, whose real name is Operation Vigilance, a computer program developed for Homeland Security that gathers and collates information from federal, state, and local law enforcement agencies. Word from Virgil strongly suggest some bad guys, possibly and probably radical Islamists, have got some weapons grade uranium into the U.S. through the Port of Charleston. Maybe one and one don't equal two in this case, but who wants to risk that? Not Willingham.

Four agents have worked themselves within twenty feet of the five foot chain link fence in front of the two thousand square foot house with all the blinds pulled and overgrown shrubs nearly enveloping the entire exterior. They popped a manhole cover and are across the street, flat and invisible on the black grass but ready to sprint on signal.

Four more agents are within ten feet of the same distance to the fence in the rear of the house, having come through the neighbor's backyard. They are the hold up. It is assumed that the enemy has set tripwires around their perimeter to sound the alarm of an imminent attack. But how far back and where did they set them? Are they motion or sound activated? How carefully are they monitoring their environment? How paranoid are they? Maybe not as paranoid as us; and certainly not with the level of patience that Willingham and Reynolds, who are running the show from a mobile command center a mile away, are exhibiting.

My patience is shot. I wonder if that means I will never call the shots on a major operation. Actually, I am not even wondering on that point.

I'm sitting with three other agents in what looks like a UPS van, about a block away. Most UPS trucks, however, don't have a 600 horse power engine and a front bumper with a six foot wide cast iron wedge that can open the side of a house as easily as a body builder hammering a screw driver through the side of a soup can. As far as I can tell, no one else is sweating and fidgeting like me.

My cell phone vibrates in four seemingly-endless rumbles for the fifth straight time. I can't remember all the specifics of our pre-event instructions—it's the FBI that calls these little assaults "events", not me—but I'm pretty sure we were supposed to leave our Nokias at home. I must have tucked mine in one of the pockets of the Batman-like utility belt that is the final accessory of my chic black on black ensemble. I can't actually see anyone else's eyes, but I think my teammates are giving me dirty looks.

I feel a new stream of sweat trace down my back. The inside of my goggles are fogging up. I'm not regular FBI so I didn't get the custom made outfit and gear the others did. My eyes are watering and I am desperate to wipe sweat from them and take care of a maddening itch.

My phone starts a sixth round of low rumbling. I absolutely know better but I can't take it anymore. I snap open the belt pocket and bring it to my ear, pushing my goggles and hood back, all in one movement.

"Mom," I hiss in a low whisper that probably isn't nearly as quiet as I want it to be. "When I don't pick up it means I'm busy. Stop hitting redial over and over."

"Kristen, there's no reason for you to talk to me that way," she says with her hurt tone, a regular part of her communication repertoire with me. "I just wanted to make sure you were meeting us in Florida on schedule."

"Mom, same as I told you last night, I'll be there. Things are winding down here quicker than I thought."

"You've been known to change plans at the last minute."

"Mom, I can't talk right now. This is a bad time."

"Honey, it never seems to be a good time for you to talk to your mom!"

I look at three sets of bug-like eyes that are now staring my direction. Oh the stories Don, my partner at CPD, could tell them right now. I wonder if it matters whether they write me up since I'm only on loan to the FBI and not an employee. Maybe if they'd given me the custom gear that doesn't let sweat get in your goggles, I wouldn't be in this position right now.

"Mom, I'll call tomorrow. I've got to go. Now."

"You are going to church every Sunday while you're there aren't you?"

I'm exasperated. "Mom, I already told you—"

A voice barks, "Now!" as the engine fires into a roar and we are thrown sideways on the uncomfortable benches we've been perched on for what seems like hours. As the turbo-charged van powers from zero to at least fifty in about five seconds, I drop my phone and nearly fall completely backward. I hear it bounce against the metal door at the back of the van. I think I can actually hear my mom calling my name.

I am on the team designated to lead the troops into the battle zone. They wait for us. Once we break through the fence across the entrance to the driveway and splinter the garage door open with the wedge, we will be spilling out the left side door and into the house through the garage entry. We have secure side straps that loop over one shoulder and halfway around the chest on the right side of the van so that we can enter the theater of conflict in a standing position.

I can barely keep my balance as we carom forward, drift to the right, and then veer hard to the left as the driver pushes the van on two wheels in the final turn to storm the fortress. I'm frantically trying to get my goggles situated on my face. The right window is covering my left eye. I don't have the strap of the goggles right, so I yank the hood off again and get the strap over and behind my ponytail. I probably waste half a second smoothing my hair back for no apparent reason. I barely have the goggles centered over my eyes and the hood up as I feel the first shudder that signifies we have gone through the gate like a hot knife through warm butter. I'm ready, my Beretta 9 millimeter in hand, when the bigger impact occurs and we cave in the garage door. There must have been a vehicle parked in there because all four of us swing forward, our legs nearly swinging to waist level with the final impact. We were told to expect this and we did.

Our squad leader is first out and unleashes a violent side kick to the entry door. I wince to myself when the door doesn't budge. That had to have hurt. Probably reinforced metal. He's unfazed and quickly reaches into a belt pocket and pulls out an MCB—a Micro Concussion Bomb—that he slaps on the door beside the handle. All four of us are out of the truck, crouched with faces to the wall and hands over ears as he wheels from the doorway and positions himself next to me. I think all three MCBs explode at once as I hear front and back doors blown inward at the same time our side door implodes. I race after my team through the smoking doorway, my head on a swivel, weapon ready to fire.

The architectural drawing of the house indicated a split level home with the main level including an enclosed kitchen featuring a shuttered picture window looking into a small dining room, and swinging doors that lead into the living room. All three attack teams will be entering on this floor. Four bedrooms and two bathrooms are up a half staircase on the opposite side of the house. A den or rec room, probably the laundry room, and another full or half bath are underneath the bedrooms a half flight below our entry point. The team coming through the front door is responsible for the upstairs. The team coming through the back door is responsible for the half basement. We are responsible for kitchen, dining room, and living room. My job is to slam through the swinging doors, do a half tumble, and come up firing at anything that doesn't have its hands straight up in the air with a white flag waving. I am then to wait for audio instructions so that I don't get shot by or shoot a team member.

As I emerge through the smoke, ready to turn left and into the living room, I half trip as my foot hits the heel of my team leader, who I'm following closely. I hear Special Agent Ted Cane shout an obscenity as he falls against the service island in the kitchen. I hit the side of a cabinet fairly hard with my right shoulder and feel a mild shoot of pain course upwards, but I instantly regain my balance. I pause and think about checking on Cane, but remember protocol—he's not my problem—and smash through the swinging doors.

I almost feel the shot in every fiber of my body as a thunderous roar sounds from behind me. The bastard must have been waiting for me. He must have headed to the corner of the room and watched the doorway as soon as he heard the MCBs explode. I don't know how he missed me; he had me at pointblank range.

I'm good at this physical stuff and improvise on the fly. I extend my tumble into a full dive and front roll. As I tumble upward to a crouch, I push myself to the side into a half roll to bring my weapon into firing position. Even as I execute a beautiful sequence of moves, I hear a voice screaming in my brain. A terrified voice. My voice. Even if I can't articulate it in real time, my peripheral vision has already seen just one target to put down. My target, however, is in an upright firing position and has a 12-gauge shot gun pressed to his shoulder, one eye gleaming down the barrel. Dad used to hunt big game with a 12-gauge. It's not a weapon you use for rabbit hunting unless you like making rabbits disappear in a fine pink mist.

Even as the voice continues to scream for me to move, I know my target isn't going to miss with his second shot no matter what I do. With a shotgun, you don't have to be a good aim.

As I torque into a crouch, my head is craned as far to the side as it will go as I pray for one shot. Just one shot. My target looks relaxed and in charge. Our eyes lock. My arm is swinging forward in the slowest slow motion I have ever experienced in my life. In that nanosecond I feel like I have time recite Marc Antony's complete speech to the Plebeians at the funeral of Caesar, something I did my sophomore or junior year of high school—doesn't matter much which year, now, does it Kristen?—and maybe add a clever limerick about a postman named Chuck that I wrote my first year in middle school and never got a chance to say in front of the class. I see my target's eyes narrow and then a streak of blue flame blaze from the end of the left barrel almost simultaneous with getting knocked backward and hitting hard on my back.

I look upward, wondering if I am going to bleed to death.

Author
Acknowledgments

I am grateful to a number of people who read early drafts of *Cuts Like a Knife* and who offered great suggestions and encouraged me to keep writing and refining. Thank you David, Troy, Stacie, Bob, Jane, Amy, Carlie, Shelley, Dave, Mark, Jessica and many others. You each know your last name!

Kudos and thanks to Bobby and Kim for designing a series look. Special thanks to Jenna, a great cover model, who has to get some training before she's allowed to hold a real gun!

A shout out to Mark for his editorial savvy and overall industry knowledge in helping me launch a wonderful character from my imagination, who I've really come to love!

To learn more about Dee Dee Apple, visit—

www.deedee-apple.com